INDOC TRIN ATION

BOOK ONE

CREATED BY

Anthony Cuizon | COLOR

"I've got my finger on the trigger
And tonight faith just ain't enough
When I look inside my heart
There's just devils and dust"

- Bruce Springsteen, 'Devils and Dust'

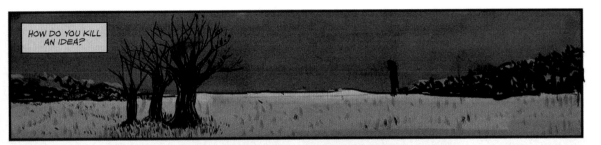

HOW DO YOU KILL AN IDEA?

THAT IS OUR BURDEN, STOPPING THIS DANGER THAT SPREADS-- THAT **INFECTS**--LIKE A VIRUS.

MAYBE THAT'S THE GREATEST TRICK IDEAS PULL-- ALIENATING YOU FROM THE WORLD WITHOUT YOU REALIZING IT.

PEOPLE LIKE TO USE THE WORD "RADICALIZE"--BUT IT DOESN'T FEEL, IN THE MOMENT, LIKE YOU'RE SO OUTSIDE SOCIETY'S NORMALIZED ATTITUDES.

THERE'S JUST THIS SLIGHT FISSURE IN YOUR PERCEPTION, AND YOUR LIFE BEGINS TO BEND AND FALL INTO THE CRACK THAT'S BEEN MADE.

BUT THERE'S NO BOTTOM TO THE FISSURE; THE MOST DANGEROUS IDEAS HAVE NO CENTER.

THEIR ONE CONSISTENT QUALITY IS CHAOS, MAKING IT IN YOU AND WITH YOU.

AND EVERY TIME THE IDEA PASSES, IT MUTATES. NORMAL CRIMES--OF PASSION, OF DESPERATION--GIVE YOU MOTIVE AND REASON.

THESE CRIMES GIVE YOU AN ENTIRE **NEW WORLD**.

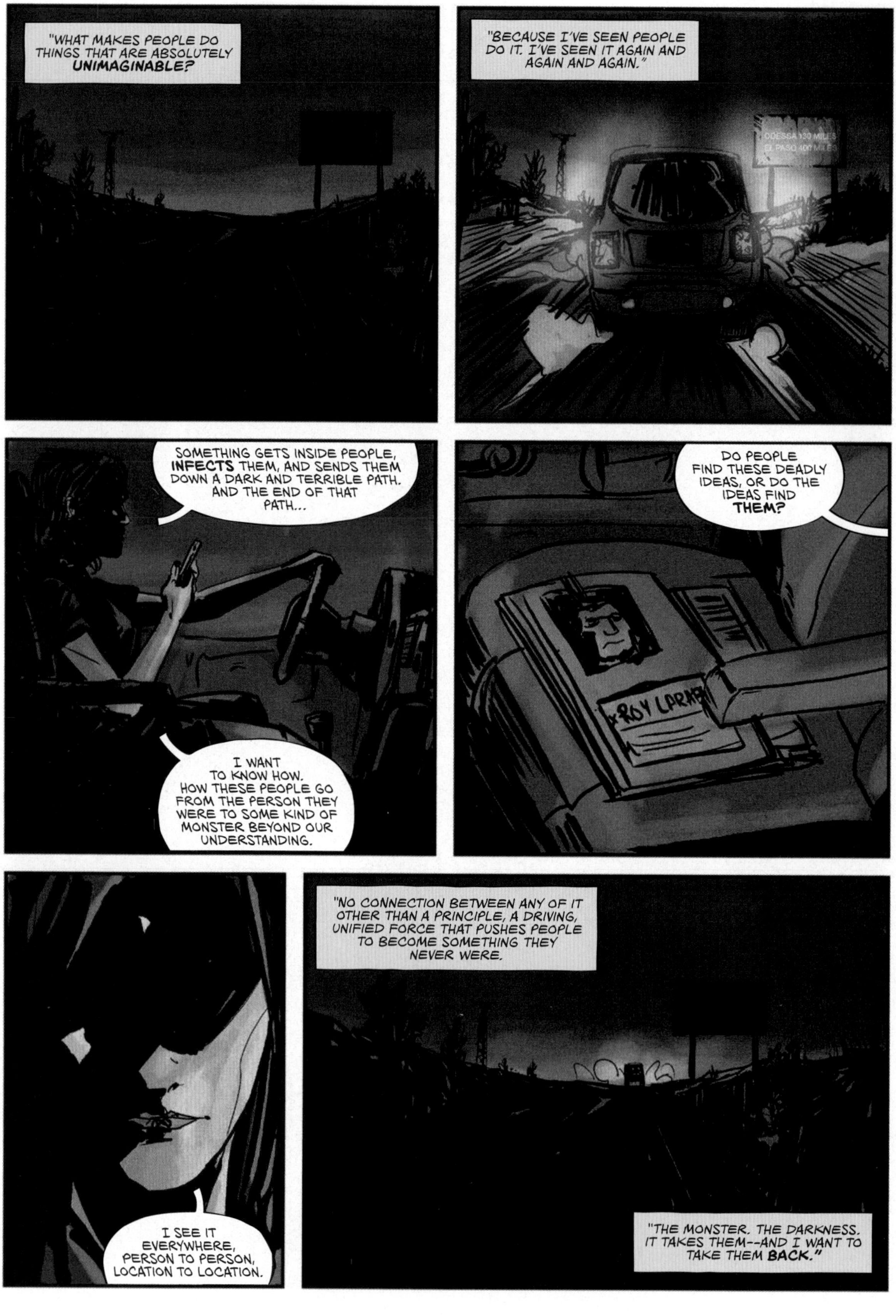
"WHAT MAKES PEOPLE DO THINGS THAT ARE ABSOLUTELY **UNIMAGINABLE?**
"BECAUSE I'VE SEEN PEOPLE DO IT. I'VE SEEN IT AGAIN AND AGAIN AND AGAIN."
SOMETHING GETS INSIDE PEOPLE, **INFECTS** THEM, AND SENDS THEM DOWN A DARK AND TERRIBLE PATH. AND THE END OF THAT PATH...
I WANT TO KNOW HOW. HOW THESE PEOPLE GO FROM THE PERSON THEY WERE TO SOME KIND OF MONSTER BEYOND OUR UNDERSTANDING.
DO PEOPLE FIND THESE DEADLY IDEAS, OR DO THE IDEAS FIND **THEM?**
I SEE IT EVERYWHERE, PERSON TO PERSON, LOCATION TO LOCATION.
"NO CONNECTION BETWEEN ANY OF IT OTHER THAN A PRINCIPLE, A DRIVING, UNIFIED FORCE THAT PUSHES PEOPLE TO BECOME SOMETHING THEY NEVER WERE.
"THE MONSTER. THE DARKNESS. IT TAKES THEM--AND I WANT TO TAKE THEM **BACK.**"

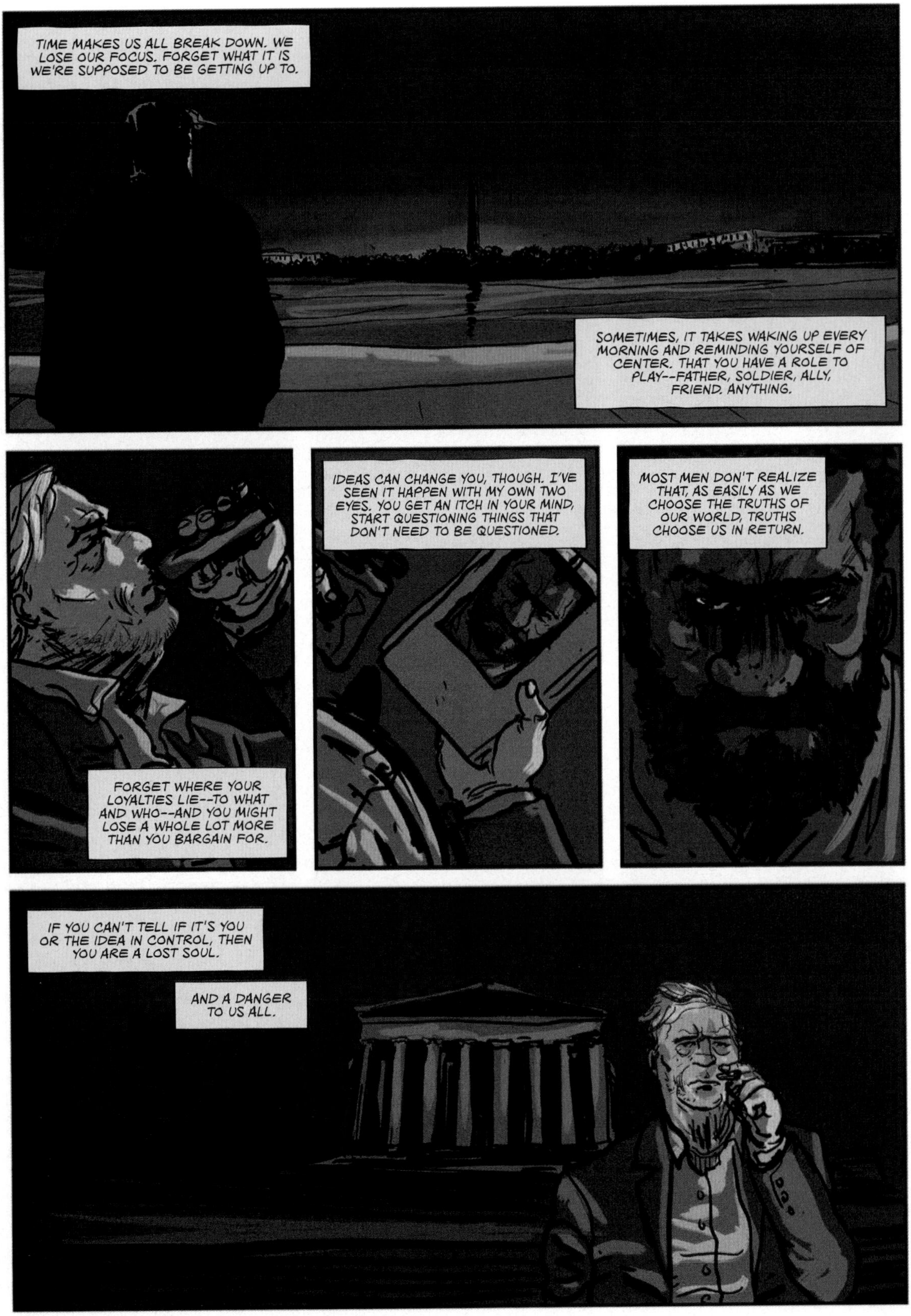
TIME MAKES US ALL BREAK DOWN. WE LOSE OUR FOCUS. FORGET WHAT IT IS WE'RE SUPPOSED TO BE GETTING UP TO.
SOMETIMES, IT TAKES WAKING UP EVERY MORNING AND REMINDING YOURSELF OF CENTER. THAT YOU HAVE A ROLE TO PLAY--FATHER, SOLDIER, ALLY, FRIEND. ANYTHING.
FORGET WHERE YOUR LOYALTIES LIE--TO WHAT AND WHO--AND YOU MIGHT LOSE A WHOLE LOT MORE THAN YOU BARGAIN FOR.
IDEAS CAN CHANGE YOU, THOUGH. I'VE SEEN IT HAPPEN WITH MY OWN TWO EYES. YOU GET AN ITCH IN YOUR MIND, START QUESTIONING THINGS THAT DON'T NEED TO BE QUESTIONED.
MOST MEN DON'T REALIZE THAT, AS EASILY AS WE CHOOSE THE TRUTHS OF OUR WORLD, TRUTHS CHOOSE US IN RETURN.
IF YOU CAN'T TELL IF IT'S YOU OR THE IDEA IN CONTROL, THEN YOU ARE A LOST SOUL.
AND A DANGER TO US ALL.

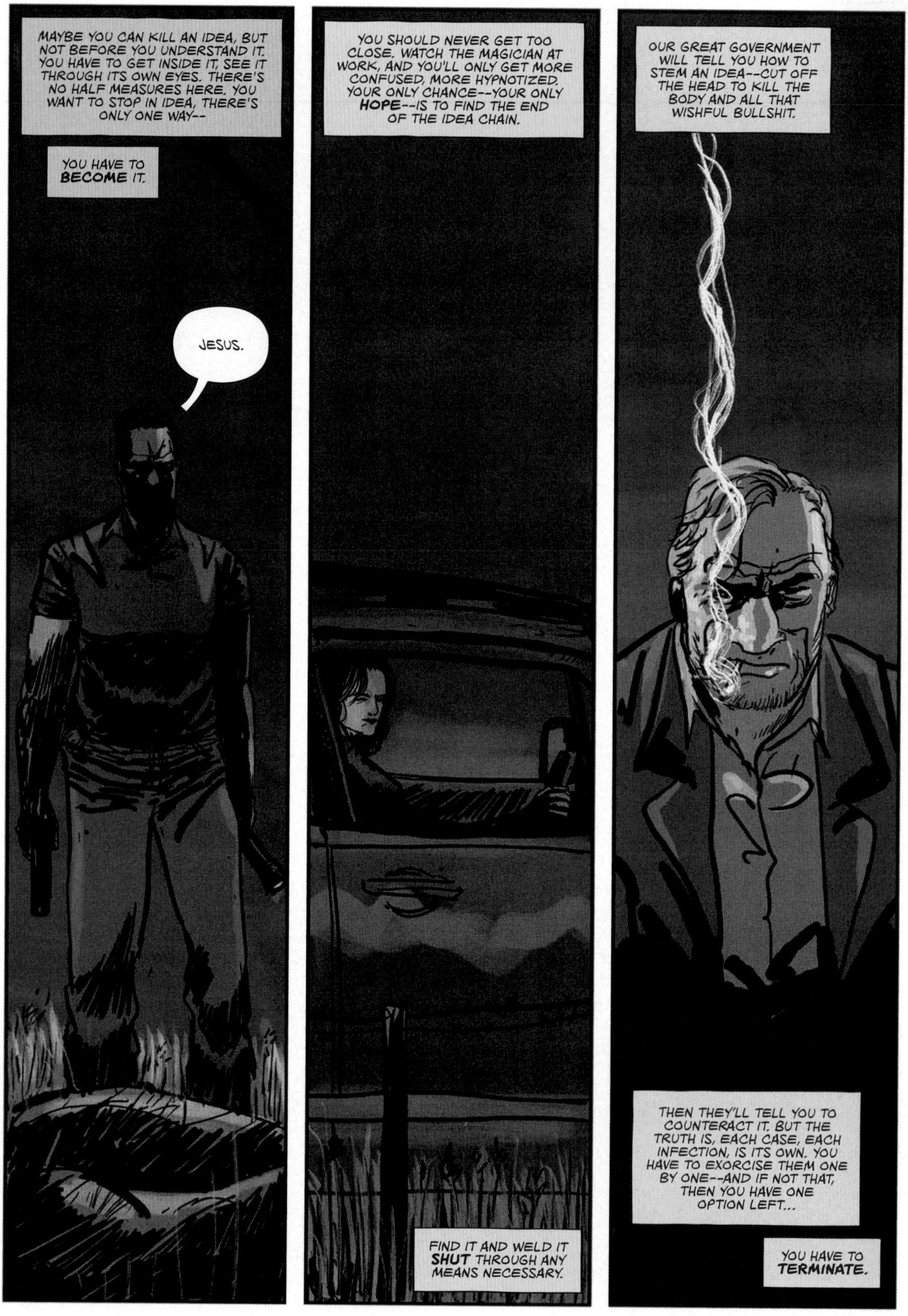
MAYBE YOU CAN KILL AN IDEA, BUT NOT BEFORE YOU UNDERSTAND IT. YOU HAVE TO GET INSIDE IT, SEE IT THROUGH ITS OWN EYES. THERE'S NO HALF MEASURES HERE. YOU WANT TO STOP IN IDEA, THERE'S ONLY ONE WAY--
YOU HAVE TO **BECOME** IT.
JESUS.
YOU SHOULD NEVER GET TOO CLOSE. WATCH THE MAGICIAN AT WORK, AND YOU'LL ONLY GET MORE CONFUSED, MORE HYPNOTIZED. YOUR ONLY CHANCE--YOUR ONLY **HOPE**--IS TO FIND THE END OF THE IDEA CHAIN.
FIND IT AND WELD IT **SHUT** THROUGH ANY MEANS NECESSARY.
OUR GREAT GOVERNMENT WILL TELL YOU HOW TO STEM AN IDEA--CUT OFF THE HEAD TO KILL THE BODY AND ALL THAT WISHFUL BULLSHIT.
THEN THEY'LL TELL YOU TO COUNTERACT IT. BUT THE TRUTH IS, EACH CASE, EACH INFECTION, IS ITS OWN. YOU HAVE TO EXORCISE THEM ONE BY ONE--AND IF NOT THAT, THEN YOU HAVE ONE OPTION LEFT...
YOU HAVE TO **TERMINATE.**

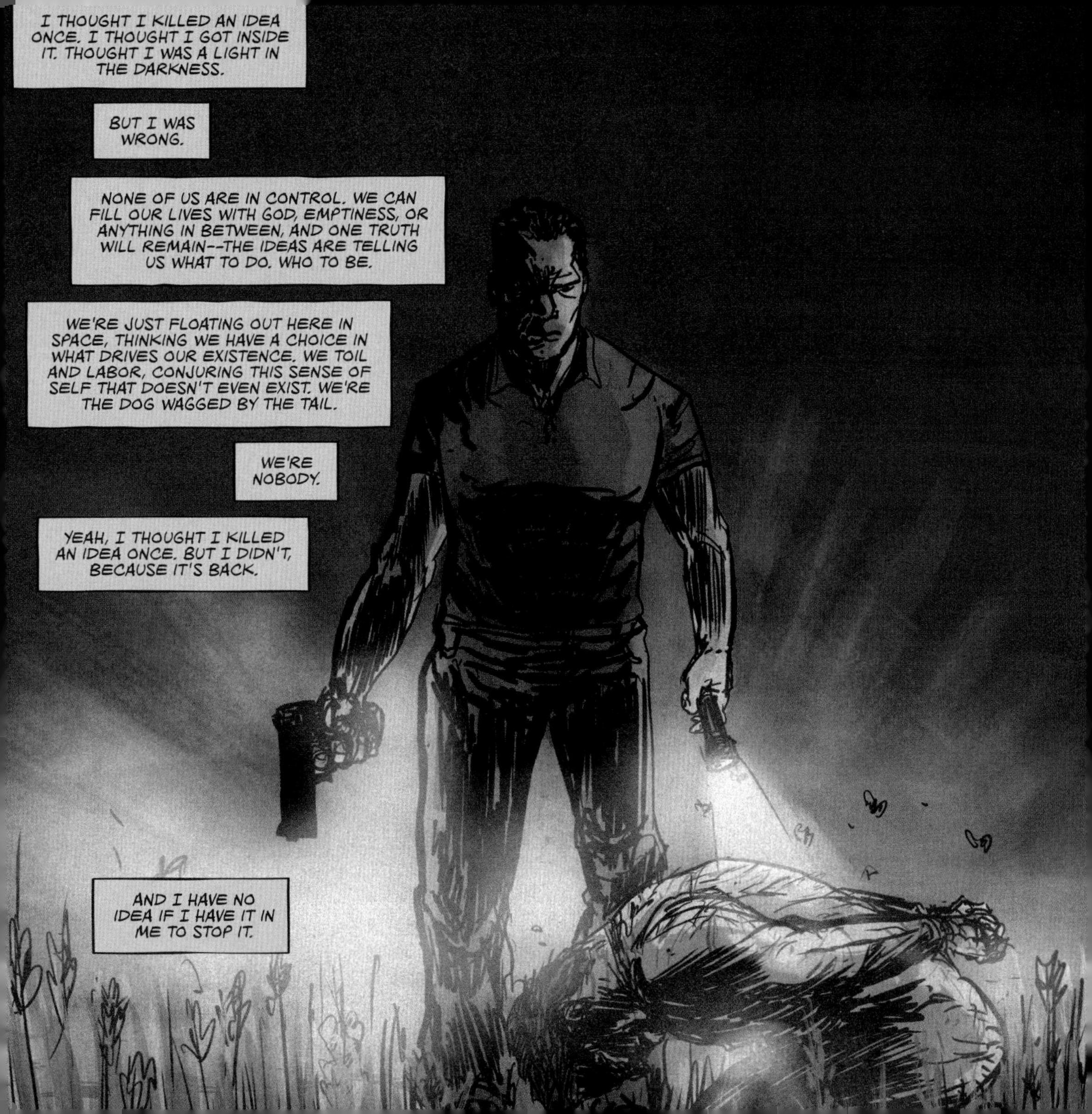
I THOUGHT I KILLED AN IDEA ONCE. I THOUGHT I GOT INSIDE IT. THOUGHT I WAS A LIGHT IN THE DARKNESS.
BUT I WAS WRONG.
NONE OF US ARE IN CONTROL. WE CAN FILL OUR LIVES WITH GOD, EMPTINESS, OR ANYTHING IN BETWEEN, AND ONE TRUTH WILL REMAIN--THE IDEAS ARE TELLING US WHAT TO DO. WHO TO BE.
WE'RE JUST FLOATING OUT HERE IN SPACE, THINKING WE HAVE A CHOICE IN WHAT DRIVES OUR EXISTENCE. WE TOIL AND LABOR, CONJURING THIS SENSE OF SELF THAT DOESN'T EVEN EXIST. WE'RE THE DOG WAGGED BY THE TAIL.
WE'RE NOBODY.
YEAH, I THOUGHT I KILLED AN IDEA ONCE. BUT I DIDN'T, BECAUSE IT'S BACK.
AND I HAVE NO IDEA IF I HAVE IT IN ME TO STOP IT.

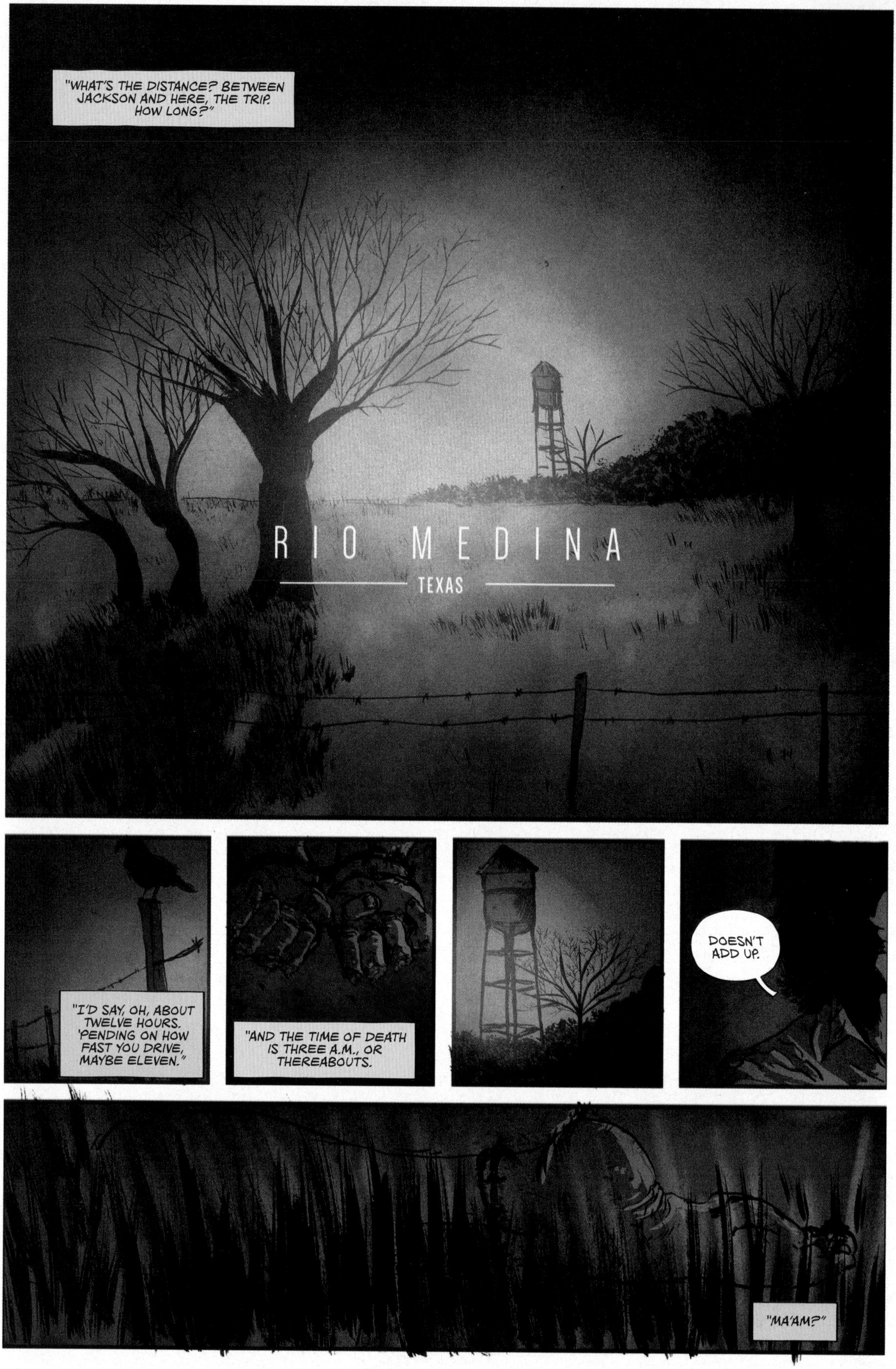
"WHAT'S THE DISTANCE? BETWEEN JACKSON AND HERE, THE TRIP. HOW LONG?"
RIO MEDINA
TEXAS
"I'D SAY, OH, ABOUT TWELVE HOURS. 'PENDING ON HOW FAST YOU DRIVE, MAYBE ELEVEN."
"AND THE TIME OF DEATH IS THREE A.M., OR THEREABOUTS.
DOESN'T ADD UP.
"MA'AM?"

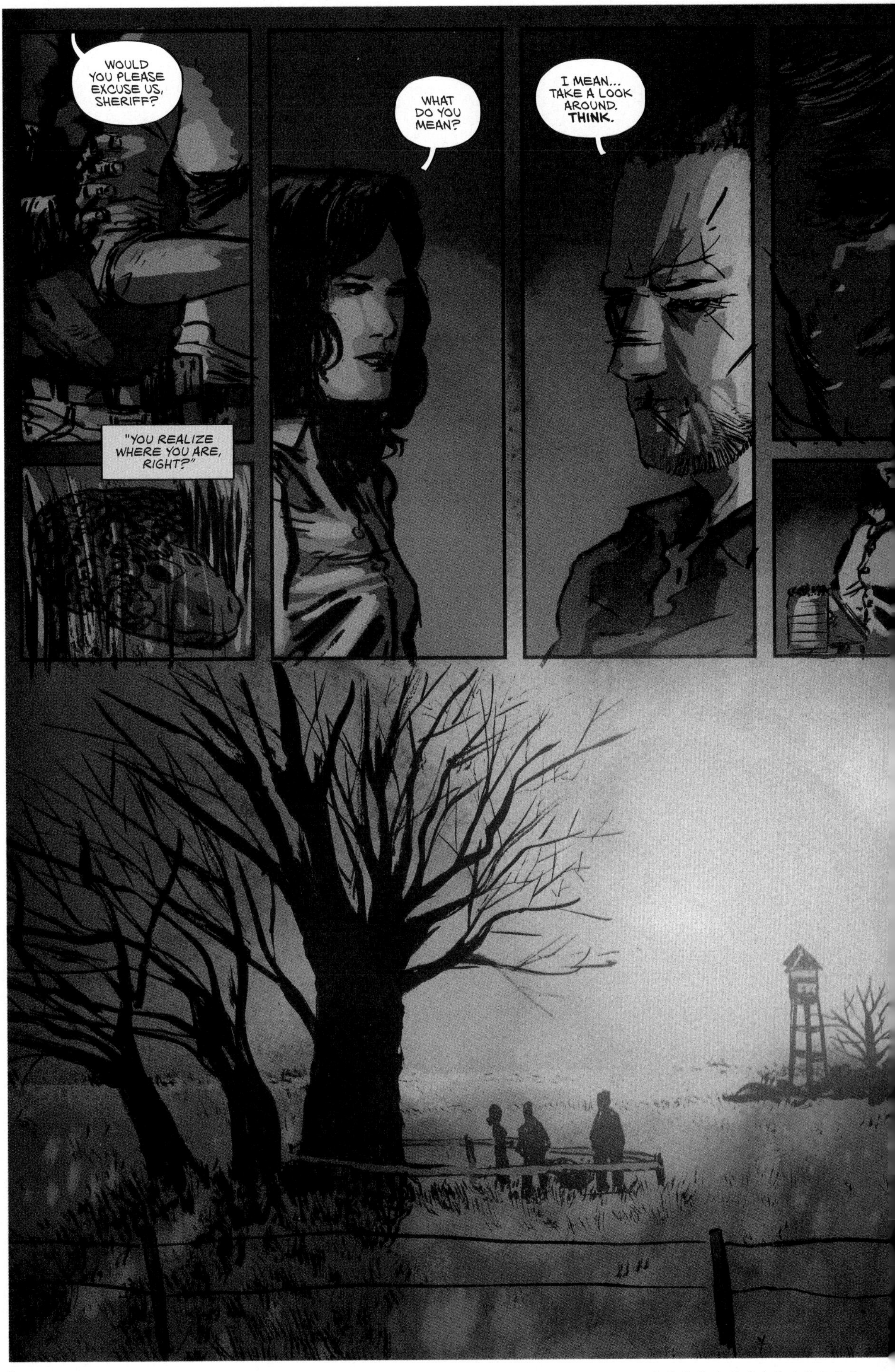
WOULD YOU PLEASE EXCUSE US, SHERIFF?
"YOU REALIZE WHERE YOU ARE, RIGHT?"
WHAT DO YOU MEAN?
I MEAN... TAKE A LOOK AROUND. THINK.

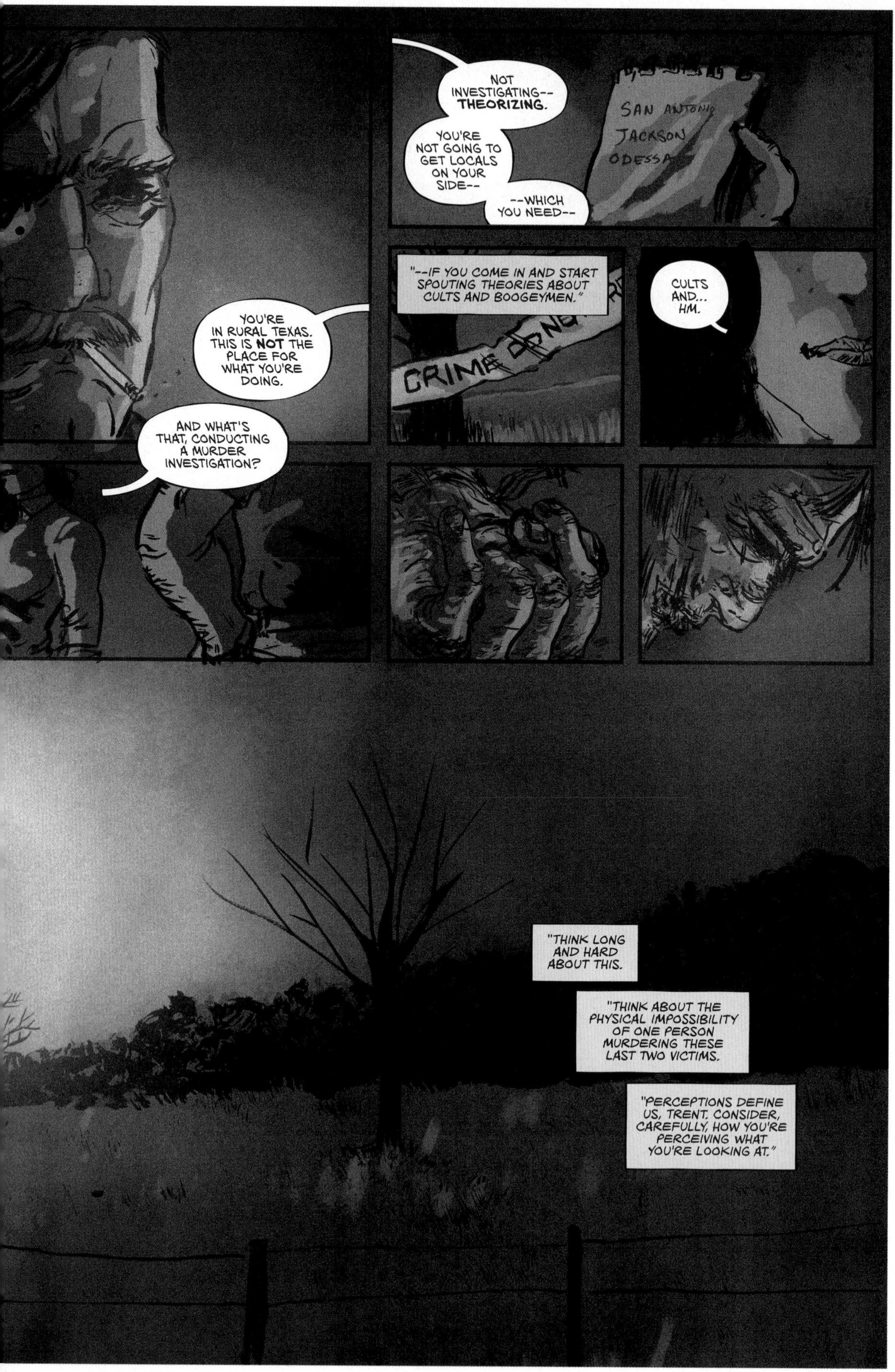
YOU'RE IN RURAL TEXAS. THIS IS **NOT** THE PLACE FOR WHAT YOU'RE DOING.
AND WHAT'S THAT, CONDUCTING A MURDER INVESTIGATION?
NOT INVESTIGATING-- **THEORIZING.**
YOU'RE NOT GOING TO GET LOCALS ON YOUR SIDE--
--WHICH YOU NEED--
JACKSON
ODESSA
"--IF YOU COME IN AND START SPOUTING THEORIES ABOUT CULTS AND BOOGEYMEN."
CRIME
CULTS AND... HM.
"THINK LONG AND HARD ABOUT THIS.
"THINK ABOUT THE PHYSICAL IMPOSSIBILITY OF ONE PERSON MURDERING THESE LAST TWO VICTIMS.
"PERCEPTIONS DEFINE US, TRENT. CONSIDER, CAREFULLY, HOW YOU'RE PERCEIVING WHAT YOU'RE LOOKING AT."

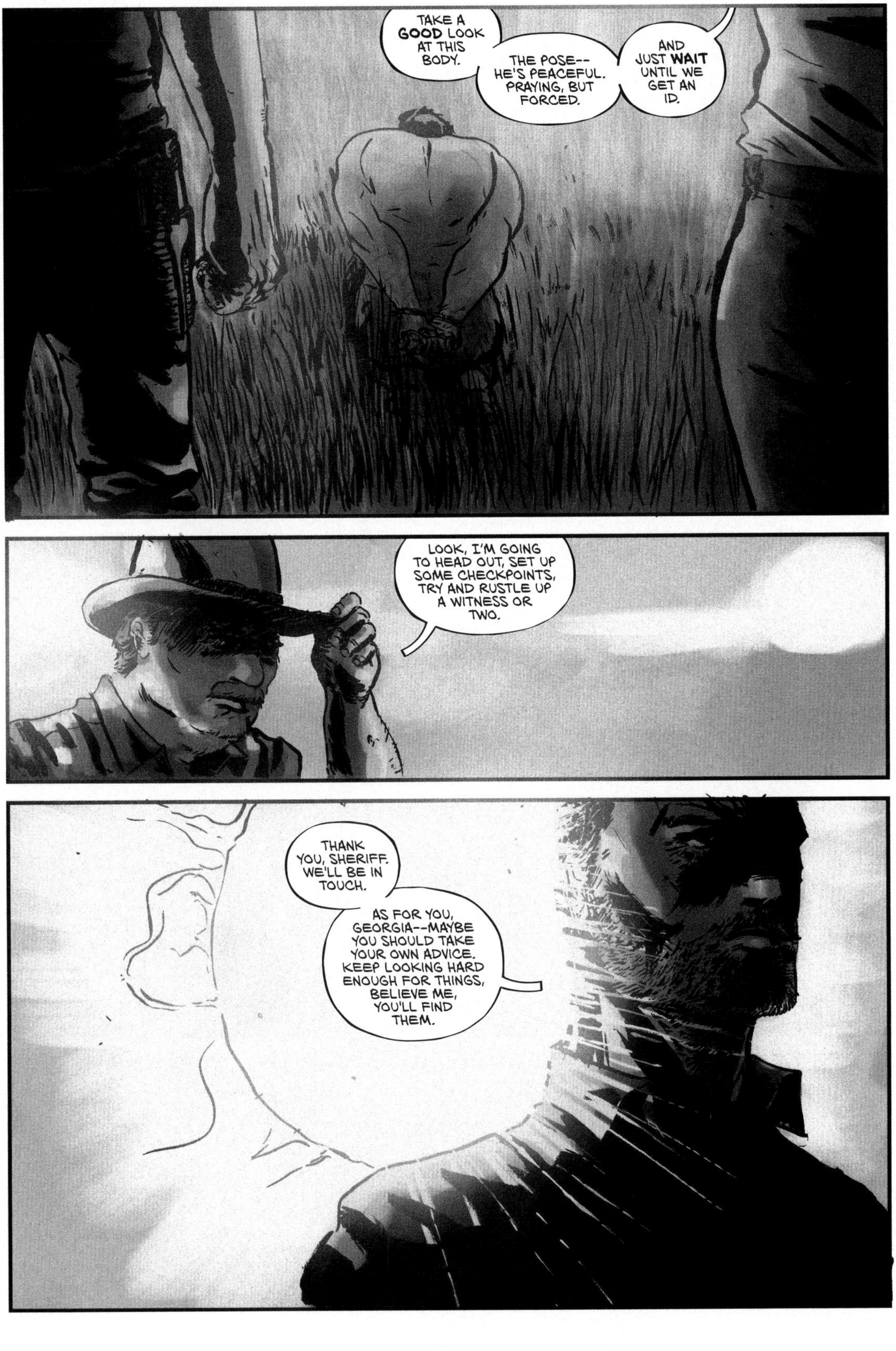
TAKE A GOOD LOOK AT THIS BODY.
THE POSE-- HE'S PEACEFUL. PRAYING, BUT FORCED.
AND JUST WAIT UNTIL WE GET AN ID.
LOOK, I'M GOING TO HEAD OUT, SET UP SOME CHECKPOINTS, TRY AND RUSTLE UP A WITNESS OR TWO.
THANK YOU, SHERIFF. WE'LL BE IN TOUCH.
AS FOR YOU, GEORGIA--MAYBE YOU SHOULD TAKE YOUR OWN ADVICE. KEEP LOOKING HARD ENOUGH FOR THINGS, BELIEVE ME, YOU'LL FIND THEM.

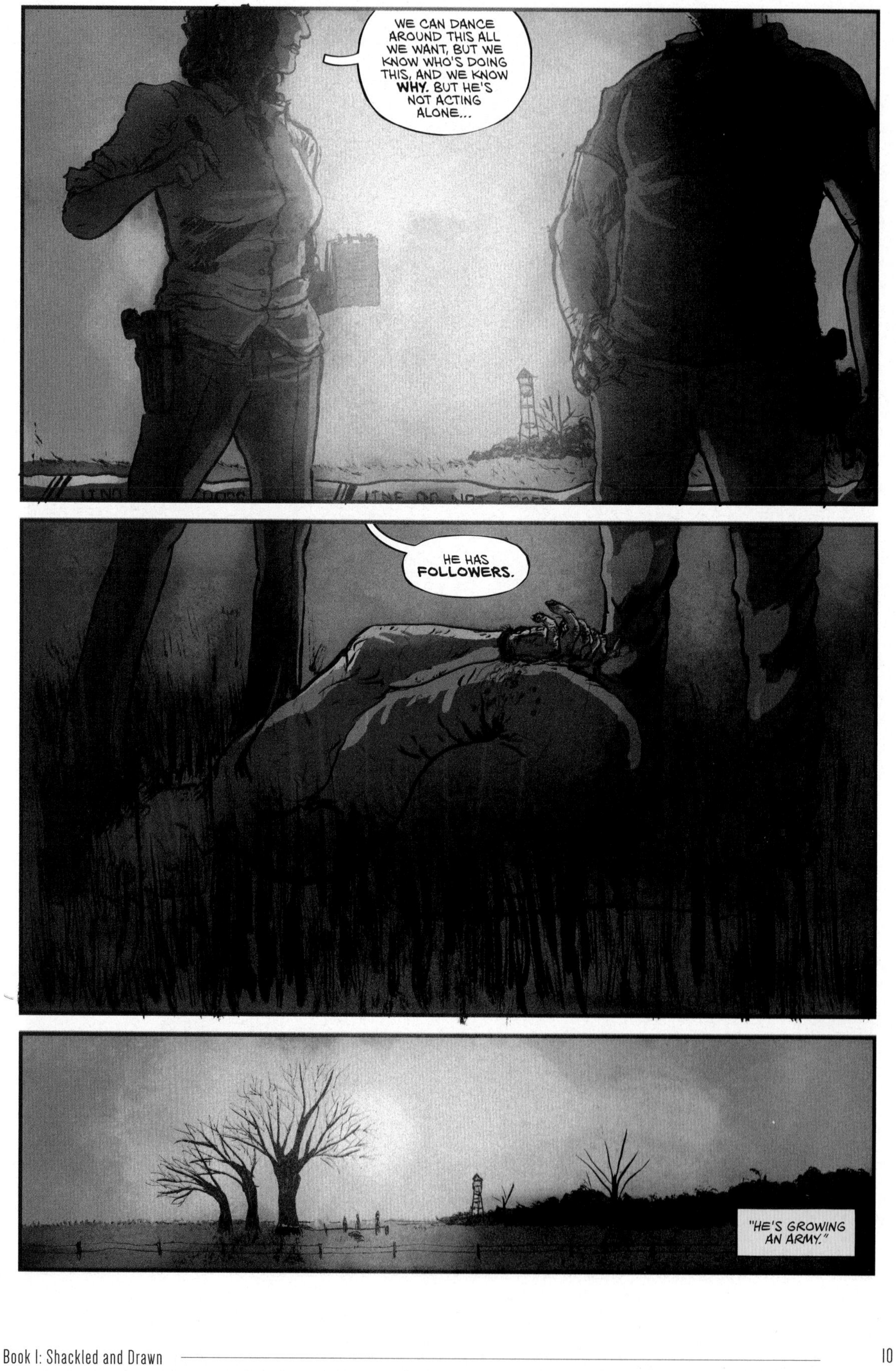
WE CAN DANCE AROUND THIS ALL WE WANT, BUT WE KNOW WHO'S DOING THIS, AND WE KNOW **WHY.** BUT HE'S NOT ACTING ALONE...
HE HAS **FOLLOWERS.**
"HE'S GROWING AN ARMY."

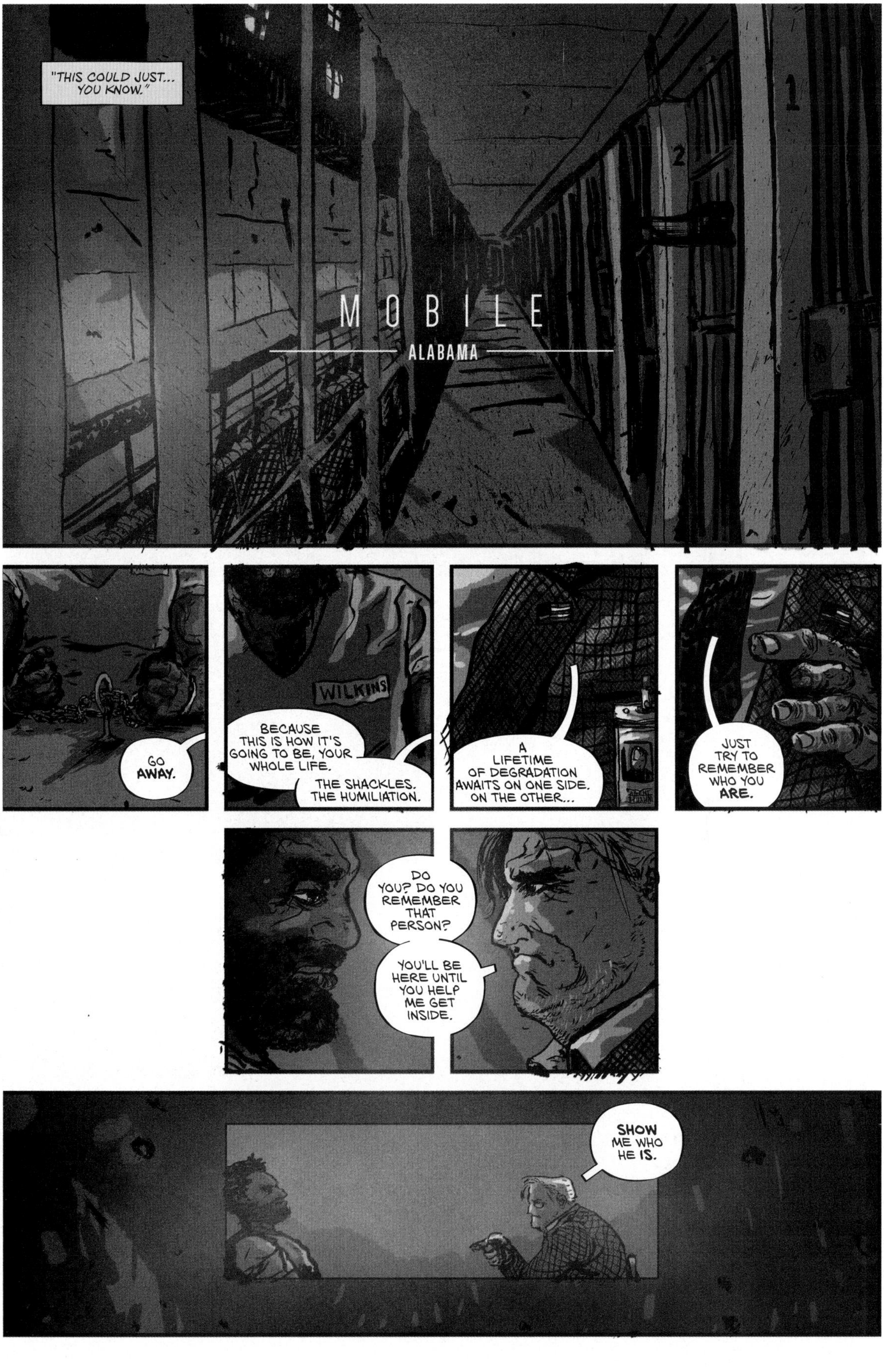
"THIS COULD JUST... YOU KNOW."
MOBILE
ALABAMA
GO AWAY.
BECAUSE THIS IS HOW IT'S GOING TO BE, YOUR WHOLE LIFE.
WILKINS
THE SHACKLES. THE HUMILIATION.
A LIFETIME OF DEGRADATION AWAITS ON ONE SIDE. ON THE OTHER...
JUST TRY TO REMEMBER WHO YOU ARE.
DO YOU? DO YOU REMEMBER THAT PERSON?
YOU'LL BE HERE UNTIL YOU HELP ME GET INSIDE.
SHOW ME WHO HE IS.

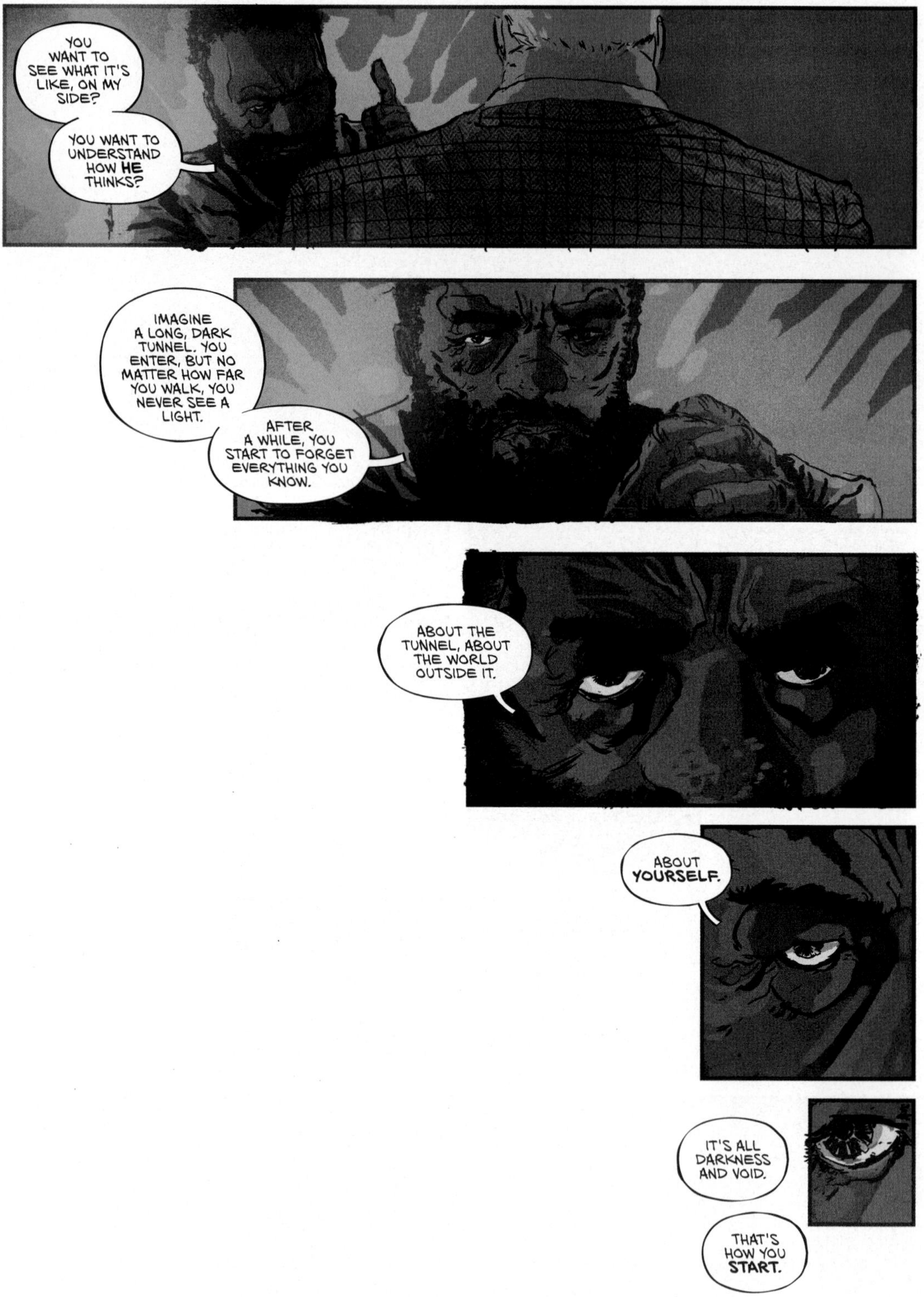
YOU WANT TO SEE WHAT IT'S LIKE, ON MY SIDE?
YOU WANT TO UNDERSTAND HOW **HE** THINKS?
IMAGINE A LONG, DARK TUNNEL. YOU ENTER, BUT NO MATTER HOW FAR YOU WALK, YOU NEVER SEE A LIGHT.
AFTER A WHILE, YOU START TO FORGET EVERYTHING YOU KNOW.
ABOUT THE TUNNEL, ABOUT THE WORLD OUTSIDE IT.
ABOUT **YOURSELF.**
IT'S ALL DARKNESS AND VOID.
THAT'S HOW YOU **START.**

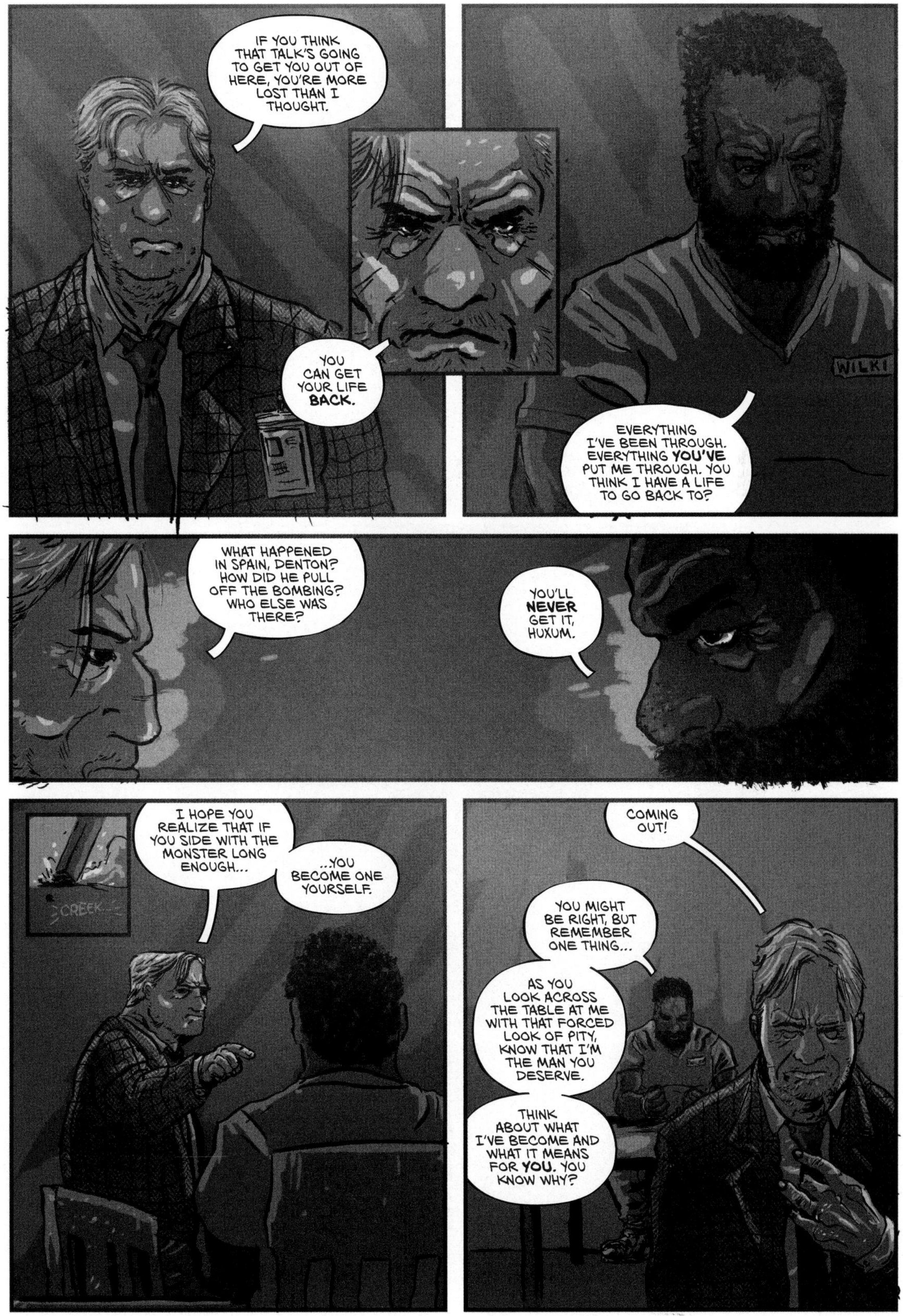
IF YOU THINK THAT TALK'S GOING TO GET YOU OUT OF HERE, YOU'RE MORE LOST THAN I THOUGHT.
YOU CAN GET YOUR LIFE **BACK.**
WILKI
EVERYTHING I'VE BEEN THROUGH. EVERYTHING **YOU'VE** PUT ME THROUGH. YOU THINK I HAVE A LIFE TO GO BACK TO?
WHAT HAPPENED IN SPAIN, DENTON? HOW DID HE PULL OFF THE BOMBING? WHO ELSE WAS THERE?
YOU'LL **NEVER** GET IT, HUXUM.
CREEK
I HOPE YOU REALIZE THAT IF YOU SIDE WITH THE MONSTER LONG ENOUGH...
...YOU BECOME ONE YOURSELF.
COMING OUT!
YOU MIGHT BE RIGHT, BUT REMEMBER ONE THING...
AS YOU LOOK ACROSS THE TABLE AT ME WITH THAT FORCED LOOK OF PITY, KNOW THAT I'M THE MAN YOU DESERVE.
THINK ABOUT WHAT I'VE BECOME AND WHAT IT MEANS FOR **YOU.** YOU KNOW WHY?

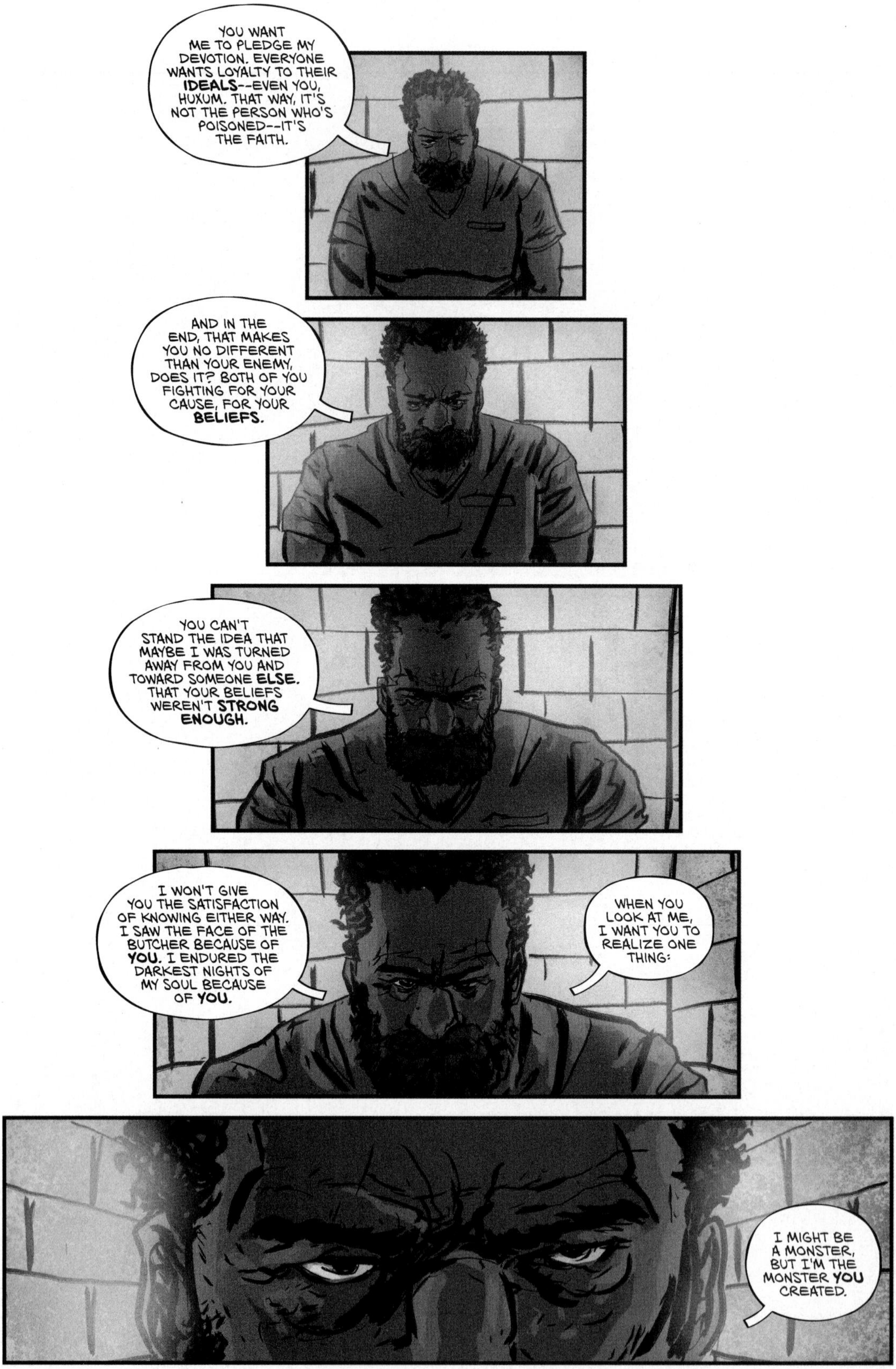
YOU WANT ME TO PLEDGE MY DEVOTION. EVERYONE WANTS LOYALTY TO THEIR IDEALS--EVEN YOU, HUXUM. THAT WAY, IT'S NOT THE PERSON WHO'S POISONED--IT'S THE FAITH.
AND IN THE END, THAT MAKES YOU NO DIFFERENT THAN YOUR ENEMY, DOES IT? BOTH OF YOU FIGHTING FOR YOUR CAUSE, FOR YOUR BELIEFS.
YOU CAN'T STAND THE IDEA THAT MAYBE I WAS TURNED AWAY FROM YOU AND TOWARD SOMEONE ELSE. THAT YOUR BELIEFS WEREN'T STRONG ENOUGH.
I WON'T GIVE YOU THE SATISFACTION OF KNOWING EITHER WAY. I SAW THE FACE OF THE BUTCHER BECAUSE OF YOU. I ENDURED THE DARKEST NIGHTS OF MY SOUL BECAUSE OF YOU.
WHEN YOU LOOK AT ME, I WANT YOU TO REALIZE ONE THING:
I MIGHT BE A MONSTER, BUT I'M THE MONSTER YOU CREATED.

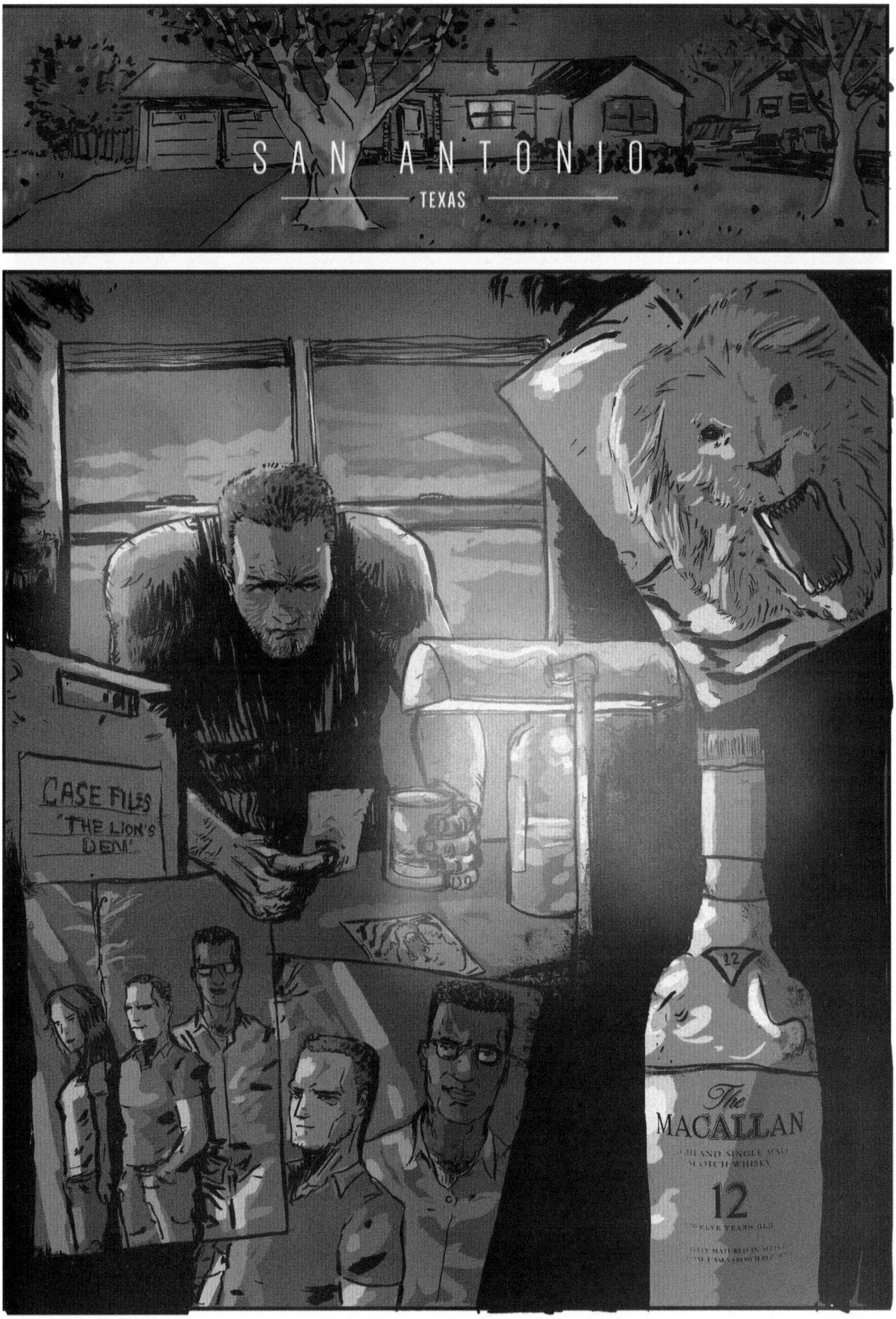
SAN ANTONIO
TEXAS
CASE FILES
"THE LION'S DEN"
The MACALLAN
12

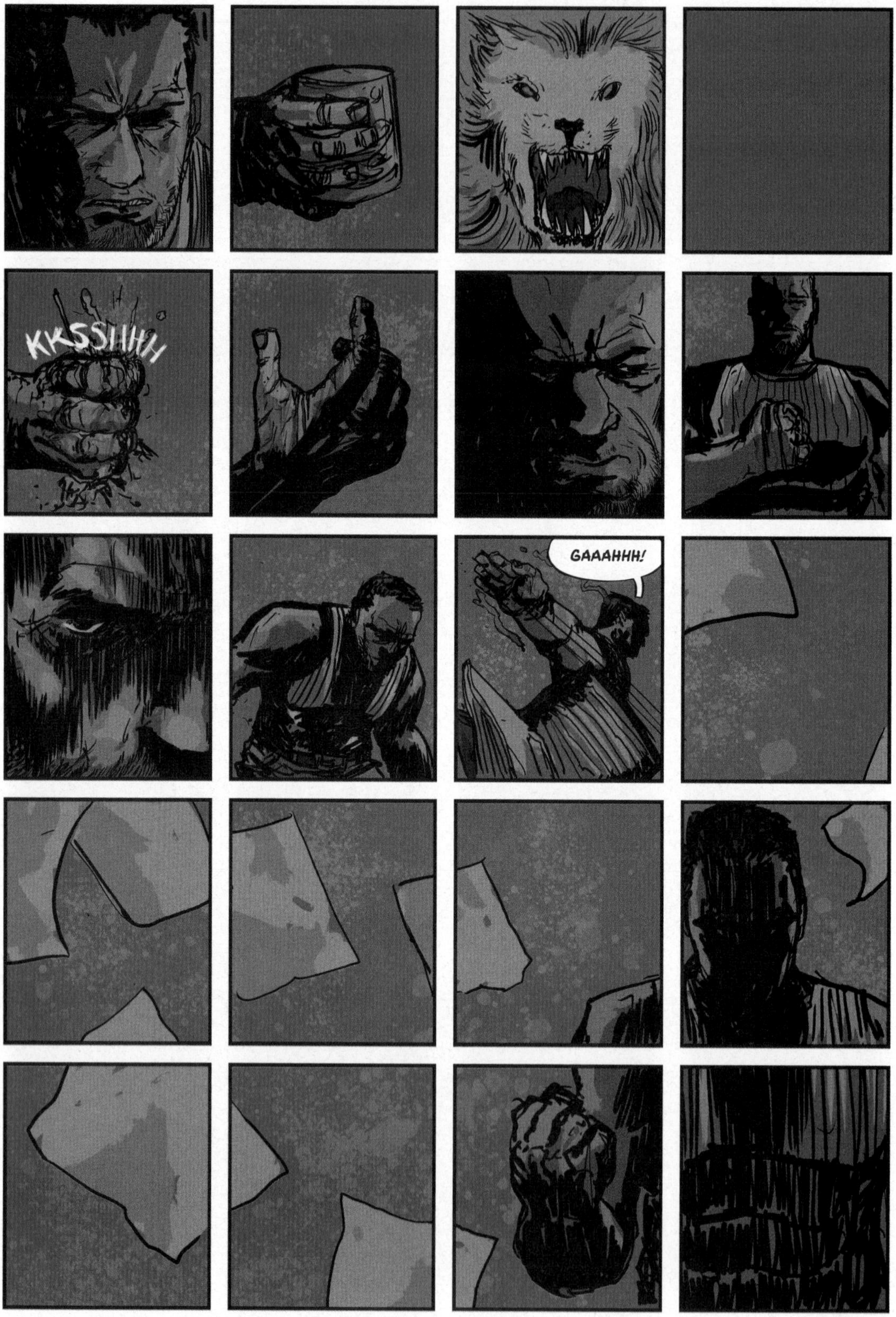
KKSSHHH
GAAAHHH!

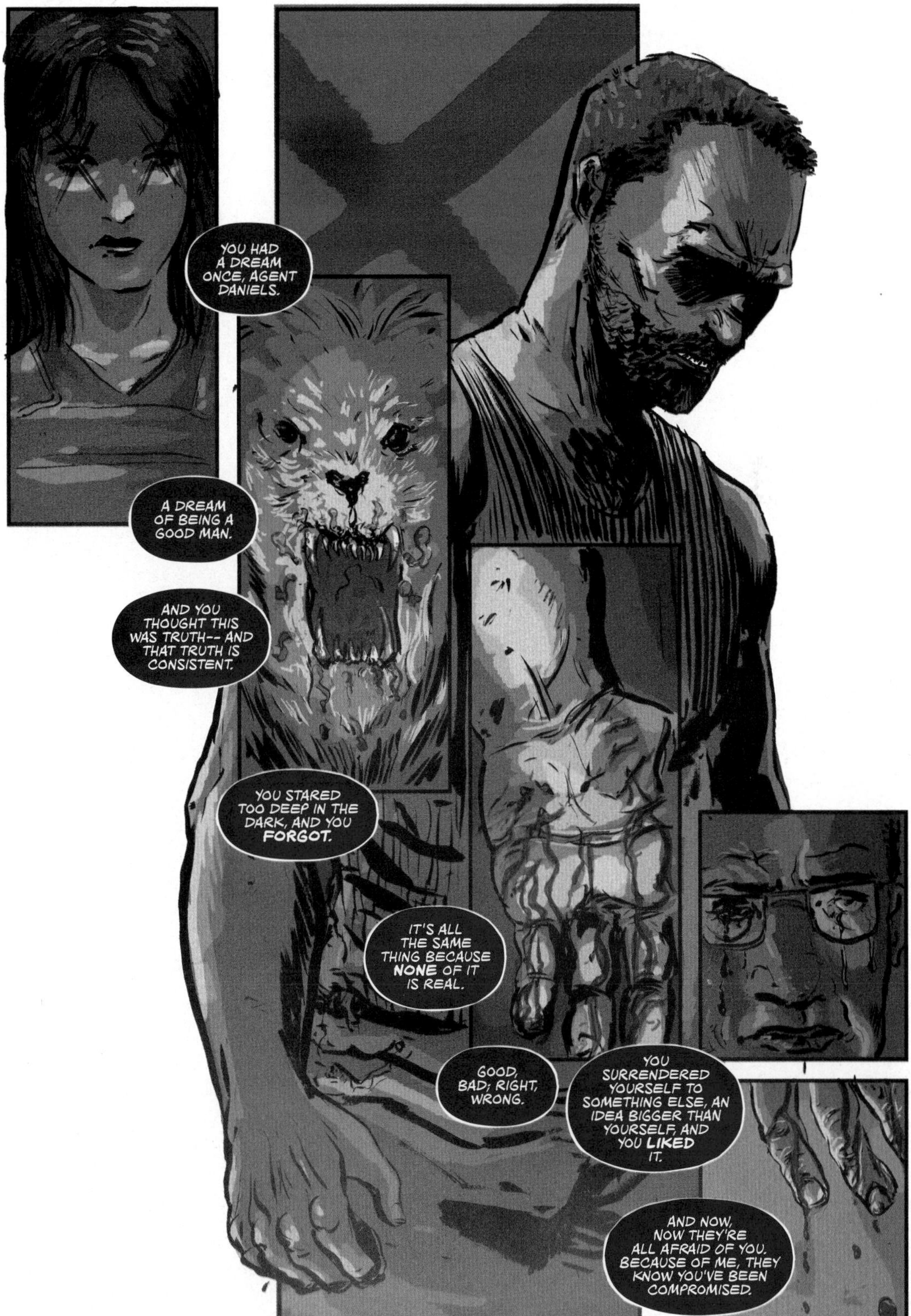
YOU HAD A DREAM ONCE, AGENT DANIELS.
A DREAM OF BEING A GOOD MAN.
AND YOU THOUGHT THIS WAS TRUTH-- AND THAT TRUTH IS CONSISTENT.
YOU STARED TOO DEEP IN THE DARK, AND YOU **FORGOT.**
IT'S ALL THE SAME THING BECAUSE **NONE** OF IT IS REAL.
GOOD, BAD; RIGHT, WRONG.
YOU SURRENDERED YOURSELF TO SOMETHING ELSE, AN IDEA BIGGER THAN YOURSELF, AND YOU **LIKED** IT.
AND NOW, NOW THEY'RE ALL AFRAID OF YOU. BECAUSE OF ME, THEY KNOW YOU'VE BEEN COMPROMISED.

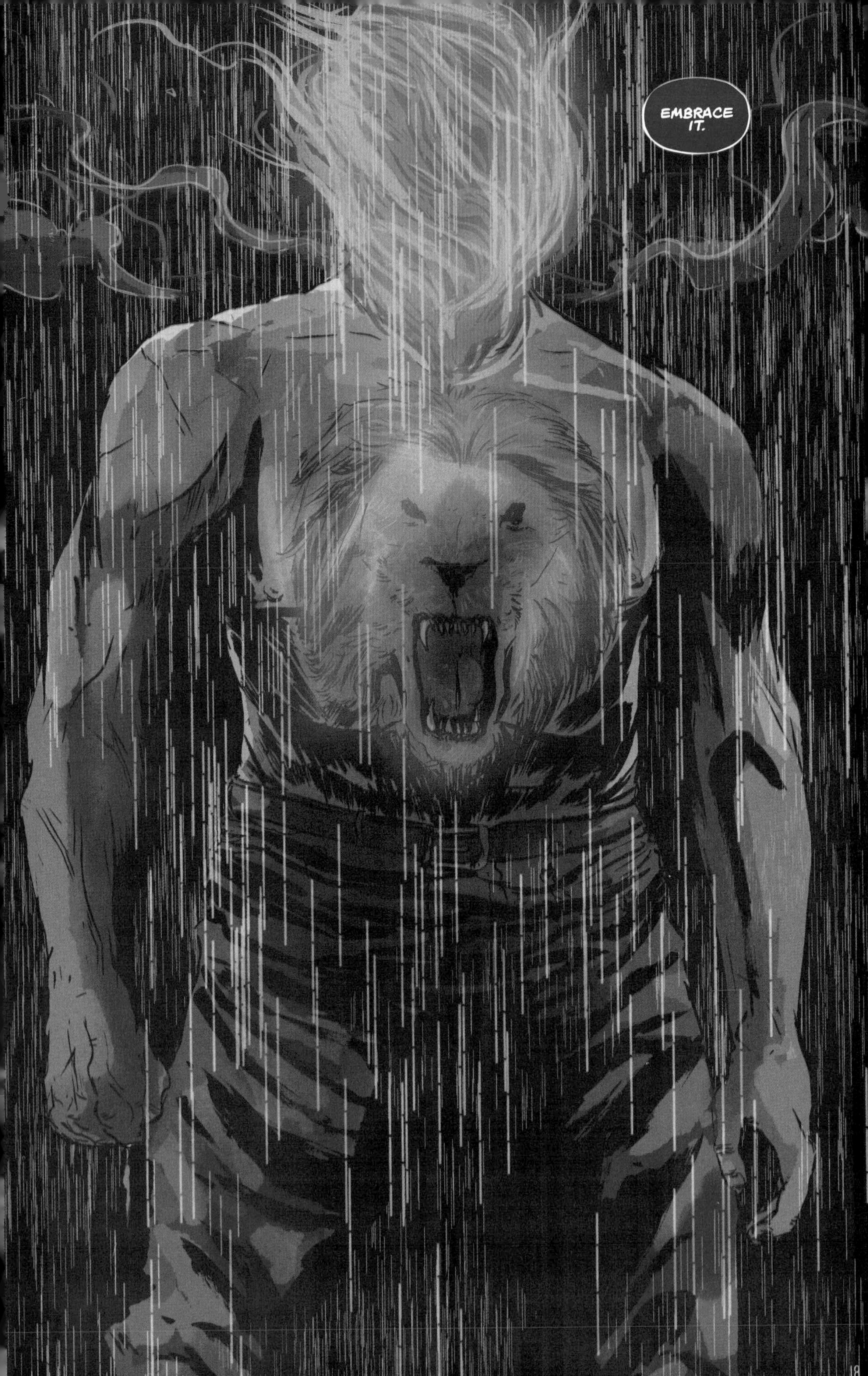
EMBRACE IT.

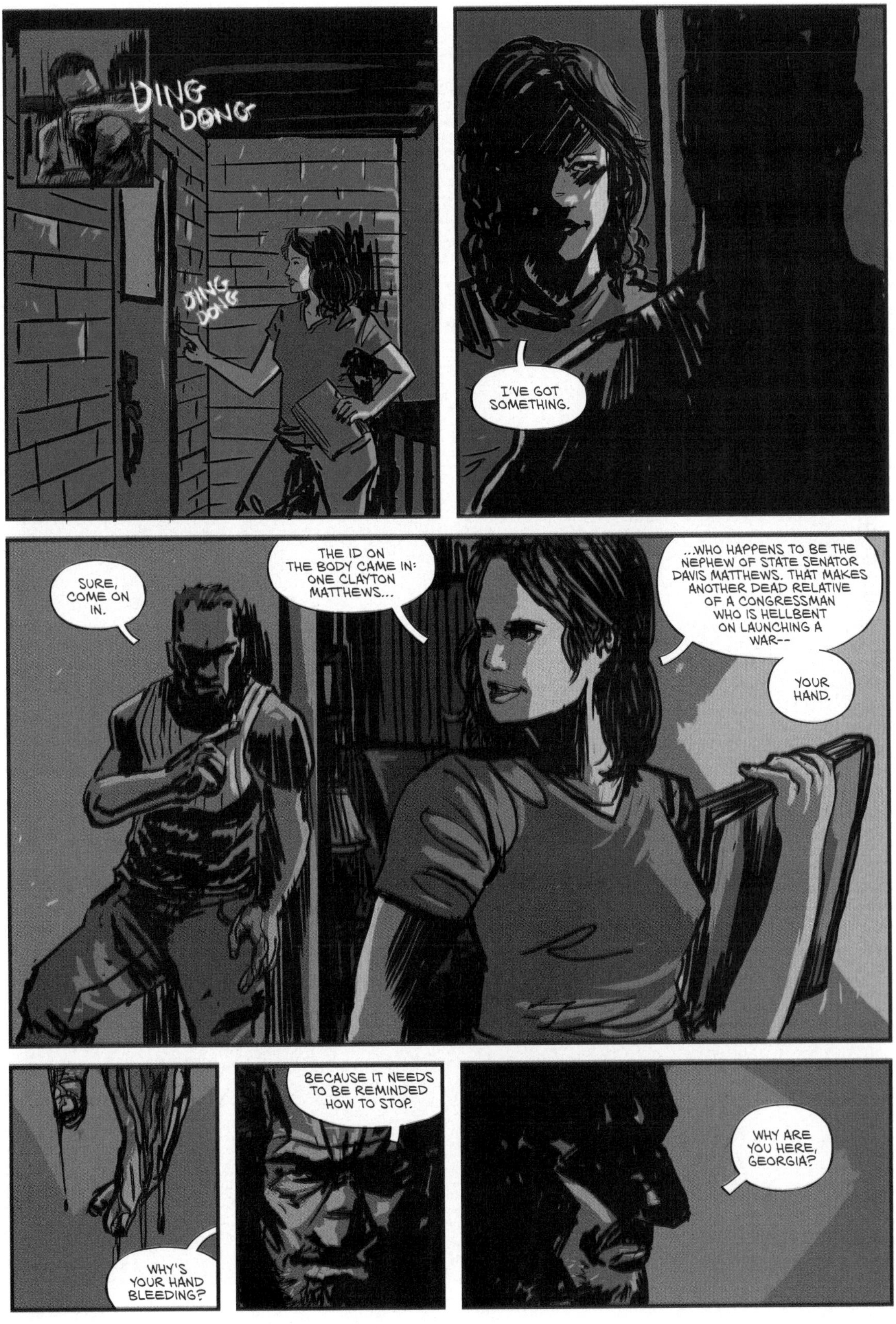
DING DONG
DING DONG
I'VE GOT SOMETHING.
SURE, COME ON IN.
THE ID ON THE BODY CAME IN: ONE CLAYTON MATTHEWS...
...WHO HAPPENS TO BE THE NEPHEW OF STATE SENATOR DAVIS MATTHEWS. THAT MAKES ANOTHER DEAD RELATIVE OF A CONGRESSMAN WHO IS HELLBENT ON LAUNCHING A WAR--
YOUR HAND.
WHY'S YOUR HAND BLEEDING?
BECAUSE IT NEEDS TO BE REMINDED HOW TO STOP.
WHY ARE YOU HERE, GEORGIA?

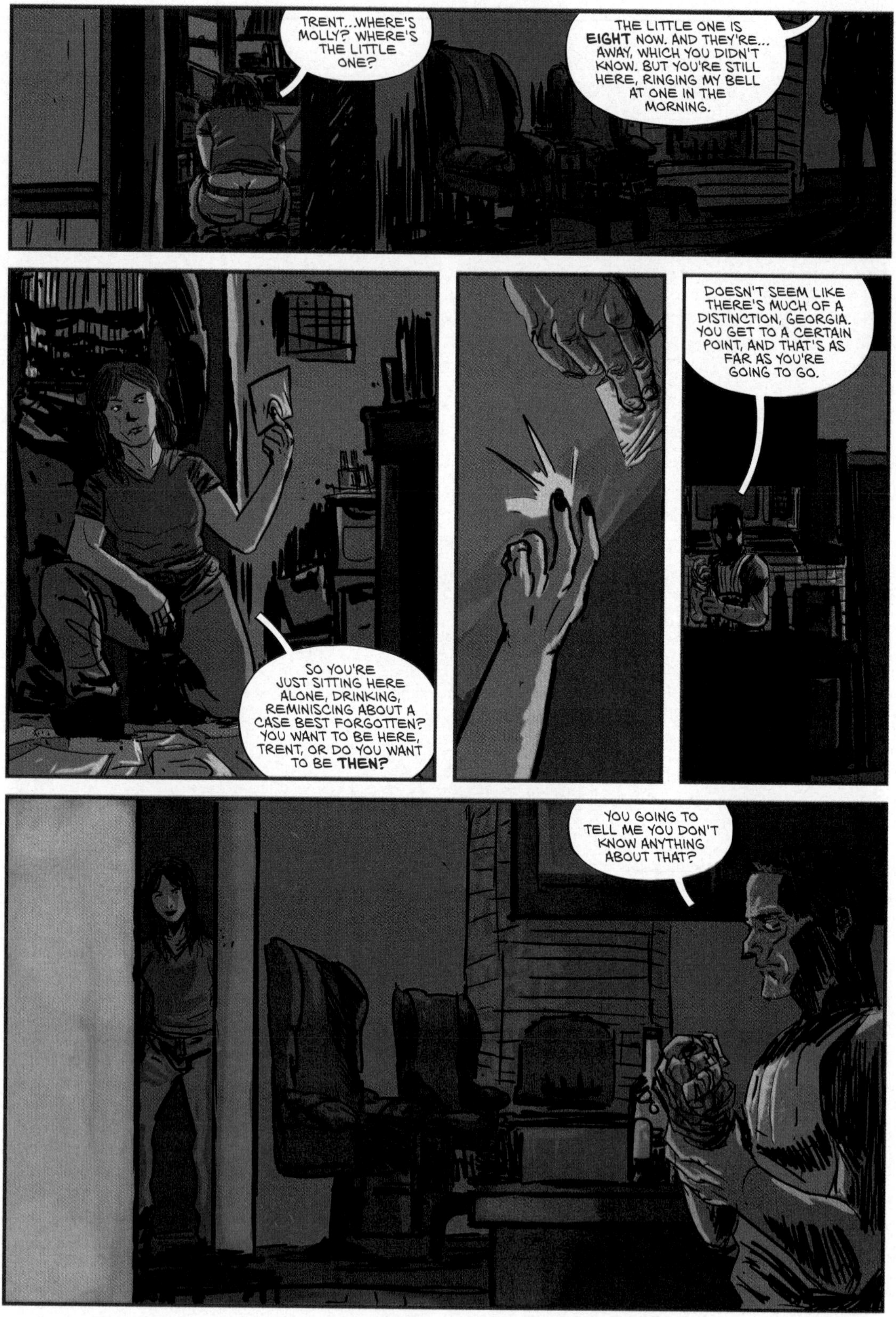
TRENT...WHERE'S MOLLY? WHERE'S THE LITTLE ONE?
THE LITTLE ONE IS EIGHT NOW. AND THEY'RE... AWAY, WHICH YOU DIDN'T KNOW. BUT YOU'RE STILL HERE, RINGING MY BELL AT ONE IN THE MORNING.
SO YOU'RE JUST SITTING HERE ALONE, DRINKING, REMINISCING ABOUT A CASE BEST FORGOTTEN? YOU WANT TO BE HERE, TRENT, OR DO YOU WANT TO BE THEN?
DOESN'T SEEM LIKE THERE'S MUCH OF A DISTINCTION, GEORGIA. YOU GET TO A CERTAIN POINT, AND THAT'S AS FAR AS YOU'RE GOING TO GO.
YOU GOING TO TELL ME YOU DON'T KNOW ANYTHING ABOUT THAT?

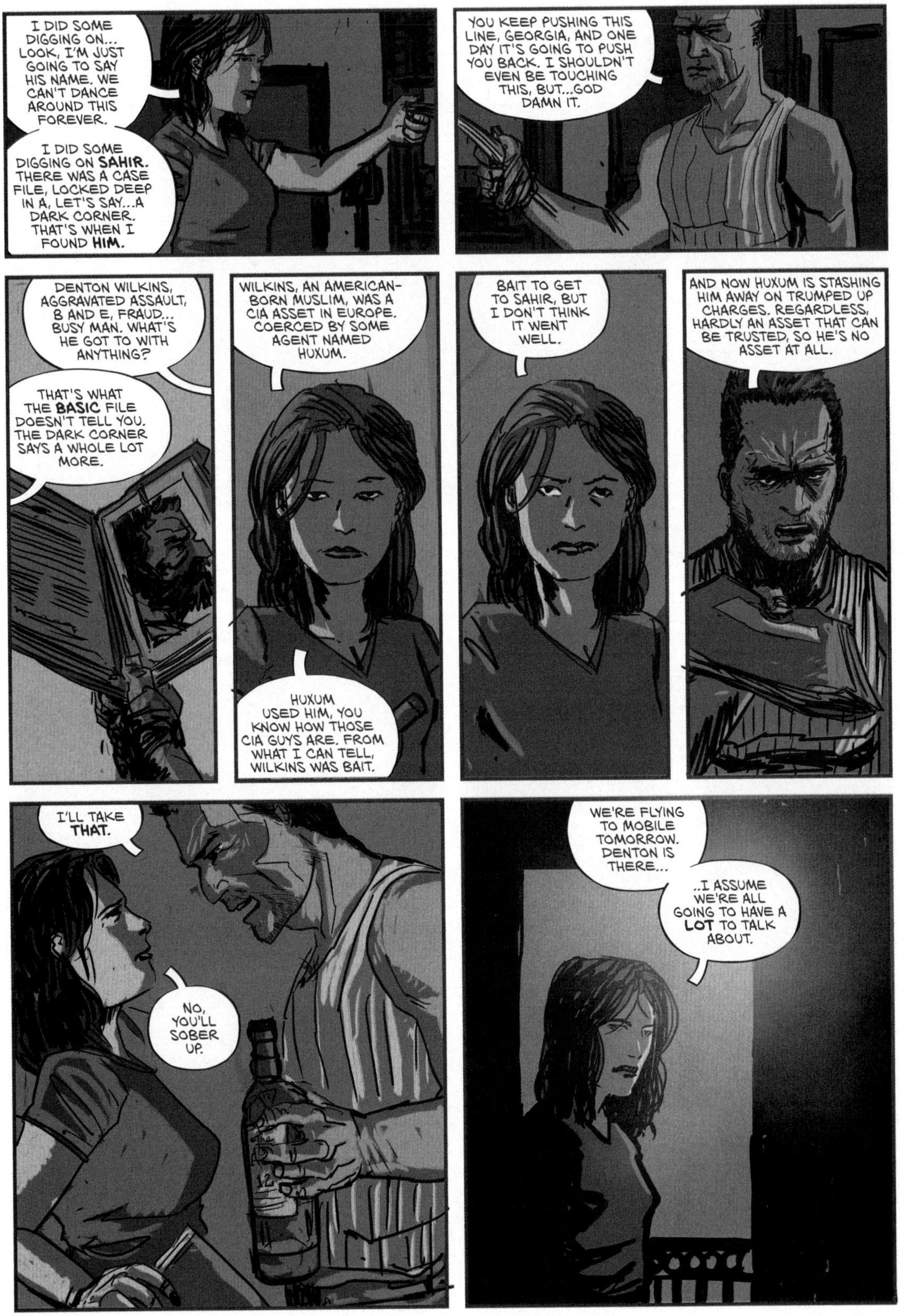
I DID SOME DIGGING ON... LOOK, I'M JUST GOING TO SAY HIS NAME. WE CAN'T DANCE AROUND THIS FOREVER.
I DID SOME DIGGING ON **SAHIR.** THERE WAS A CASE FILE, LOCKED DEEP IN A, LET'S SAY...A DARK CORNER. THAT'S WHEN I FOUND **HIM.**
YOU KEEP PUSHING THIS LINE, GEORGIA, AND ONE DAY IT'S GOING TO PUSH YOU BACK. I SHOULDN'T EVEN BE TOUCHING THIS, BUT...GOD DAMN IT.
DENTON WILKINS, AGGRAVATED ASSAULT, B AND E, FRAUD... BUSY MAN. WHAT'S HE GOT TO WITH ANYTHING?
THAT'S WHAT THE **BASIC** FILE DOESN'T TELL YOU. THE DARK CORNER SAYS A WHOLE LOT MORE.
WILKINS, AN AMERICAN-BORN MUSLIM, WAS A CIA ASSET IN EUROPE. COERCED BY SOME AGENT NAMED HUXUM.
HUXUM USED HIM, YOU KNOW HOW THOSE CIA GUYS ARE. FROM WHAT I CAN TELL, WILKINS WAS BAIT.
BAIT TO GET TO SAHIR, BUT I DON'T THINK IT WENT WELL.
AND NOW HUXUM IS STASHING HIM AWAY ON TRUMPED UP CHARGES. REGARDLESS, HARDLY AN ASSET THAT CAN BE TRUSTED, SO HE'S NO ASSET AT ALL.
I'LL TAKE **THAT.**
NO, YOU'LL SOBER UP.
WE'RE FLYING TO MOBILE TOMORROW. DENTON IS THERE...
..I ASSUME WE'RE ALL GOING TO HAVE A **LOT** TO TALK ABOUT.

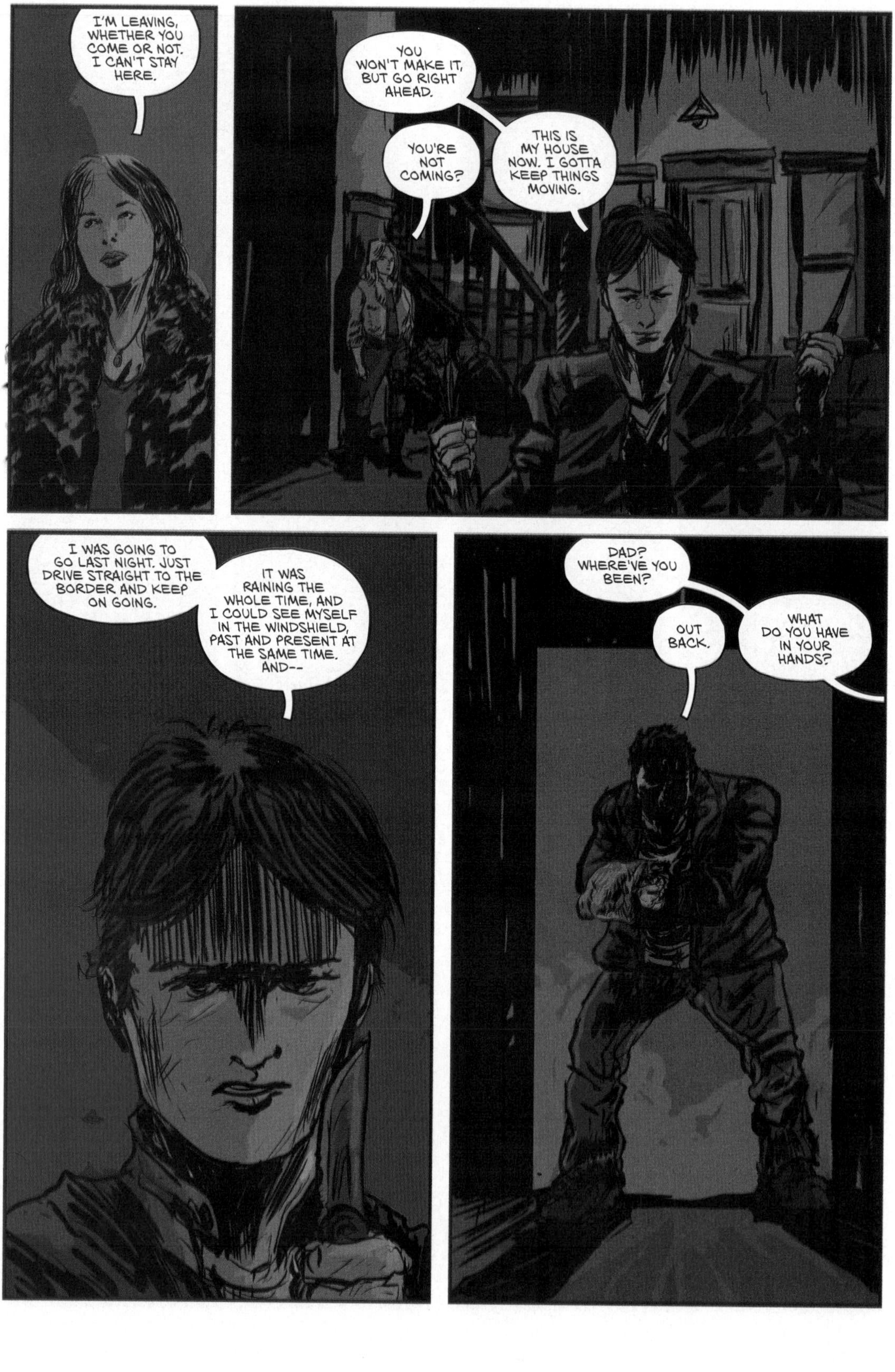
I'M LEAVING, WHETHER YOU COME OR NOT. I CAN'T STAY HERE.
YOU WON'T MAKE IT, BUT GO RIGHT AHEAD.
YOU'RE NOT COMING?
THIS IS MY HOUSE NOW. I GOTTA KEEP THINGS MOVING.
I WAS GOING TO GO LAST NIGHT. JUST DRIVE STRAIGHT TO THE BORDER AND KEEP ON GOING.
IT WAS RAINING THE WHOLE TIME, AND I COULD SEE MYSELF IN THE WINDSHIELD, PAST AND PRESENT AT THE SAME TIME. AND--
DAD? WHERE'VE YOU BEEN?
OUT BACK.
WHAT DO YOU HAVE IN YOUR HANDS?

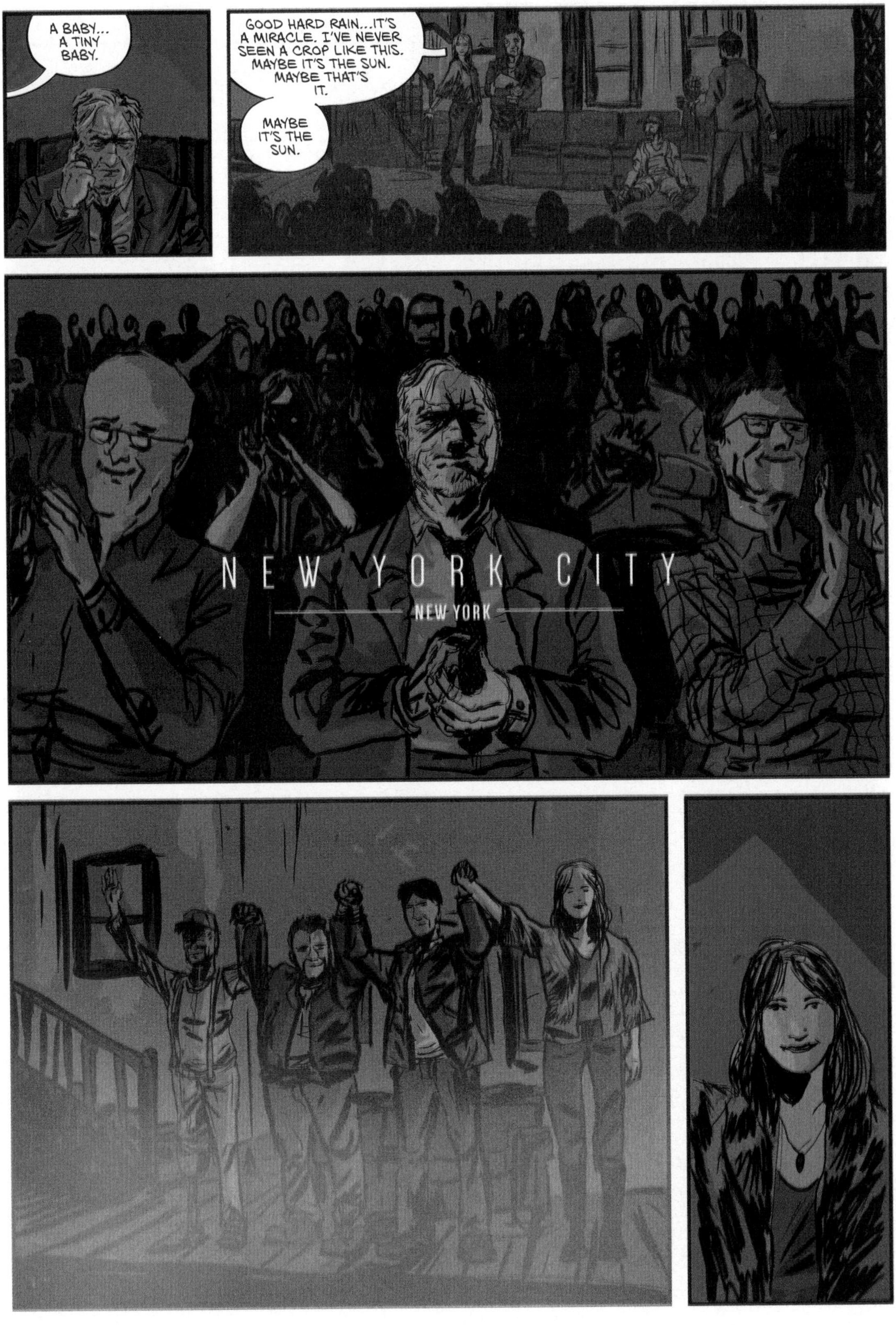
A BABY... A TINY BABY.
GOOD HARD RAIN...IT'S A MIRACLE. I'VE NEVER SEEN A CROP LIKE THIS. MAYBE IT'S THE SUN. MAYBE THAT'S IT.
MAYBE IT'S THE SUN.
NEW YORK CITY
NEW YORK

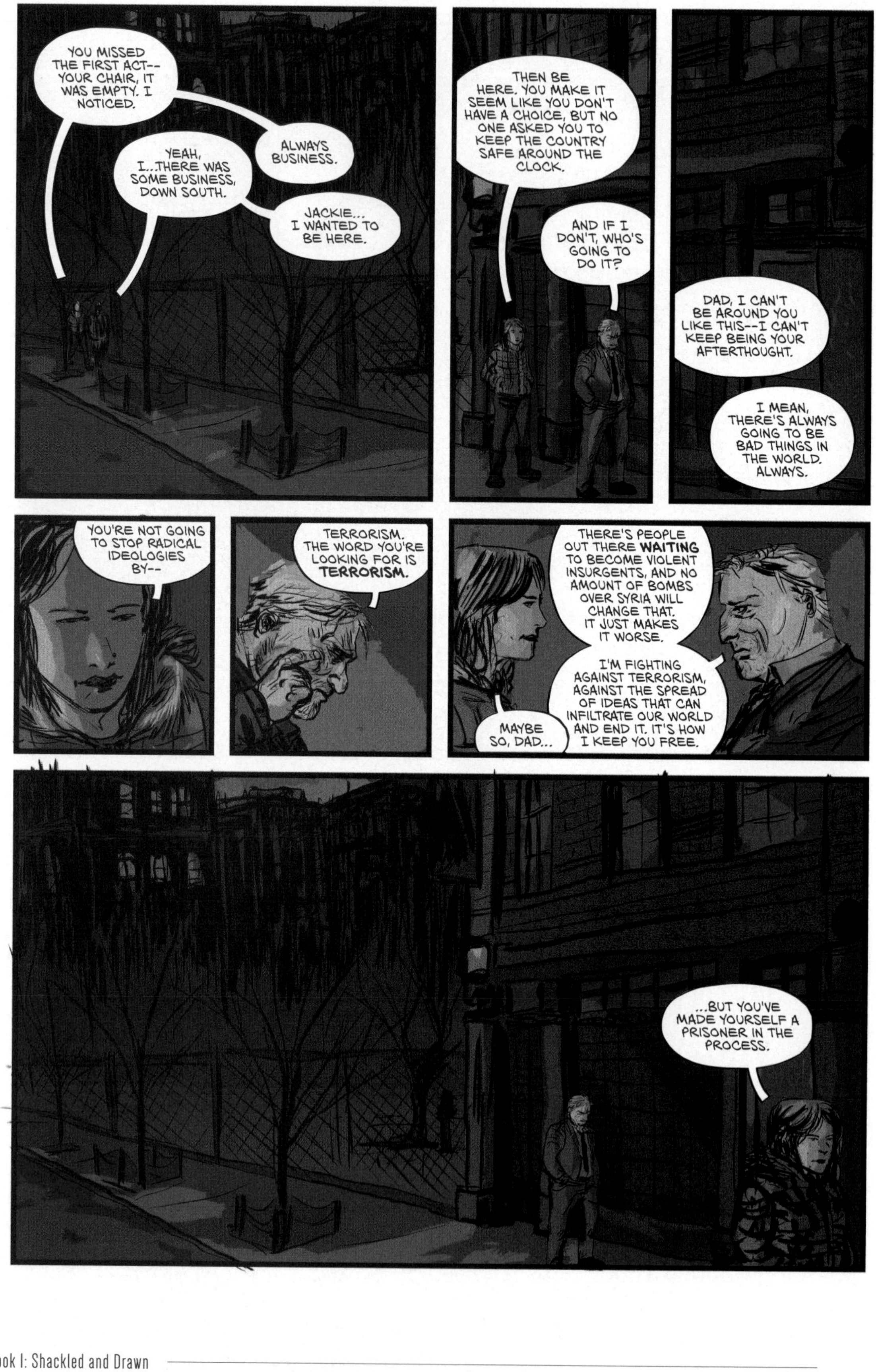
YOU MISSED THE FIRST ACT-- YOUR CHAIR, IT WAS EMPTY. I NOTICED.
YEAH, I...THERE WAS SOME BUSINESS, DOWN SOUTH.
ALWAYS BUSINESS.
JACKIE... I WANTED TO BE HERE.
THEN BE HERE. YOU MAKE IT SEEM LIKE YOU DON'T HAVE A CHOICE, BUT NO ONE ASKED YOU TO KEEP THE COUNTRY SAFE AROUND THE CLOCK.
AND IF I DON'T, WHO'S GOING TO DO IT?
DAD, I CAN'T BE AROUND YOU LIKE THIS--I CAN'T KEEP BEING YOUR AFTERTHOUGHT.
I MEAN, THERE'S ALWAYS GOING TO BE BAD THINGS IN THE WORLD. ALWAYS.
YOU'RE NOT GOING TO STOP RADICAL IDEOLOGIES BY--
TERRORISM. THE WORD YOU'RE LOOKING FOR IS **TERRORISM.**
THERE'S PEOPLE OUT THERE **WAITING** TO BECOME VIOLENT INSURGENTS, AND NO AMOUNT OF BOMBS OVER SYRIA WILL CHANGE THAT. IT JUST MAKES IT WORSE.
I'M FIGHTING AGAINST TERRORISM, AGAINST THE SPREAD OF IDEAS THAT CAN INFILTRATE OUR WORLD AND END IT. IT'S HOW I KEEP YOU FREE.
MAYBE SO, DAD...
...BUT YOU'VE MADE YOURSELF A PRISONER IN THE PROCESS.

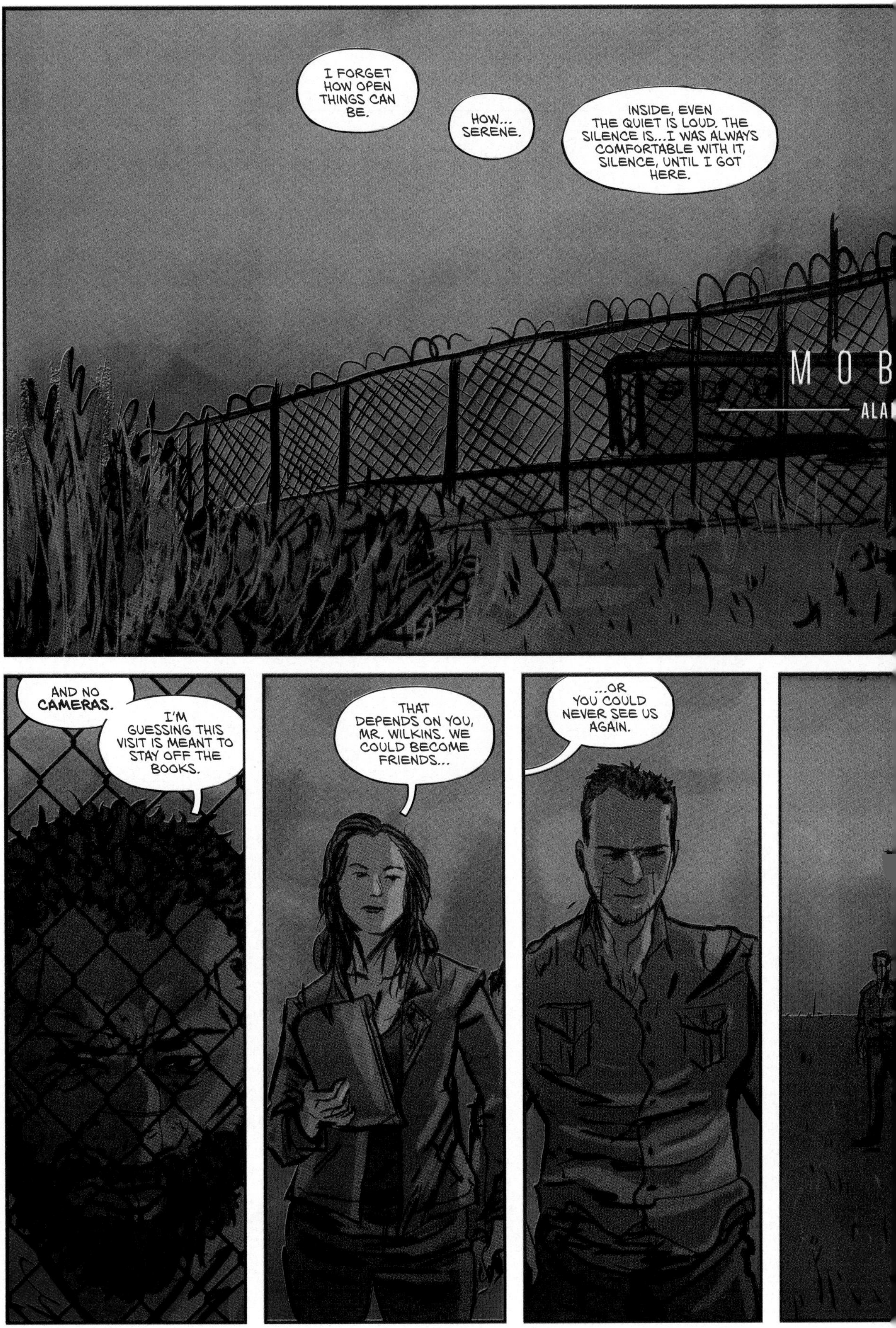
I FORGET HOW OPEN THINGS CAN BE.
HOW... SERENE.
INSIDE, EVEN THE QUIET IS LOUD. THE SILENCE IS...I WAS ALWAYS COMFORTABLE WITH IT, SILENCE, UNTIL I GOT HERE.
M O B
AND NO CAMERAS.
I'M GUESSING THIS VISIT IS MEANT TO STAY OFF THE BOOKS.
THAT DEPENDS ON YOU, MR. WILKINS. WE COULD BECOME FRIENDS...
...OR YOU COULD NEVER SEE US AGAIN.

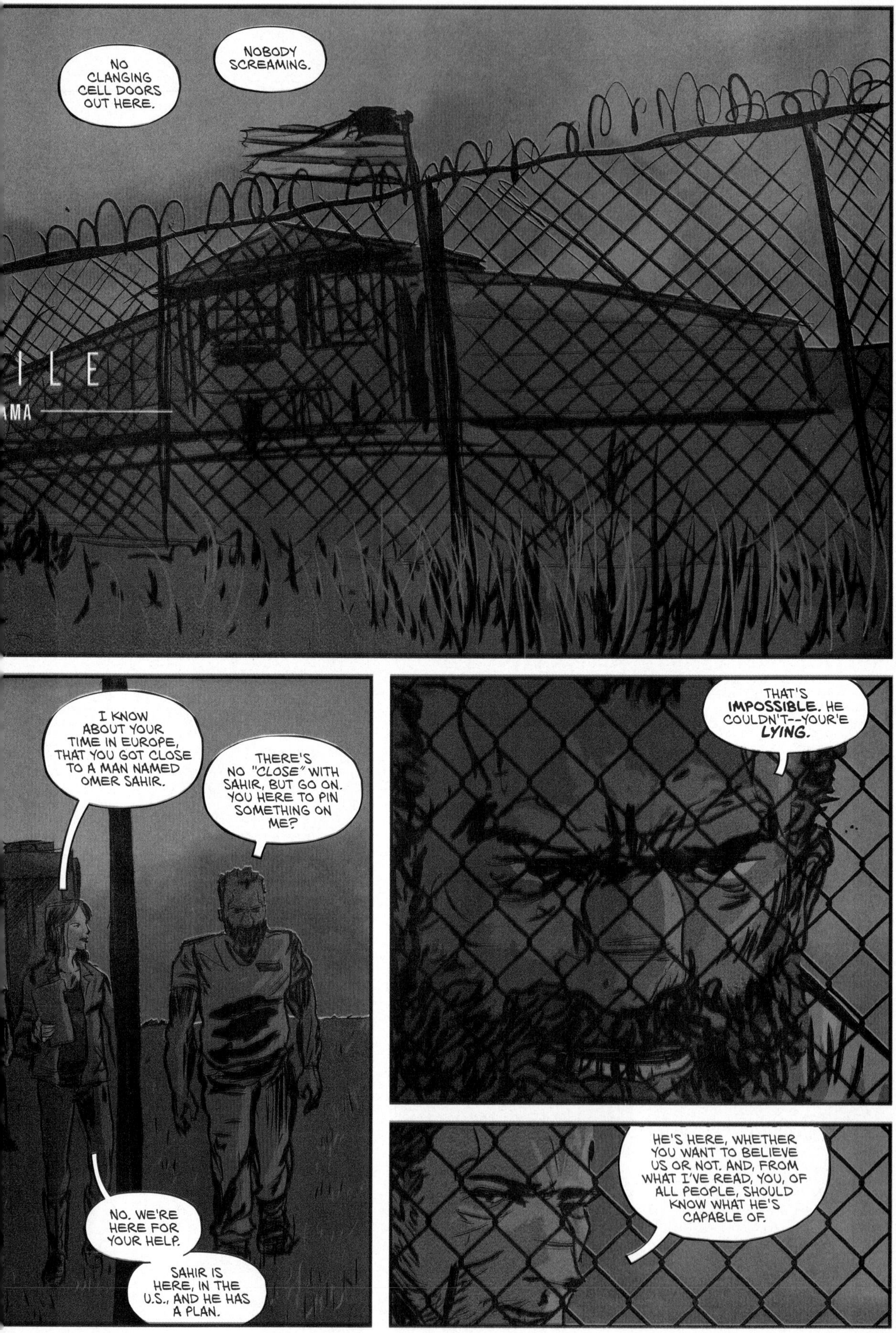
NO CLANGING CELL DOORS OUT HERE.
NOBODY SCREAMING.
I KNOW ABOUT YOUR TIME IN EUROPE, THAT YOU GOT CLOSE TO A MAN NAMED OMER SAHIR.
THERE'S NO "CLOSE" WITH SAHIR, BUT GO ON. YOU HERE TO PIN SOMETHING ON ME?
NO. WE'RE HERE FOR YOUR HELP.
SAHIR IS HERE, IN THE U.S., AND HE HAS A PLAN.
THAT'S **IMPOSSIBLE.** HE COULDN'T--YOUR'E ***LYING.***
HE'S HERE, WHETHER YOU WANT TO BELIEVE US OR NOT. AND, FROM WHAT I'VE READ, YOU, OF ALL PEOPLE, SHOULD KNOW WHAT HE'S CAPABLE OF.

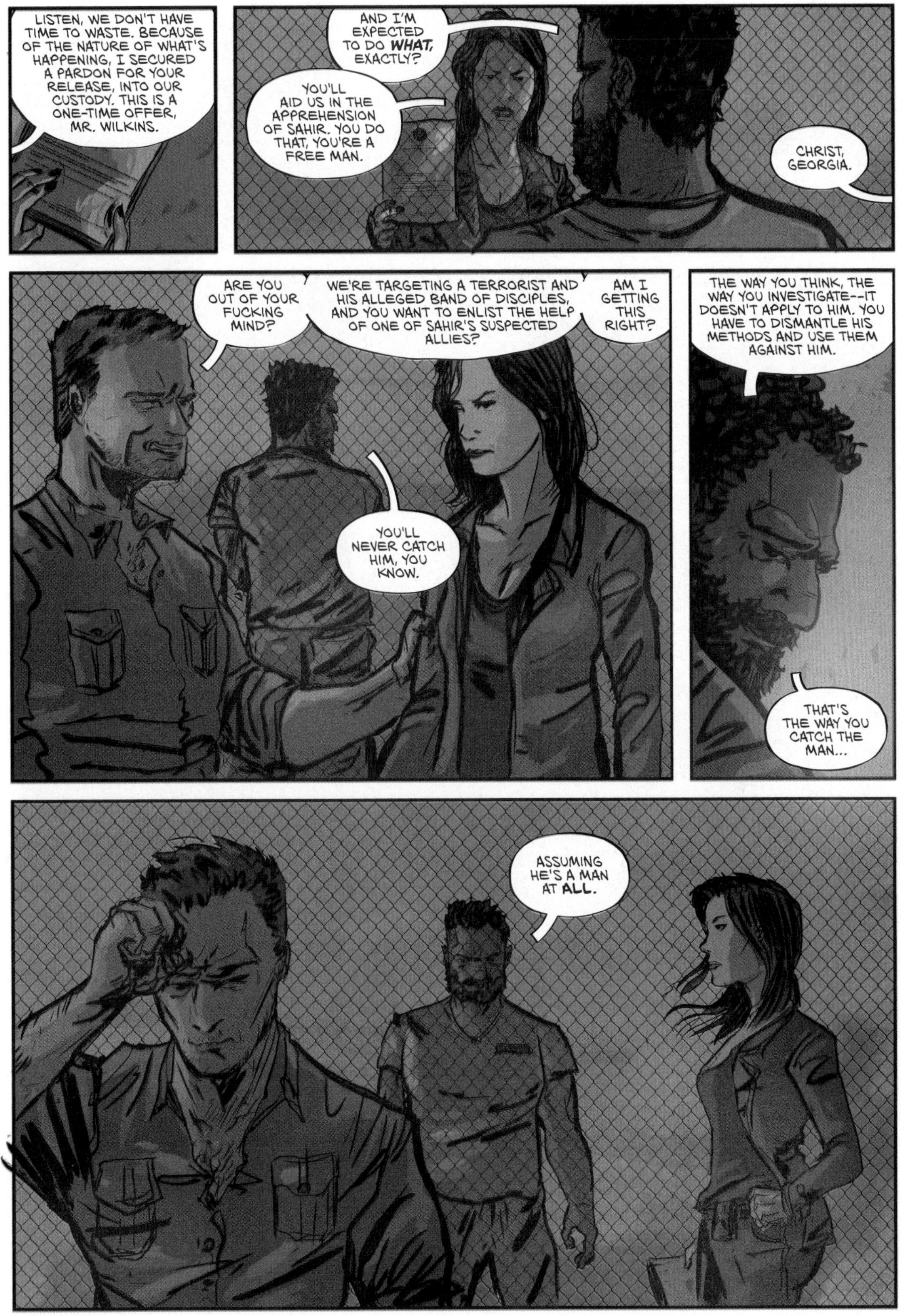
LISTEN, WE DON'T HAVE TIME TO WASTE. BECAUSE OF THE NATURE OF WHAT'S HAPPENING, I SECURED A PARDON FOR YOUR RELEASE, INTO OUR CUSTODY. THIS IS A ONE-TIME OFFER, MR. WILKINS.
AND I'M EXPECTED TO DO **WHAT,** EXACTLY?
YOU'LL AID US IN THE APPREHENSION OF SAHIR. YOU DO THAT, YOU'RE A FREE MAN.
CHRIST, GEORGIA.
ARE YOU OUT OF YOUR FUCKING MIND?
WE'RE TARGETING A TERRORIST AND HIS ALLEGED BAND OF DISCIPLES, AND YOU WANT TO ENLIST THE HELP OF ONE OF SAHIR'S SUSPECTED ALLIES?
AM I GETTING THIS RIGHT?
YOU'LL NEVER CATCH HIM, YOU KNOW.
THE WAY YOU THINK, THE WAY YOU INVESTIGATE--IT DOESN'T APPLY TO HIM. YOU HAVE TO DISMANTLE HIS METHODS AND USE THEM AGAINST HIM.
THAT'S THE WAY YOU CATCH THE MAN...
ASSUMING HE'S A MAN AT **ALL.**

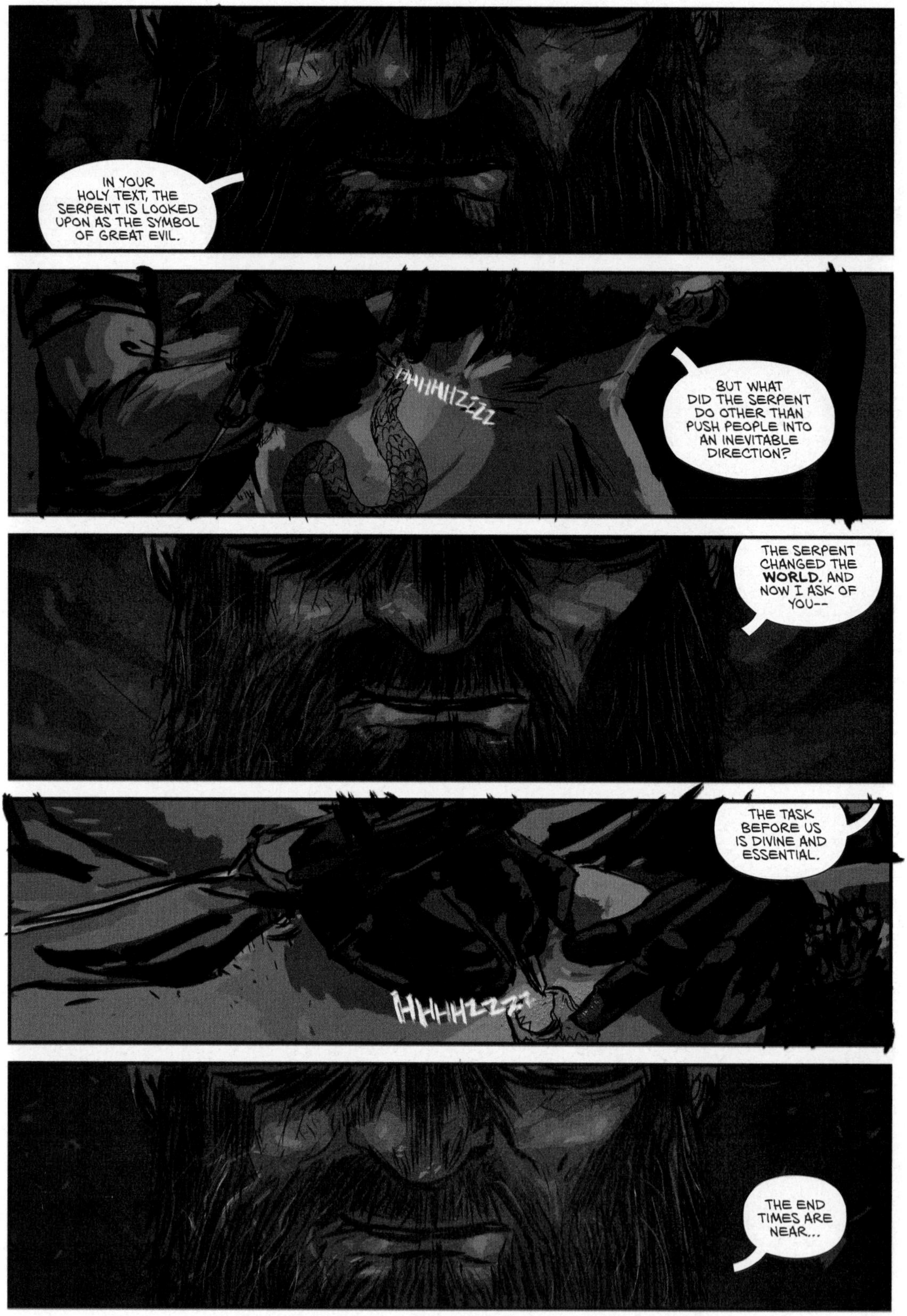
IN YOUR HOLY TEXT, THE SERPENT IS LOOKED UPON AS THE SYMBOL OF GREAT EVIL.
HHHHHZZZZ
BUT WHAT DID THE SERPENT DO OTHER THAN PUSH PEOPLE INTO AN INEVITABLE DIRECTION?
THE SERPENT CHANGED THE **WORLD.** AND NOW I ASK OF YOU--
THE TASK BEFORE US IS DIVINE AND ESSENTIAL.
HHHHHZZZZ
THE END TIMES ARE NEAR...

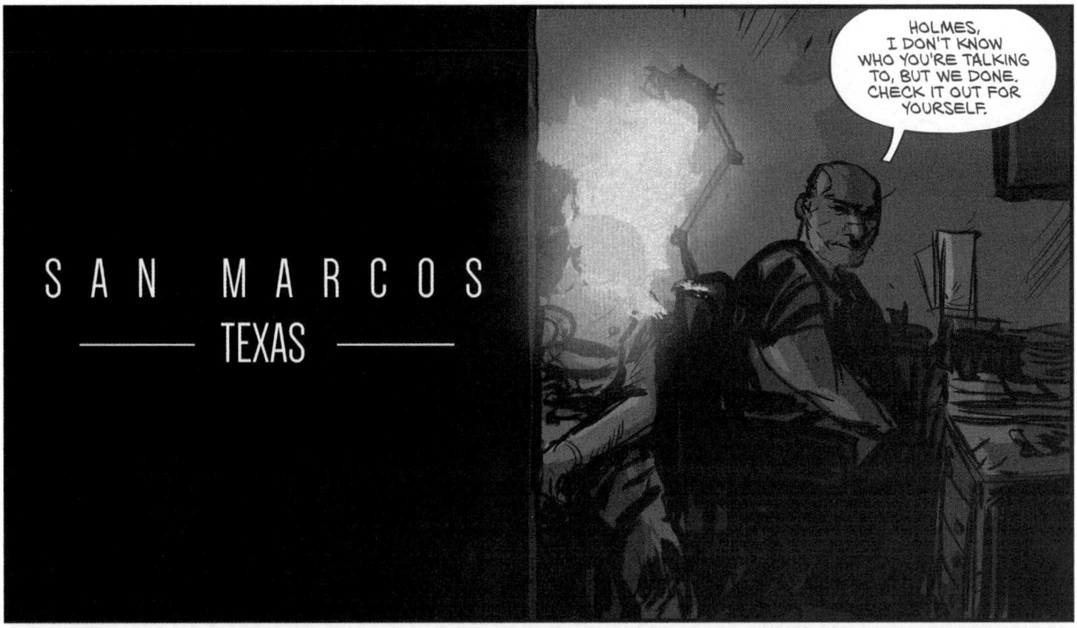
SAN MARCOS
TEXAS
HOLMES, I DON'T KNOW WHO YOU'RE TALKING TO, BUT WE DONE. CHECK IT OUT FOR YOURSELF.

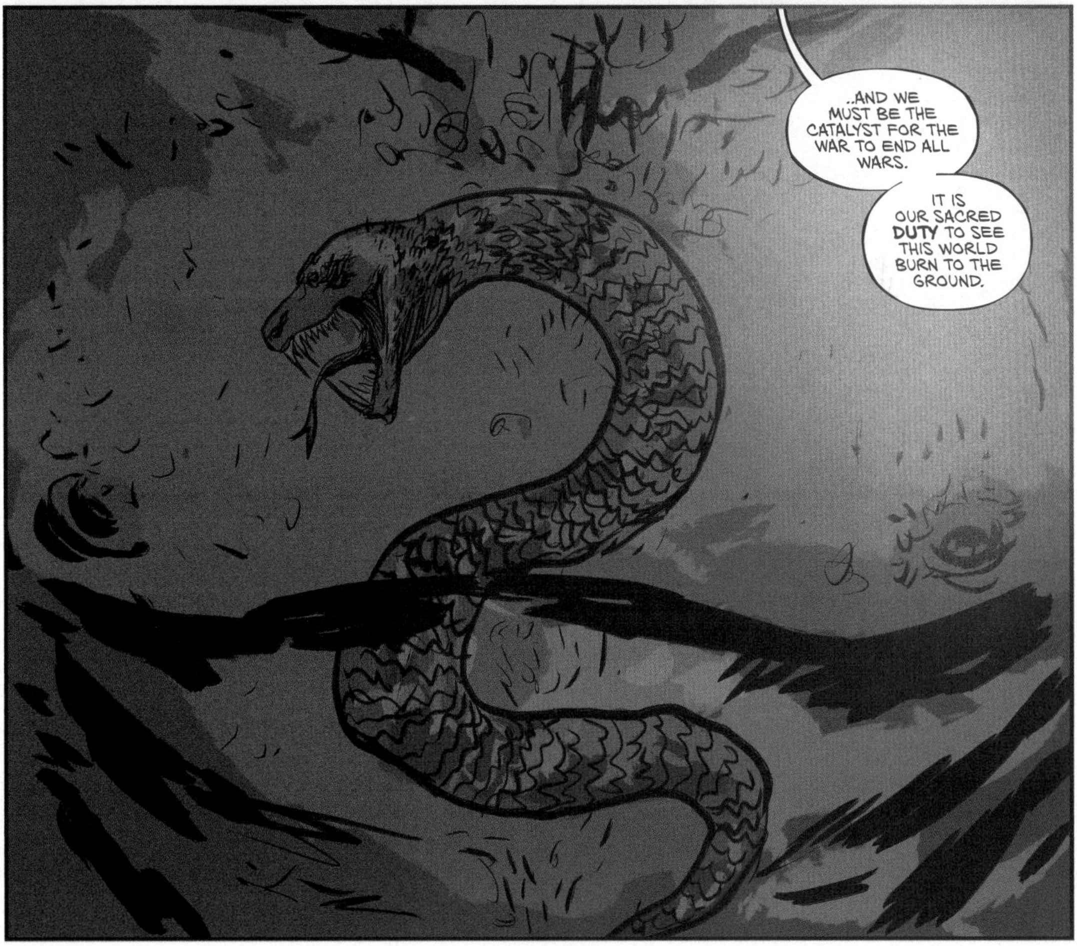
..AND WE MUST BE THE CATALYST FOR THE WAR TO END ALL WARS.
IT IS OUR SACRED **DUTY** TO SEE THIS WORLD BURN TO THE GROUND.

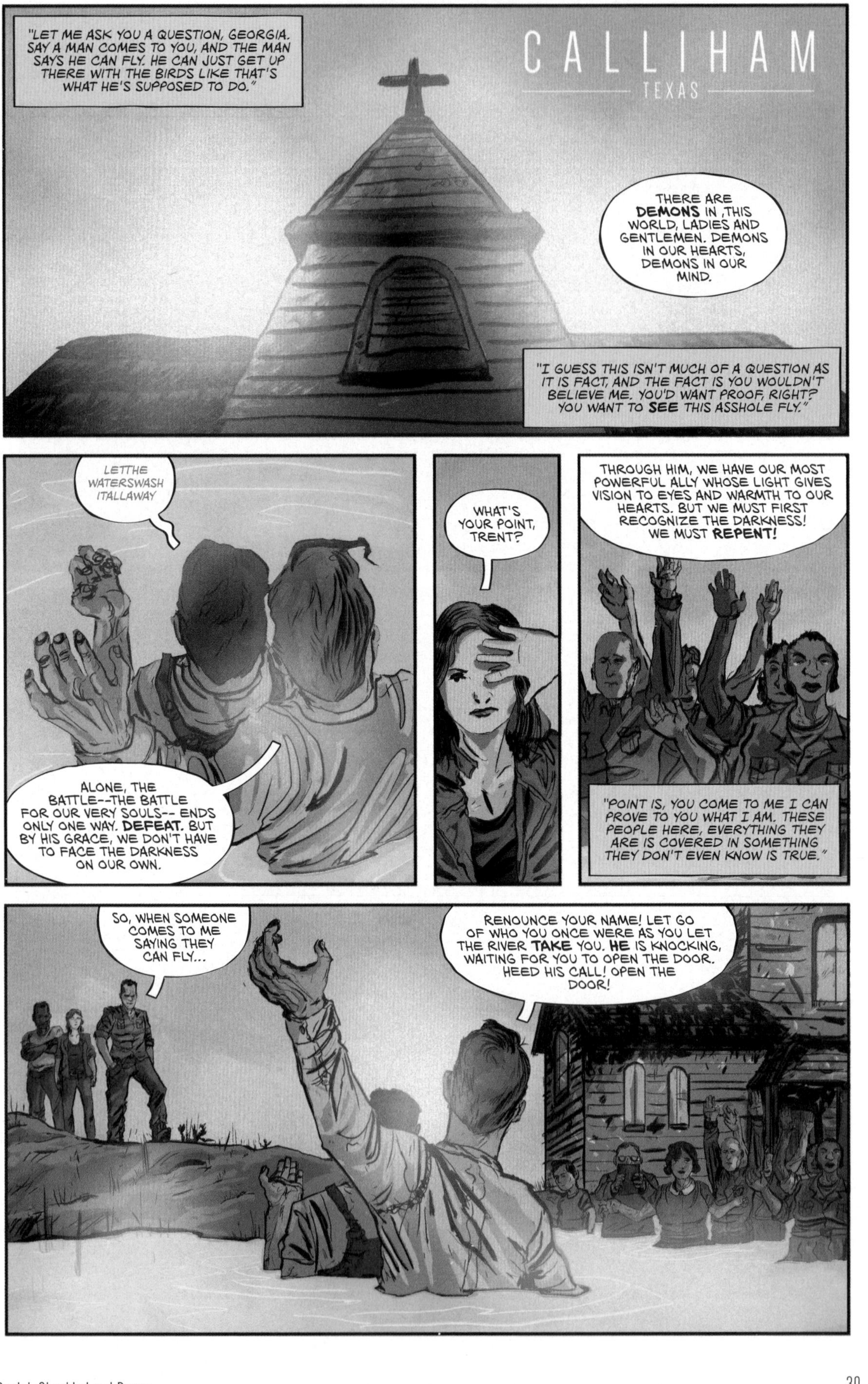
"LET ME ASK YOU A QUESTION, GEORGIA. SAY A MAN COMES TO YOU, AND THE MAN SAYS HE CAN FLY. HE CAN JUST GET UP THERE WITH THE BIRDS LIKE THAT'S WHAT HE'S SUPPOSED TO DO."
CALLIHAM
TEXAS
THERE ARE DEMONS IN ,THIS WORLD, LADIES AND GENTLEMEN. DEMONS IN OUR HEARTS, DEMONS IN OUR MIND.
"I GUESS THIS ISN'T MUCH OF A QUESTION AS IT IS FACT, AND THE FACT IS YOU WOULDN'T BELIEVE ME. YOU'D WANT PROOF, RIGHT? YOU WANT TO SEE THIS ASSHOLE FLY."
LETTHE WATERSWASH ITALLAWAY
ALONE, THE BATTLE--THE BATTLE FOR OUR VERY SOULS-- ENDS ONLY ONE WAY. DEFEAT. BUT BY HIS GRACE, WE DON'T HAVE TO FACE THE DARKNESS ON OUR OWN.
WHAT'S YOUR POINT, TRENT?
THROUGH HIM, WE HAVE OUR MOST POWERFUL ALLY WHOSE LIGHT GIVES VISION TO EYES AND WARMTH TO OUR HEARTS. BUT WE MUST FIRST RECOGNIZE THE DARKNESS! WE MUST REPENT!
"POINT IS, YOU COME TO ME I CAN PROVE TO YOU WHAT I AM. THESE PEOPLE HERE, EVERYTHING THEY ARE IS COVERED IN SOMETHING THEY DON'T EVEN KNOW IS TRUE."
SO, WHEN SOMEONE COMES TO ME SAYING THEY CAN FLY...
RENOUNCE YOUR NAME! LET GO OF WHO YOU ONCE WERE AS YOU LET THE RIVER TAKE YOU. HE IS KNOCKING, WAITING FOR YOU TO OPEN THE DOOR. HEED HIS CALL! OPEN THE DOOR!

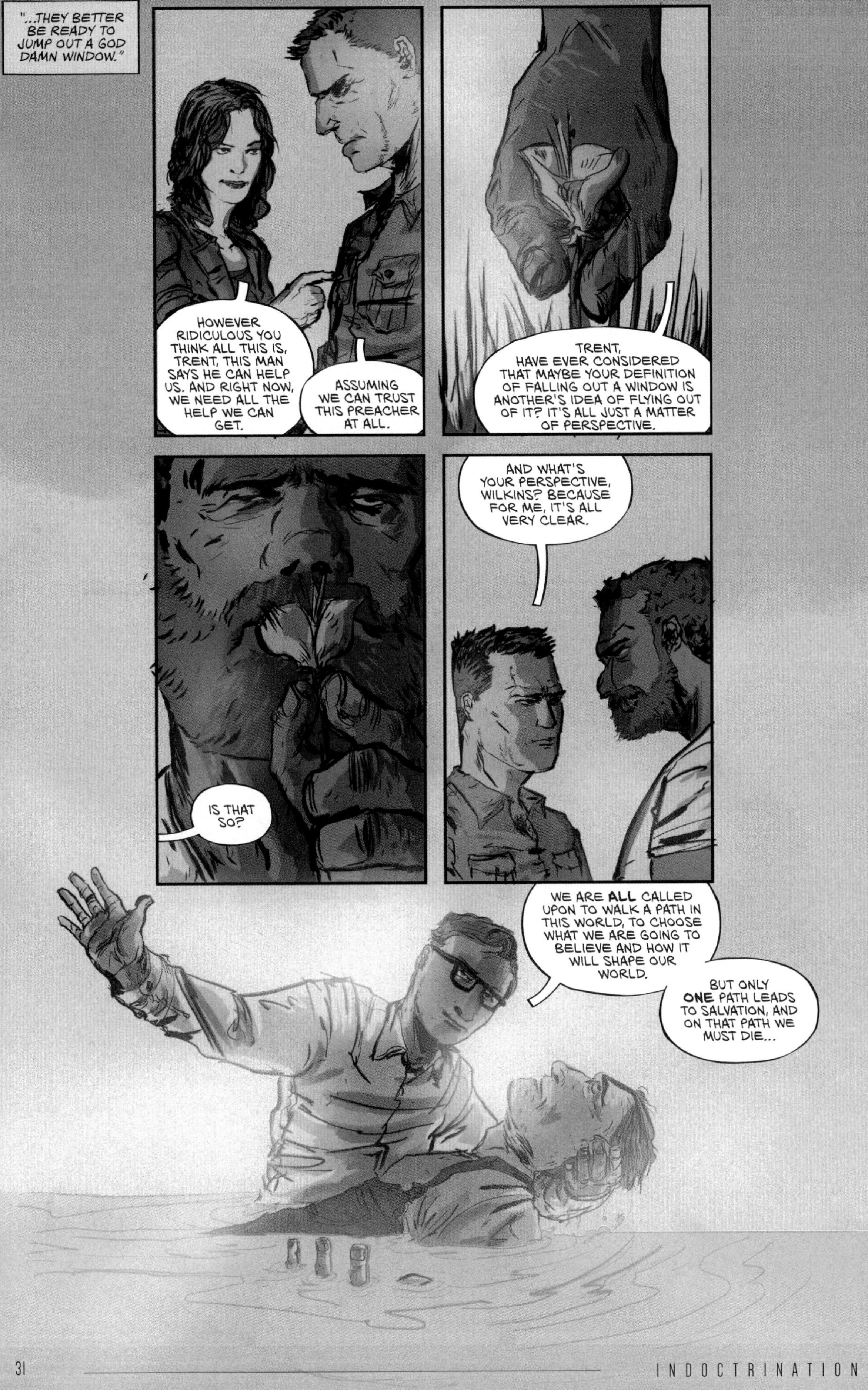
"...THEY BETTER BE READY TO JUMP OUT A GOD DAMN WINDOW."
HOWEVER RIDICULOUS YOU THINK ALL THIS IS, TRENT, THIS MAN SAYS HE CAN HELP US. AND RIGHT NOW, WE NEED ALL THE HELP WE CAN GET.
ASSUMING WE CAN TRUST THIS PREACHER AT ALL.
TRENT, HAVE EVER CONSIDERED THAT MAYBE YOUR DEFINITION OF FALLING OUT A WINDOW IS ANOTHER'S IDEA OF FLYING OUT OF IT? IT'S ALL JUST A MATTER OF PERSPECTIVE.
IS THAT SO?
AND WHAT'S YOUR PERSPECTIVE, WILKINS? BECAUSE FOR ME, IT'S ALL VERY CLEAR.
WE ARE **ALL** CALLED UPON TO WALK A PATH IN THIS WORLD, TO CHOOSE WHAT WE ARE GOING TO BELIEVE AND HOW IT WILL SHAPE OUR WORLD.
BUT ONLY **ONE** PATH LEADS TO SALVATION, AND ON THAT PATH WE MUST DIE...

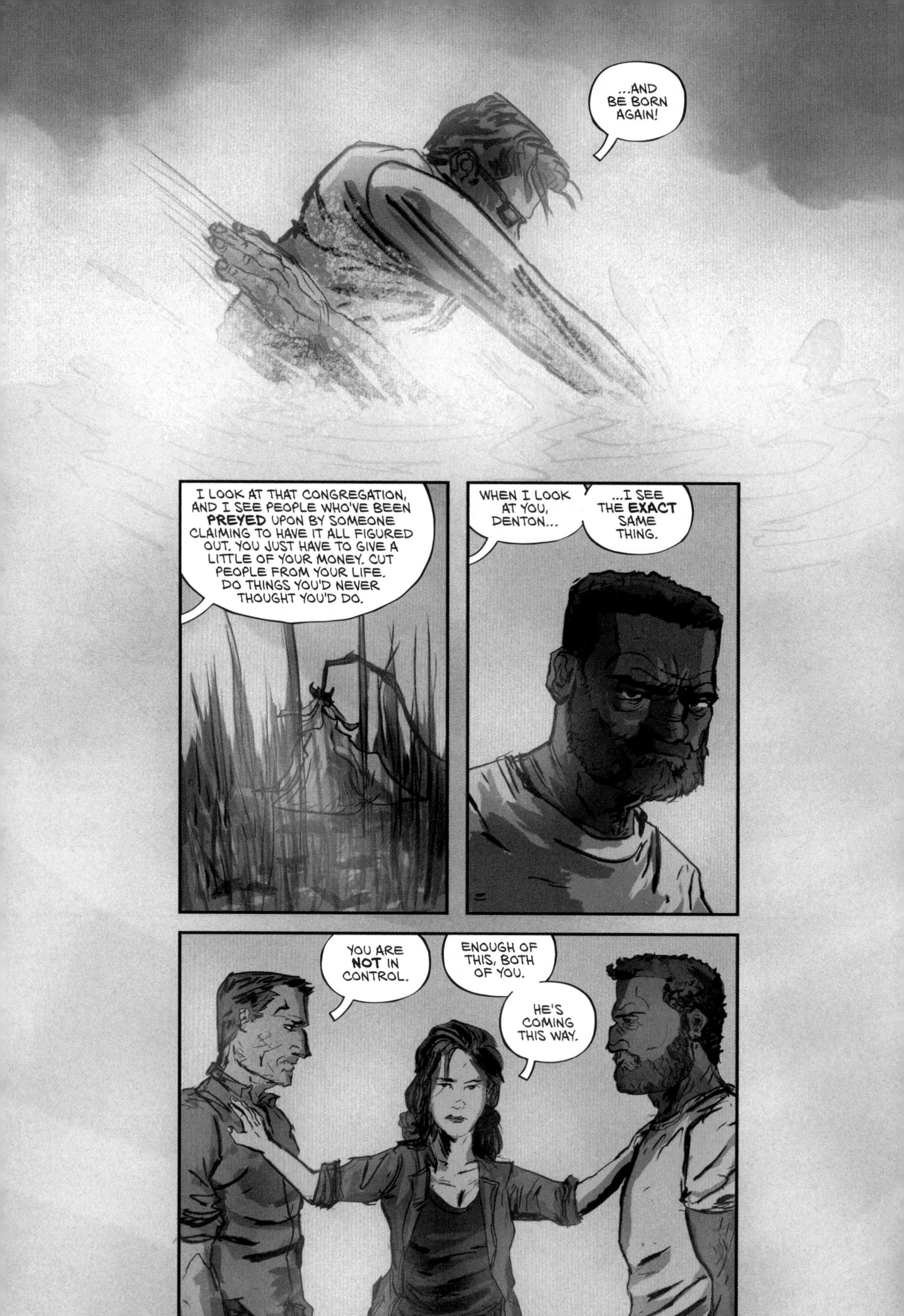
...AND BE BORN AGAIN!
I LOOK AT THAT CONGREGATION, AND I SEE PEOPLE WHO'VE BEEN **PREYED** UPON BY SOMEONE CLAIMING TO HAVE IT ALL FIGURED OUT. YOU JUST HAVE TO GIVE A LITTLE OF YOUR MONEY. CUT PEOPLE FROM YOUR LIFE. DO THINGS YOU'D NEVER THOUGHT YOU'D DO.
WHEN I LOOK AT YOU, DENTON...
...I SEE THE **EXACT** SAME THING.
YOU ARE **NOT** IN CONTROL.
ENOUGH OF THIS, BOTH OF YOU.
HE'S COMING THIS WAY.

AGENTS, THANK YOU FOR COMING TO SEE ME ON THIS BLESSED DAY.

WE'RE HAPPY TO BE HERE.

I UNDERSTAND YOU HAVE INFORMATION TO SHARE WITH US, BUT YOU COULDN'T GO TO LOCAL AUTHORITIES WITH IT?

OH I DID--A FRIEND OF MINE IN THE SHERIFF'S OFFICE POINTED ME IN YOUR DIRECTION.

SEE, THE INFORMATION I HAVE NEEDS TO REMAIN, LET'S SAY... DISCREET.

YOU UNDERSTAND WE NEED TO PRESS YOU ON THAT.

I DO. THE PERSON WHO NEEDS TO SPEAK WITH YOU, HE'S A MEMBER OF MY CONGREGATION. AND THAT MAKES HIM FAMILY.

HE WAS ATTACKED, NEARLY KILLED, AND I WILL NOT ALLOW FURTHER HARM TO COME TO SOMEONE I SEE AS KIN.

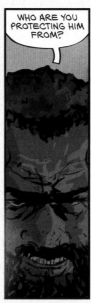

WHO ARE YOU PROTECTING HIM FROM?

HIS BROTHER, A PROMINENT CONGRESSMAN. THIS MEMBER OF MY FLOCK, HE HAS CERTAIN... SEXUAL APPETITES THAT, SHOULD THEY COME TO LIGHT, WOULD REFLECT POORLY ON HIS BROTHER'S VALUES.

SO HE REMAINS WITH ME, HIDDEN.

PASS. UNRELIABLE AND MORE TROUBLE THAN IT'S WORTH.

HE CAN IDENTIFY HIS ATTACKER, AGENT. A DISTINGUISHING MARK...

A TATTOO OF A SERPENT. BIG. RIGHT OVER HIS CHEST.

TAKE US TO HIM.

NOW.

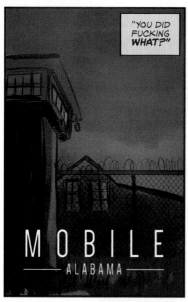

"YOU DID FUCKING **WHAT?**"

TWO AGENTS CAME IN HERE WITH A PARDON FROM THE GOVERNOR HISSELF. I VERIFIED--IT ALL CHECKED OUT.

THEY TOOK HIM THAT VERY DAY, AND BEFORE YOU ASK, NO, I DON'T KNOW WHERE THEY WENT.

GOD DAMN IT, VAUGHN. YOU KNOW HOW IMPORTANT-- HOW **DANGEROUS**-- DENTON WILKINS IS?

DON'T YOU SIT THERE WITH THAT BURNED OUT LOOK ON YOUR FACE. I TOLD YOU **MONTHS** AGO HOW TO EXTRACT INFORMATION FROM THIS MAN, AND YOU DID **NOTHING.**

THAT'S **NOT** HOW I RUN MY PRISON.

WHAT ABOUT THESE AGENTS WHO GAVE WILKINS THE GOVERNOR'S SWEET DELIVERANCE--WHO WERE THEY?

BUREAU AGENTS, BOTH OF 'EM.

FBI? CHRIST.

WHO ARE THEY? NAMES, BOTH OF THEM.

DON'T THINK I CAN GIVE YOU THAT, HUXUM.

UNFORTUNATE TIMING, WITH WILKINS GETTING SPRUNG AND ALL.

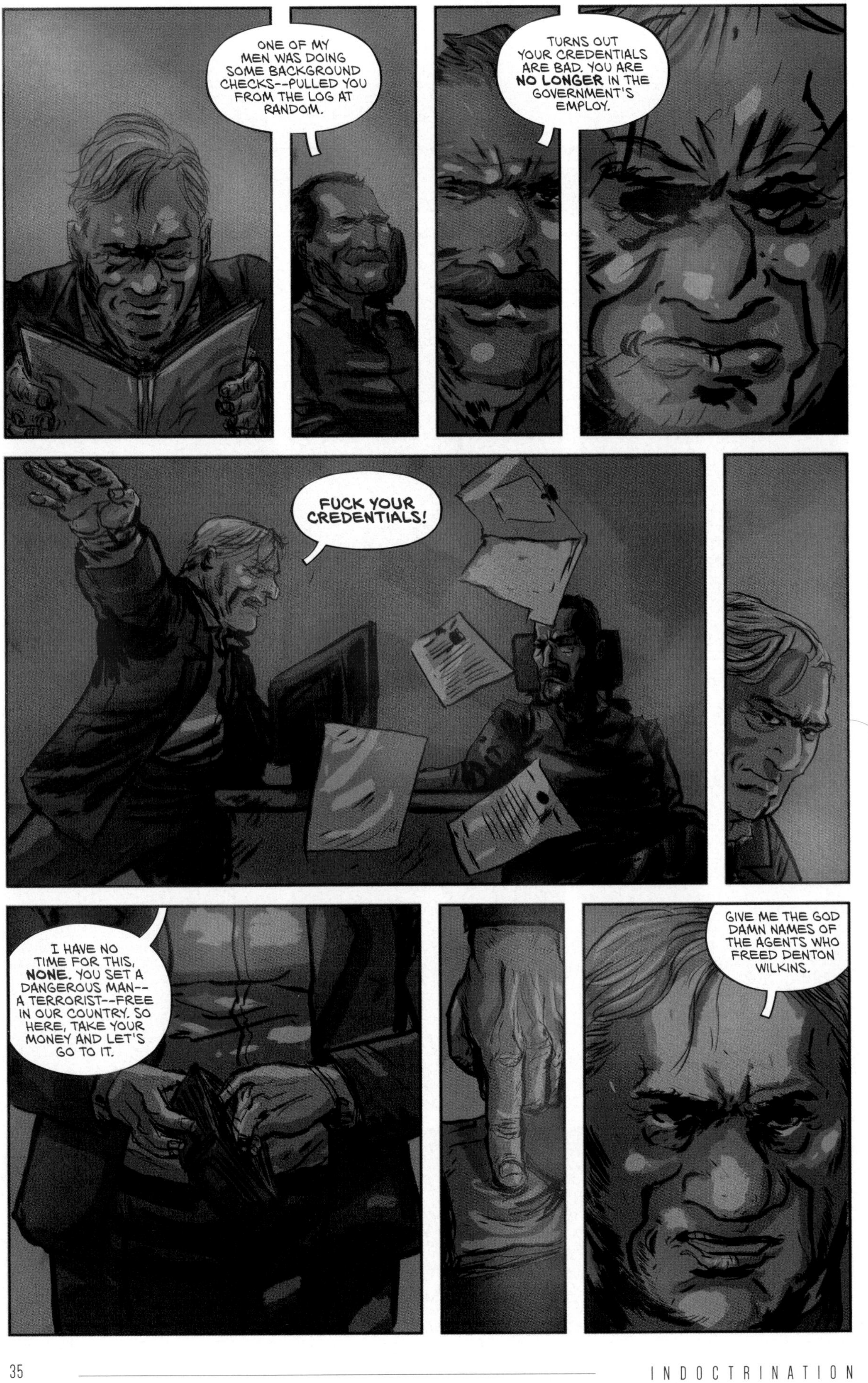
ONE OF MY MEN WAS DOING SOME BACKGROUND CHECKS--PULLED YOU FROM THE LOG AT RANDOM.
TURNS OUT YOUR CREDENTIALS ARE BAD. YOU ARE **NO LONGER** IN THE GOVERNMENT'S EMPLOY.
FUCK YOUR CREDENTIALS!
I HAVE NO TIME FOR THIS, **NONE.** YOU SET A DANGEROUS MAN--A TERRORIST--FREE IN OUR COUNTRY. SO HERE, TAKE YOUR MONEY AND LET'S GO TO IT.
GIVE ME THE GOD DAMN NAMES OF THE AGENTS WHO FREED DENTON WILKINS.

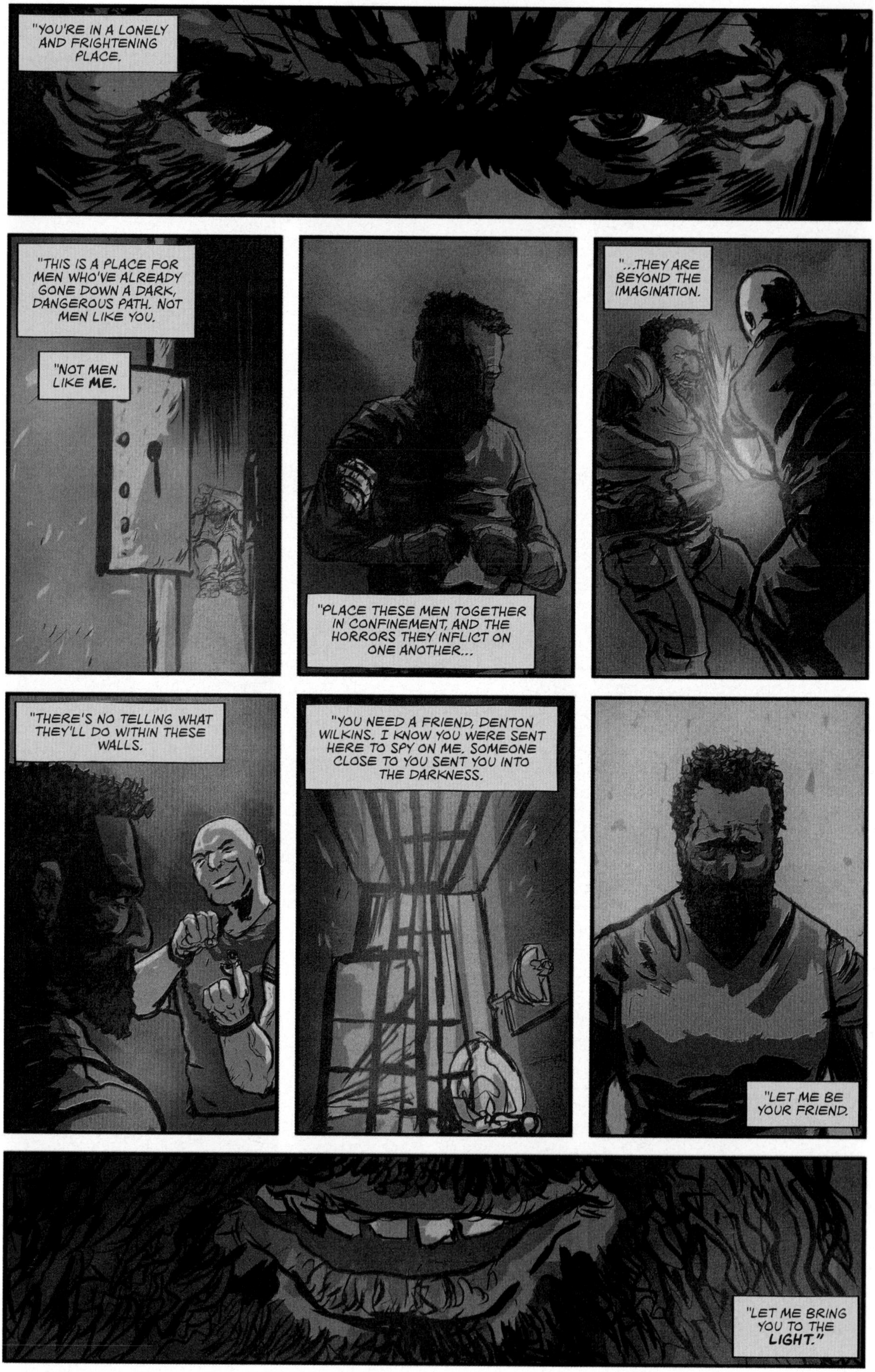
"YOU'RE IN A LONELY AND FRIGHTENING PLACE.
"THIS IS A PLACE FOR MEN WHO'VE ALREADY GONE DOWN A DARK, DANGEROUS PATH. NOT MEN LIKE YOU.
"NOT MEN LIKE ME.
"PLACE THESE MEN TOGETHER IN CONFINEMENT, AND THE HORRORS THEY INFLICT ON ONE ANOTHER...
"...THEY ARE BEYOND THE IMAGINATION.
"THERE'S NO TELLING WHAT THEY'LL DO WITHIN THESE WALLS.
"YOU NEED A FRIEND, DENTON WILKINS. I KNOW YOU WERE SENT HERE TO SPY ON ME. SOMEONE CLOSE TO YOU SENT YOU INTO THE DARKNESS.
"LET ME BE YOUR FRIEND.
"LET ME BRING YOU TO THE LIGHT."

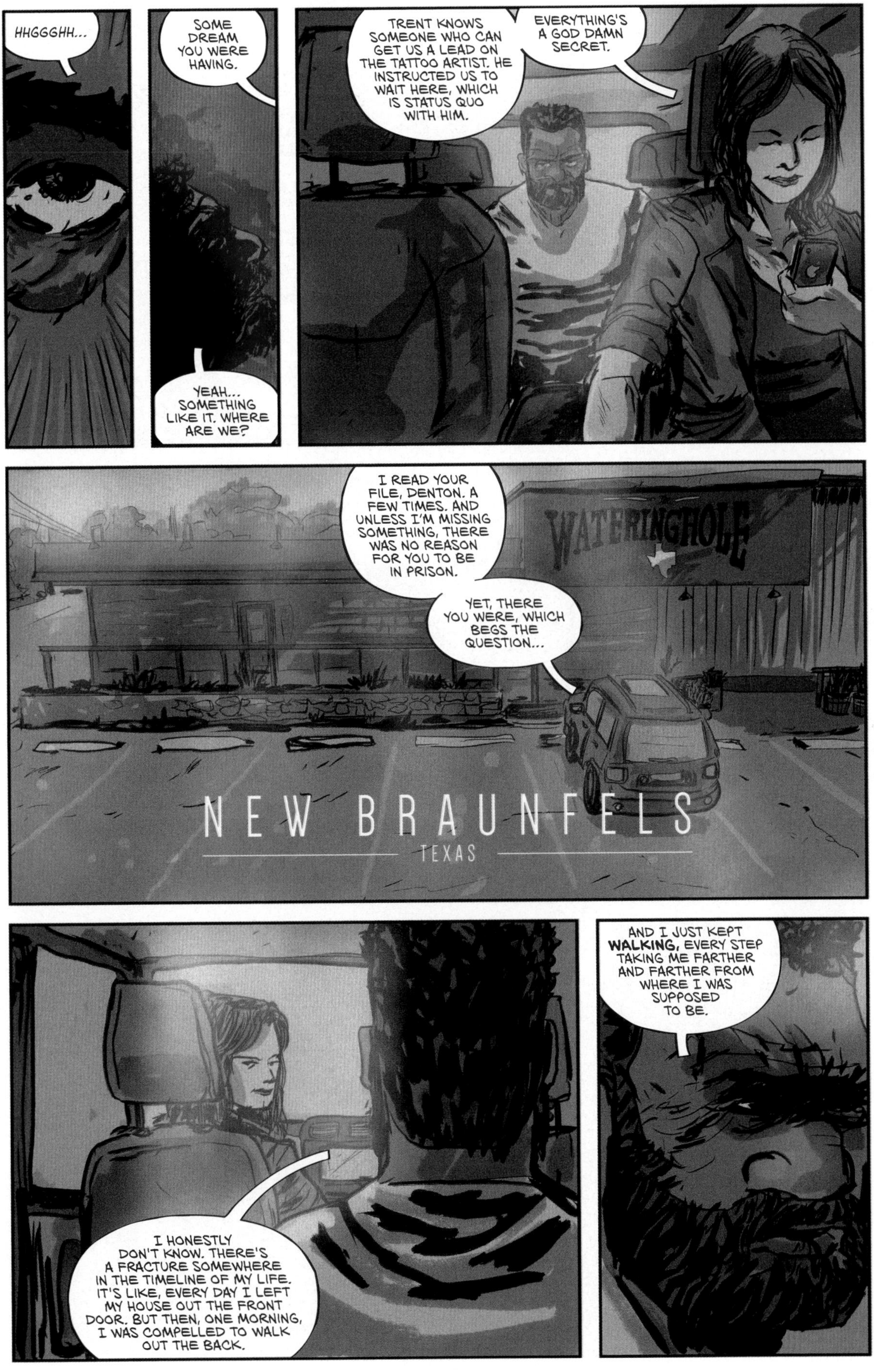
HHGGGHH...
SOME DREAM YOU WERE HAVING.
YEAH... SOMETHING LIKE IT. WHERE ARE WE?
TRENT KNOWS SOMEONE WHO CAN GET US A LEAD ON THE TATTOO ARTIST. HE INSTRUCTED US TO WAIT HERE, WHICH IS STATUS QUO WITH HIM.
EVERYTHING'S A GOD DAMN SECRET.
WATERINGHOLE
I READ YOUR FILE, DENTON. A FEW TIMES. AND UNLESS I'M MISSING SOMETHING, THERE WAS NO REASON FOR YOU TO BE IN PRISON.
YET, THERE YOU WERE, WHICH BEGS THE QUESTION...
NEW BRAUNFELS
TEXAS
I HONESTLY DON'T KNOW. THERE'S A FRACTURE SOMEWHERE IN THE TIMELINE OF MY LIFE. IT'S LIKE, EVERY DAY I LEFT MY HOUSE OUT THE FRONT DOOR. BUT THEN, ONE MORNING, I WAS COMPELLED TO WALK OUT THE BACK.
AND I JUST KEPT **WALKING**, EVERY STEP TAKING ME FARTHER AND FARTHER FROM WHERE I WAS SUPPOSED TO BE.

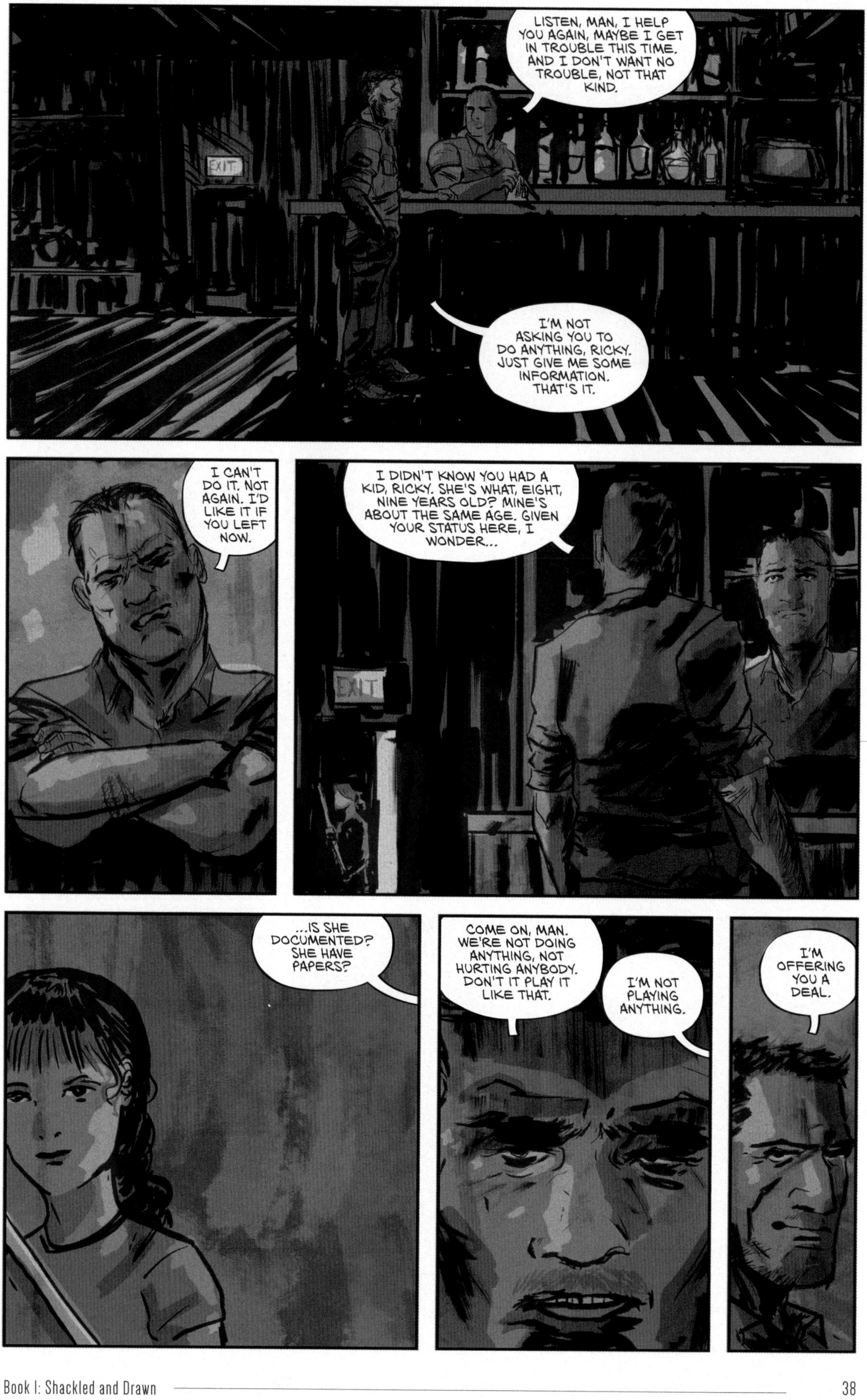
LISTEN, MAN, I HELP YOU AGAIN, MAYBE I GET IN TROUBLE THIS TIME. AND I DON'T WANT NO TROUBLE, NOT THAT KIND.
EXIT
I'M NOT ASKING YOU TO DO ANYTHING, RICKY. JUST GIVE ME SOME INFORMATION. THAT'S IT.
I CAN'T DO IT. NOT AGAIN. I'D LIKE IT IF YOU LEFT NOW.
I DIDN'T KNOW YOU HAD A KID, RICKY. SHE'S WHAT, EIGHT, NINE YEARS OLD? MINE'S ABOUT THE SAME AGE. GIVEN YOUR STATUS HERE, I WONDER...
EXIT
...IS SHE DOCUMENTED? SHE HAVE PAPERS?
COME ON, MAN. WE'RE NOT DOING ANYTHING, NOT HURTING ANYBODY. DON'T IT PLAY IT LIKE THAT.
I'M NOT PLAYING ANYTHING.
I'M OFFERING YOU A DEAL.

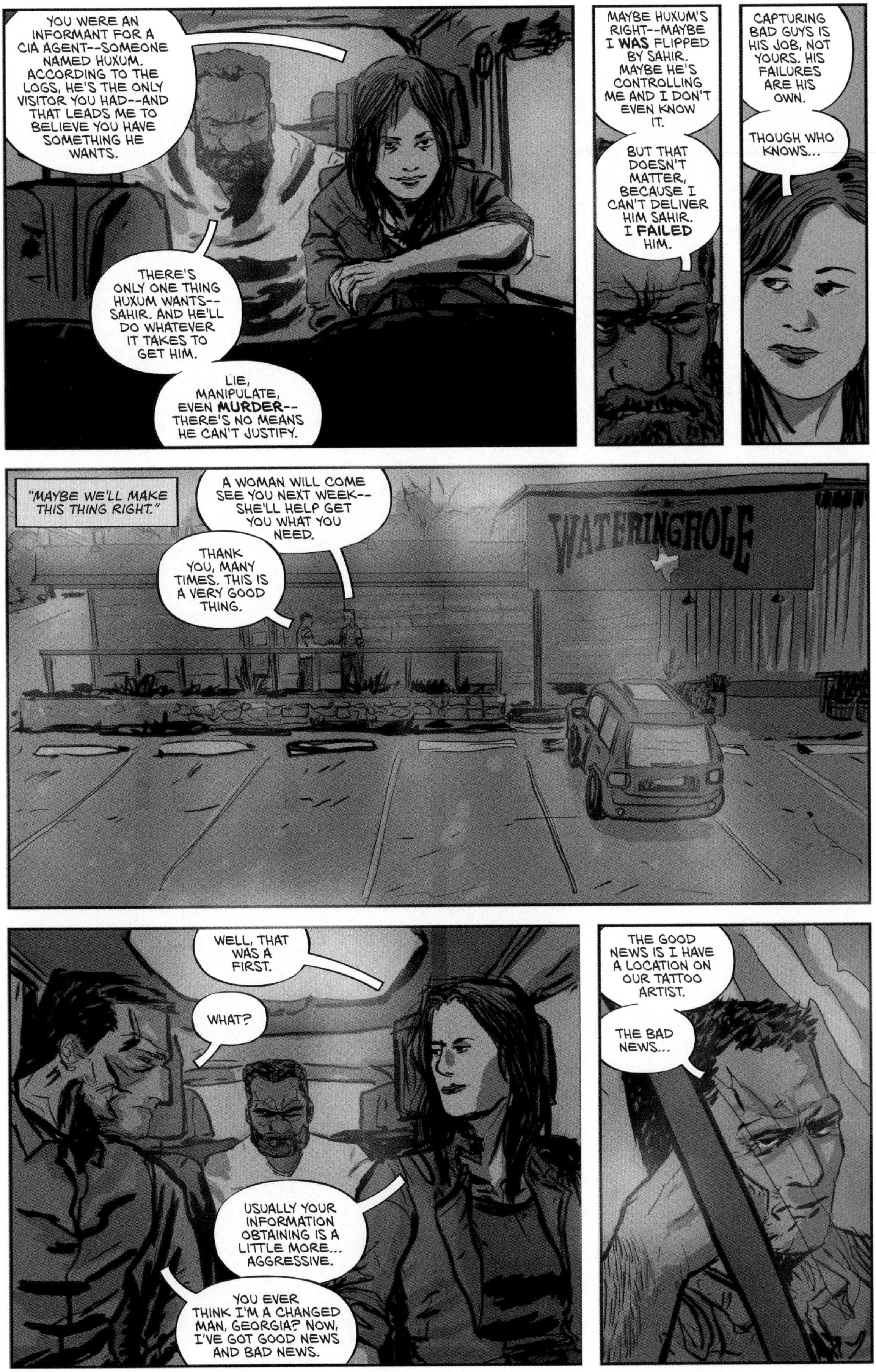
YOU WERE AN INFORMANT FOR A CIA AGENT--SOMEONE NAMED HUXUM. ACCORDING TO THE LOGS, HE'S THE ONLY VISITOR YOU HAD--AND THAT LEADS ME TO BELIEVE YOU HAVE SOMETHING HE WANTS.
THERE'S ONLY ONE THING HUXUM WANTS--SAHIR. AND HE'LL DO WHATEVER IT TAKES TO GET HIM.
LIE, MANIPULATE, EVEN **MURDER**--THERE'S NO MEANS HE CAN'T JUSTIFY.
MAYBE HUXUM'S RIGHT--MAYBE I **WAS** FLIPPED BY SAHIR. MAYBE HE'S CONTROLLING ME AND I DON'T EVEN KNOW IT.
BUT THAT DOESN'T MATTER, BECAUSE I CAN'T DELIVER HIM SAHIR. I **FAILED** HIM.
CAPTURING BAD GUYS IS HIS JOB, NOT YOURS. HIS FAILURES ARE HIS OWN.
THOUGH WHO KNOWS...
"MAYBE WE'LL MAKE THIS THING RIGHT."
A WOMAN WILL COME SEE YOU NEXT WEEK--SHE'LL HELP GET YOU WHAT YOU NEED.
THANK YOU, MANY TIMES. THIS IS A VERY GOOD THING.
WATERINGHOLE
WELL, THAT WAS A FIRST.
WHAT?
USUALLY YOUR INFORMATION OBTAINING IS A LITTLE MORE... AGGRESSIVE.
YOU EVER THINK I'M A CHANGED MAN, GEORGIA? NOW, I'VE GOT GOOD NEWS AND BAD NEWS.
THE GOOD NEWS IS I HAVE A LOCATION ON OUR TATTOO ARTIST.
THE BAD NEWS...

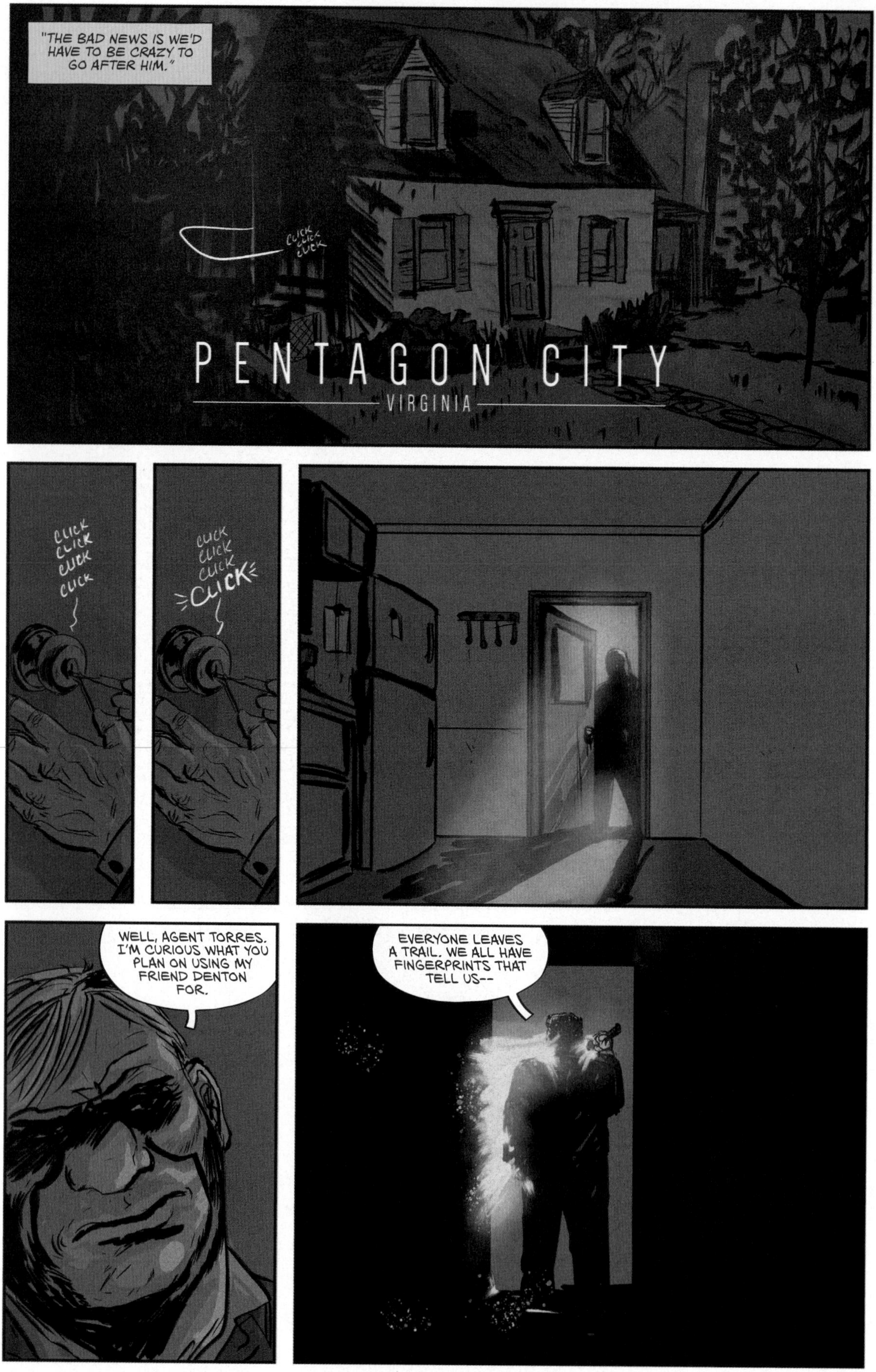
"THE BAD NEWS IS WE'D HAVE TO BE CRAZY TO GO AFTER HIM."
CLICK CLICK CLICK
PENTAGON CITY
VIRGINIA
CLICK CLICK CLICK CLICK
CLICK CLICK CLICK CLICK
WELL, AGENT TORRES. I'M CURIOUS WHAT YOU PLAN ON USING MY FRIEND DENTON FOR.
EVERYONE LEAVES A TRAIL. WE ALL HAVE FINGERPRINTS THAT TELL US--

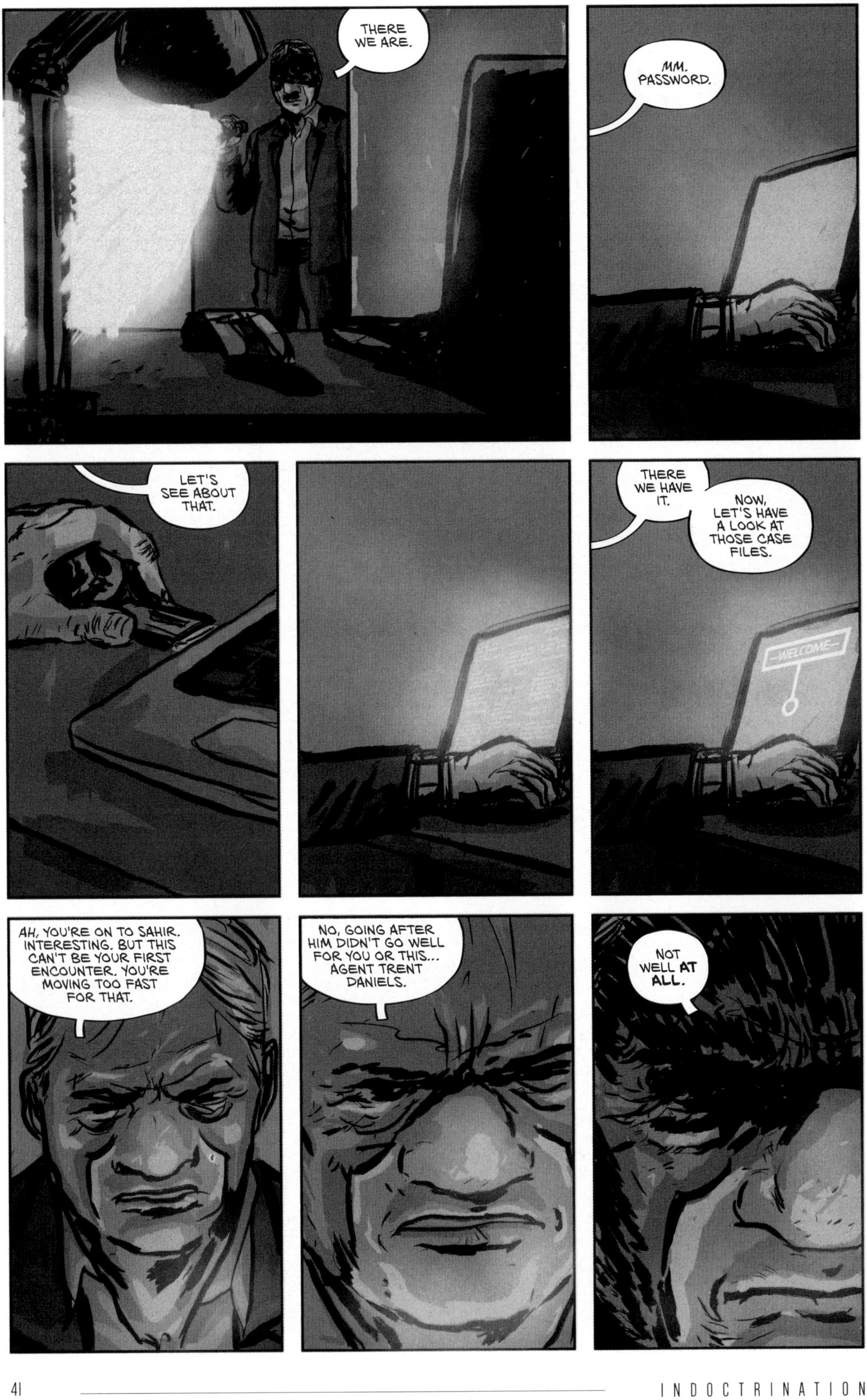
THERE WE ARE.
MM. PASSWORD.
LET'S SEE ABOUT THAT.
THERE WE HAVE IT.
NOW, LET'S HAVE A LOOK AT THOSE CASE FILES.
WELCOME
AH, YOU'RE ON TO SAHIR. INTERESTING. BUT THIS CAN'T BE YOUR FIRST ENCOUNTER. YOU'RE MOVING TOO FAST FOR THAT.
NO, GOING AFTER HIM DIDN'T GO WELL FOR YOU OR THIS... AGENT TRENT DANIELS.
NOT WELL **AT ALL**.

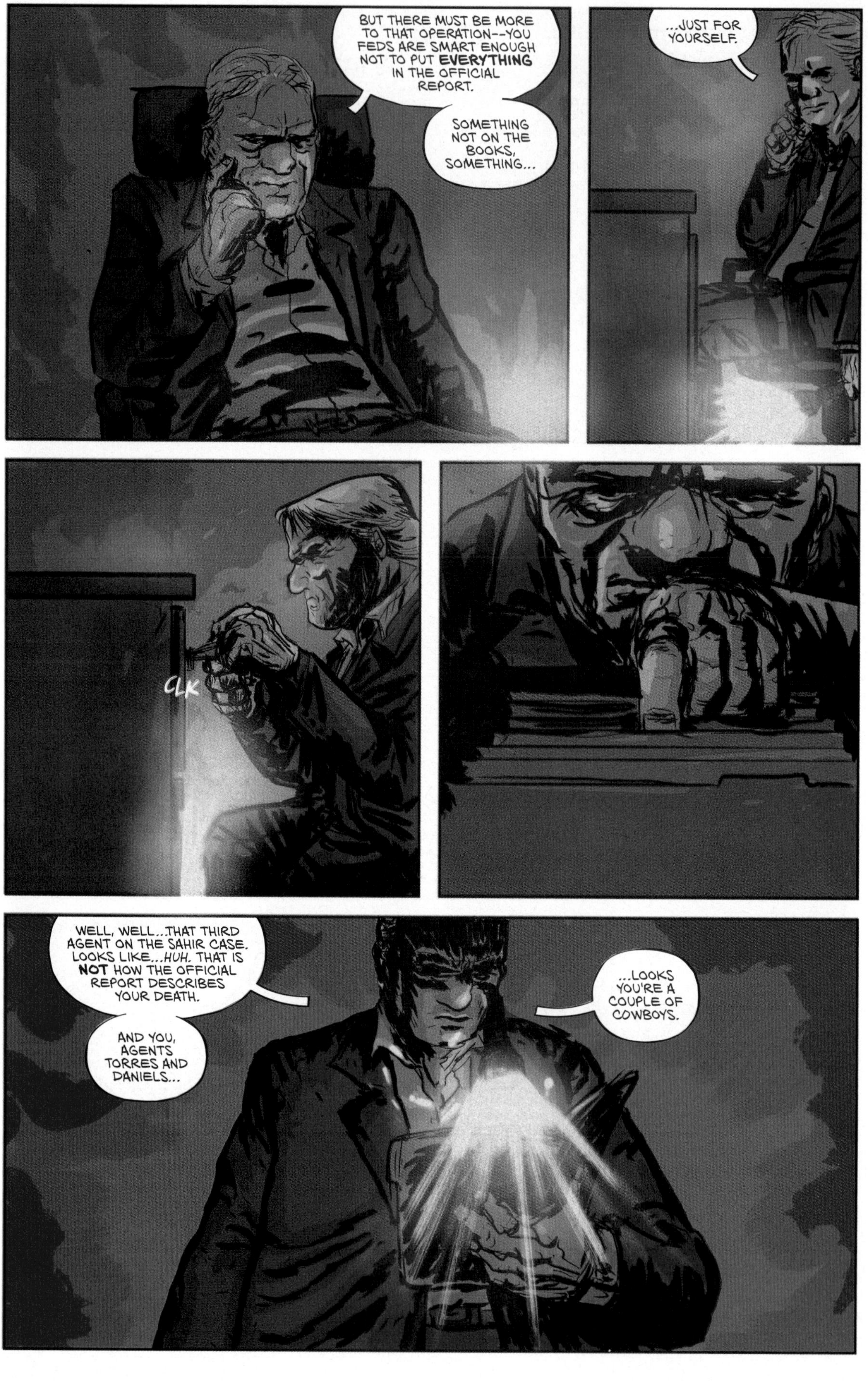
BUT THERE MUST BE MORE TO THAT OPERATION--YOU FEDS ARE SMART ENOUGH NOT TO PUT **EVERYTHING** IN THE OFFICIAL REPORT.
SOMETHING NOT ON THE BOOKS, SOMETHING...
...JUST FOR YOURSELF.
CLK
WELL, WELL...THAT THIRD AGENT ON THE SAHIR CASE. LOOKS LIKE...*HUH.* THAT IS **NOT** HOW THE OFFICIAL REPORT DESCRIBES YOUR DEATH.
AND YOU, AGENTS TORRES AND DANIELS...
...LOOKS YOU'RE A COUPLE OF COWBOYS.

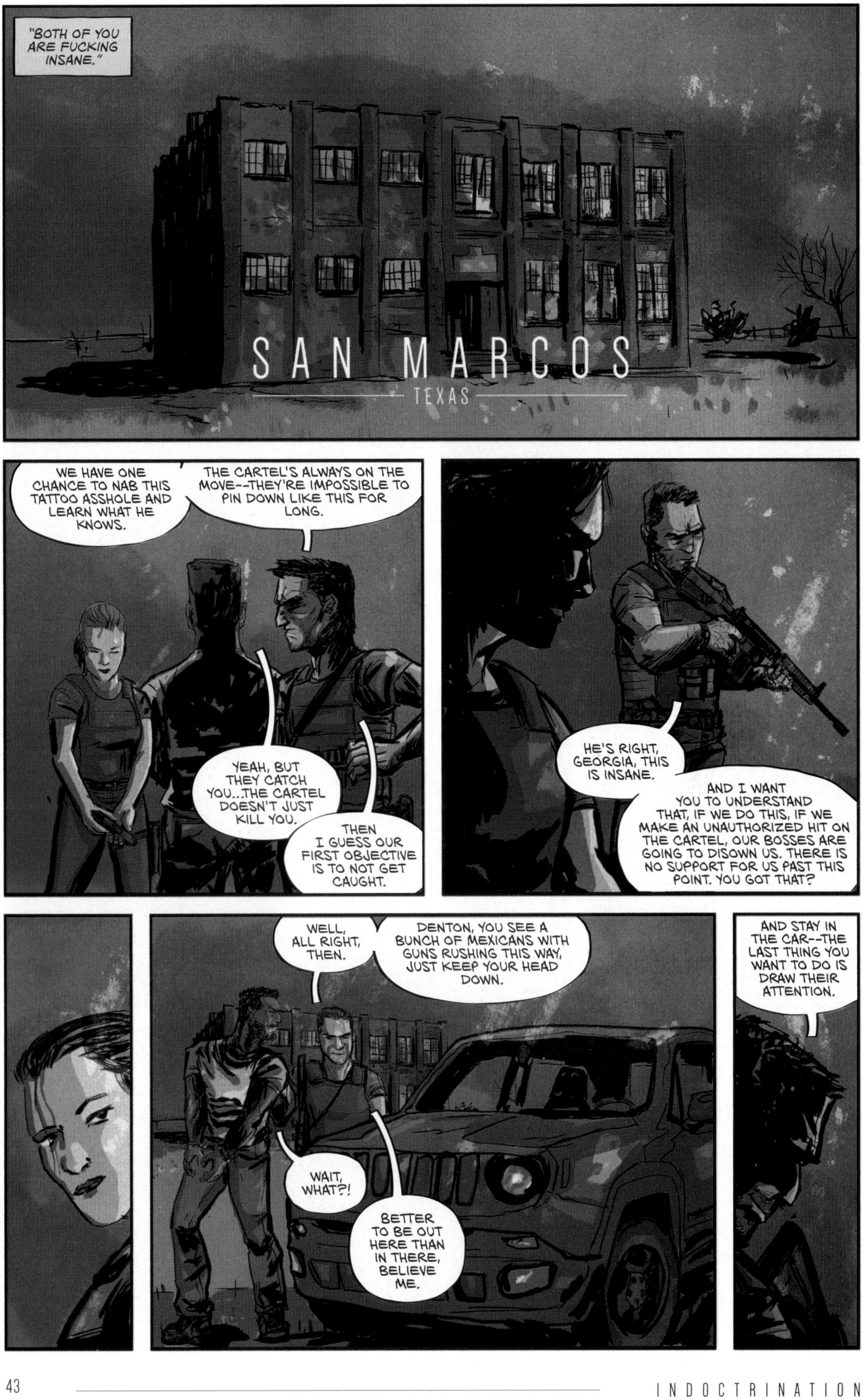
"BOTH OF YOU ARE FUCKING INSANE."
SAN MARCOS
TEXAS
WE HAVE ONE CHANCE TO NAB THIS TATTOO ASSHOLE AND LEARN WHAT HE KNOWS.
THE CARTEL'S ALWAYS ON THE MOVE--THEY'RE IMPOSSIBLE TO PIN DOWN LIKE THIS FOR LONG.
YEAH, BUT THEY CATCH YOU...THE CARTEL DOESN'T JUST KILL YOU.
THEN I GUESS OUR FIRST OBJECTIVE IS TO NOT GET CAUGHT.
HE'S RIGHT, GEORGIA, THIS IS INSANE.
AND I WANT YOU TO UNDERSTAND THAT, IF WE DO THIS, IF WE MAKE AN UNAUTHORIZED HIT ON THE CARTEL, OUR BOSSES ARE GOING TO DISOWN US. THERE IS NO SUPPORT FOR US PAST THIS POINT. YOU GOT THAT?
WELL, ALL RIGHT, THEN.
DENTON, YOU SEE A BUNCH OF MEXICANS WITH GUNS RUSHING THIS WAY, JUST KEEP YOUR HEAD DOWN.
WAIT, WHAT?!
BETTER TO BE OUT HERE THAN IN THERE, BELIEVE ME.
AND STAY IN THE CAR--THE LAST THING YOU WANT TO DO IS DRAW THEIR ATTENTION.

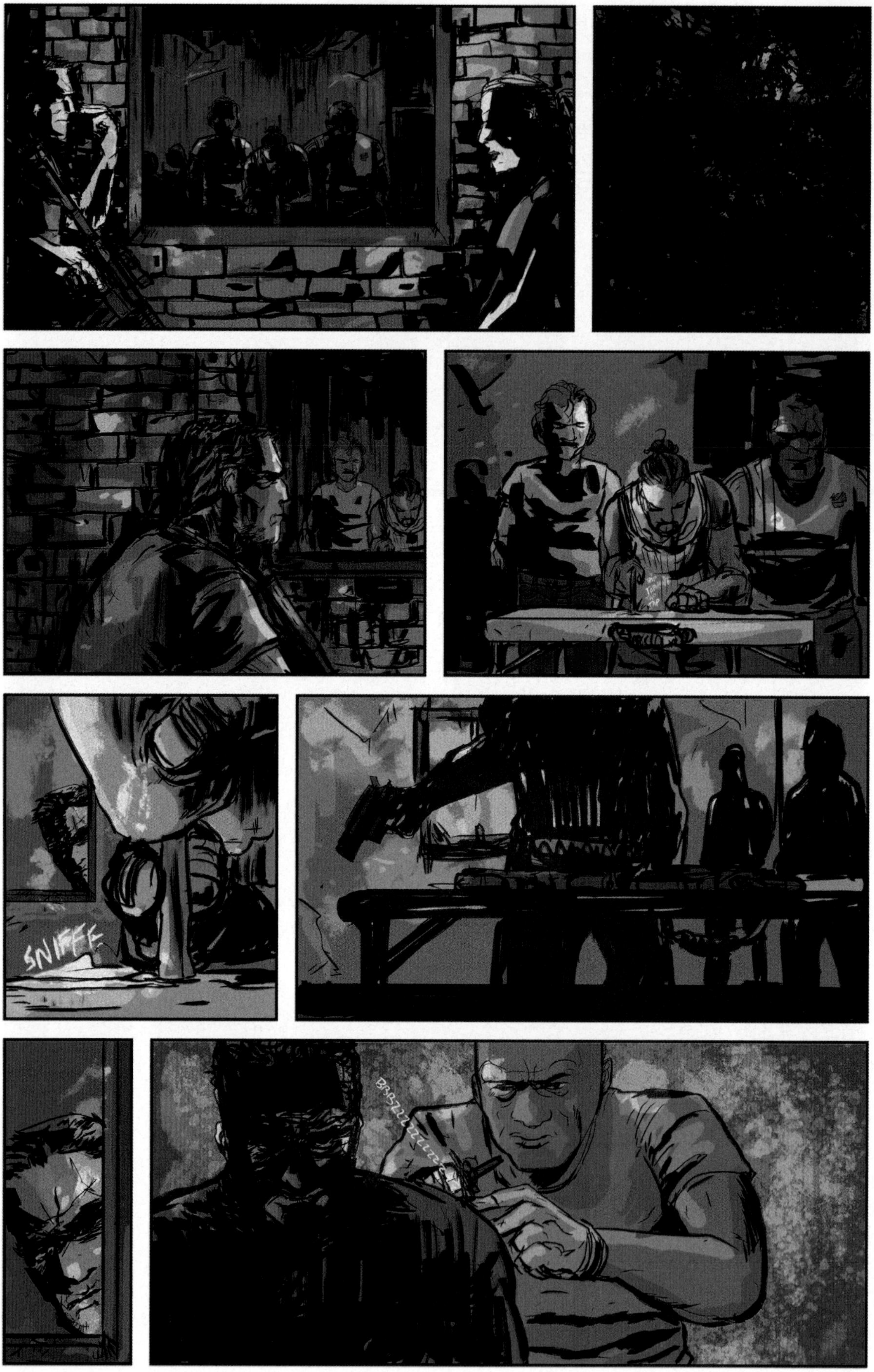
SNIFFF
BRRZZZZZZZZZZZ

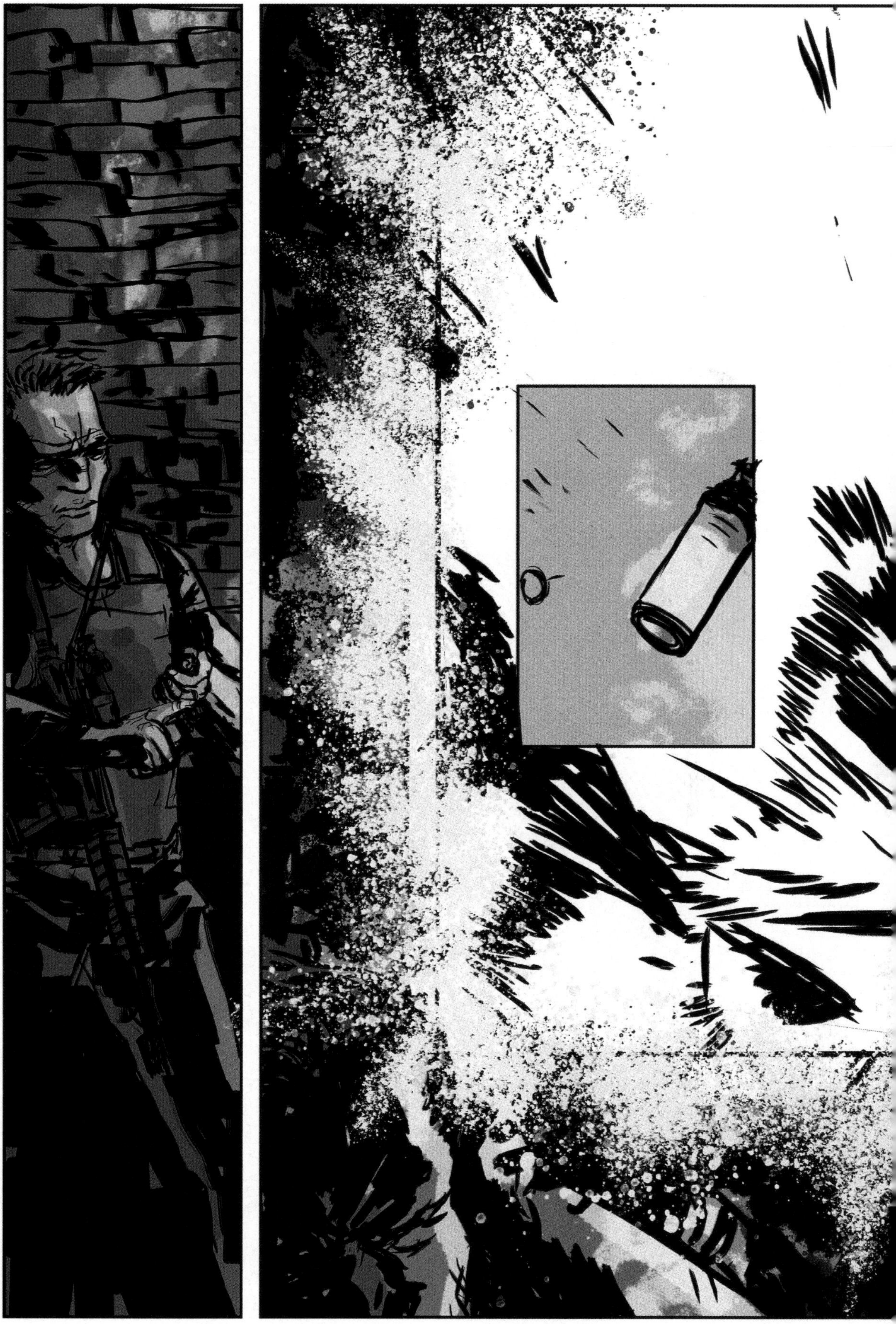

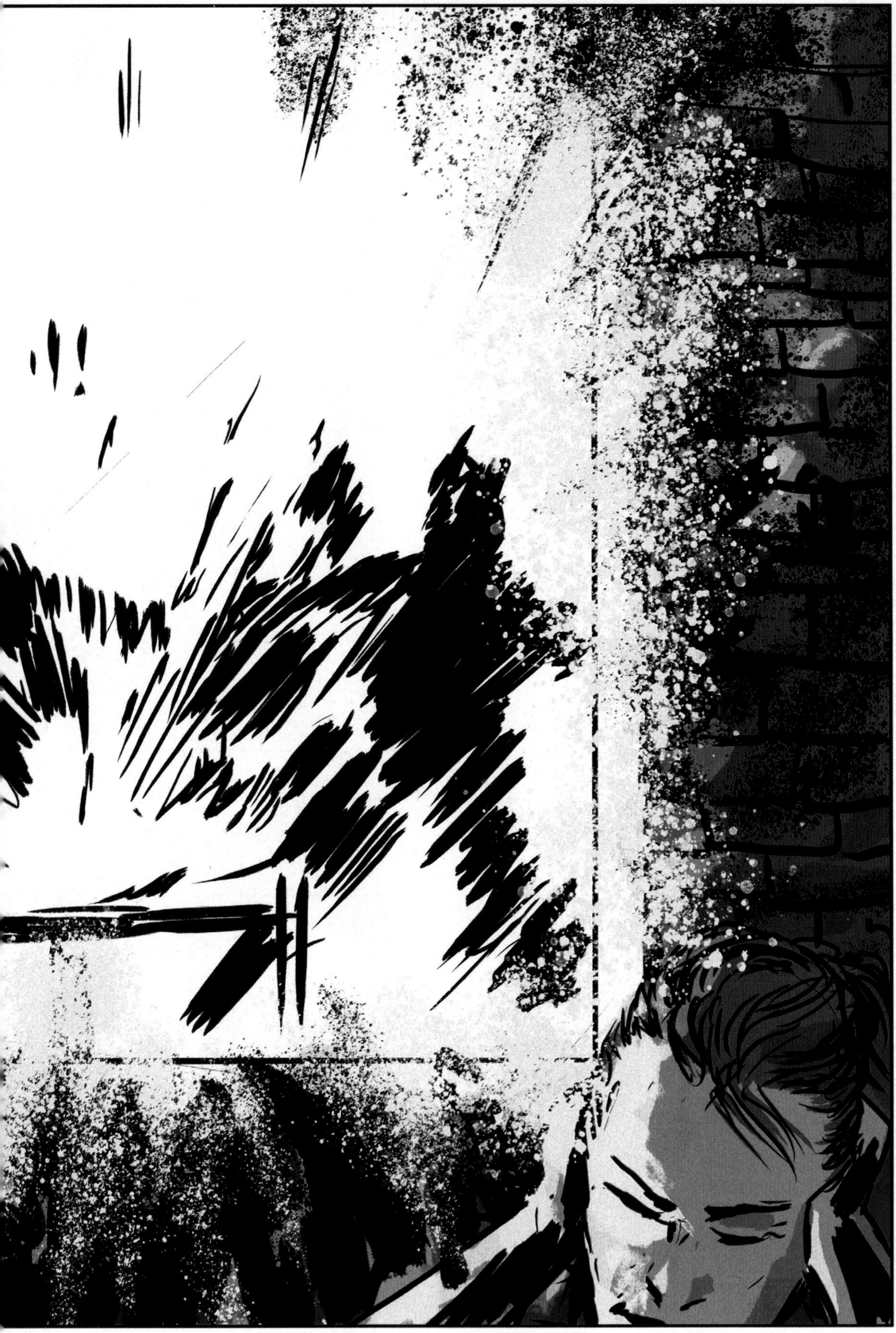

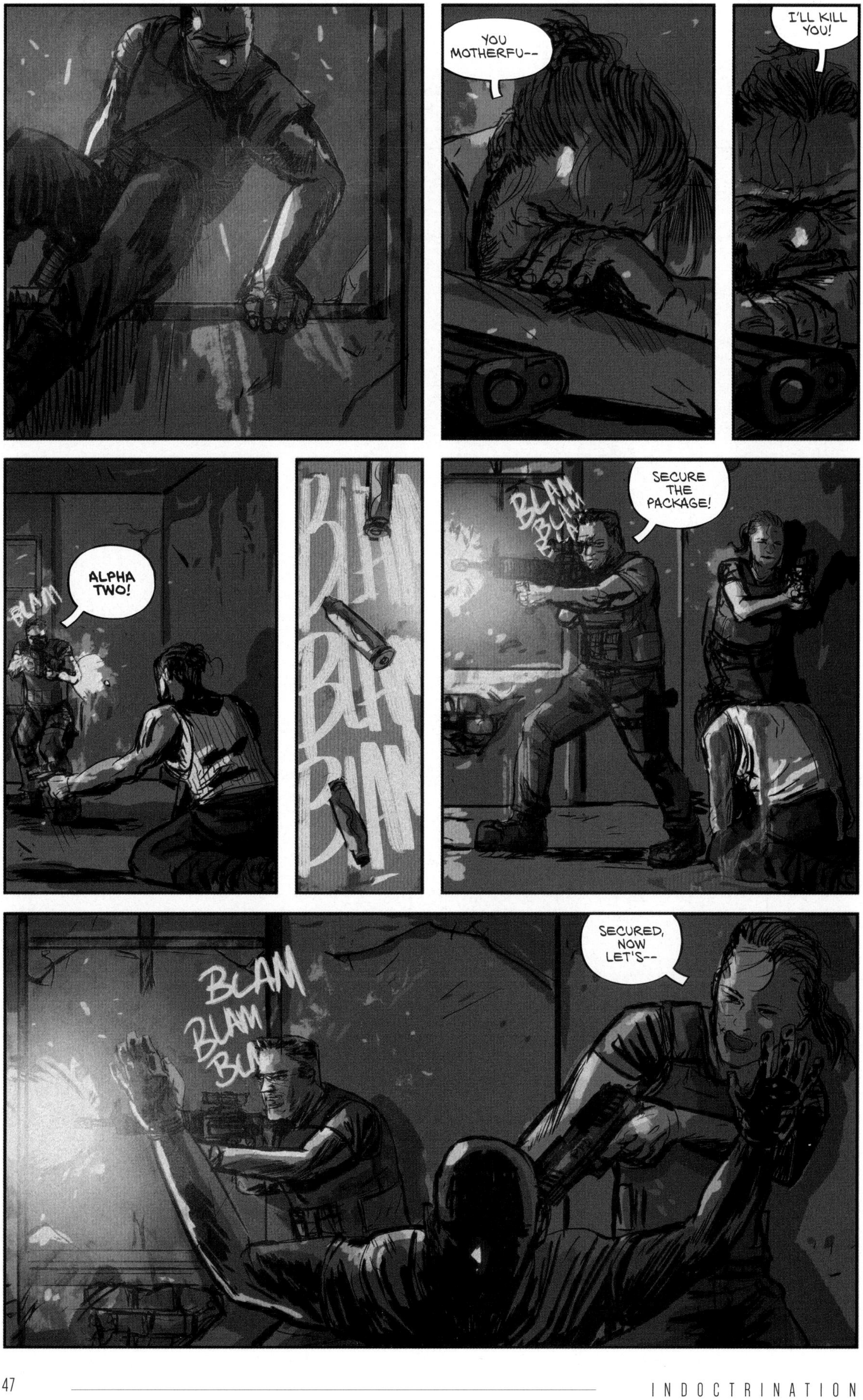
YOU MOTHERFU--
I'LL KILL YOU!
BLAM
ALPHA TWO!
BLAM
BLAM
BLAM
BLAM
BLAM
BLA
SECURE THE PACKAGE!
BLAM
BLAM
BLA
SECURED, NOW LET'S--

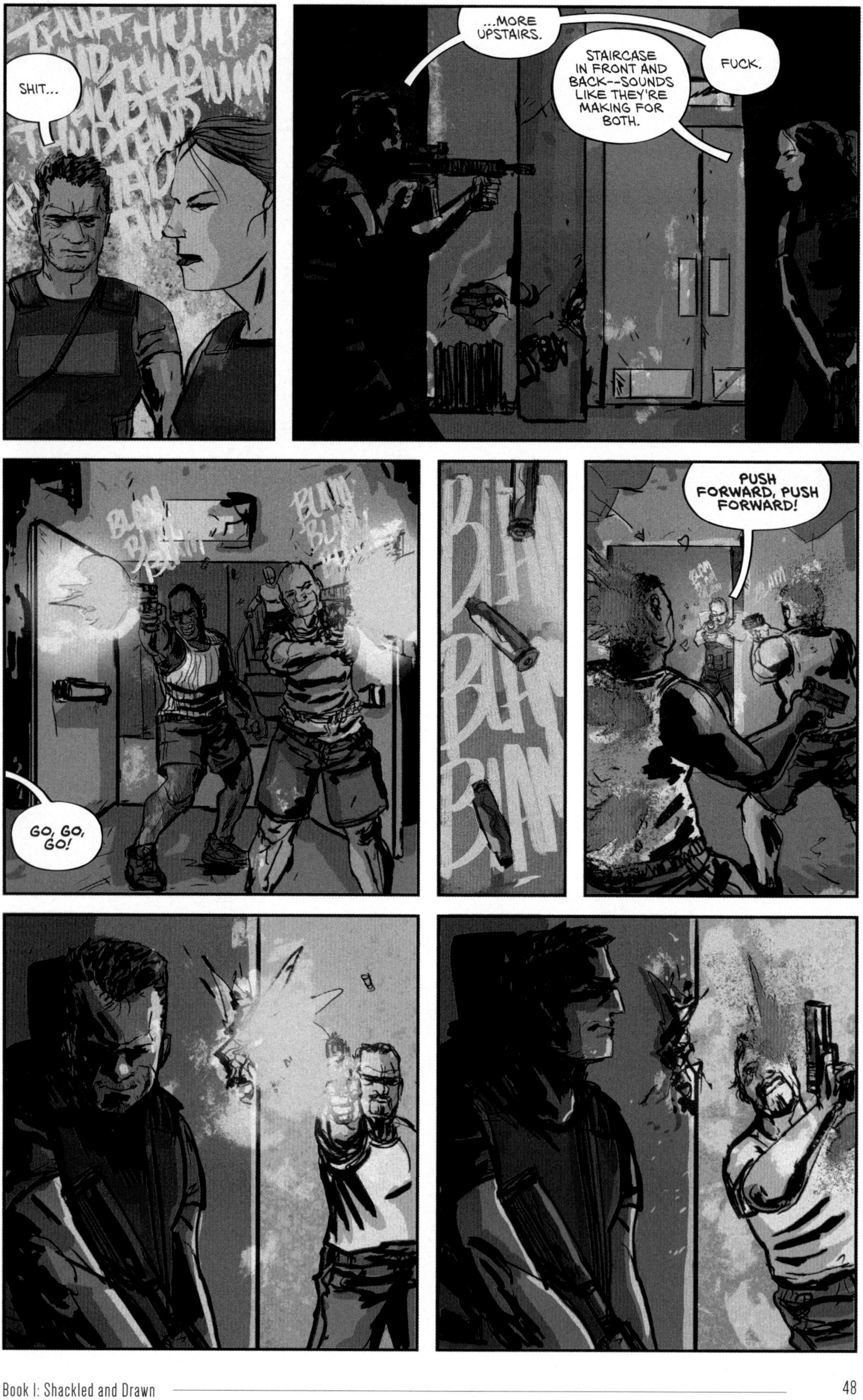
THUD THUMP THUD THUD THUMP
SHIT...
...MORE UPSTAIRS.
STAIRCASE IN FRONT AND BACK--SOUNDS LIKE THEY'RE MAKING FOR BOTH.
FUCK.
BLAM BLAM BLAM
BLAM BLAM
GO, GO, GO!
BLAM BLAM BLAM BLAM
PUSH FORWARD, PUSH FORWARD!

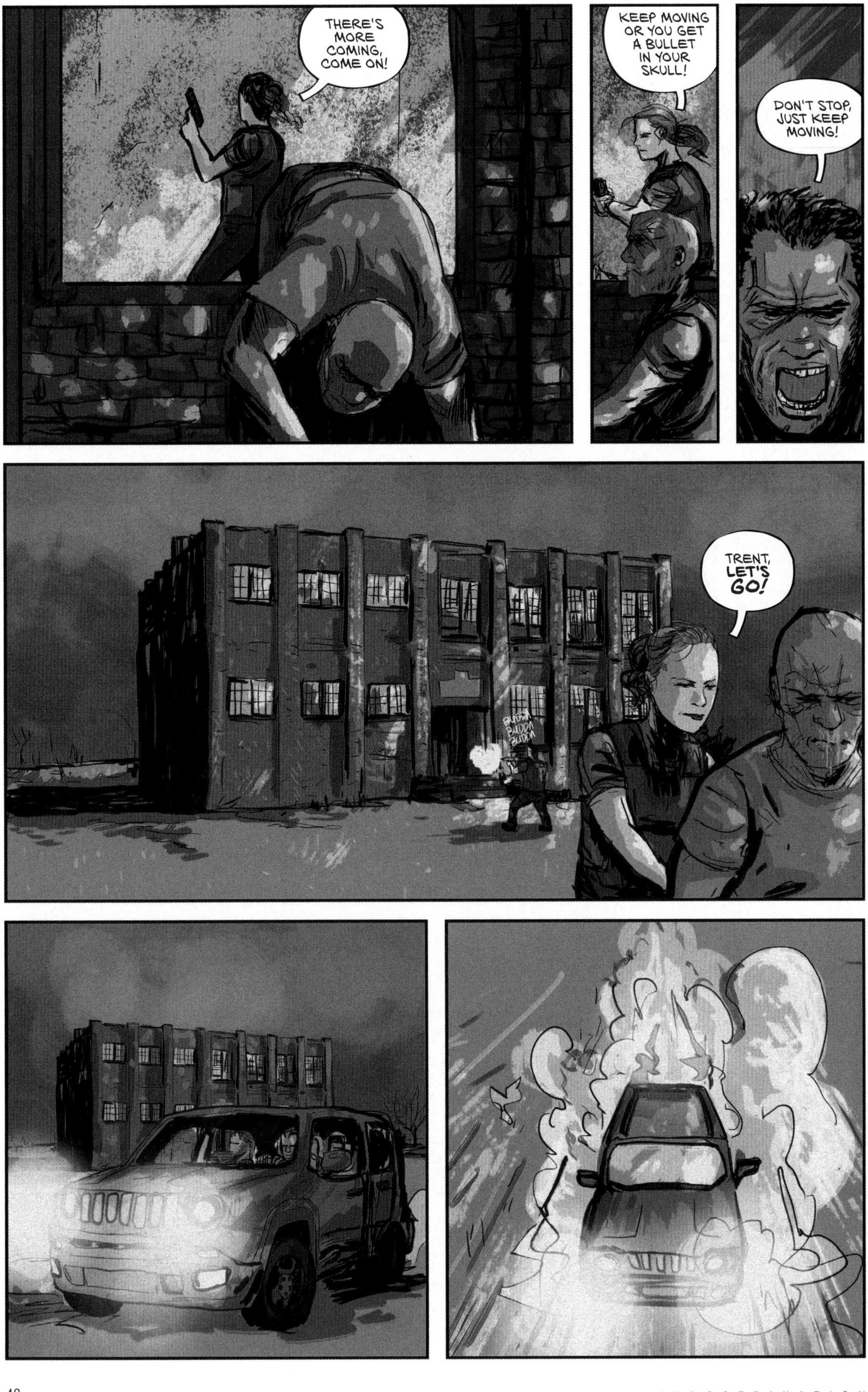
THERE'S MORE COMING, COME ON!
KEEP MOVING OR YOU GET A BULLET IN YOUR SKULL!
DON'T STOP, JUST KEEP MOVING!
BUDDA BUDDA BUDDA
TRENT, LET'S GO!

"AS LONG AS HE'S MORE AFRAID OF THE CARTEL THAN HE IS OF US..."

...HE'S NOT GOING TO GIVE US A **THING.**

I THINK THIS SITUATION NEEDS A MORE... **DIRECT** METHOD OF INTERROGATION.

A DIRECT-- WAIT, WHAT?

WHAT ARE YOU SAYING?

WE DON'T HAVE TIME TO MESS AROUND, TRENT.

THIS MAN IS OUR ONLY LINK TO THE KILLER, AND IF HE DOESN'T TALK, WE'VE GOT **NOTHING.**

SO WHAT I'M SAYING IS I'M GOING TO LEAVE THIS ROOM WITH THE TWO OF YOU IN IT. WHATEVER HAPPENS FROM THAT POINT IS UP TO YOU.

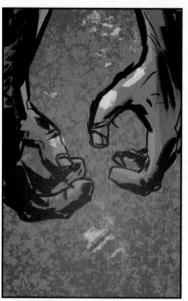

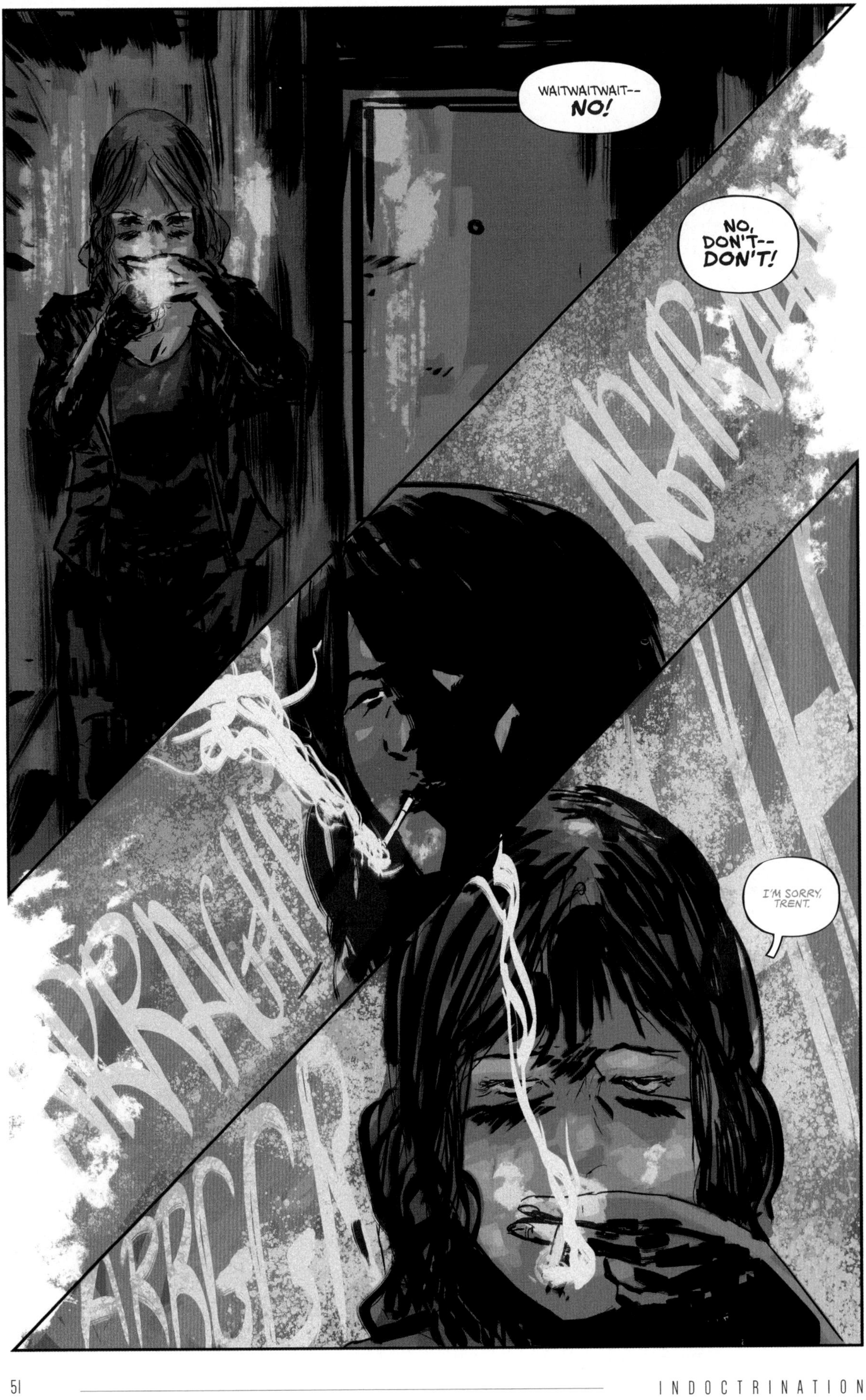
WAITWAITWAIT--
NO!
NO, DON'T-- DON'T!
I'M SORRY, TRENT.

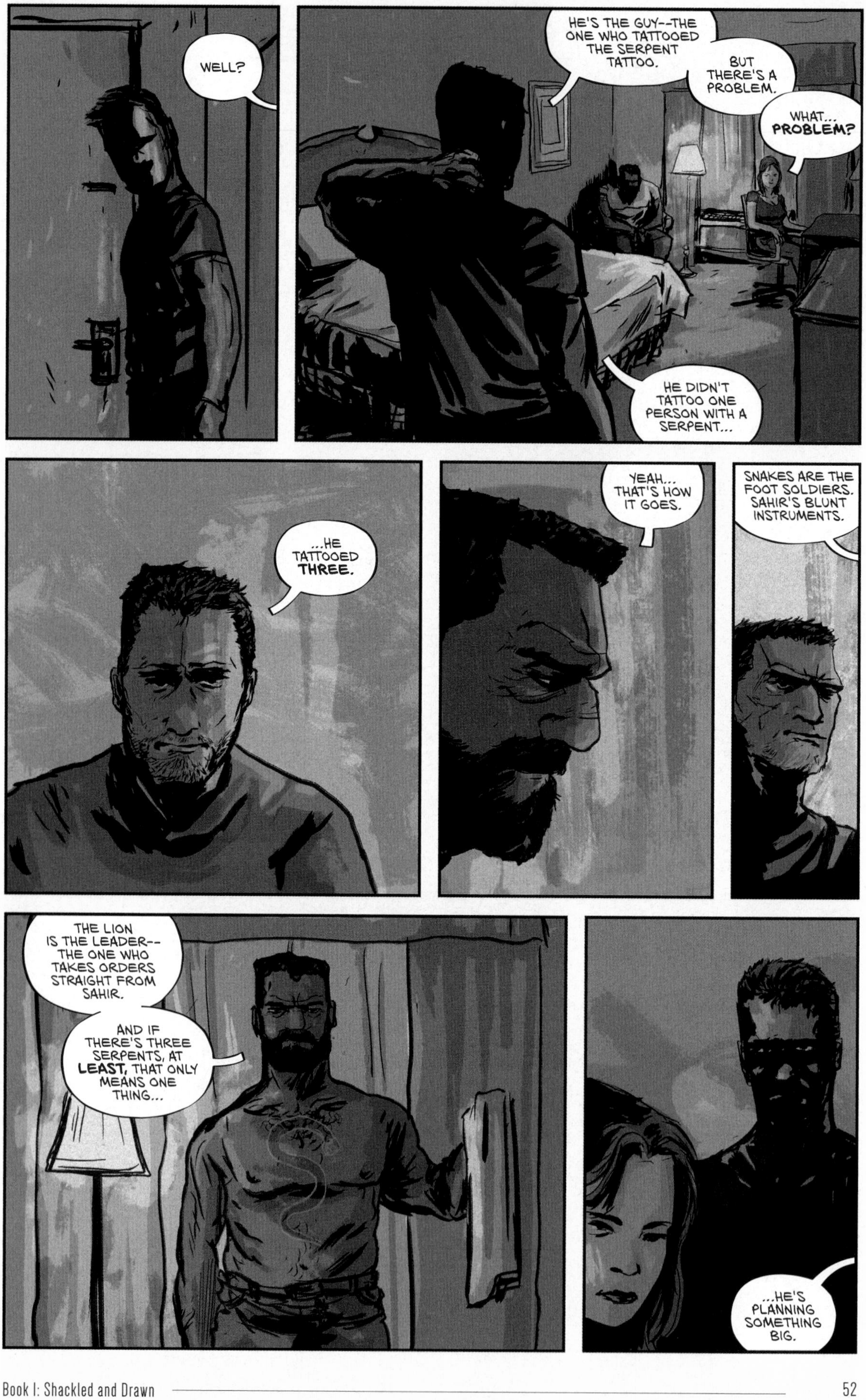
WELL?
HE'S THE GUY--THE ONE WHO TATTOOED THE SERPENT TATTOO.
BUT THERE'S A PROBLEM.
WHAT... **PROBLEM?**
HE DIDN'T TATTOO ONE PERSON WITH A SERPENT...
...HE TATTOOED **THREE.**
YEAH... THAT'S HOW IT GOES.
SNAKES ARE THE FOOT SOLDIERS. SAHIR'S BLUNT INSTRUMENTS.
THE LION IS THE LEADER-- THE ONE WHO TAKES ORDERS STRAIGHT FROM SAHIR.
AND IF THERE'S THREE SERPENTS, AT **LEAST,** THAT ONLY MEANS ONE THING...
...HE'S PLANNING SOMETHING BIG.

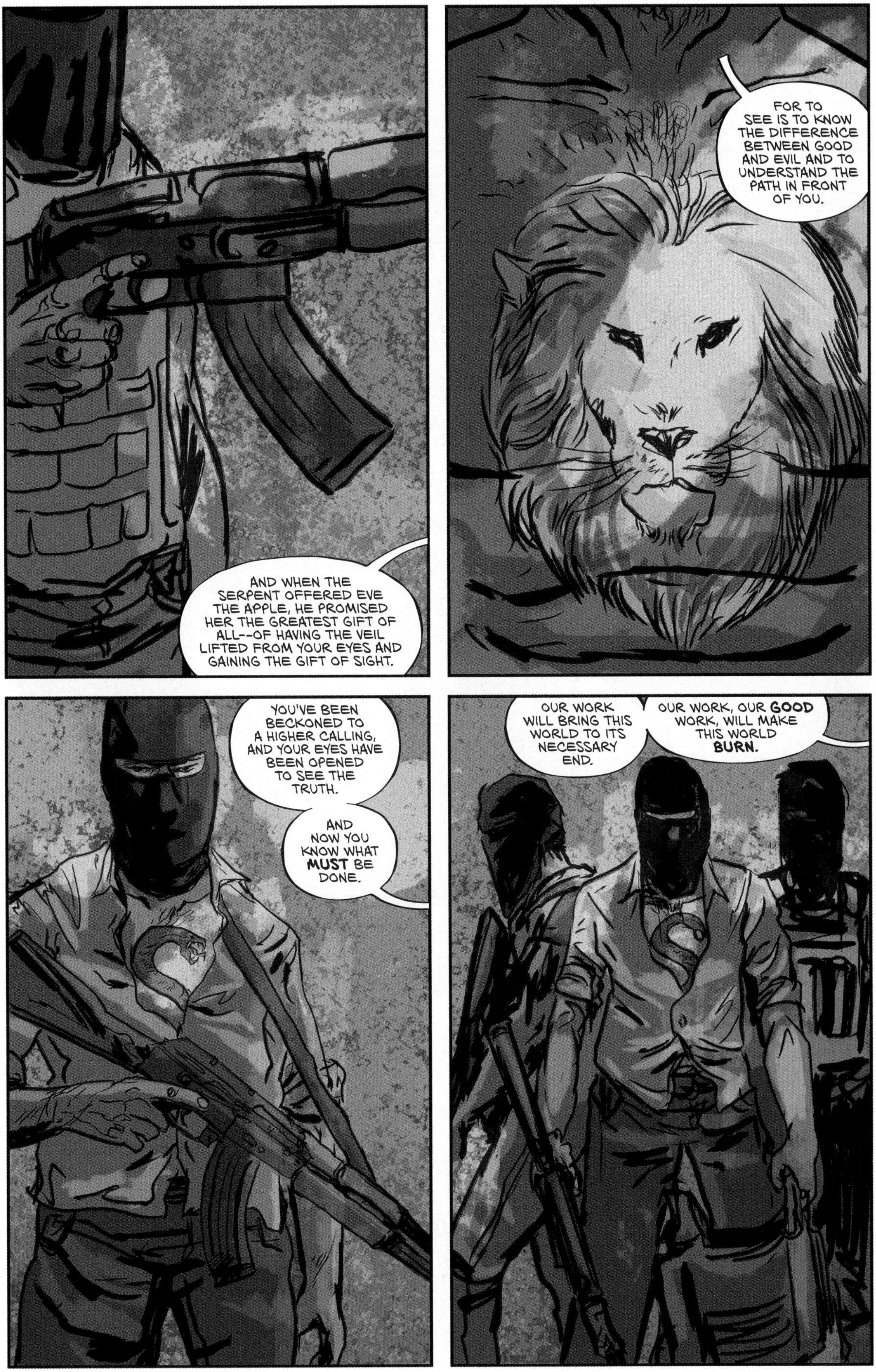
AND WHEN THE SERPENT OFFERED EVE THE APPLE, HE PROMISED HER THE GREATEST GIFT OF ALL--OF HAVING THE VEIL LIFTED FROM YOUR EYES AND GAINING THE GIFT OF SIGHT.
FOR TO SEE IS TO KNOW THE DIFFERENCE BETWEEN GOOD AND EVIL AND TO UNDERSTAND THE PATH IN FRONT OF YOU.
YOU'VE BEEN BECKONED TO A HIGHER CALLING, AND YOUR EYES HAVE BEEN OPENED TO SEE THE TRUTH.
AND NOW YOU KNOW WHAT **MUST** BE DONE.
OUR WORK WILL BRING THIS WORLD TO ITS NECESSARY END.
OUR WORK, OUR **GOOD** WORK, WILL MAKE THIS WORLD **BURN.**

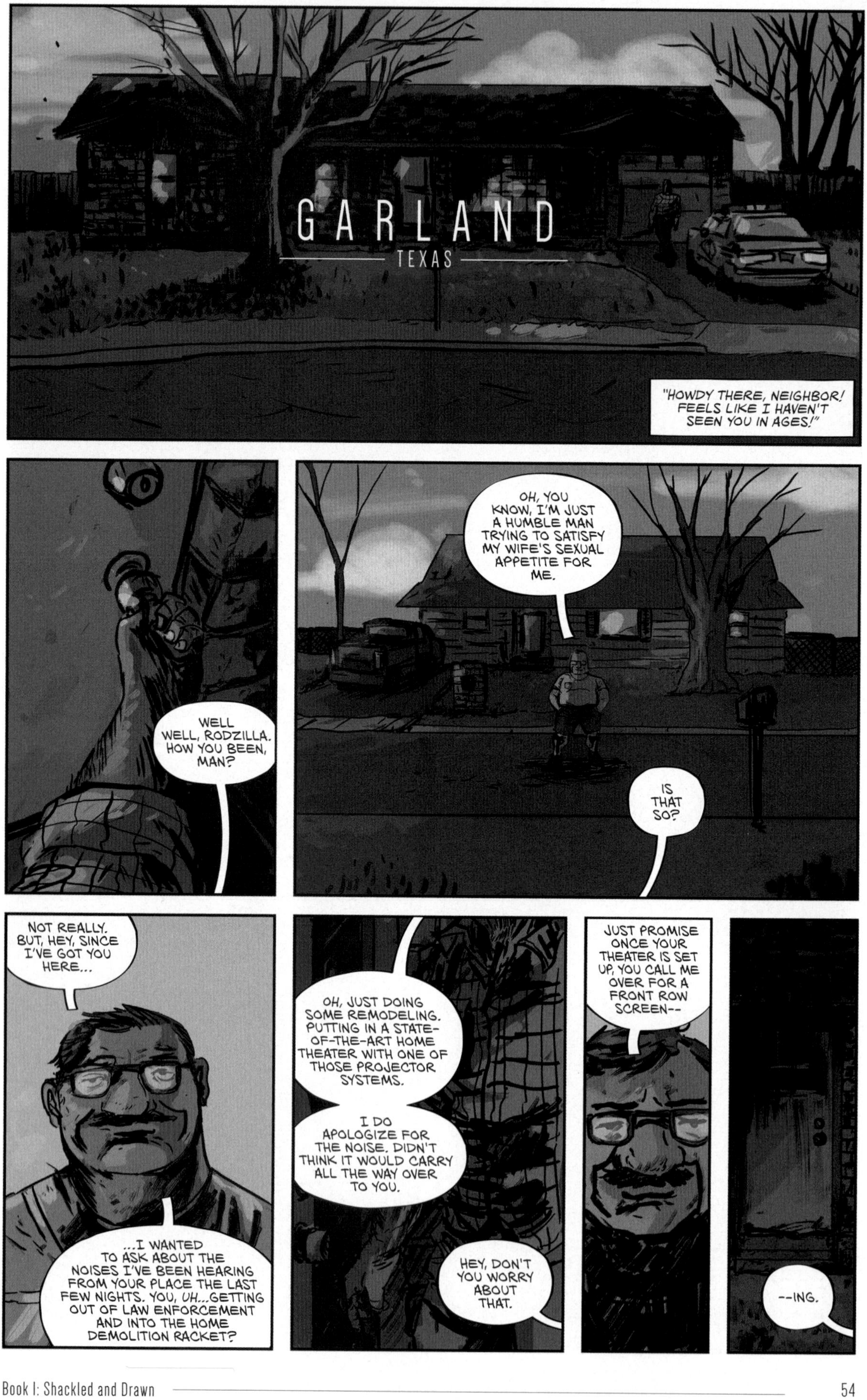
GARLAND
TEXAS
"HOWDY THERE, NEIGHBOR! FEELS LIKE I HAVEN'T SEEN YOU IN AGES!"
WELL WELL, RODZILLA. HOW YOU BEEN, MAN?
OH, YOU KNOW, I'M JUST A HUMBLE MAN TRYING TO SATISFY MY WIFE'S SEXUAL APPETITE FOR ME.
IS THAT SO?
NOT REALLY. BUT, HEY, SINCE I'VE GOT YOU HERE...
...I WANTED TO ASK ABOUT THE NOISES I'VE BEEN HEARING FROM YOUR PLACE THE LAST FEW NIGHTS. YOU, UH...GETTING OUT OF LAW ENFORCEMENT AND INTO THE HOME DEMOLITION RACKET?
OH, JUST DOING SOME REMODELING. PUTTING IN A STATE-OF-THE-ART HOME THEATER WITH ONE OF THOSE PROJECTOR SYSTEMS.
I DO APOLOGIZE FOR THE NOISE. DIDN'T THINK IT WOULD CARRY ALL THE WAY OVER TO YOU.
HEY, DON'T YOU WORRY ABOUT THAT.
JUST PROMISE ONCE YOUR THEATER IS SET UP, YOU CALL ME OVER FOR A FRONT ROW SCREEN--
--ING.

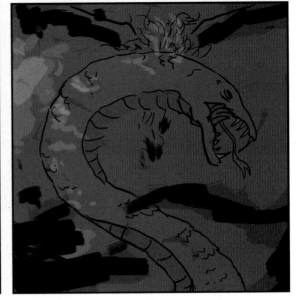

PLEASE... PLEASE LET ME...LET ME GO *HOME.*

CLICK

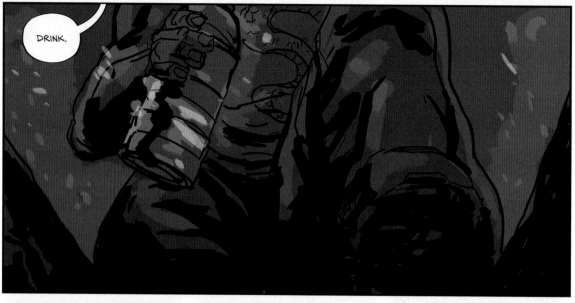

DRINK.

NONONO PLEASE DON'T, DON'T CLOSE IT, DO--

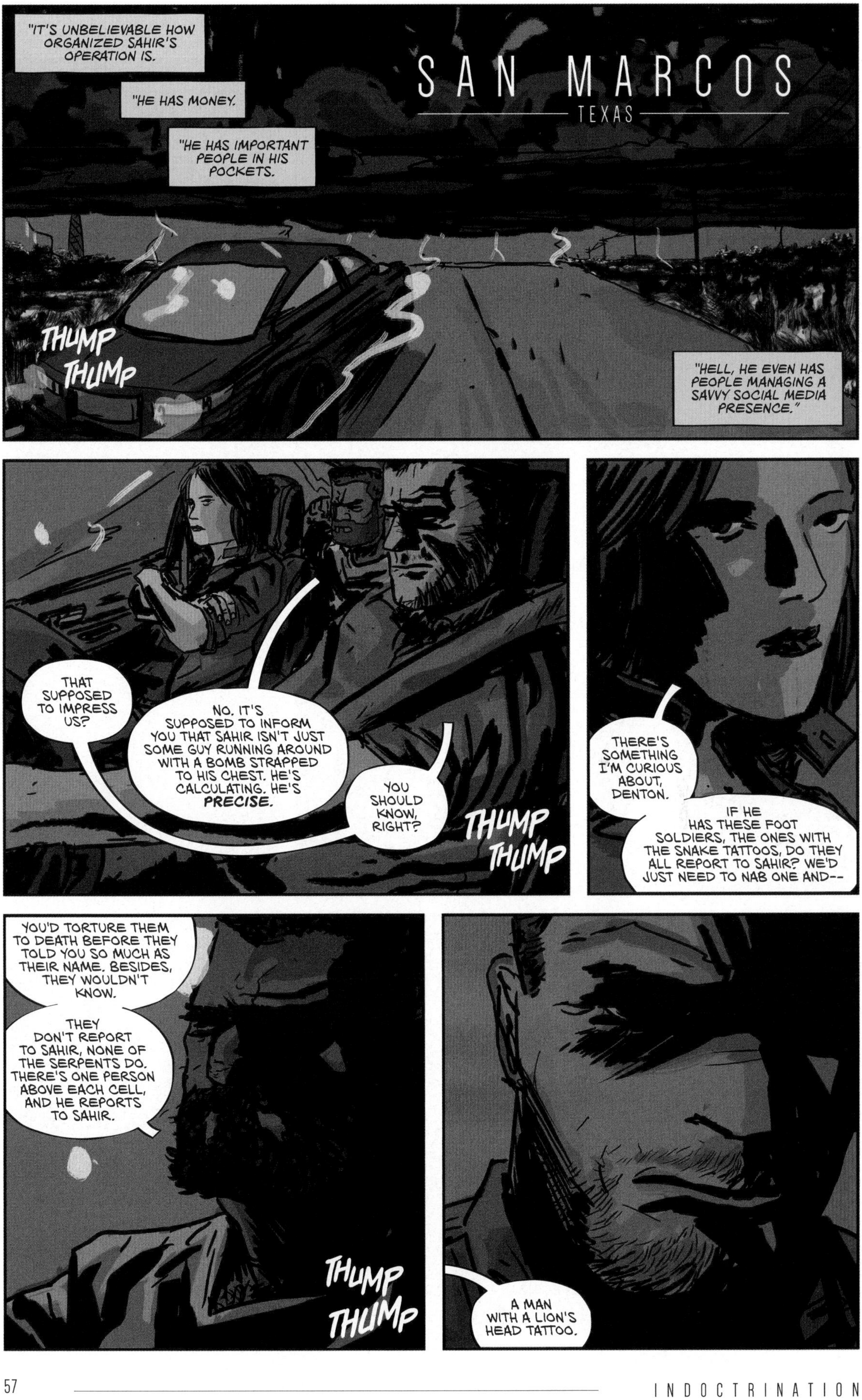
"IT'S UNBELIEVABLE HOW ORGANIZED SAHIR'S OPERATION IS.
SAN MARCOS TEXAS
"HE HAS MONEY.
"HE HAS IMPORTANT PEOPLE IN HIS POCKETS.
THUMP THUMP
"HELL, HE EVEN HAS PEOPLE MANAGING A SAVVY SOCIAL MEDIA PRESENCE."
THAT SUPPOSED TO IMPRESS US?
NO. IT'S SUPPOSED TO INFORM YOU THAT SAHIR ISN'T JUST SOME GUY RUNNING AROUND WITH A BOMB STRAPPED TO HIS CHEST. HE'S CALCULATING. HE'S **PRECISE.**
YOU SHOULD KNOW, RIGHT?
THUMP THUMP
THERE'S SOMETHING I'M CURIOUS ABOUT, DENTON.
IF HE HAS THESE FOOT SOLDIERS, THE ONES WITH THE SNAKE TATTOOS, DO THEY ALL REPORT TO SAHIR? WE'D JUST NEED TO NAB ONE AND--
YOU'D TORTURE THEM TO DEATH BEFORE THEY TOLD YOU SO MUCH AS THEIR NAME. BESIDES, THEY WOULDN'T KNOW.
THEY DON'T REPORT TO SAHIR, NONE OF THE SERPENTS DO. THERE'S ONE PERSON ABOVE EACH CELL, AND HE REPORTS TO SAHIR.
THUMP THUMP
A MAN WITH A LION'S HEAD TATTOO.

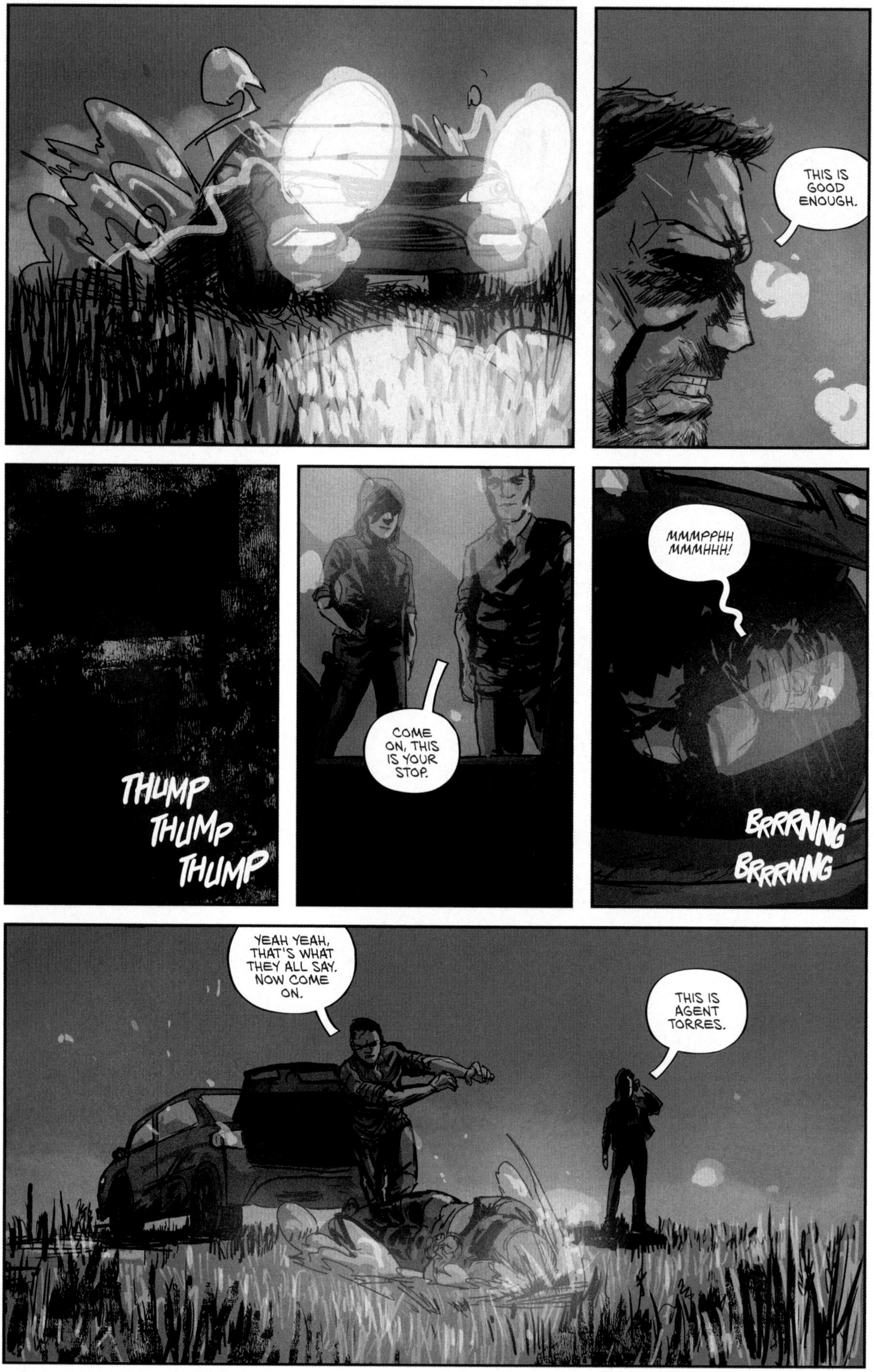
THIS IS GOOD ENOUGH.
THUMP
THUMP
THUMP
COME ON, THIS IS YOUR STOP.
MMMPPHH MMMHHH!
BRRRNNG
BRRRNNG
YEAH YEAH, THAT'S WHAT THEY ALL SAY. NOW COME ON.
THIS IS AGENT TORRES.

TRY ANYTHING STUPID, AND YOU'LL BE LEFT OUT HERE WITH MORE, LET'S SAY, **PERMANENCE.**

THAT'S THE CASE I'VE BEEN WORKING, WHY?

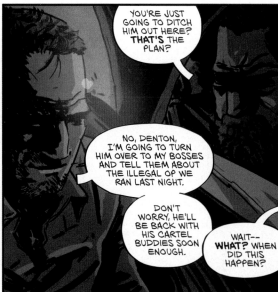

YOU'RE JUST GOING TO DITCH HIM OUT HERE? **THAT'S** THE PLAN?

NO, DENTON, I'M GOING TO TURN HIM OVER TO MY BOSSES AND TELL THEM ABOUT THE ILLEGAL OP WE RAN LAST NIGHT.

DON'T WORRY, HE'LL BE BACK WITH HIS CARTEL BUDDIES SOON ENOUGH.

WAIT-- **WHAT?** WHEN DID THIS HAPPEN?

WHAT IS IT?

OKAY, WE'LL BE BACK IN DALLAS TONIGHT.

ANDALE, ASSHOLE. WE'RE THROUGH WITH YOU.

SOMETHING'S WRONG--WHAT ARE WE LOOKING AT?

THAT WAS GONZALEZ. GOVERNOR RIDLEY'S DAUGHTER-- SHE'S BEEN KIDNAPPED.

SHIIIIT.

YEAH, AND THAT'S NOT ALL. THEY HAVE A VIDEO...

...AND IT FEATURES A MAN WITH A SERPENT TATTOOED OVER HIS CHEST.

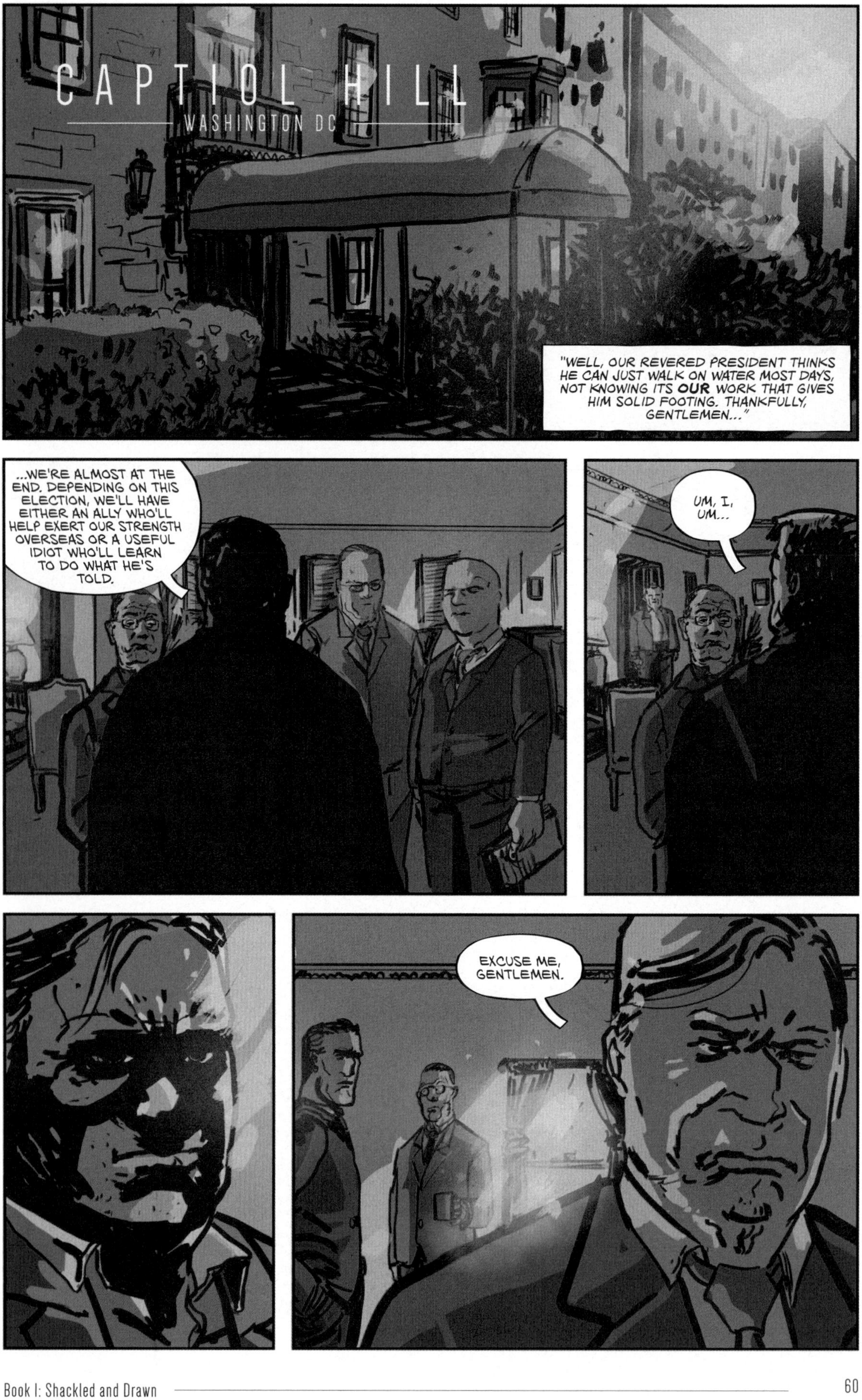
CAPTIOL HILL
WASHINGTON DC
"WELL, OUR REVERED PRESIDENT THINKS HE CAN JUST WALK ON WATER MOST DAYS, NOT KNOWING ITS **OUR** WORK THAT GIVES HIM SOLID FOOTING. THANKFULLY, GENTLEMEN..."
...WE'RE ALMOST AT THE END. DEPENDING ON THIS ELECTION, WE'LL HAVE EITHER AN ALLY WHO'LL HELP EXERT OUR STRENGTH OVERSEAS OR A USEFUL IDIOT WHO'LL LEARN TO DO WHAT HE'S TOLD.
UM, I, UM...
EXCUSE ME, GENTLEMEN.

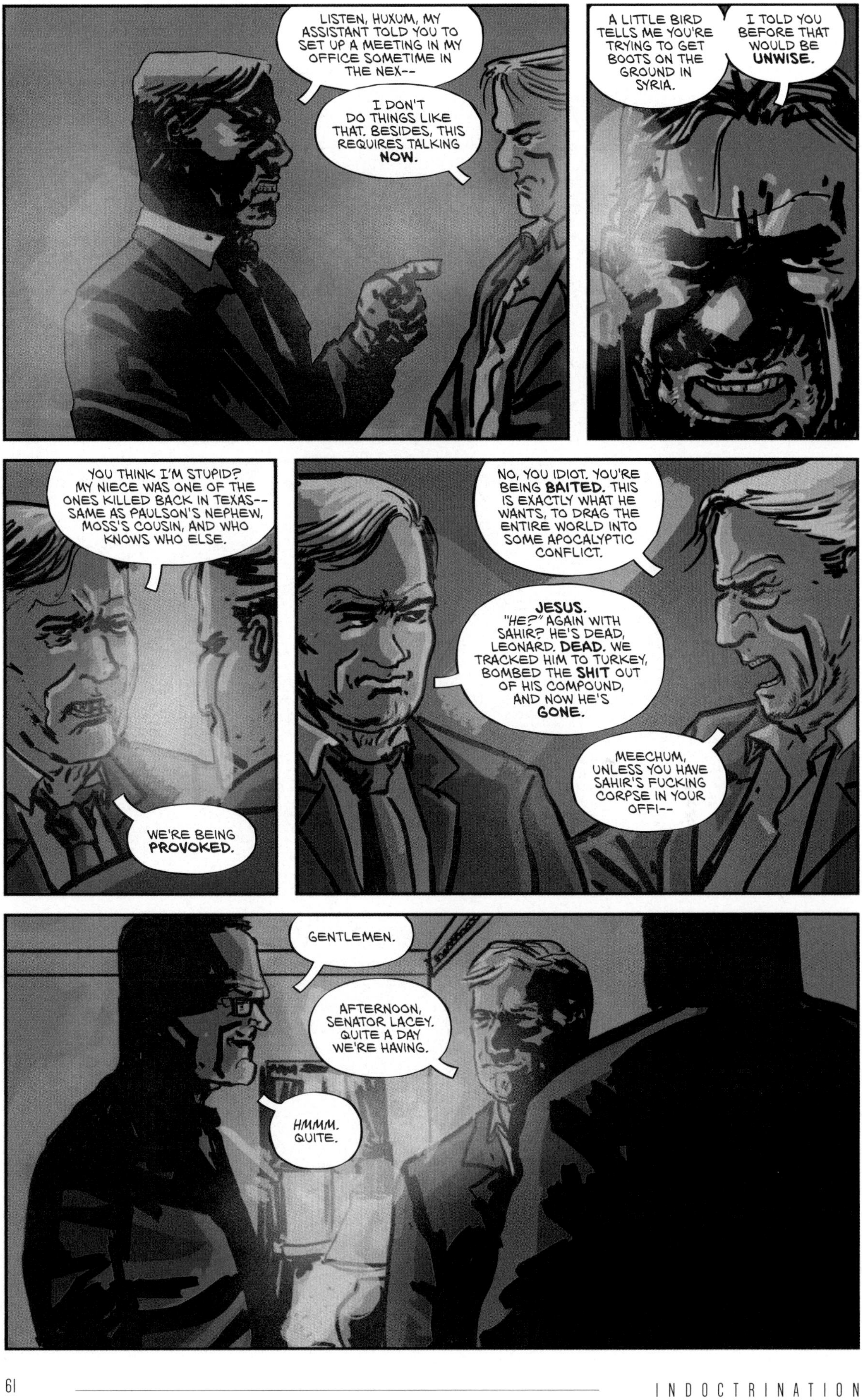
LISTEN, HUXUM, MY ASSISTANT TOLD YOU TO SET UP A MEETING IN MY OFFICE SOMETIME IN THE NEX--
I DON'T DO THINGS LIKE THAT. BESIDES, THIS REQUIRES TALKING **NOW.**
A LITTLE BIRD TELLS ME YOU'RE TRYING TO GET BOOTS ON THE GROUND IN SYRIA.
I TOLD YOU BEFORE THAT WOULD BE **UNWISE.**
YOU THINK I'M STUPID? MY NIECE WAS ONE OF THE ONES KILLED BACK IN TEXAS-- SAME AS PAULSON'S NEPHEW, MOSS'S COUSIN, AND WHO KNOWS WHO ELSE.
WE'RE BEING **PROVOKED.**
NO, YOU IDIOT. YOU'RE BEING **BAITED.** THIS IS EXACTLY WHAT HE WANTS, TO DRAG THE ENTIRE WORLD INTO SOME APOCALYPTIC CONFLICT.
JESUS. *"HE?"* AGAIN WITH SAHIR? HE'S DEAD, LEONARD. **DEAD.** WE TRACKED HIM TO TURKEY, BOMBED THE **SHIT** OUT OF HIS COMPOUND, AND NOW HE'S **GONE.**
MEECHUM, UNLESS YOU HAVE SAHIR'S FUCKING CORPSE IN YOUR OFFI--
GENTLEMEN.
AFTERNOON, SENATOR LACEY. QUITE A DAY WE'RE HAVING.
HMMM. QUITE.

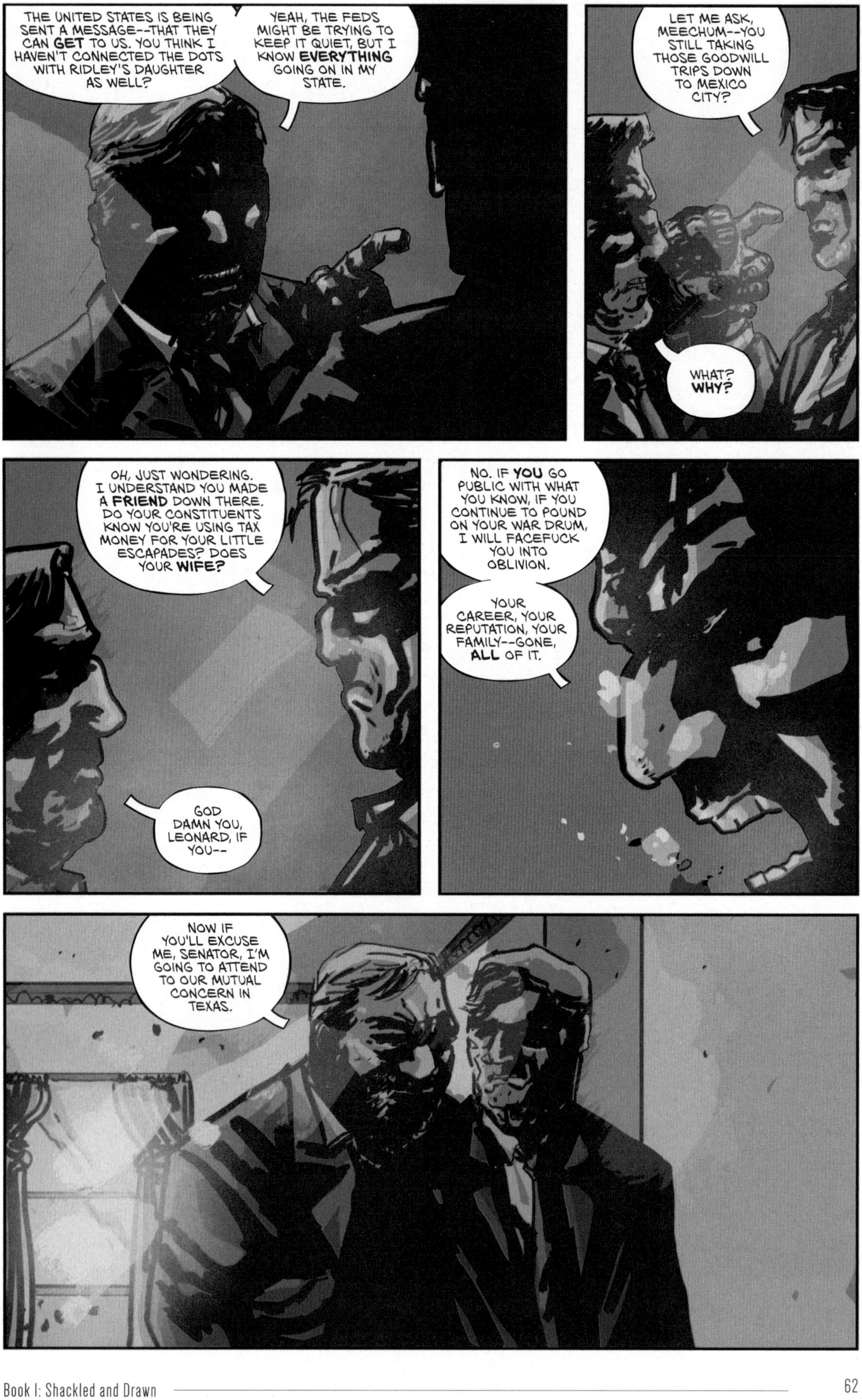
THE UNITED STATES IS BEING SENT A MESSAGE--THAT THEY CAN **GET** TO US. YOU THINK I HAVEN'T CONNECTED THE DOTS WITH RIDLEY'S DAUGHTER AS WELL?
YEAH, THE FEDS MIGHT BE TRYING TO KEEP IT QUIET, BUT I KNOW **EVERYTHING** GOING ON IN MY STATE.
LET ME ASK, MEECHUM--YOU STILL TAKING THOSE GOODWILL TRIPS DOWN TO MEXICO CITY?
WHAT? **WHY?**
OH, JUST WONDERING. I UNDERSTAND YOU MADE A **FRIEND** DOWN THERE. DO YOUR CONSTITUENTS KNOW YOU'RE USING TAX MONEY FOR YOUR LITTLE ESCAPADES? DOES YOUR **WIFE?**
GOD DAMN YOU, LEONARD, IF YOU--
NO. IF **YOU** GO PUBLIC WITH WHAT YOU KNOW, IF YOU CONTINUE TO POUND ON YOUR WAR DRUM, I WILL FACEFUCK YOU INTO OBLIVION.
YOUR CAREER, YOUR REPUTATION, YOUR FAMILY--GONE, **ALL** OF IT.
NOW IF YOU'LL EXCUSE ME, SENATOR, I'M GOING TO ATTEND TO OUR MUTUAL CONCERN IN TEXAS.

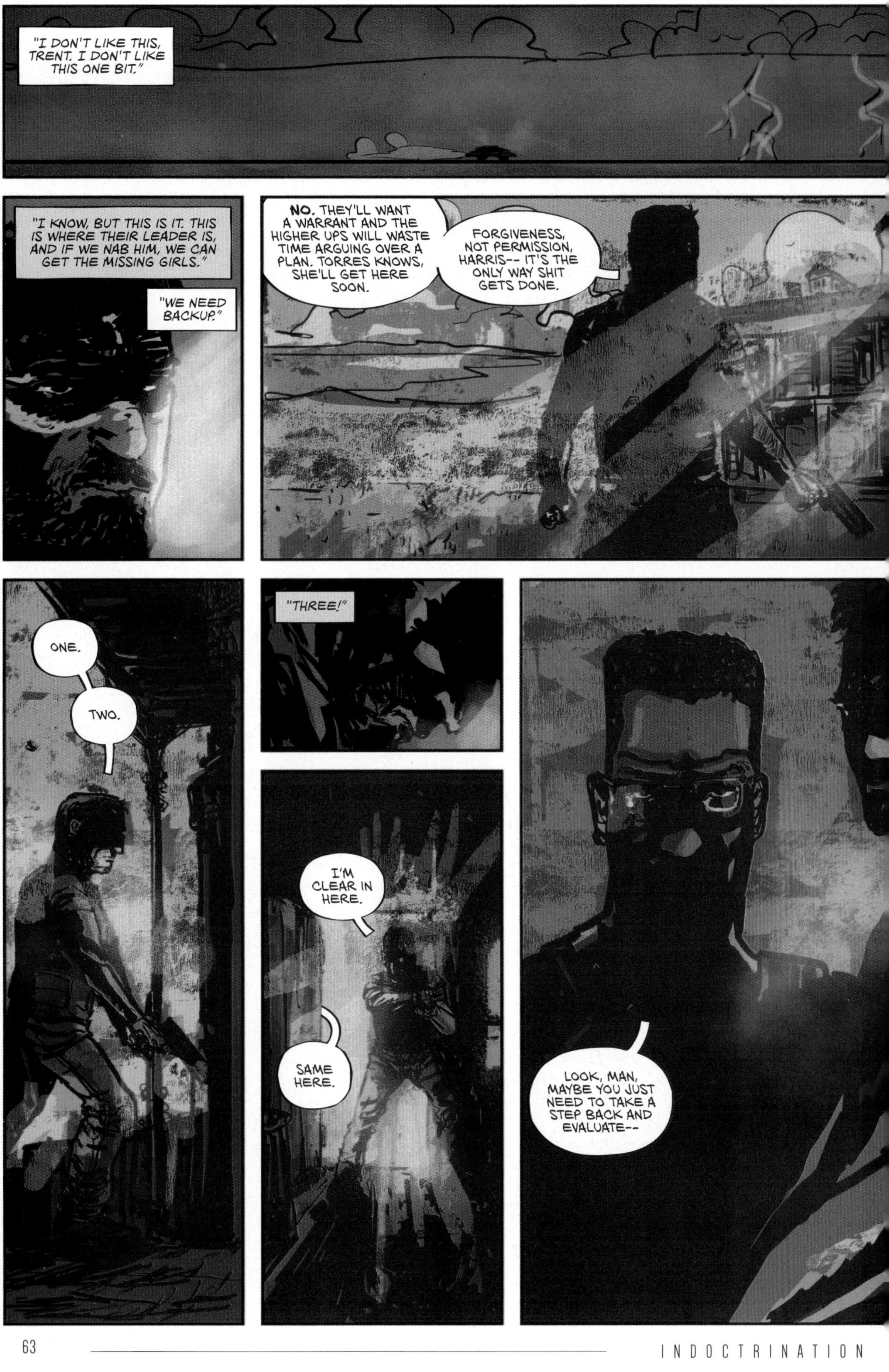
"I DON'T LIKE THIS, TRENT. I DON'T LIKE THIS ONE BIT."
"I KNOW, BUT THIS IS IT. THIS IS WHERE THEIR LEADER IS, AND IF WE NAB HIM, WE CAN GET THE MISSING GIRLS."
"WE NEED BACKUP."
NO. THEY'LL WANT A WARRANT AND THE HIGHER UPS WILL WASTE TIME ARGUING OVER A PLAN. TORRES KNOWS, SHE'LL GET HERE SOON.
FORGIVENESS, NOT PERMISSION, HARRIS-- IT'S THE ONLY WAY SHIT GETS DONE.
ONE.
TWO.
"THREE!"
I'M CLEAR IN HERE.
SAME HERE.
LOOK, MAN, MAYBE YOU JUST NEED TO TAKE A STEP BACK AND EVALUATE--

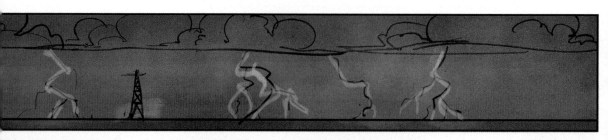

"FINE, BUT THIS GOES SOUTH--"

"IT'S ON ME.

"AND, LISTEN, THE KID I'VE BEEN WORKING--I WANT HIM SAFE,"

HEEELLLPPPP! HEL--

"TRENT?"

TRENT, YOU CANNOT GO DOWN THERE, THEY WILL BE WAITING FOR US.

TRENT?

"TRENT--YOU ALL RIGHT?"

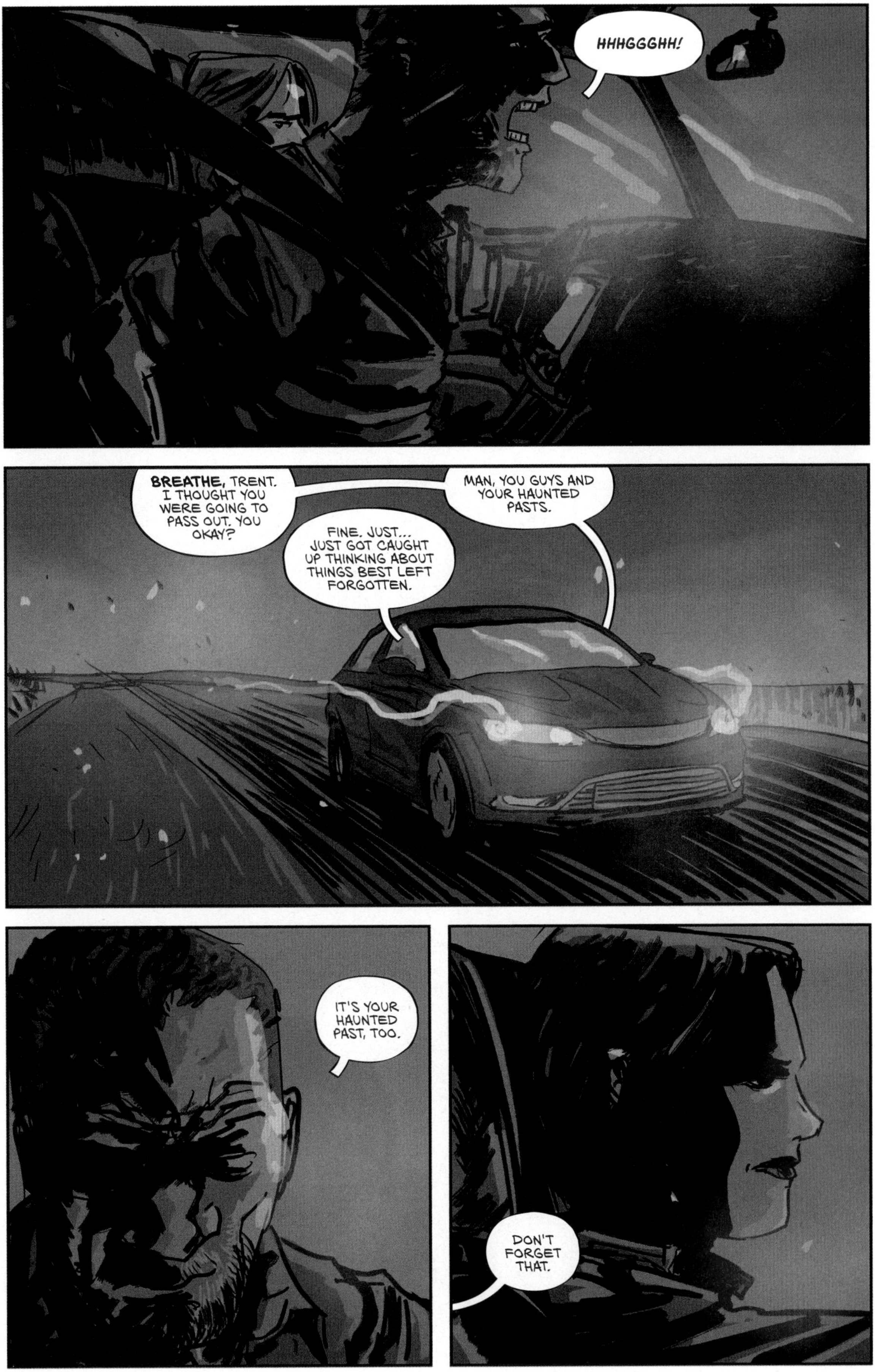
HHHGGGHH!
BREATHE, TRENT. I THOUGHT YOU WERE GOING TO PASS OUT. YOU OKAY?
FINE. JUST... JUST GOT CAUGHT UP THINKING ABOUT THINGS BEST LEFT FORGOTTEN.
MAN, YOU GUYS AND YOUR HAUNTED PASTS.
IT'S YOUR HAUNTED PAST, TOO.
DON'T FORGET THAT.

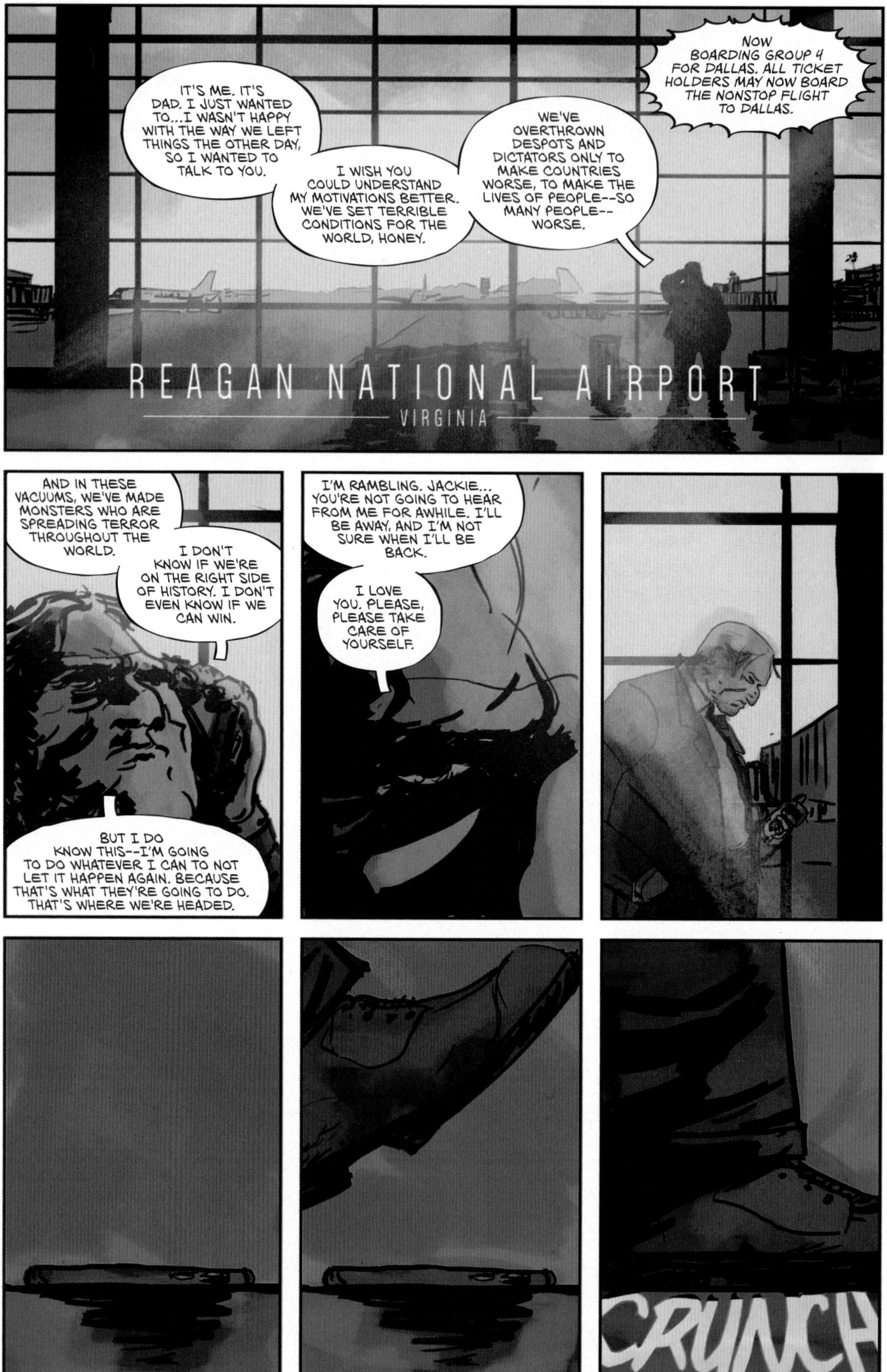
IT'S ME. IT'S DAD. I JUST WANTED TO...I WASN'T HAPPY WITH THE WAY WE LEFT THINGS THE OTHER DAY, SO I WANTED TO TALK TO YOU.
I WISH YOU COULD UNDERSTAND MY MOTIVATIONS BETTER. WE'VE SET TERRIBLE CONDITIONS FOR THE WORLD, HONEY.
WE'VE OVERTHROWN DESPOTS AND DICTATORS ONLY TO MAKE COUNTRIES WORSE, TO MAKE THE LIVES OF PEOPLE--SO MANY PEOPLE--WORSE.
NOW BOARDING GROUP 4 FOR DALLAS. ALL TICKET HOLDERS MAY NOW BOARD THE NONSTOP FLIGHT TO DALLAS.
REAGAN NATIONAL AIRPORT
VIRGINIA
AND IN THESE VACUUMS, WE'VE MADE MONSTERS WHO ARE SPREADING TERROR THROUGHOUT THE WORLD.
I DON'T KNOW IF WE'RE ON THE RIGHT SIDE OF HISTORY. I DON'T EVEN KNOW IF WE CAN WIN.
BUT I DO KNOW THIS--I'M GOING TO DO WHATEVER I CAN TO NOT LET IT HAPPEN AGAIN. BECAUSE THAT'S WHAT THEY'RE GOING TO DO. THAT'S WHERE WE'RE HEADED.
I'M RAMBLING. JACKIE... YOU'RE NOT GOING TO HEAR FROM ME FOR AWHILE. I'LL BE AWAY, AND I'M NOT SURE WHEN I'LL BE BACK.
I LOVE YOU. PLEASE, PLEASE TAKE CARE OF YOURSELF.
CRUNCH

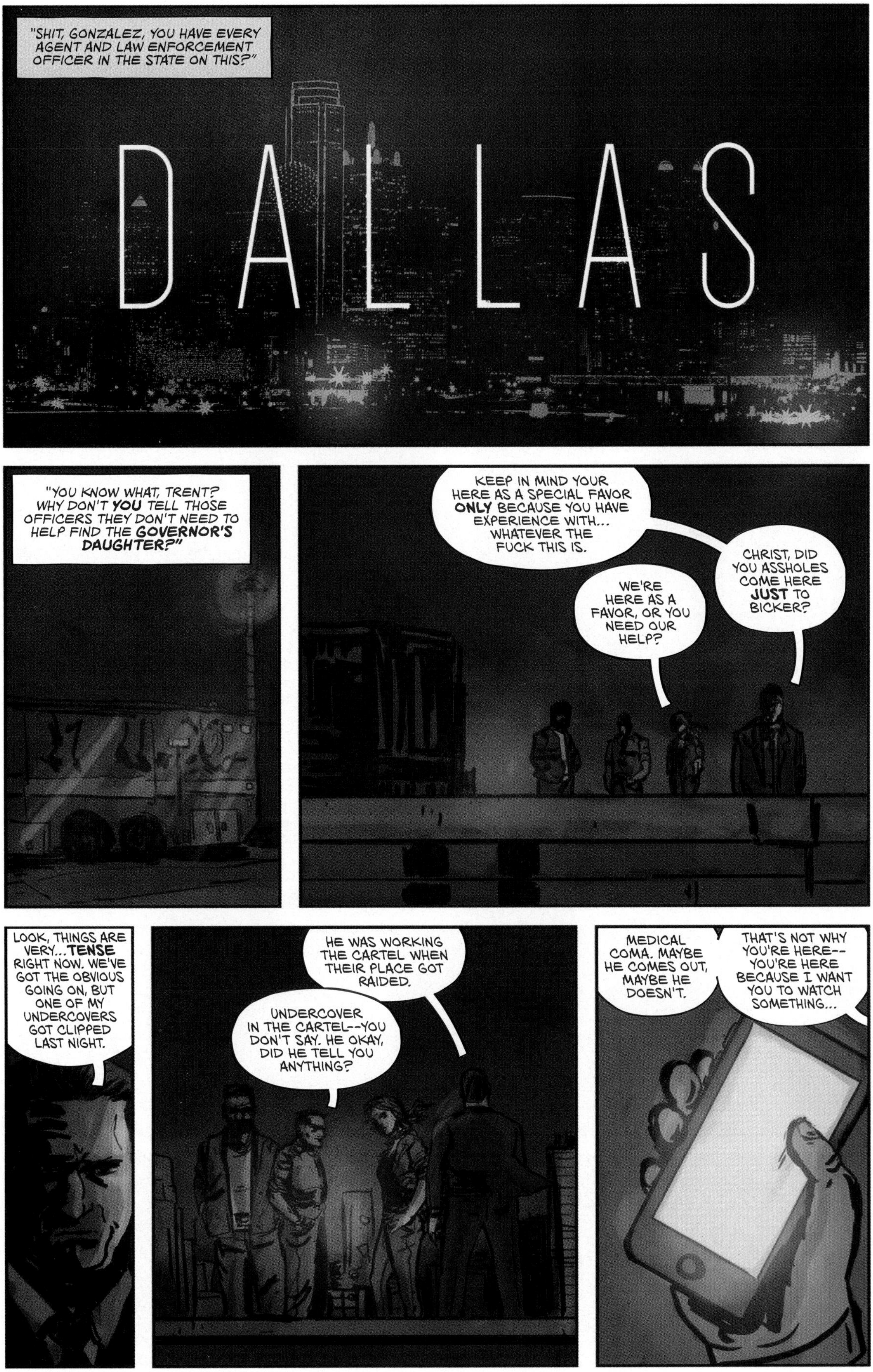
"SHIT, GONZALEZ, YOU HAVE EVERY AGENT AND LAW ENFORCEMENT OFFICER IN THE STATE ON THIS?"
DALLAS
"YOU KNOW WHAT, TRENT? WHY DON'T YOU TELL THOSE OFFICERS THEY DON'T NEED TO HELP FIND THE GOVERNOR'S DAUGHTER?"
KEEP IN MIND YOUR HERE AS A SPECIAL FAVOR ONLY BECAUSE YOU HAVE EXPERIENCE WITH... WHATEVER THE FUCK THIS IS.
WE'RE HERE AS A FAVOR, OR YOU NEED OUR HELP?
CHRIST, DID YOU ASSHOLES COME HERE JUST TO BICKER?
LOOK, THINGS ARE VERY...TENSE RIGHT NOW. WE'VE GOT THE OBVIOUS GOING ON, BUT ONE OF MY UNDERCOVERS GOT CLIPPED LAST NIGHT.
UNDERCOVER IN THE CARTEL--YOU DON'T SAY. HE OKAY, DID HE TELL YOU ANYTHING?
HE WAS WORKING THE CARTEL WHEN THEIR PLACE GOT RAIDED.
MEDICAL COMA. MAYBE HE COMES OUT, MAYBE HE DOESN'T.
THAT'S NOT WHY YOU'RE HERE--YOU'RE HERE BECAUSE I WANT YOU TO WATCH SOMETHING...

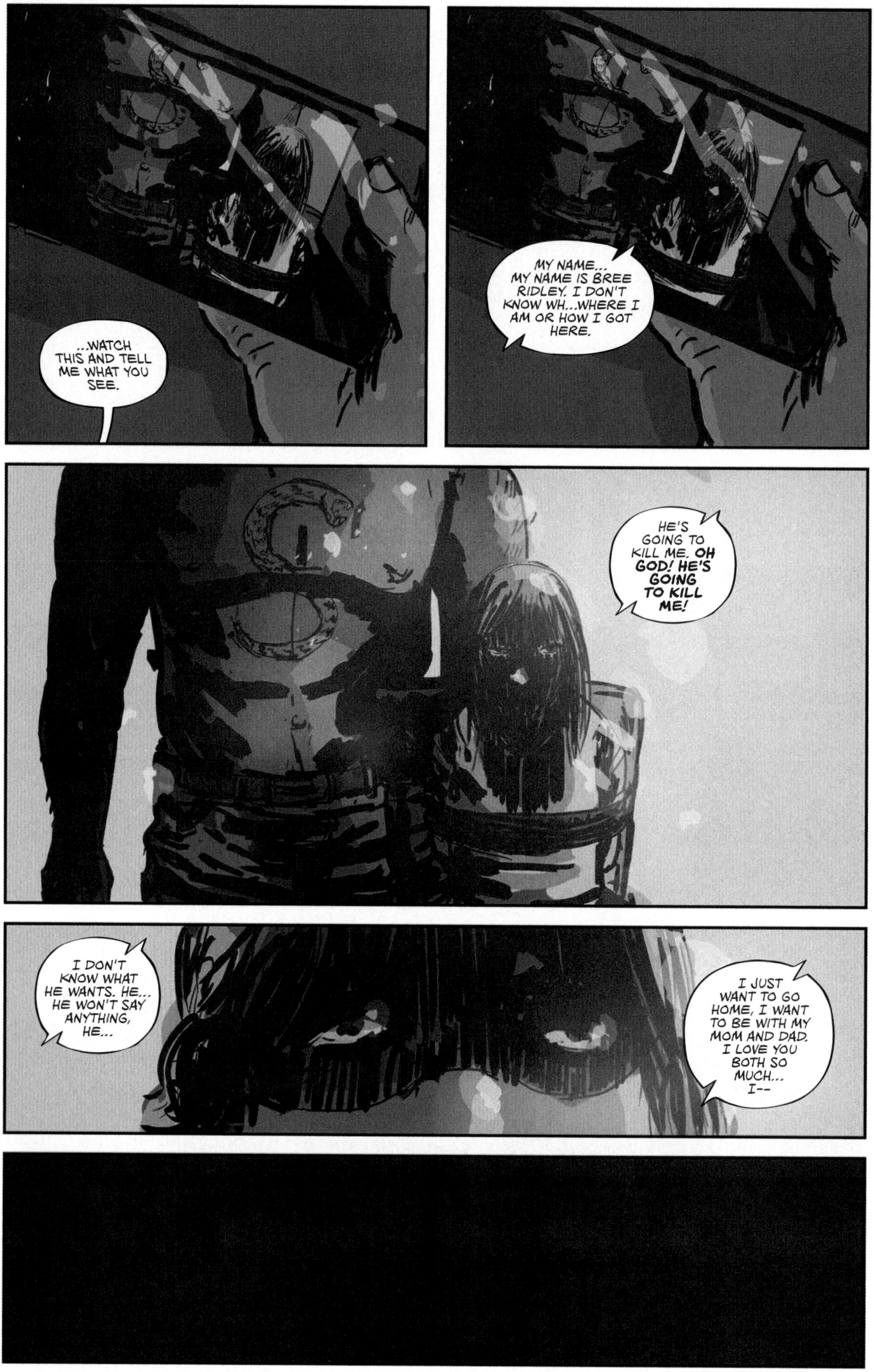
...WATCH THIS AND TELL ME WHAT YOU SEE.
MY NAME... MY NAME IS BREE RIDLEY. I DON'T KNOW WH...WHERE I AM OR HOW I GOT HERE.
HE'S GOING TO KILL ME. **OH GOD! HE'S GOING TO KILL ME!**
I DON'T KNOW WHAT HE WANTS. HE... HE WON'T SAY ANYTHING, HE...
I JUST WANT TO GO HOME, I WANT TO BE WITH MY MOM AND DAD. I LOVE YOU BOTH SO MUCH... I--

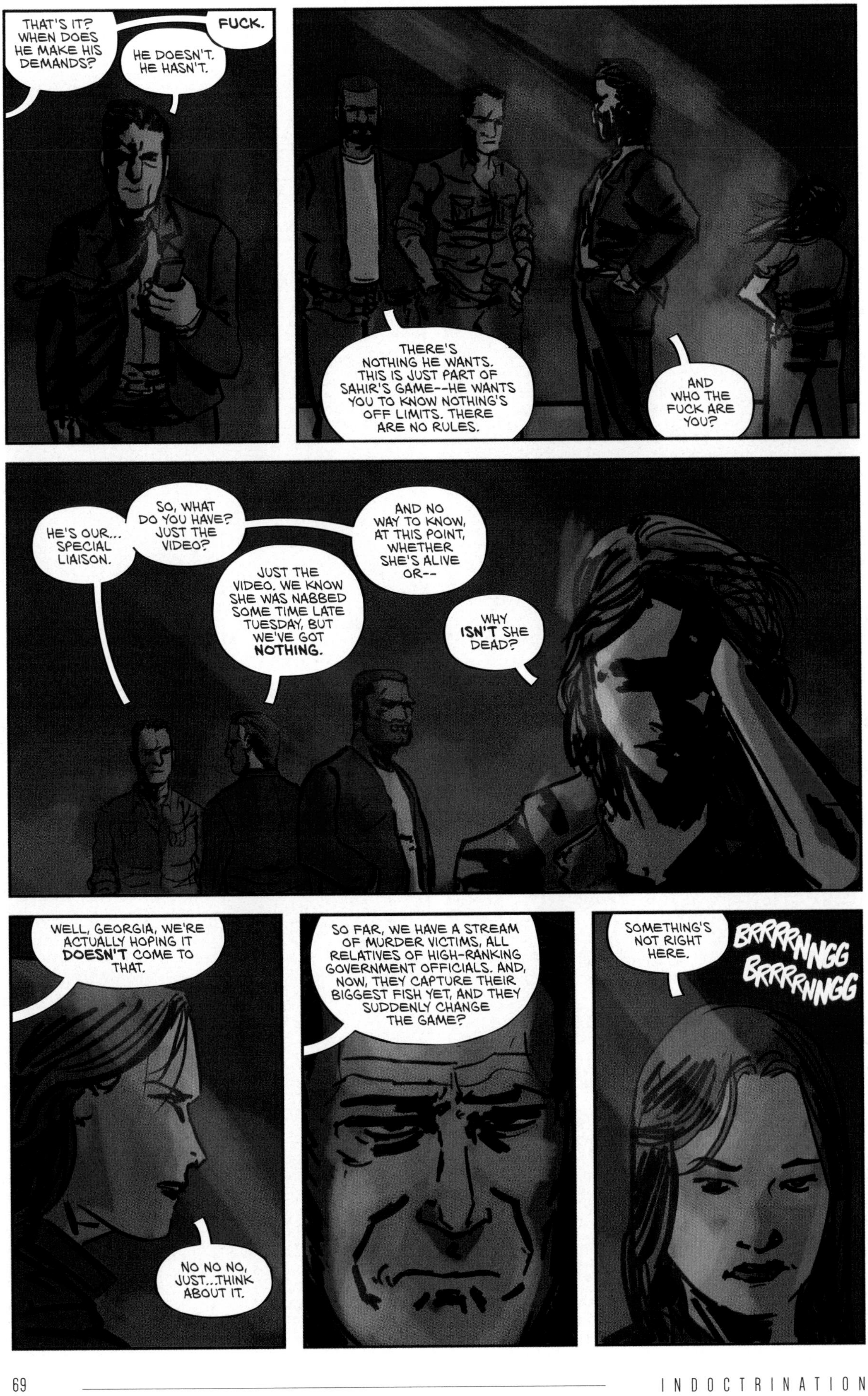
THAT'S IT? WHEN DOES HE MAKE HIS DEMANDS?
HE DOESN'T. HE HASN'T.
FUCK.
THERE'S NOTHING HE WANTS. THIS IS JUST PART OF SAHIR'S GAME--HE WANTS YOU TO KNOW NOTHING'S OFF LIMITS. THERE ARE NO RULES.
AND WHO THE FUCK ARE YOU?
HE'S OUR... SPECIAL LIAISON.
SO, WHAT DO YOU HAVE? JUST THE VIDEO?
JUST THE VIDEO. WE KNOW SHE WAS NABBED SOME TIME LATE TUESDAY, BUT WE'VE GOT NOTHING.
AND NO WAY TO KNOW, AT THIS POINT, WHETHER SHE'S ALIVE OR--
WHY ISN'T SHE DEAD?
WELL, GEORGIA, WE'RE ACTUALLY HOPING IT DOESN'T COME TO THAT.
NO NO NO, JUST...THINK ABOUT IT.
SO FAR, WE HAVE A STREAM OF MURDER VICTIMS, ALL RELATIVES OF HIGH-RANKING GOVERNMENT OFFICIALS. AND, NOW, THEY CAPTURE THEIR BIGGEST FISH YET, AND THEY SUDDENLY CHANGE THE GAME?
SOMETHING'S NOT RIGHT HERE.
BRRRRNNGG BRRRRNNGG

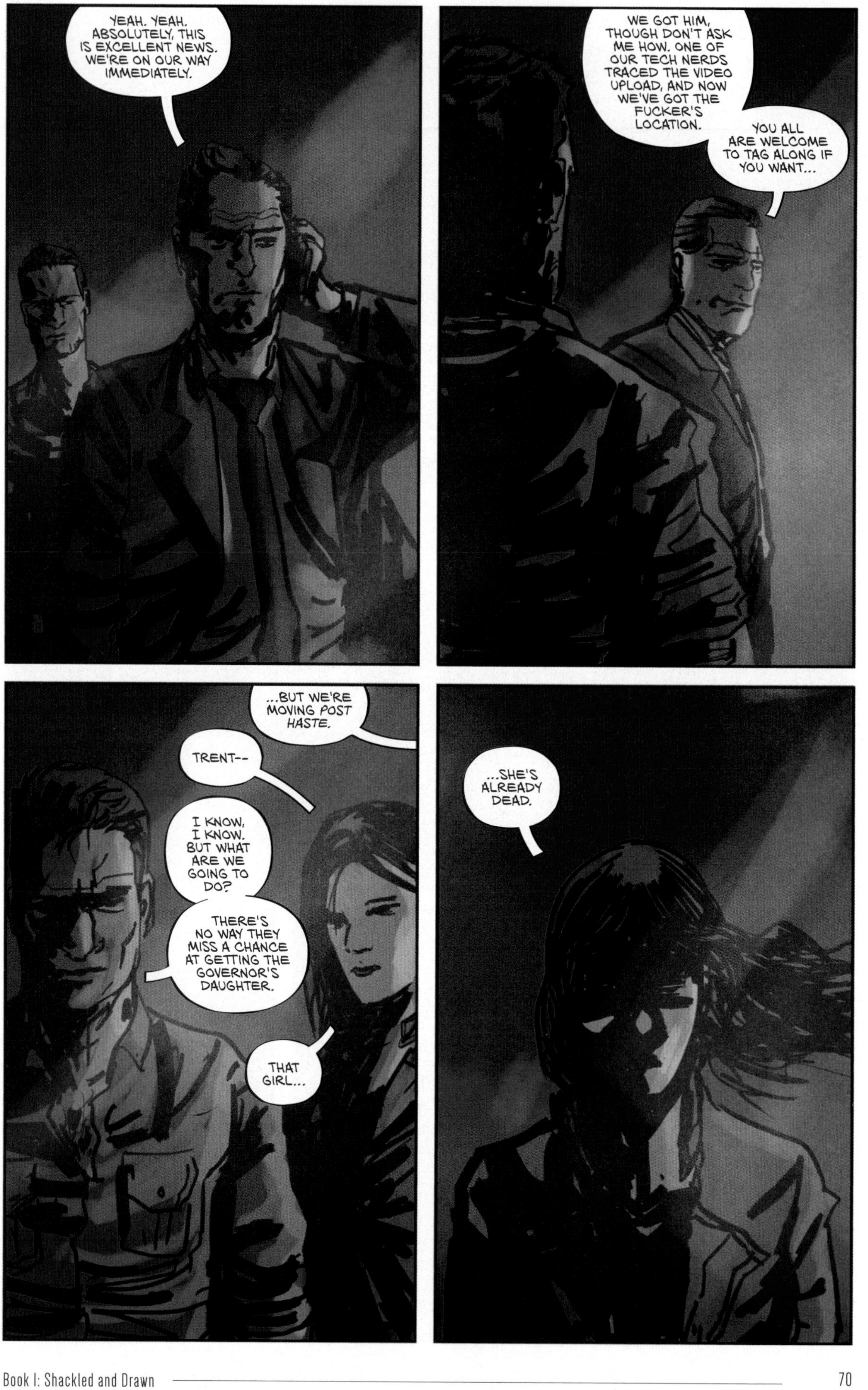
YEAH. YEAH. ABSOLUTELY, THIS IS EXCELLENT NEWS. WE'RE ON OUR WAY IMMEDIATELY.
WE GOT HIM, THOUGH DON'T ASK ME HOW. ONE OF OUR TECH NERDS TRACED THE VIDEO UPLOAD, AND NOW WE'VE GOT THE FUCKER'S LOCATION.
YOU ALL ARE WELCOME TO TAG ALONG IF YOU WANT...
...BUT WE'RE MOVING POST HASTE.
TRENT--
I KNOW, I KNOW. BUT WHAT ARE WE GOING TO DO?
THERE'S NO WAY THEY MISS A CHANCE AT GETTING THE GOVERNOR'S DAUGHTER.
THAT GIRL...
...SHE'S ALREADY DEAD.

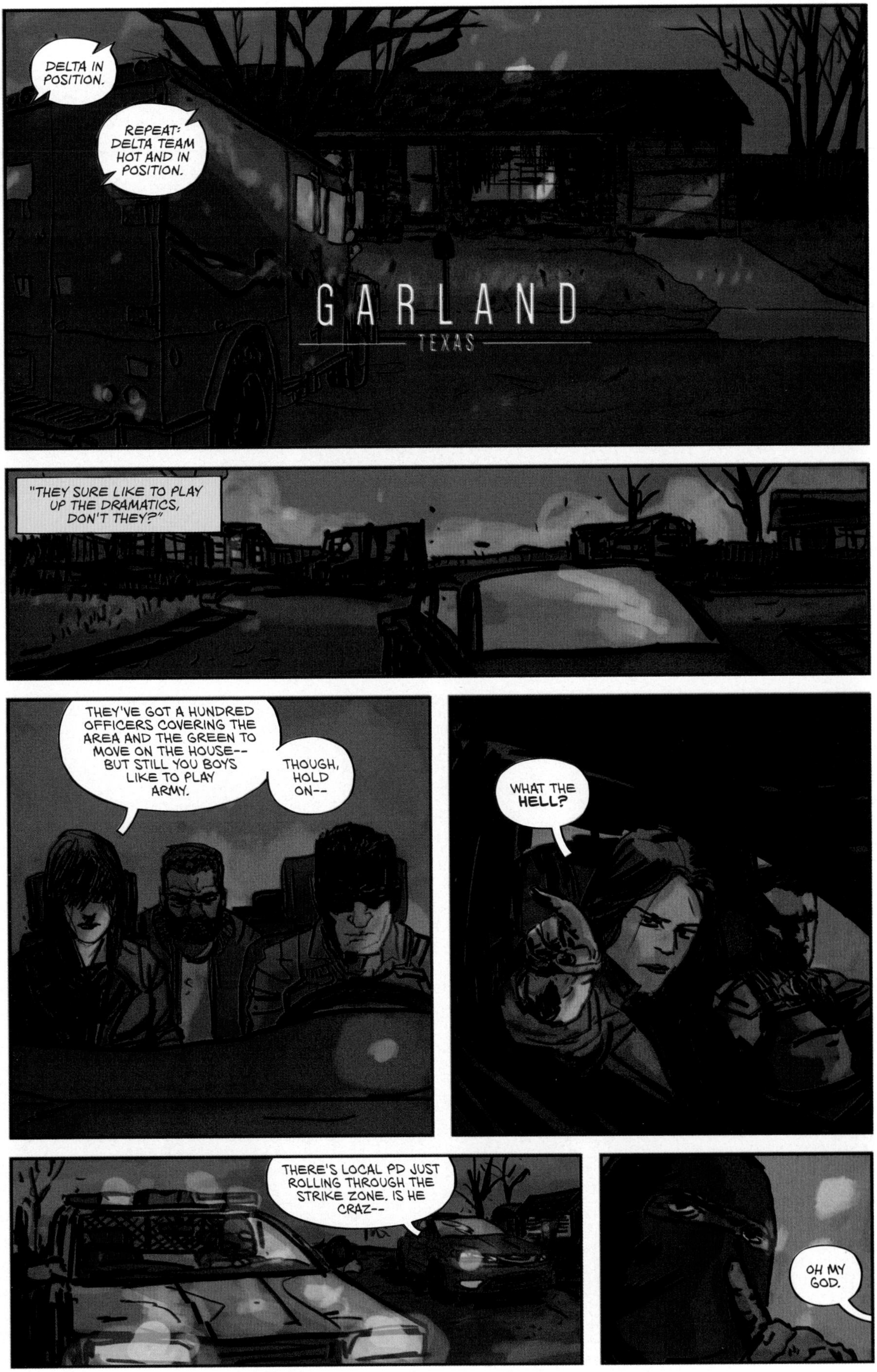
DELTA IN POSITION.
REPEAT: DELTA TEAM HOT AND IN POSITION.
GARLAND
TEXAS
"THEY SURE LIKE TO PLAY UP THE DRAMATICS, DON'T THEY?"
THEY'VE GOT A HUNDRED OFFICERS COVERING THE AREA AND THE GREEN TO MOVE ON THE HOUSE-- BUT STILL YOU BOYS LIKE TO PLAY ARMY.
THOUGH, HOLD ON--
WHAT THE HELL?
THERE'S LOCAL PD JUST ROLLING THROUGH THE STRIKE ZONE. IS HE CRAZ--
OH MY GOD.

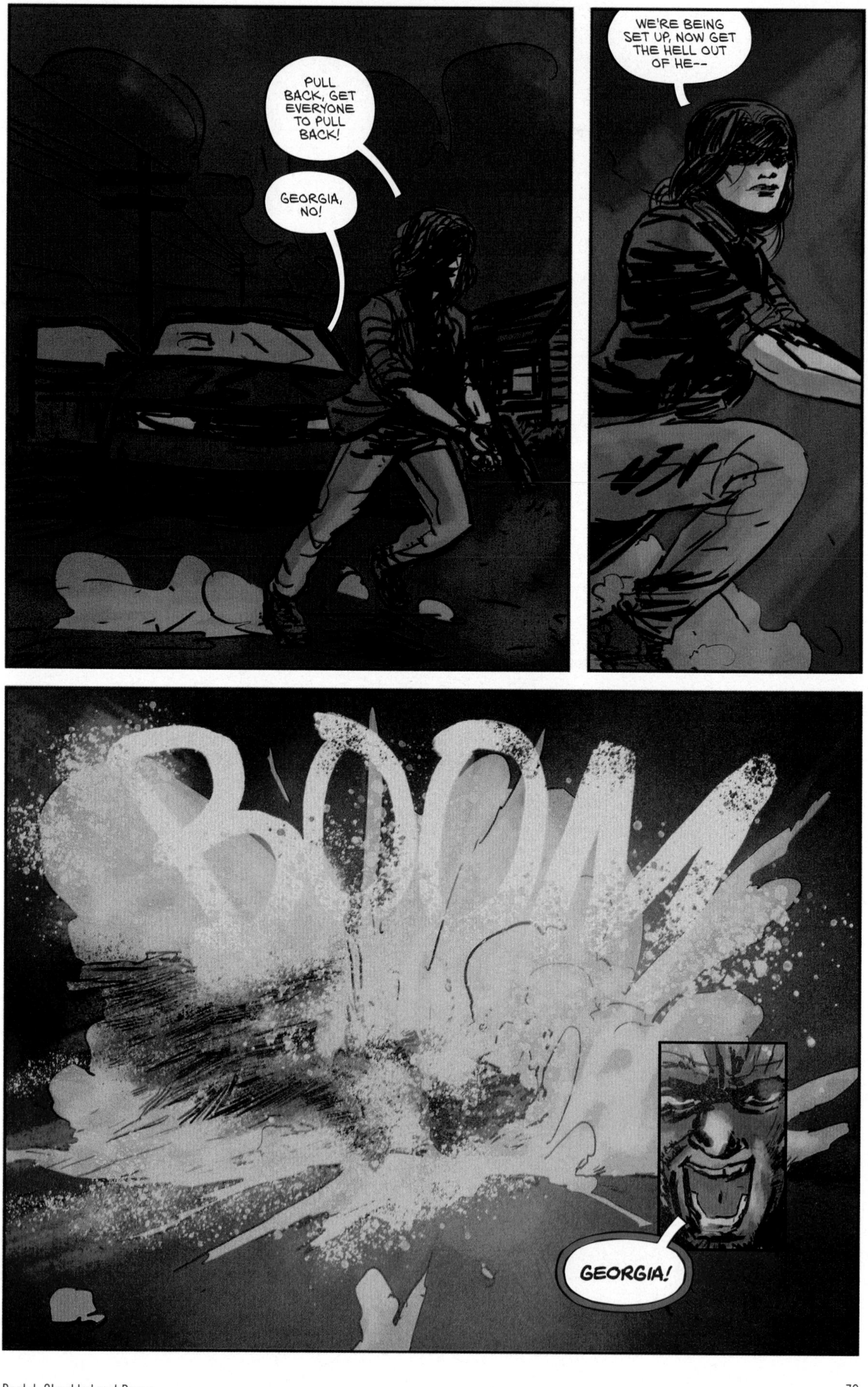
PULL BACK, GET EVERYONE TO PULL BACK!
GEORGIA, NO!
WE'RE BEING SET UP, NOW GET THE HELL OUT OF HE--
BOOM
GEORGIA!

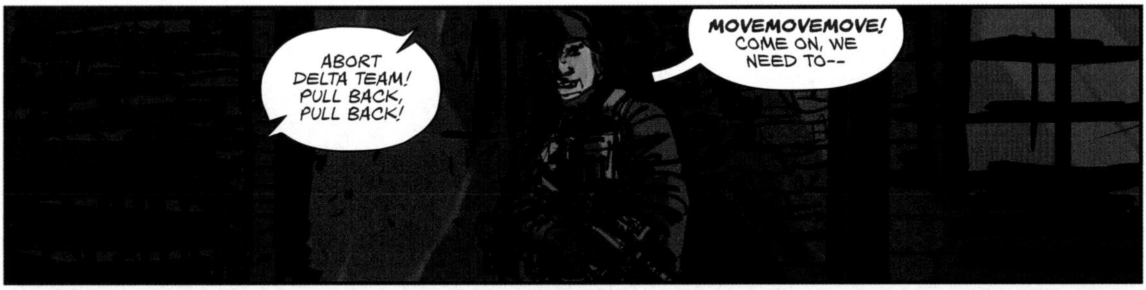

ABORT DELTA TEAM! PULL BACK, PULL BACK!
MOVEMOVEMOVE! COME ON, WE NEED TO--

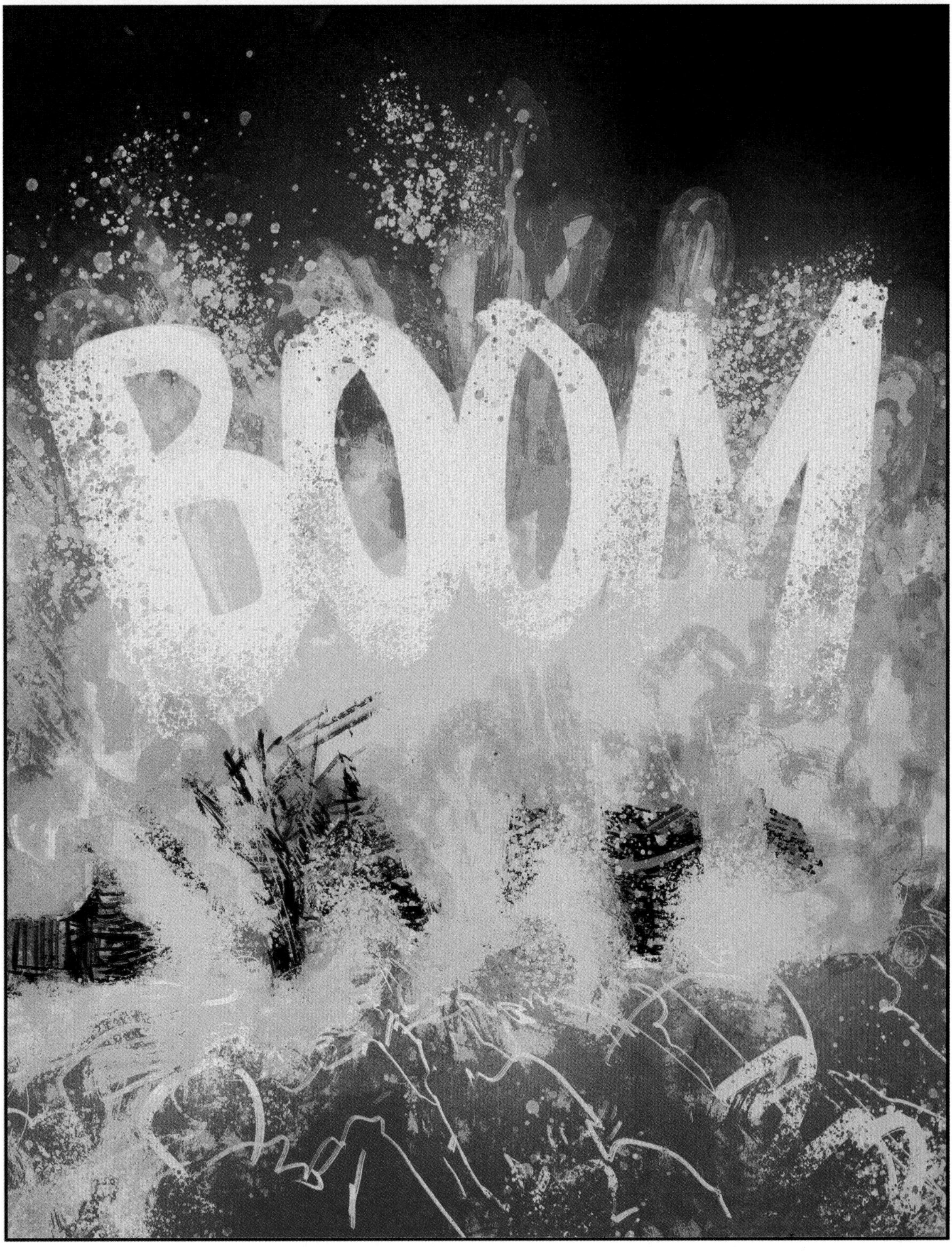

BOOM

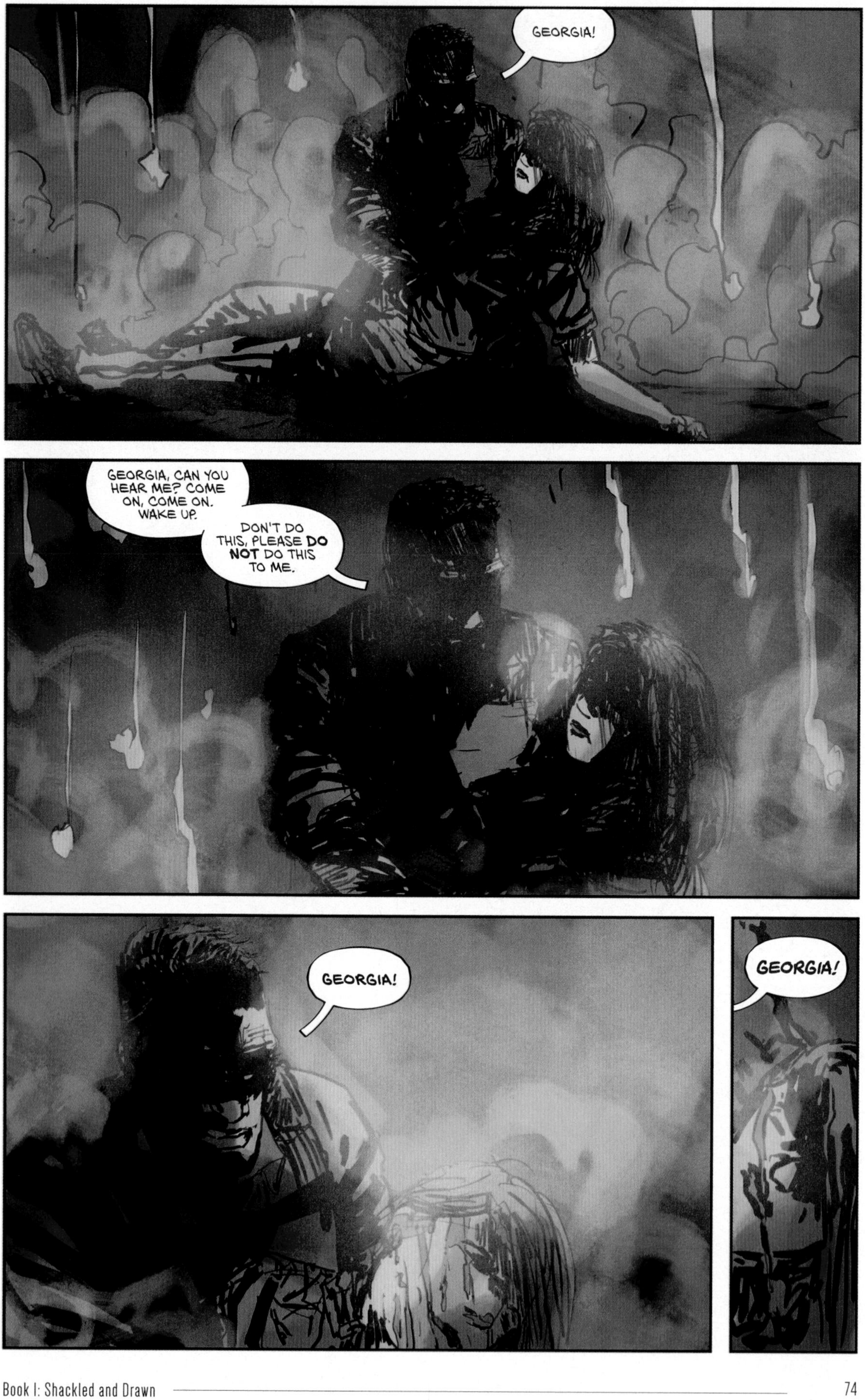
GEORGIA!
GEORGIA, CAN YOU HEAR ME? COME ON, COME ON. WAKE UP.
DON'T DO THIS, PLEASE DO NOT DO THIS TO ME.
GEORGIA!
GEORGIA!

"I sink 'neath the river cool and clear

Drifting down I disappear

I see you on the other side

I search for the peace in your eyes

But they're as empty as paradise

They're as empty as paradise"

- Bruce Springsteen, 'Paradise'

"I NEVER TOLD YOU ABOUT MY OLD MAN, DID I?"

"ALL THOSE YEARS WE PARTNERED UP, AND HE NEVER CAME UP ONCE, DID HE?"

DALLAS
— TEXAS —

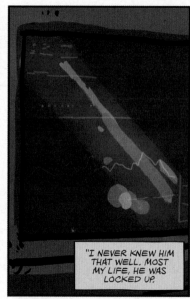

"I NEVER KNEW HIM THAT WELL. MOST MY LIFE, HE WAS LOCKED UP."

"I CAN'T EVEN REMEMBER WHAT FOR—HE HAD SO MANY BRUSHES WITH THE LAW, AND I WAS SO YOUNG, I CAN'T REMEMBER WHAT IT WAS THAT PUT HIM AWAY."

"NEVER CARED TO FIND OUT, EITHER."

"MY MOM ONLY TOOK ME TO VISIT HIM ONE TIME. I WAS PROBABLY ELEVEN, TWELVE YEARS OLD."

"AND I REMEMBER HIM SITTING THERE BEHIND THE GLASS, THIS OLD MAN I BARELY KNEW, AND HE JUST KINDA SHRUGGED AT ME, LIKE HE DIDN'T KNOW WHAT TO SAY, AND HE DIDN'T CARE, EITHER."

"HE SAID TO ME—HE SAID, "KID, EVERY MAN'S GOTTA FOLLOW A PATH."

"THEN HE GOT UP, AND HE WALKED AWAY.""

I NEVER SAW HIM AGAIN.

THE THING IS, THOUGH...

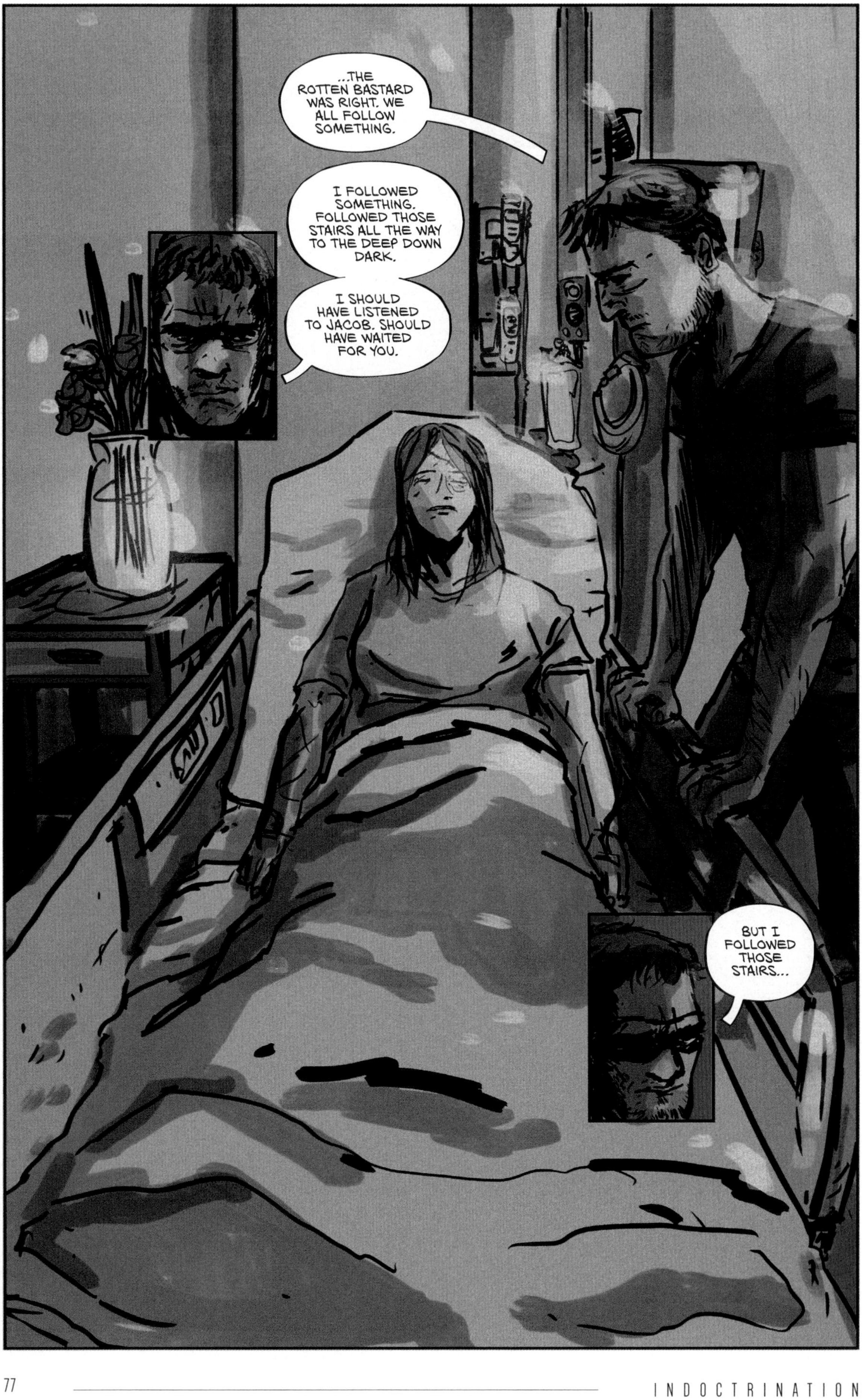
...THE ROTTEN BASTARD WAS RIGHT. WE ALL FOLLOW SOMETHING.
I FOLLOWED SOMETHING. FOLLOWED THOSE STAIRS ALL THE WAY TO THE DEEP DOWN DARK.
I SHOULD HAVE LISTENED TO JACOB. SHOULD HAVE WAITED FOR YOU.
BUT I FOLLOWED THOSE STAIRS...

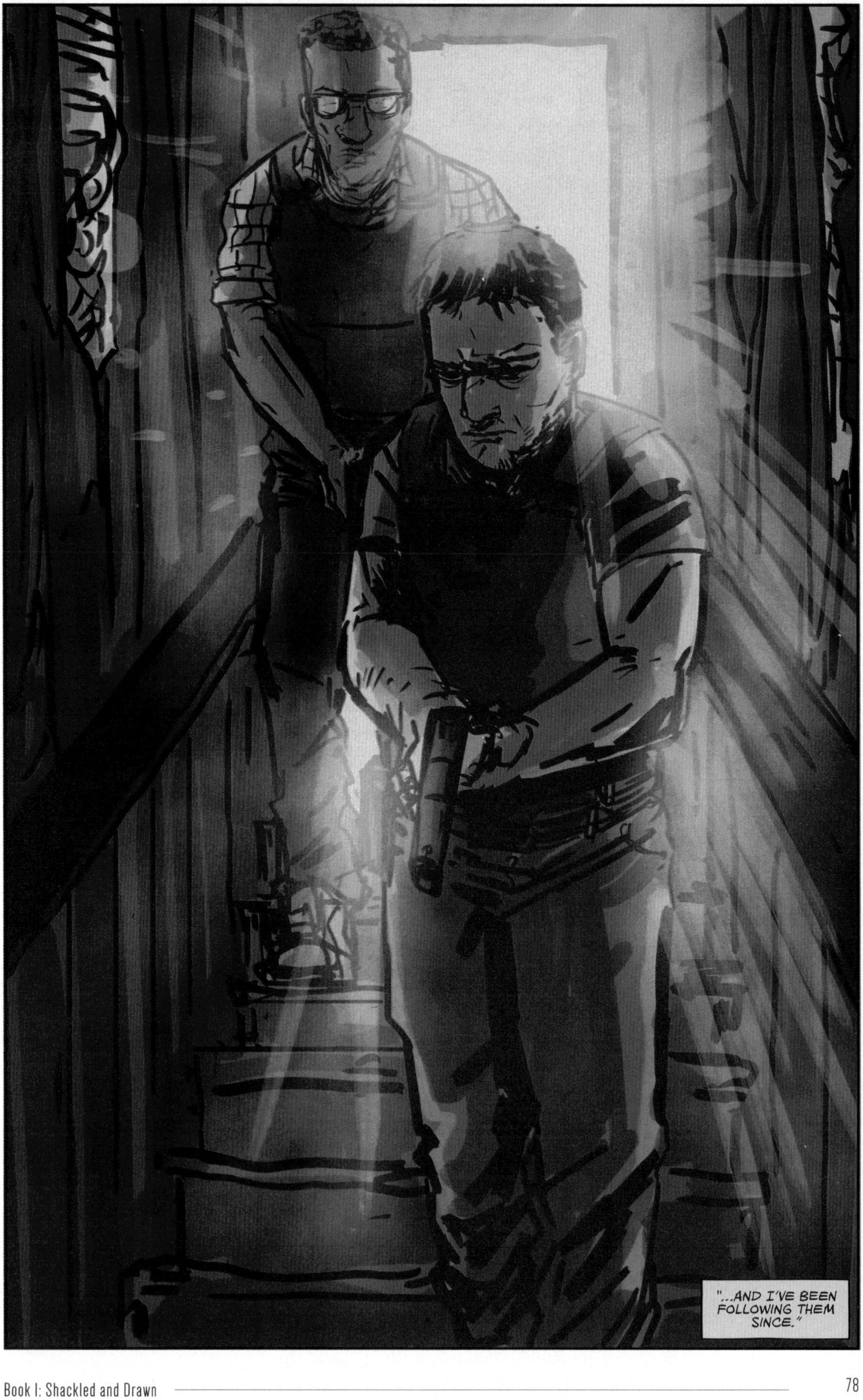
"...AND I'VE BEEN FOLLOWING THEM SINCE."

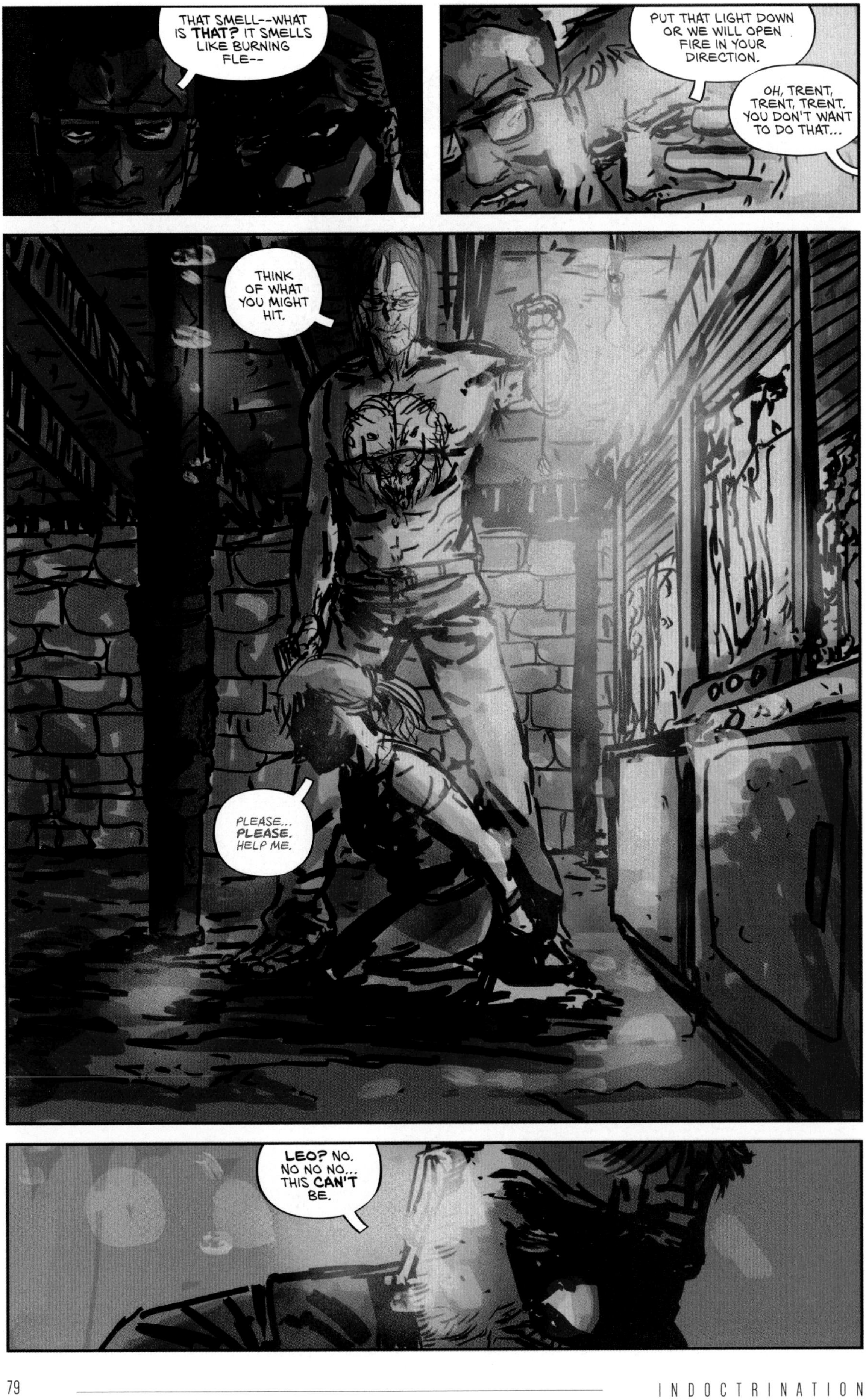
THAT SMELL--WHAT IS **THAT?** IT SMELLS LIKE BURNING FLE--
PUT THAT LIGHT DOWN OR WE WILL OPEN FIRE IN YOUR DIRECTION.
OH, TRENT, TRENT, TRENT. YOU DON'T WANT TO DO THAT...
THINK OF WHAT YOU MIGHT HIT.
*PLEASE... **PLEASE.** HELP ME.*
LEO? NO. NO NO NO... THIS **CAN'T** BE.

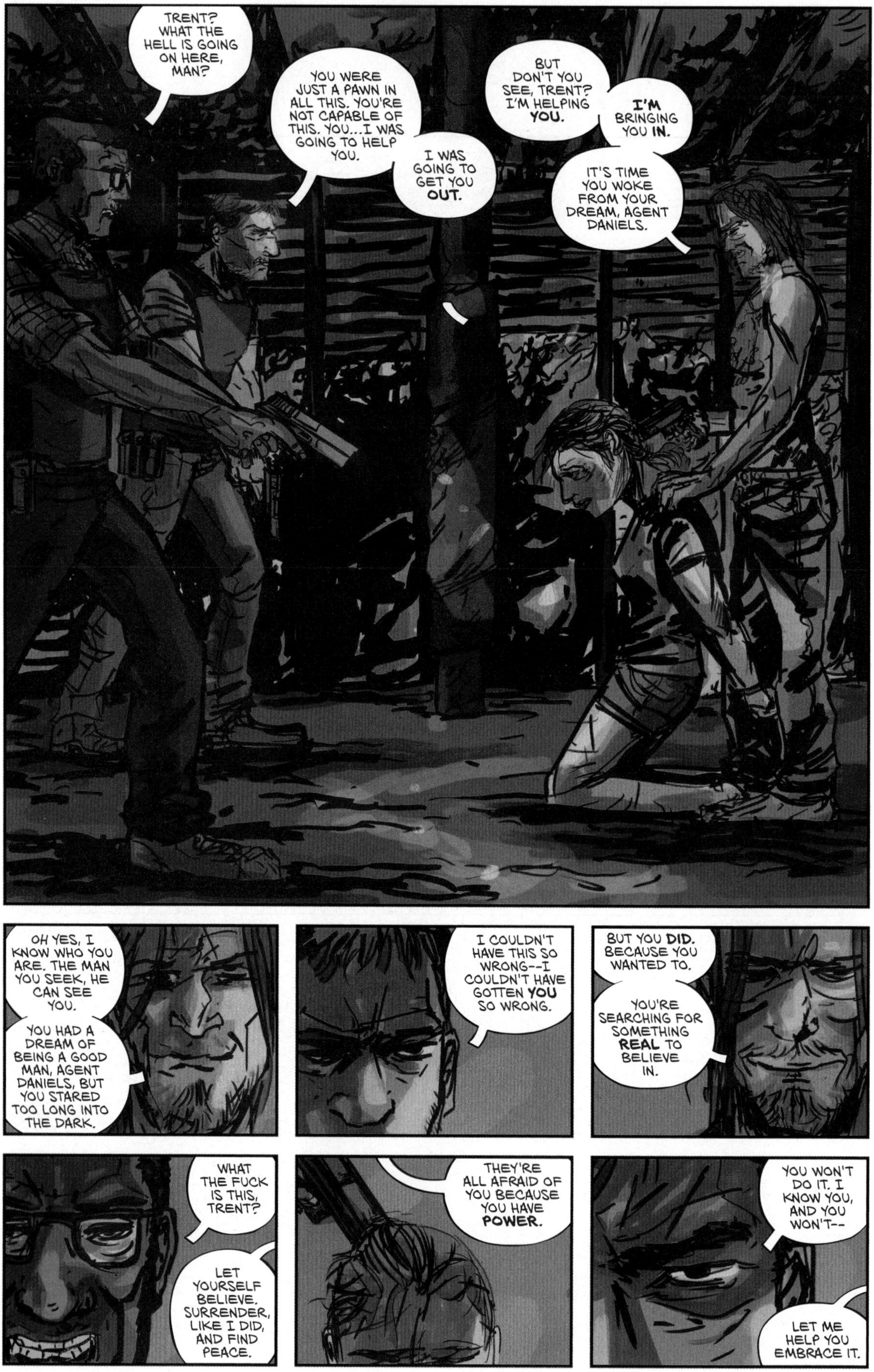
TRENT? WHAT THE HELL IS GOING ON HERE, MAN?
YOU WERE JUST A PAWN IN ALL THIS. YOU'RE NOT CAPABLE OF THIS. YOU... I WAS GOING TO HELP YOU.
I WAS GOING TO GET YOU OUT.
BUT DON'T YOU SEE, TRENT? I'M HELPING YOU.
I'M BRINGING YOU IN.
IT'S TIME YOU WOKE FROM YOUR DREAM, AGENT DANIELS.
OH YES, I KNOW WHO YOU ARE. THE MAN YOU SEEK, HE CAN SEE YOU.
YOU HAD A DREAM OF BEING A GOOD MAN, AGENT DANIELS, BUT YOU STARED TOO LONG INTO THE DARK.
I COULDN'T HAVE THIS SO WRONG--I COULDN'T HAVE GOTTEN YOU SO WRONG.
BUT YOU DID. BECAUSE YOU WANTED TO.
YOU'RE SEARCHING FOR SOMETHING REAL TO BELIEVE IN.
WHAT THE FUCK IS THIS, TRENT?
LET YOURSELF BELIEVE. SURRENDER, LIKE I DID, AND FIND PEACE.
THEY'RE ALL AFRAID OF YOU BECAUSE YOU HAVE POWER.
YOU WON'T DO IT. I KNOW YOU, AND YOU WON'T--
LET ME HELP YOU EMBRACE IT.

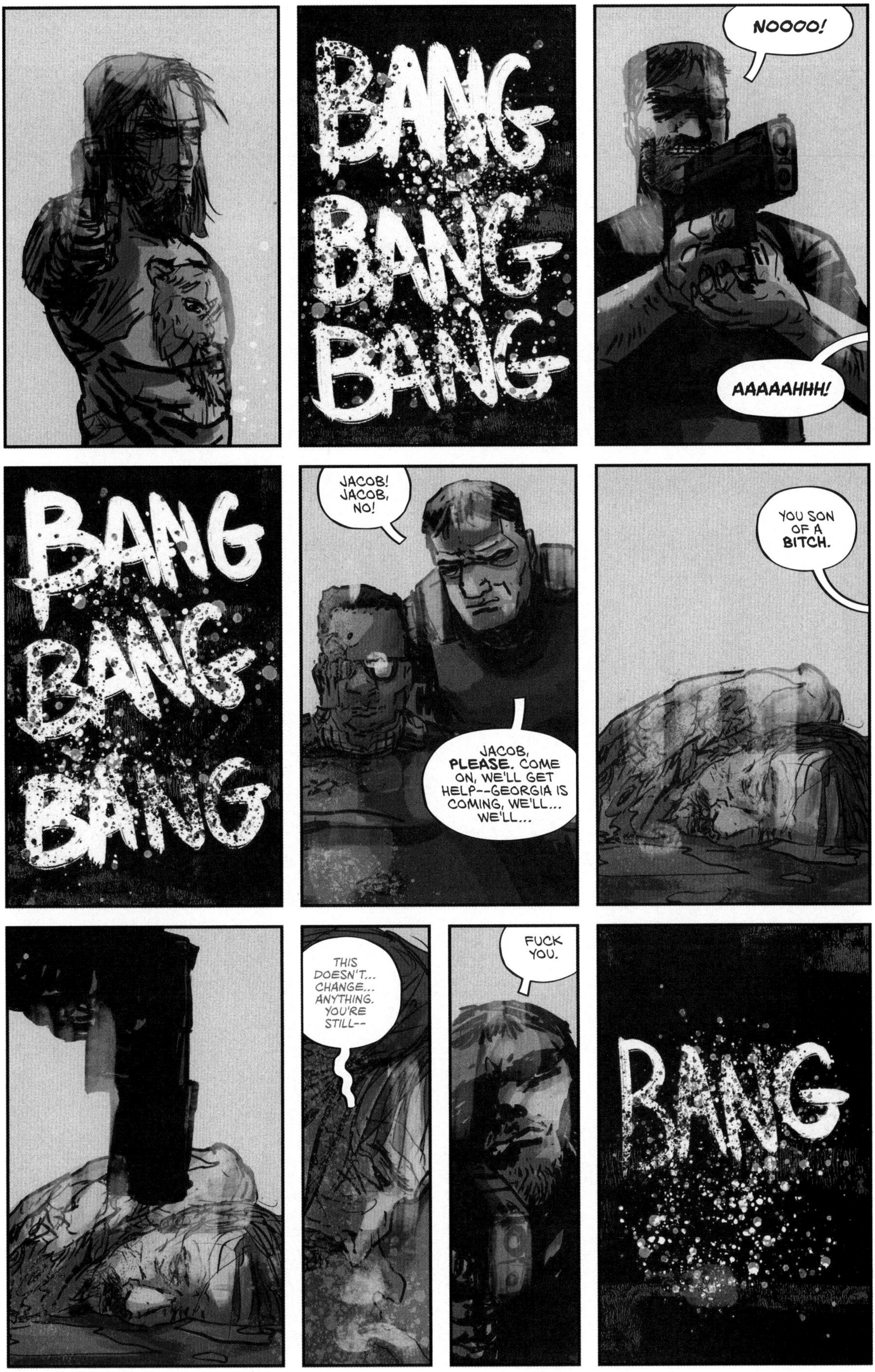
BANG
BANG
BANG
NOOOO!
AAAAAHHH!
BANG
BANG
BANG
JACOB! JACOB, NO!
JACOB, PLEASE. COME ON, WE'LL GET HELP--GEORGIA IS COMING, WE'LL... WE'LL...
YOU SON OF A BITCH.
THIS DOESN'T... CHANGE... ANYTHING. YOU'RE STILL--
FUCK YOU.
BANG

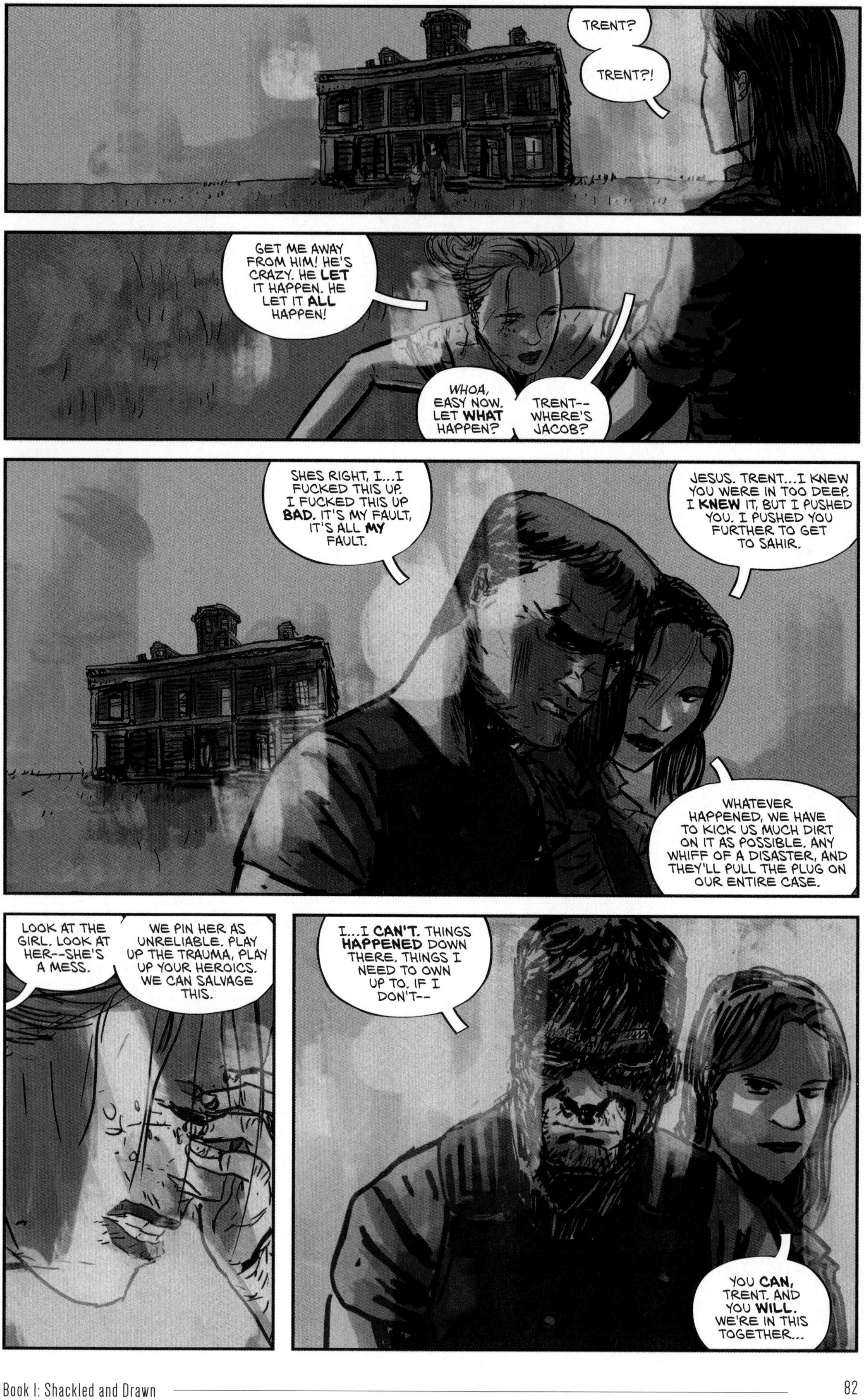
TRENT?
TRENT?!
GET ME AWAY FROM HIM! HE'S CRAZY. HE LET IT HAPPEN. HE LET IT ALL HAPPEN!
WHOA, EASY NOW. LET WHAT HAPPEN?
TRENT--WHERE'S JACOB?
SHES RIGHT, I...I FUCKED THIS UP. I FUCKED THIS UP BAD. IT'S MY FAULT, IT'S ALL MY FAULT.
JESUS. TRENT...I KNEW YOU WERE IN TOO DEEP. I KNEW IT, BUT I PUSHED YOU. I PUSHED YOU FURTHER TO GET TO SAHIR.
WHATEVER HAPPENED, WE HAVE TO KICK US MUCH DIRT ON IT AS POSSIBLE. ANY WHIFF OF A DISASTER, AND THEY'LL PULL THE PLUG ON OUR ENTIRE CASE.
LOOK AT THE GIRL. LOOK AT HER--SHE'S A MESS.
WE PIN HER AS UNRELIABLE. PLAY UP THE TRAUMA, PLAY UP YOUR HEROICS. WE CAN SALVAGE THIS.
I...I CAN'T. THINGS HAPPENED DOWN THERE. THINGS I NEED TO OWN UP TO. IF I DON'T--
YOU CAN, TRENT. AND YOU WILL. WE'RE IN THIS TOGETHER...

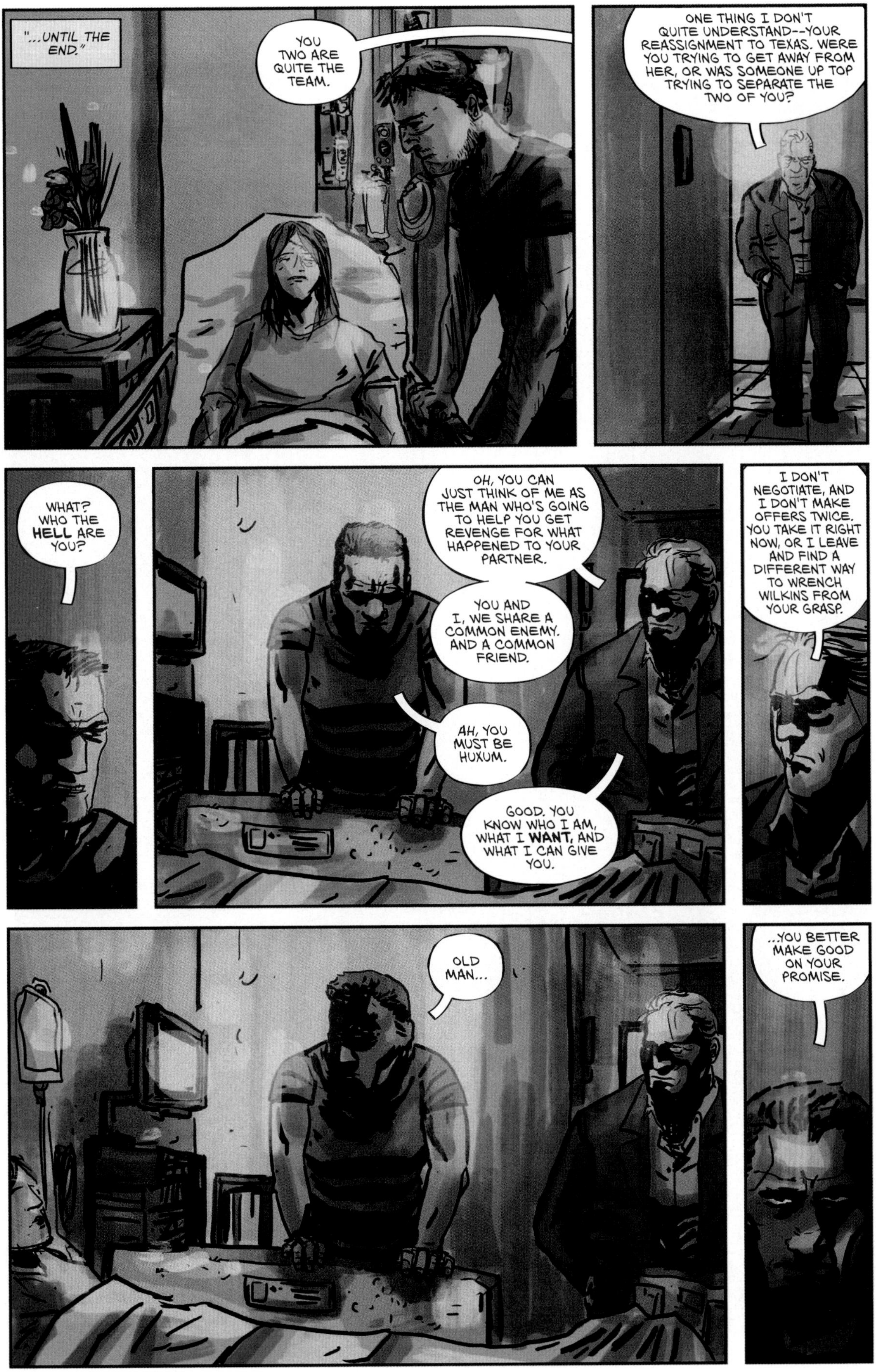
"...UNTIL THE END."
YOU TWO ARE QUITE THE TEAM.
ONE THING I DON'T QUITE UNDERSTAND--YOUR REASSIGNMENT TO TEXAS. WERE YOU TRYING TO GET AWAY FROM HER, OR WAS SOMEONE UP TOP TRYING TO SEPARATE THE TWO OF YOU?
WHAT? WHO THE HELL ARE YOU?
OH, YOU CAN JUST THINK OF ME AS THE MAN WHO'S GOING TO HELP YOU GET REVENGE FOR WHAT HAPPENED TO YOUR PARTNER.
YOU AND I, WE SHARE A COMMON ENEMY. AND A COMMON FRIEND.
AH, YOU MUST BE HUXUM.
GOOD. YOU KNOW WHO I AM, WHAT I WANT, AND WHAT I CAN GIVE YOU.
I DON'T NEGOTIATE, AND I DON'T MAKE OFFERS TWICE. YOU TAKE IT RIGHT NOW, OR I LEAVE AND FIND A DIFFERENT WAY TO WRENCH WILKINS FROM YOUR GRASP.
OLD MAN...
...YOU BETTER MAKE GOOD ON YOUR PROMISE.

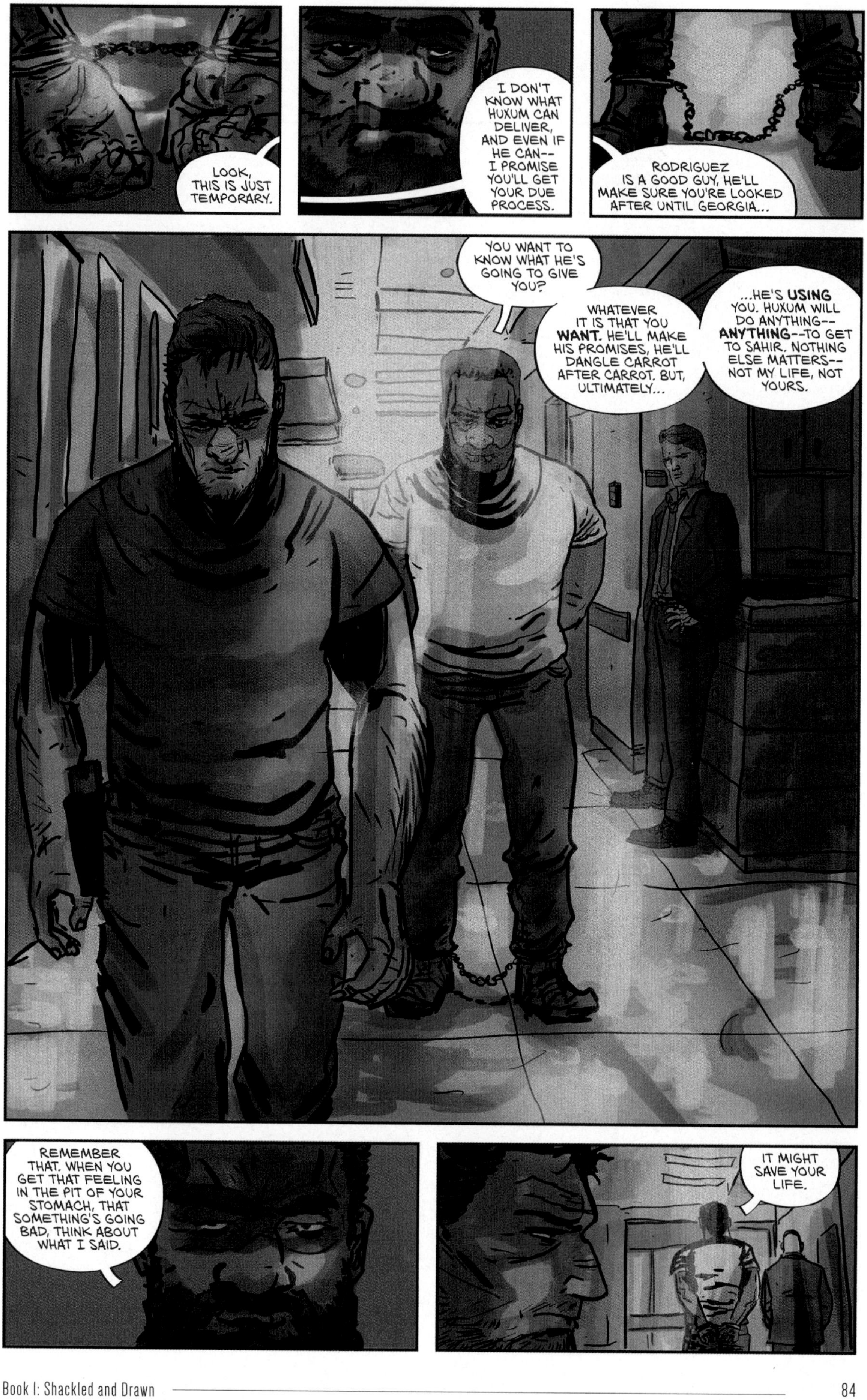
LOOK, THIS IS JUST TEMPORARY.
I DON'T KNOW WHAT HUXUM CAN DELIVER, AND EVEN IF HE CAN-- I PROMISE YOU'LL GET YOUR DUE PROCESS.
RODRIGUEZ IS A GOOD GUY, HE'LL MAKE SURE YOU'RE LOOKED AFTER UNTIL GEORGIA...
YOU WANT TO KNOW WHAT HE'S GOING TO GIVE YOU?
WHATEVER IT IS THAT YOU **WANT**. HE'LL MAKE HIS PROMISES, HE'LL DANGLE CARROT AFTER CARROT. BUT, ULTIMATELY...
...HE'S **USING** YOU. HUXUM WILL DO ANYTHING-- **ANYTHING**--TO GET TO SAHIR. NOTHING ELSE MATTERS-- NOT MY LIFE, NOT YOURS.
REMEMBER THAT. WHEN YOU GET THAT FEELING IN THE PIT OF YOUR STOMACH, THAT SOMETHING'S GOING BAD, THINK ABOUT WHAT I SAID.
IT MIGHT SAVE YOUR LIFE.

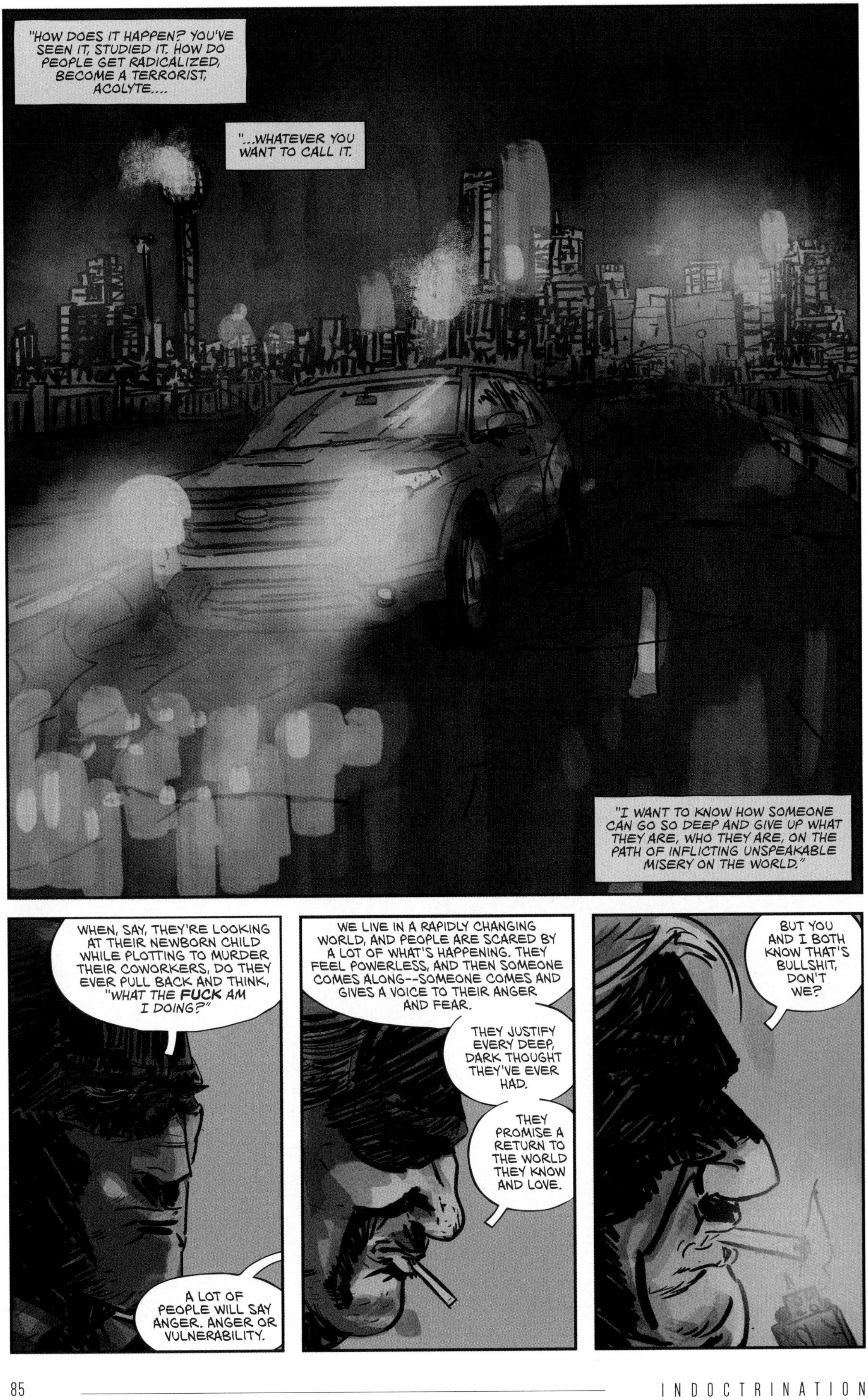
"HOW DOES IT HAPPEN? YOU'VE SEEN IT, STUDIED IT. HOW DO PEOPLE GET RADICALIZED, BECOME A TERRORIST, ACOLYTE....
"...WHATEVER YOU WANT TO CALL IT.
"I WANT TO KNOW HOW SOMEONE CAN GO SO DEEP AND GIVE UP WHAT THEY ARE, WHO THEY ARE, ON THE PATH OF INFLICTING UNSPEAKABLE MISERY ON THE WORLD."
WHEN, SAY, THEY'RE LOOKING AT THEIR NEWBORN CHILD WHILE PLOTTING TO MURDER THEIR COWORKERS, DO THEY EVER PULL BACK AND THINK, "WHAT THE FUCK AM I DOING?"
A LOT OF PEOPLE WILL SAY ANGER. ANGER OR VULNERABILITY.
WE LIVE IN A RAPIDLY CHANGING WORLD, AND PEOPLE ARE SCARED BY A LOT OF WHAT'S HAPPENING. THEY FEEL POWERLESS, AND THEN SOMEONE COMES ALONG--SOMEONE COMES AND GIVES A VOICE TO THEIR ANGER AND FEAR.
THEY JUSTIFY EVERY DEEP, DARK THOUGHT THEY'VE EVER HAD.
THEY PROMISE A RETURN TO THE WORLD THEY KNOW AND LOVE.
BUT YOU AND I BOTH KNOW THAT'S BULLSHIT, DON'T WE?

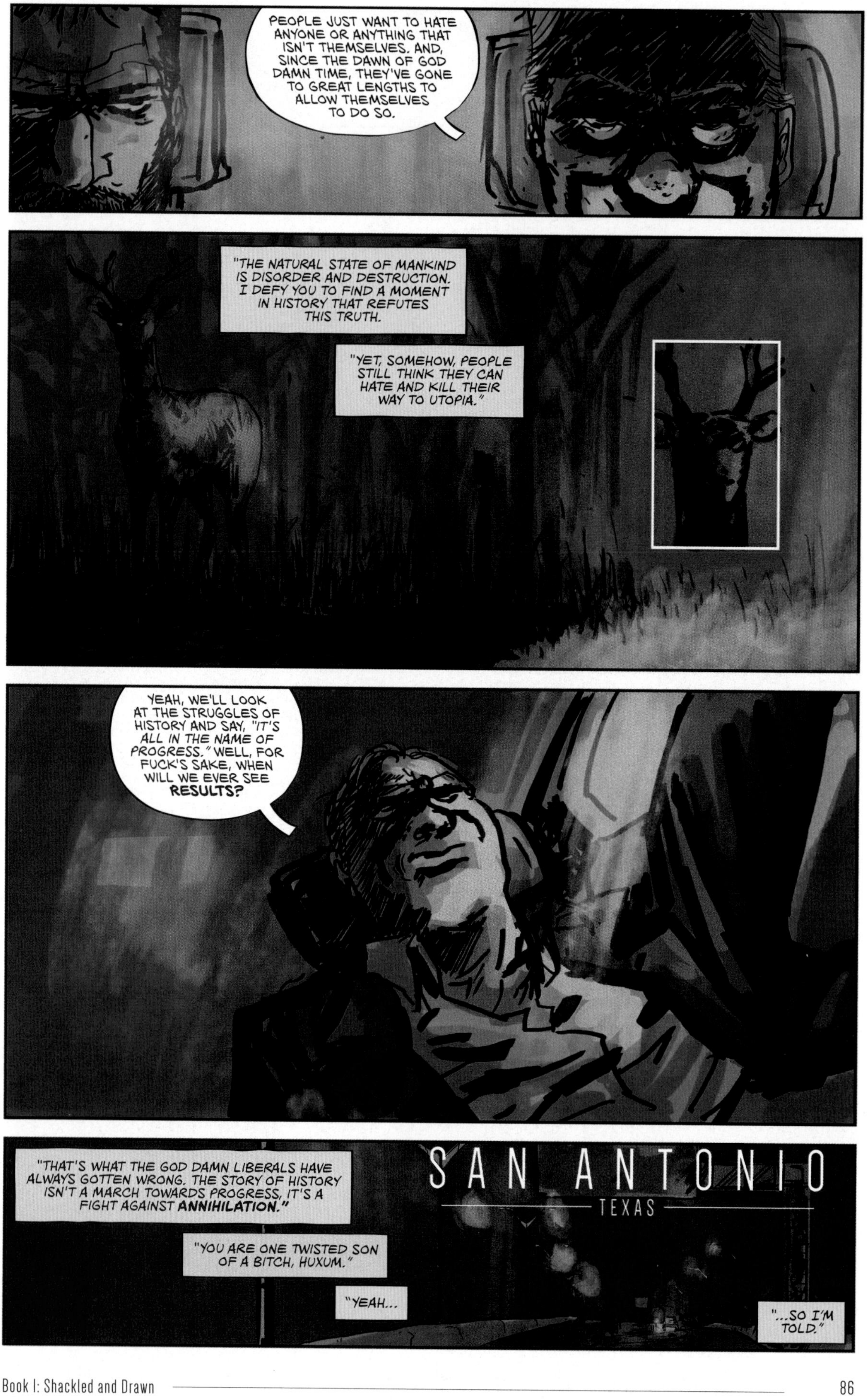

PEOPLE JUST WANT TO HATE ANYONE OR ANYTHING THAT ISN'T THEMSELVES. AND, SINCE THE DAWN OF GOD DAMN TIME, THEY'VE GONE TO GREAT LENGTHS TO ALLOW THEMSELVES TO DO SO.
"THE NATURAL STATE OF MANKIND IS DISORDER AND DESTRUCTION. I DEFY YOU TO FIND A MOMENT IN HISTORY THAT REFUTES THIS TRUTH.
"YET, SOMEHOW, PEOPLE STILL THINK THEY CAN HATE AND KILL THEIR WAY TO UTOPIA."
YEAH, WE'LL LOOK AT THE STRUGGLES OF HISTORY AND SAY, "IT'S ALL IN THE NAME OF PROGRESS." WELL, FOR FUCK'S SAKE, WHEN WILL WE EVER SEE **RESULTS?**
"THAT'S WHAT THE GOD DAMN LIBERALS HAVE ALWAYS GOTTEN WRONG. THE STORY OF HISTORY ISN'T A MARCH TOWARDS PROGRESS, IT'S A FIGHT AGAINST **ANNIHILATION.**"
SAN ANTONIO
TEXAS
"YOU ARE ONE TWISTED SON OF A BITCH, HUXUM."
"YEAH...
"...SO I'M TOLD."

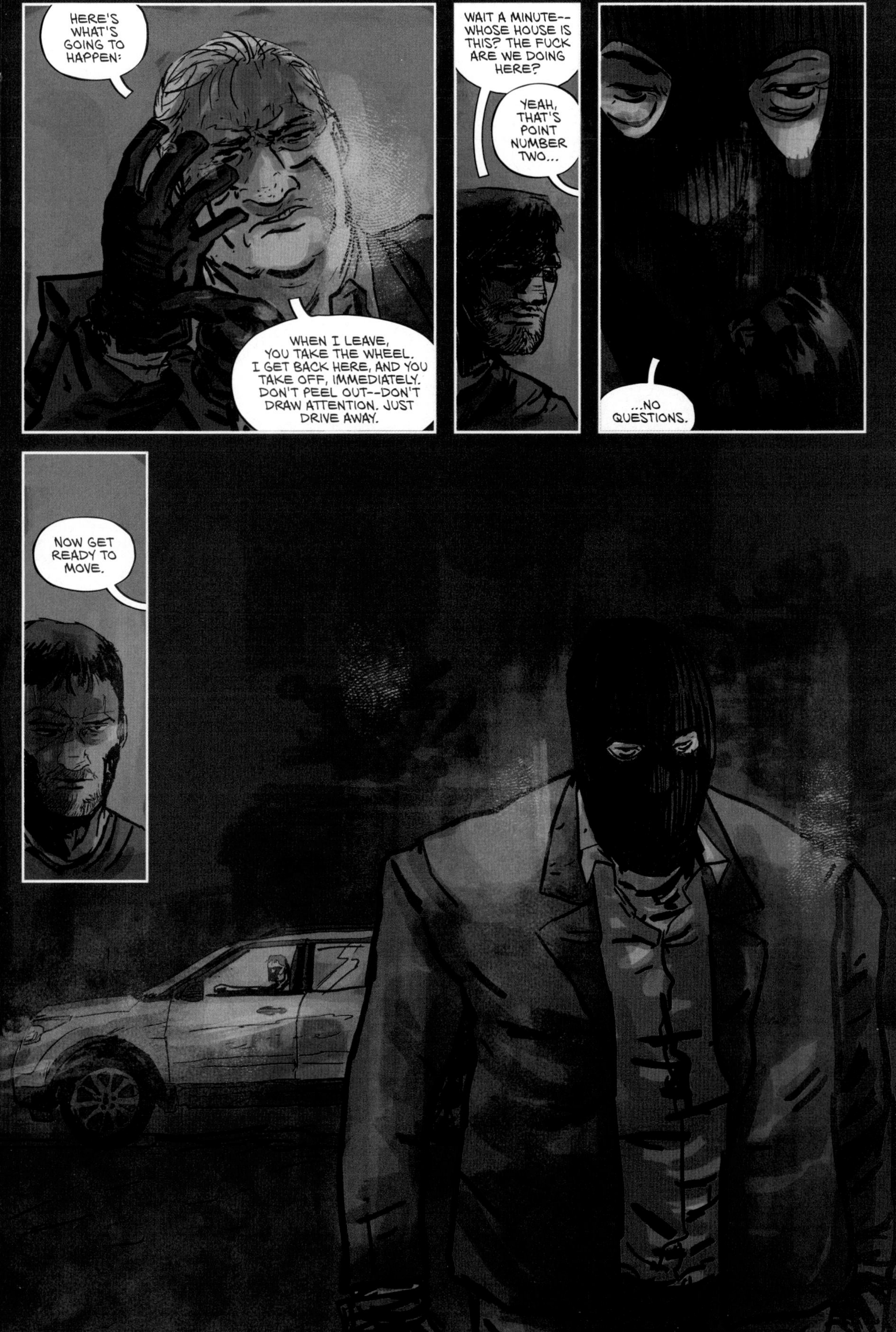
HERE'S WHAT'S GOING TO HAPPEN:
WHEN I LEAVE, YOU TAKE THE WHEEL. I GET BACK HERE, AND YOU TAKE OFF, IMMEDIATELY. DON'T PEEL OUT--DON'T DRAW ATTENTION. JUST DRIVE AWAY.
WAIT A MINUTE--WHOSE HOUSE IS THIS? THE FUCK ARE WE DOING HERE?
YEAH, THAT'S POINT NUMBER TWO...
...NO QUESTIONS.
NOW GET READY TO MOVE.

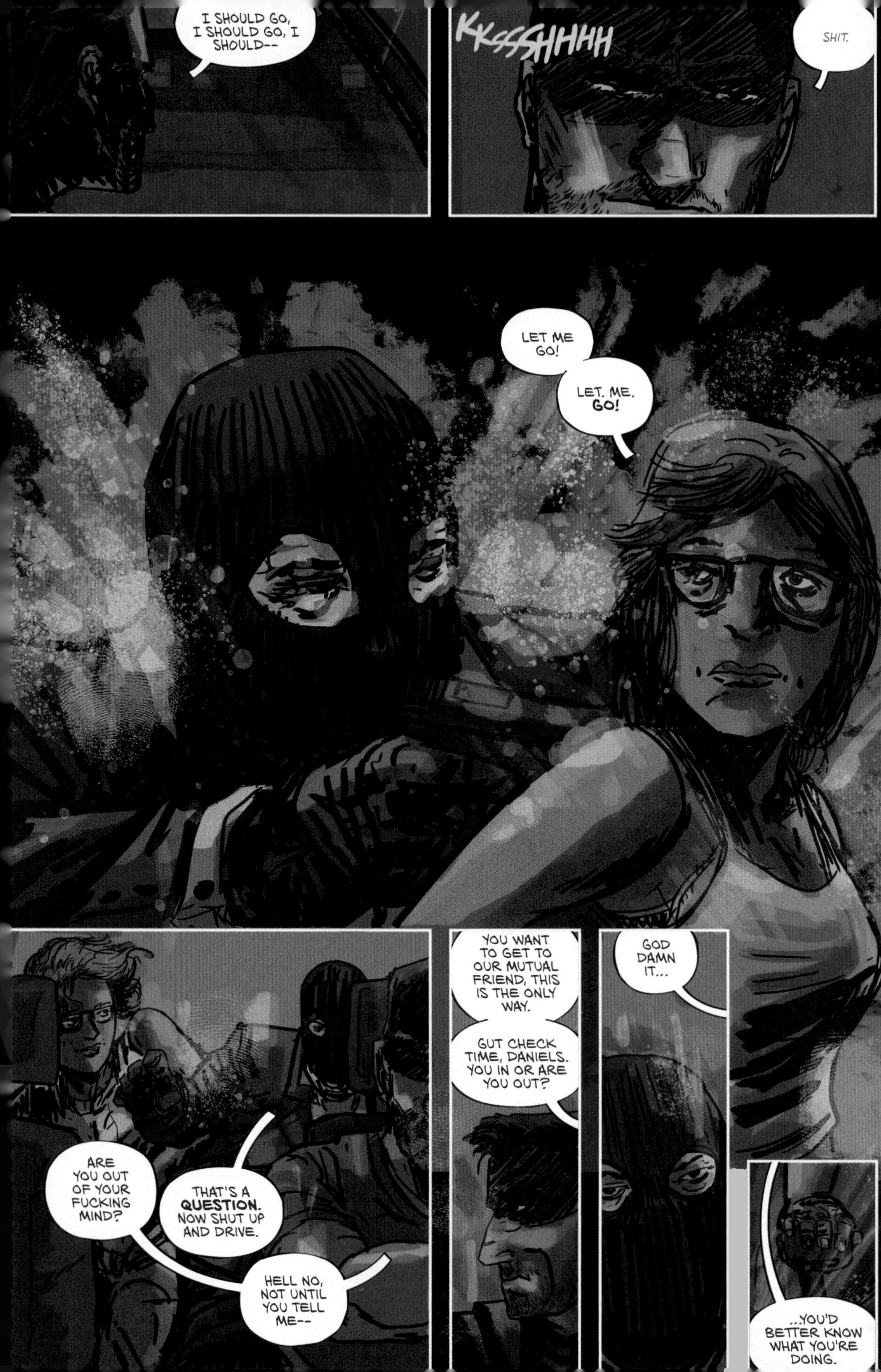
I SHOULD GO, I SHOULD GO, I SHOULD--
KKSSSHHHH
SHIT.
LET ME GO!
LET. ME. GO!
ARE YOU OUT OF YOUR FUCKING MIND?
THAT'S A QUESTION. NOW SHUT UP AND DRIVE.
HELL NO, NOT UNTIL YOU TELL ME--
YOU WANT TO GET TO OUR MUTUAL FRIEND, THIS IS THE ONLY WAY.
GUT CHECK TIME, DANIELS. YOU IN OR ARE YOU OUT?
GOD DAMN IT...
...YOU'D BETTER KNOW WHAT YOU'RE DOING.

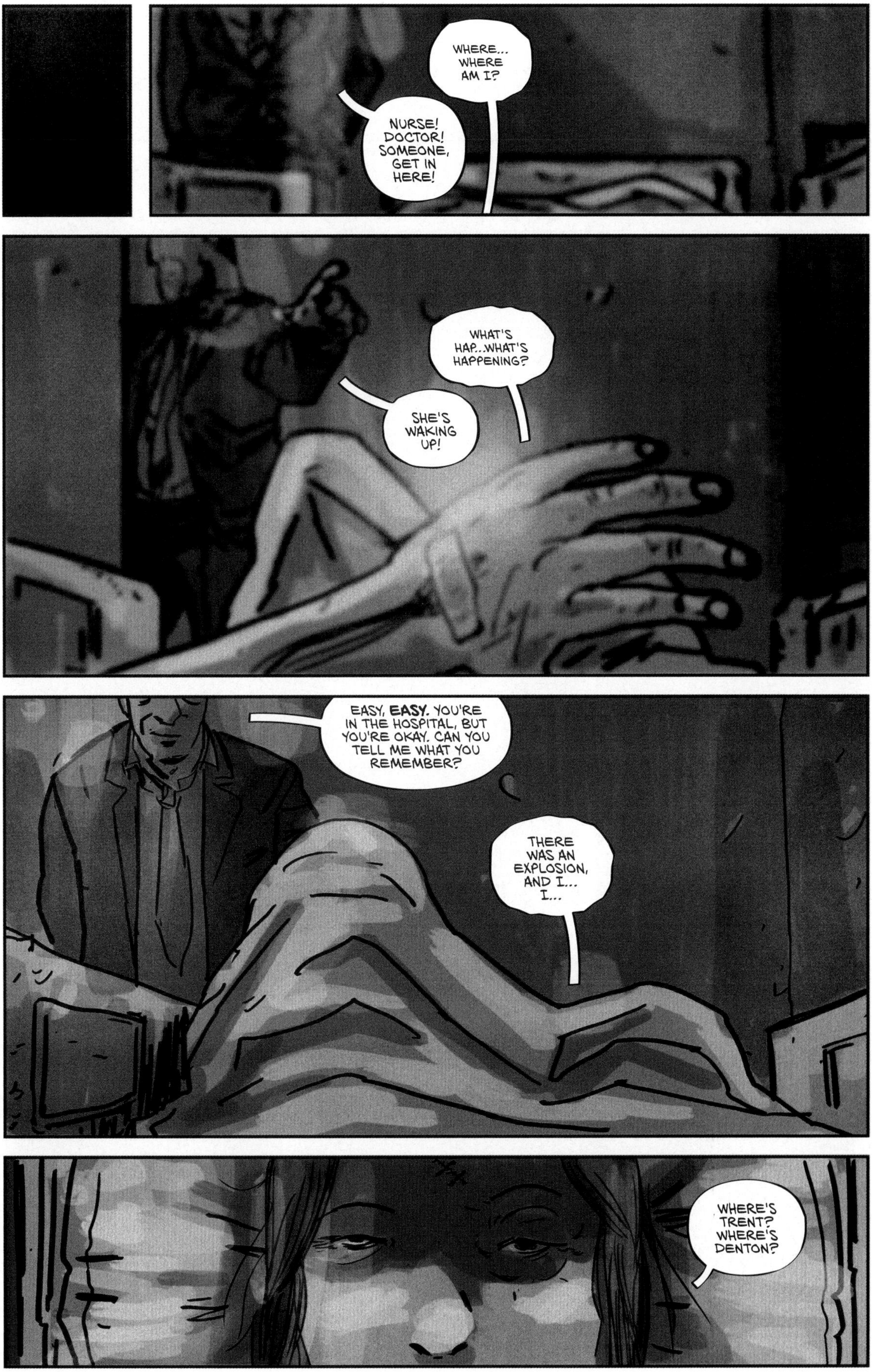
WHERE... WHERE AM I?
NURSE! DOCTOR! SOMEONE, GET IN HERE!
WHAT'S HAP...WHAT'S HAPPENING?
SHE'S WAKING UP!
EASY, **EASY.** YOU'RE IN THE HOSPITAL, BUT YOU'RE OKAY. CAN YOU TELL ME WHAT YOU REMEMBER?
THERE WAS AN EXPLOSION, AND I... I...
WHERE'S TRENT? WHERE'S DENTON?

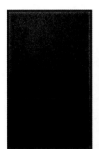

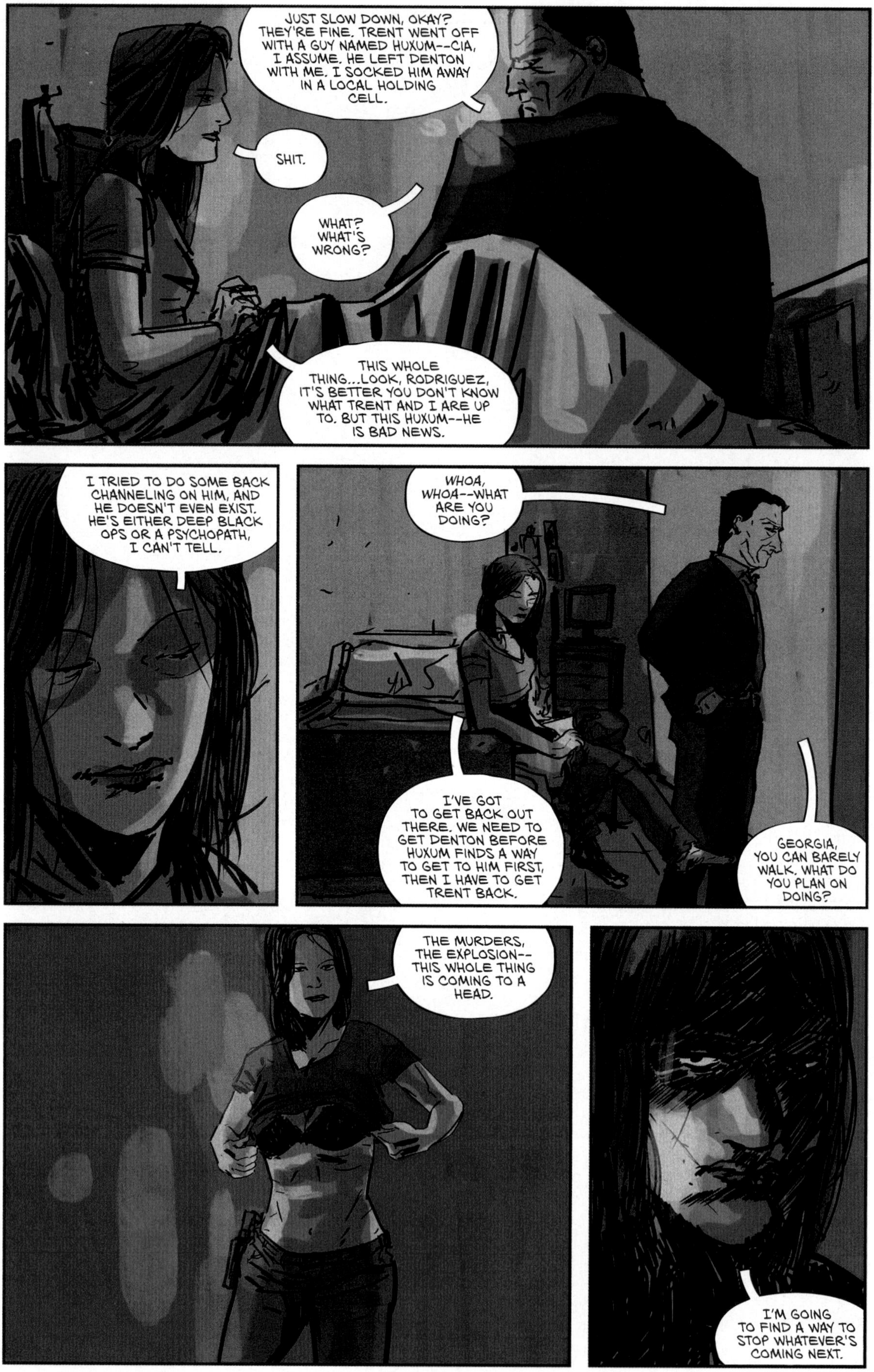
JUST SLOW DOWN, OKAY? THEY'RE FINE. TRENT WENT OFF WITH A GUY NAMED HUXUM--CIA, I ASSUME. HE LEFT DENTON WITH ME. I SOCKED HIM AWAY IN A LOCAL HOLDING CELL.
SHIT.
WHAT? WHAT'S WRONG?
THIS WHOLE THING...LOOK, RODRIGUEZ, IT'S BETTER YOU DON'T KNOW WHAT TRENT AND I ARE UP TO. BUT THIS HUXUM--HE IS BAD NEWS.
I TRIED TO DO SOME BACK CHANNELING ON HIM, AND HE DOESN'T EVEN EXIST. HE'S EITHER DEEP BLACK OPS OR A PSYCHOPATH, I CAN'T TELL.
WHOA, WHOA--WHAT ARE YOU DOING?
I'VE GOT TO GET BACK OUT THERE. WE NEED TO GET DENTON BEFORE HUXUM FINDS A WAY TO GET TO HIM FIRST, THEN I HAVE TO GET TRENT BACK.
GEORGIA, YOU CAN BARELY WALK. WHAT DO YOU PLAN ON DOING?
THE MURDERS, THE EXPLOSION-- THIS WHOLE THING IS COMING TO A HEAD.
I'M GOING TO FIND A WAY TO STOP WHATEVER'S COMING NEXT.

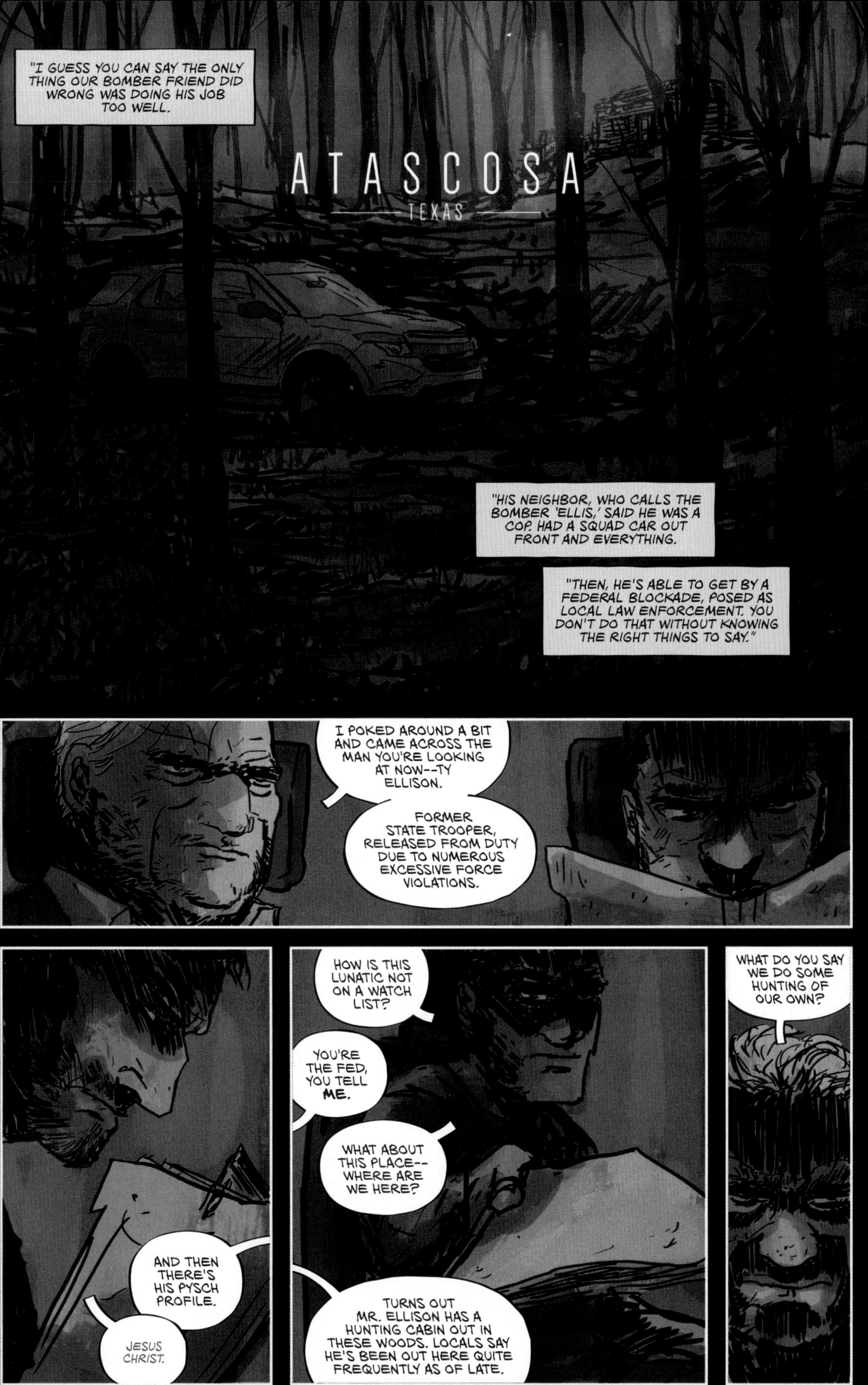
"I GUESS YOU CAN SAY THE ONLY THING OUR BOMBER FRIEND DID WRONG WAS DOING HIS JOB TOO WELL.
ATASCOSA
TEXAS
"HIS NEIGHBOR, WHO CALLS THE BOMBER 'ELLIS,' SAID HE WAS A COP. HAD A SQUAD CAR OUT FRONT AND EVERYTHING.
"THEN, HE'S ABLE TO GET BY A FEDERAL BLOCKADE, POSED AS LOCAL LAW ENFORCEMENT. YOU DON'T DO THAT WITHOUT KNOWING THE RIGHT THINGS TO SAY."
I POKED AROUND A BIT AND CAME ACROSS THE MAN YOU'RE LOOKING AT NOW--TY ELLISON.
FORMER STATE TROOPER, RELEASED FROM DUTY DUE TO NUMEROUS EXCESSIVE FORCE VIOLATIONS.
AND THEN THERE'S HIS PYSCH PROFILE.
JESUS CHRIST.
HOW IS THIS LUNATIC NOT ON A WATCH LIST?
YOU'RE THE FED, YOU TELL ME.
WHAT ABOUT THIS PLACE-- WHERE ARE WE HERE?
TURNS OUT MR. ELLISON HAS A HUNTING CABIN OUT IN THESE WOODS. LOCALS SAY HE'S BEEN OUT HERE QUITE FREQUENTLY AS OF LATE.
WHAT DO YOU SAY WE DO SOME HUNTING OF OUR OWN?

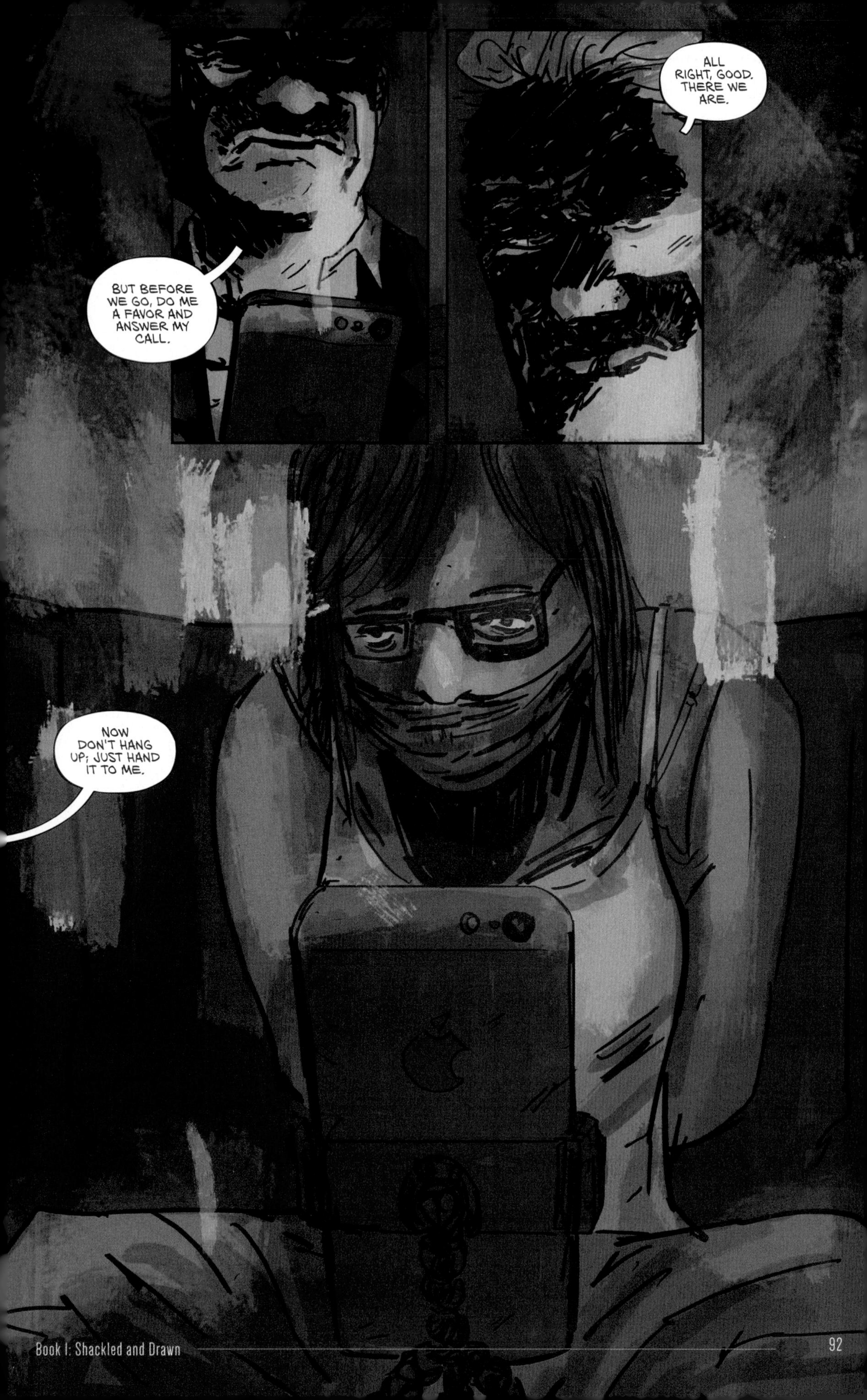
BUT BEFORE WE GO, DO ME A FAVOR AND ANSWER MY CALL.
ALL RIGHT, GOOD. THERE WE ARE.
NOW DON'T HANG UP; JUST HAND IT TO ME.

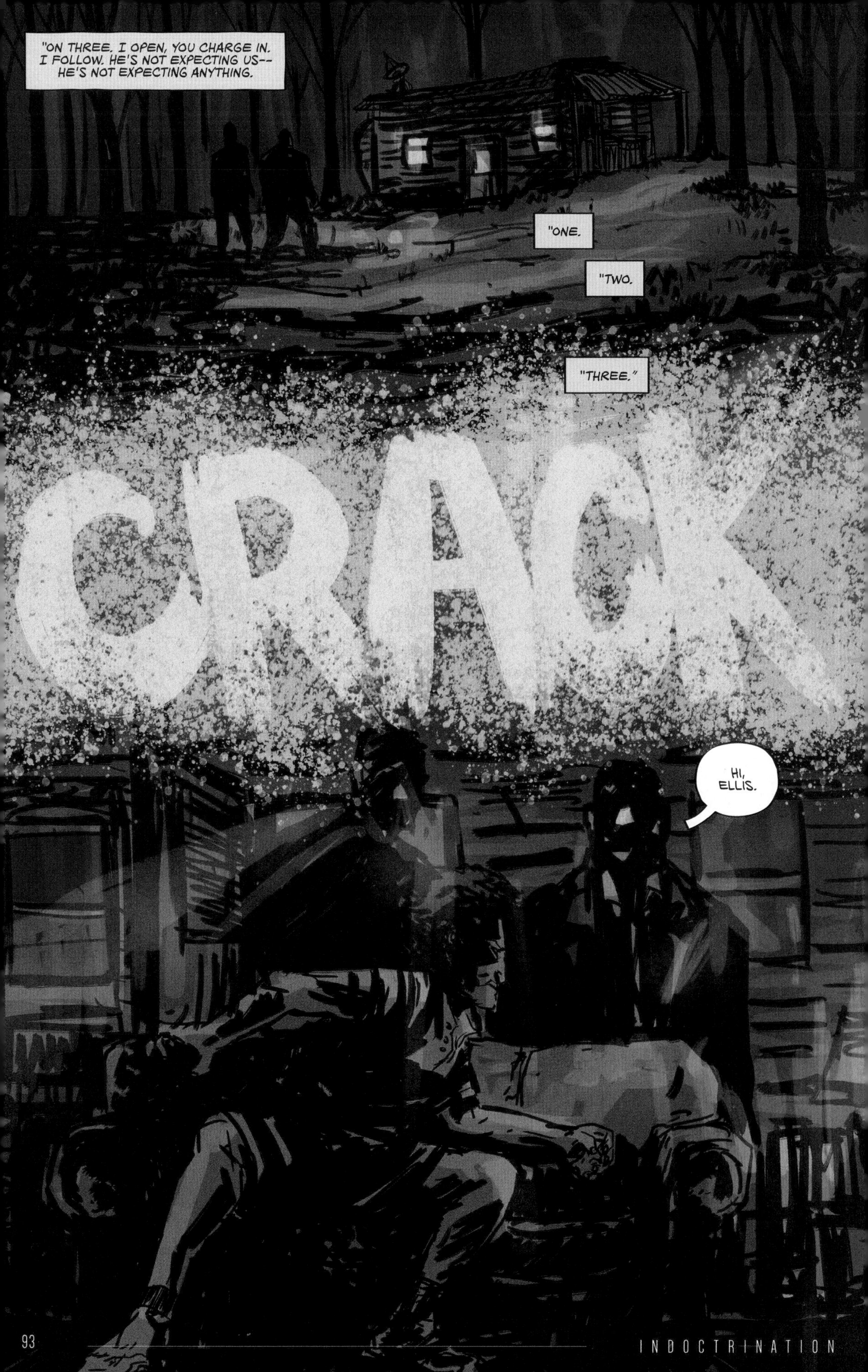
"ON THREE. I OPEN, YOU CHARGE IN. I FOLLOW. HE'S NOT EXPECTING US-- HE'S NOT EXPECTING ANYTHING.
"ONE.
"TWO.
"THREE."
CRACK
HI, ELLIS.

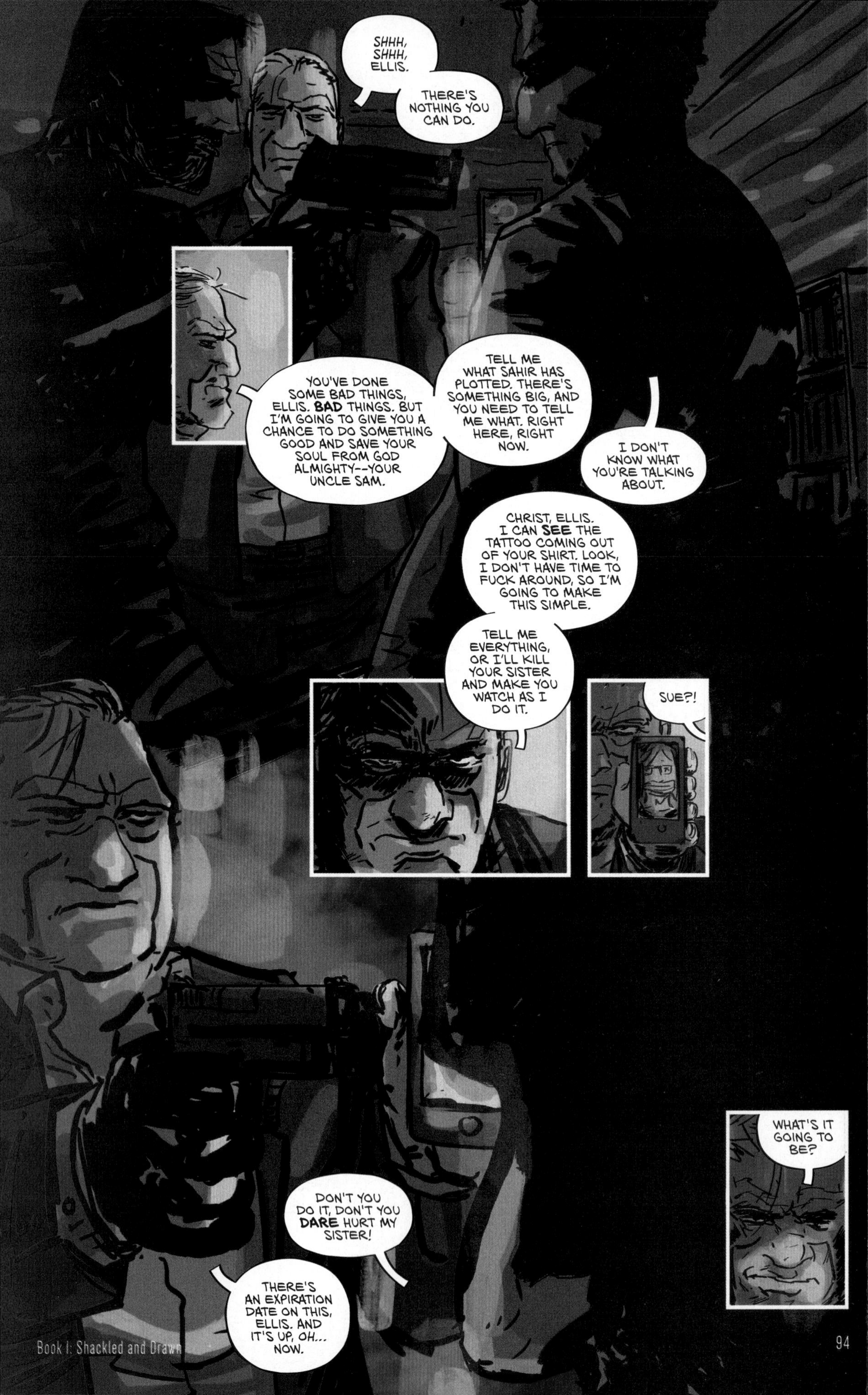
SHHH, SHHH, ELLIS.
THERE'S NOTHING YOU CAN DO.
YOU'VE DONE SOME BAD THINGS, ELLIS. BAD THINGS. BUT I'M GOING TO GIVE YOU A CHANCE TO DO SOMETHING GOOD AND SAVE YOUR SOUL FROM GOD ALMIGHTY--YOUR UNCLE SAM.
TELL ME WHAT SAHIR HAS PLOTTED. THERE'S SOMETHING BIG, AND YOU NEED TO TELL ME WHAT. RIGHT HERE, RIGHT NOW.
I DON'T KNOW WHAT YOU'RE TALKING ABOUT.
CHRIST, ELLIS. I CAN SEE THE TATTOO COMING OUT OF YOUR SHIRT. LOOK, I DON'T HAVE TIME TO FUCK AROUND, SO I'M GOING TO MAKE THIS SIMPLE.
TELL ME EVERYTHING, OR I'LL KILL YOUR SISTER AND MAKE YOU WATCH AS I DO IT.
SUE?!
DON'T YOU DO IT, DON'T YOU DARE HURT MY SISTER!
THERE'S AN EXPIRATION DATE ON THIS, ELLIS. AND IT'S UP, OH... NOW.
WHAT'S IT GOING TO BE?

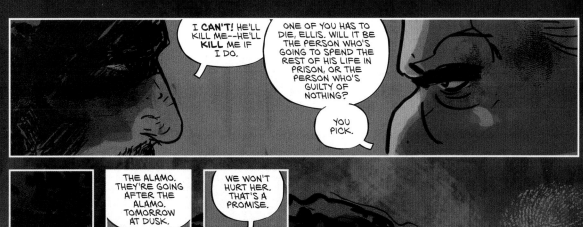

I **CAN'T!** HE'LL KILL ME--HE'LL **KILL** ME IF I DO.

ONE OF YOU HAS TO DIE, ELLIS. WILL IT BE THE PERSON WHO'S GOING TO SPEND THE REST OF HIS LIFE IN PRISON, OR THE PERSON WHO'S GUILTY OF NOTHING?

YOU PICK.

THE ALAMO. THEY'RE GOING AFTER THE ALAMO. TOMORROW AT DUSK.

NOW PLEASE, **PLEASE**... SUE...

WE WON'T HURT HER. THAT'S A PROMISE.

HE SEES YOU, YOU KNOW. HE SEES EVERYTHING. THIS IS ALL HAPPENING EXACTLY AS IT'S SUPPOSED TO-- EVEN THIS.

IT'S ALL PART OF HIS PLAN.

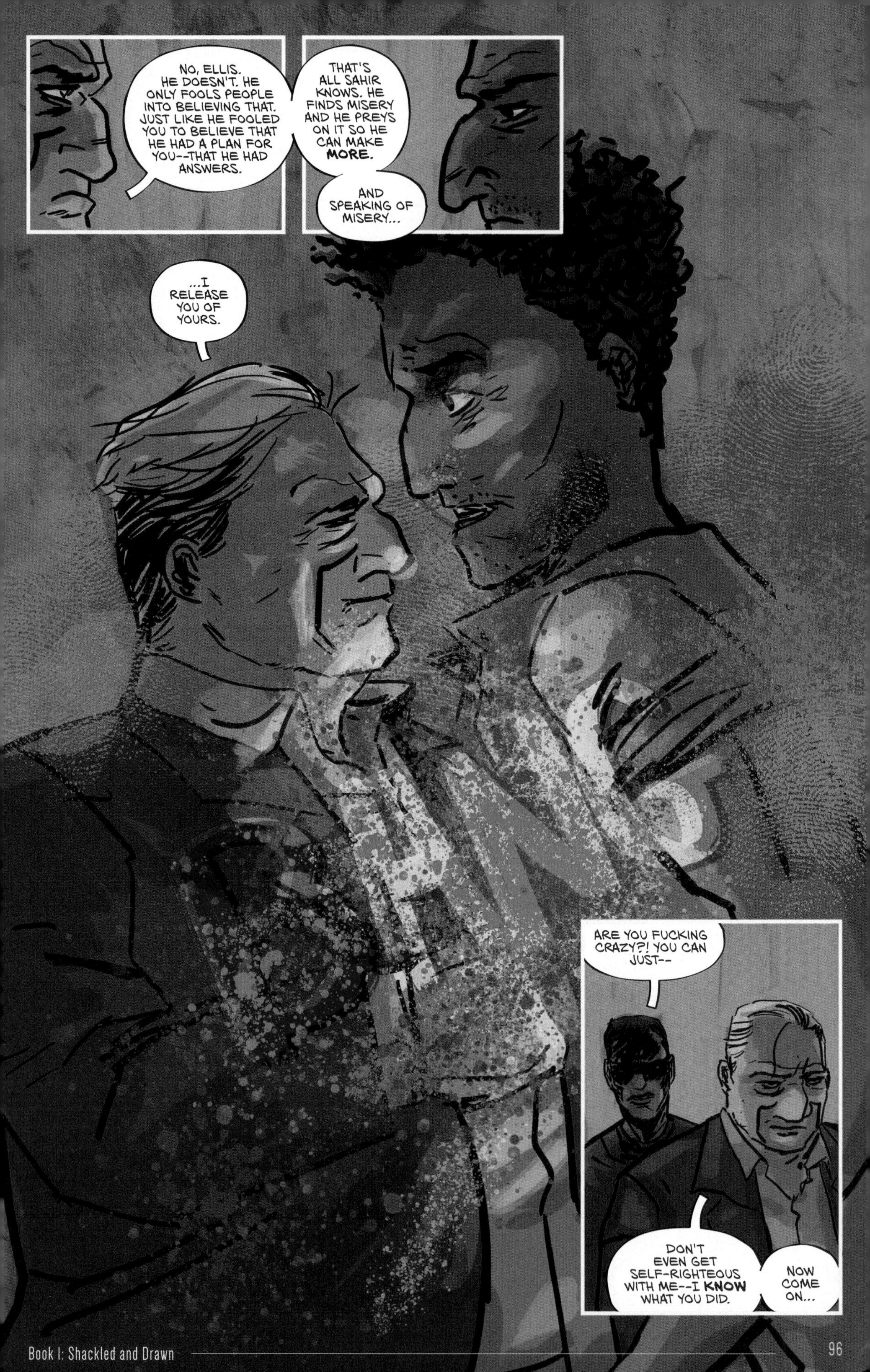
NO, ELLIS. HE DOESN'T. HE ONLY FOOLS PEOPLE INTO BELIEVING THAT. JUST LIKE HE FOOLED YOU TO BELIEVE THAT HE HAD A PLAN FOR YOU--THAT HE HAD ANSWERS.
THAT'S ALL SAHIR KNOWS. HE FINDS MISERY AND HE PREYS ON IT SO HE CAN MAKE **MORE.**
AND SPEAKING OF MISERY...
...I RELEASE YOU OF YOURS.
ARE YOU FUCKING CRAZY?! YOU CAN JUST--
DON'T EVEN GET SELF-RIGHTEOUS WITH ME--I **KNOW** WHAT YOU DID.
NOW COME ON...

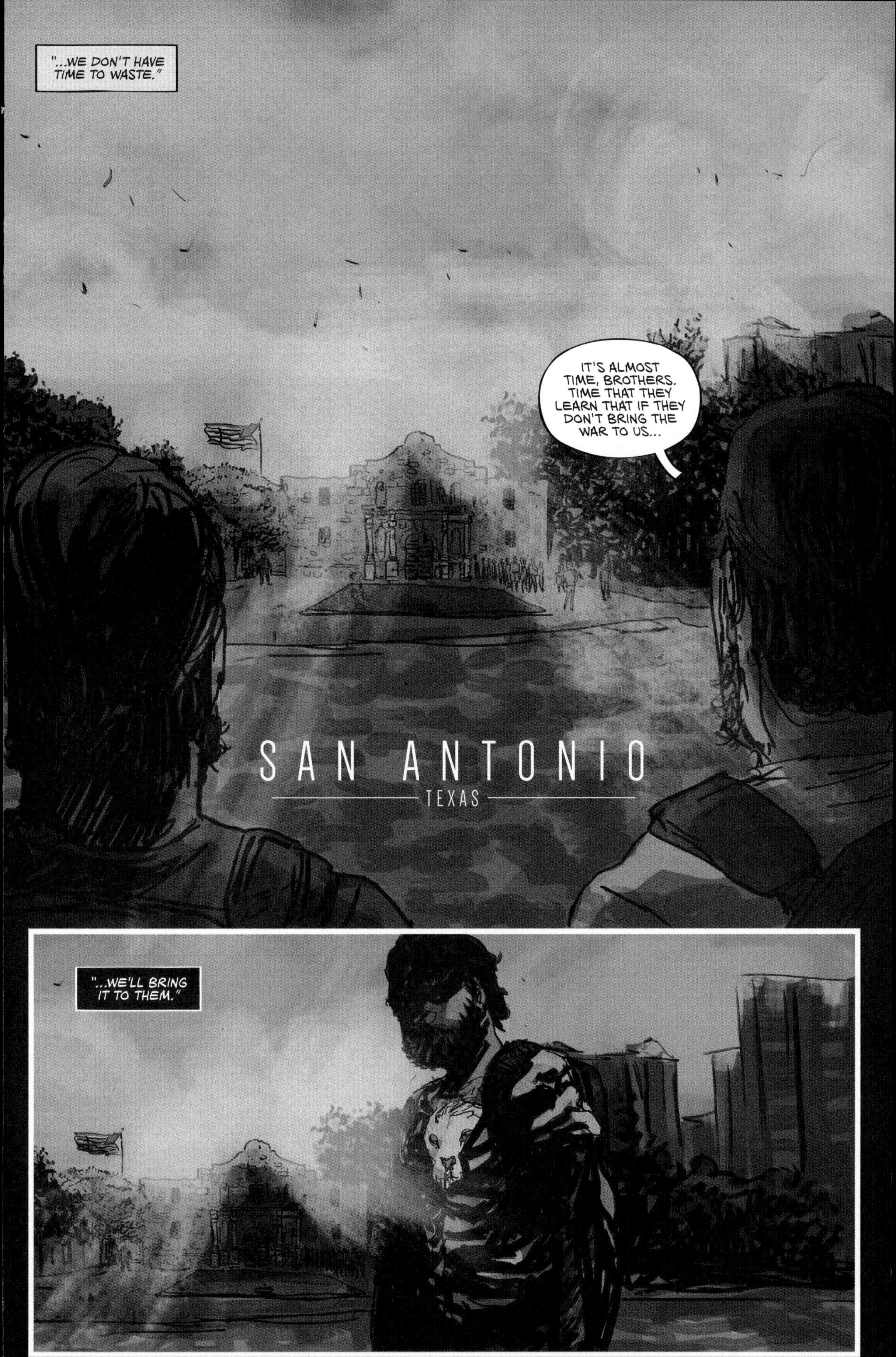
"...WE DON'T HAVE TIME TO WASTE."
IT'S ALMOST TIME, BROTHERS. TIME THAT THEY LEARN THAT IF THEY DON'T BRING THE WAR TO US...
SAN ANTONIO
TEXAS
"...WE'LL BRING IT TO THEM."

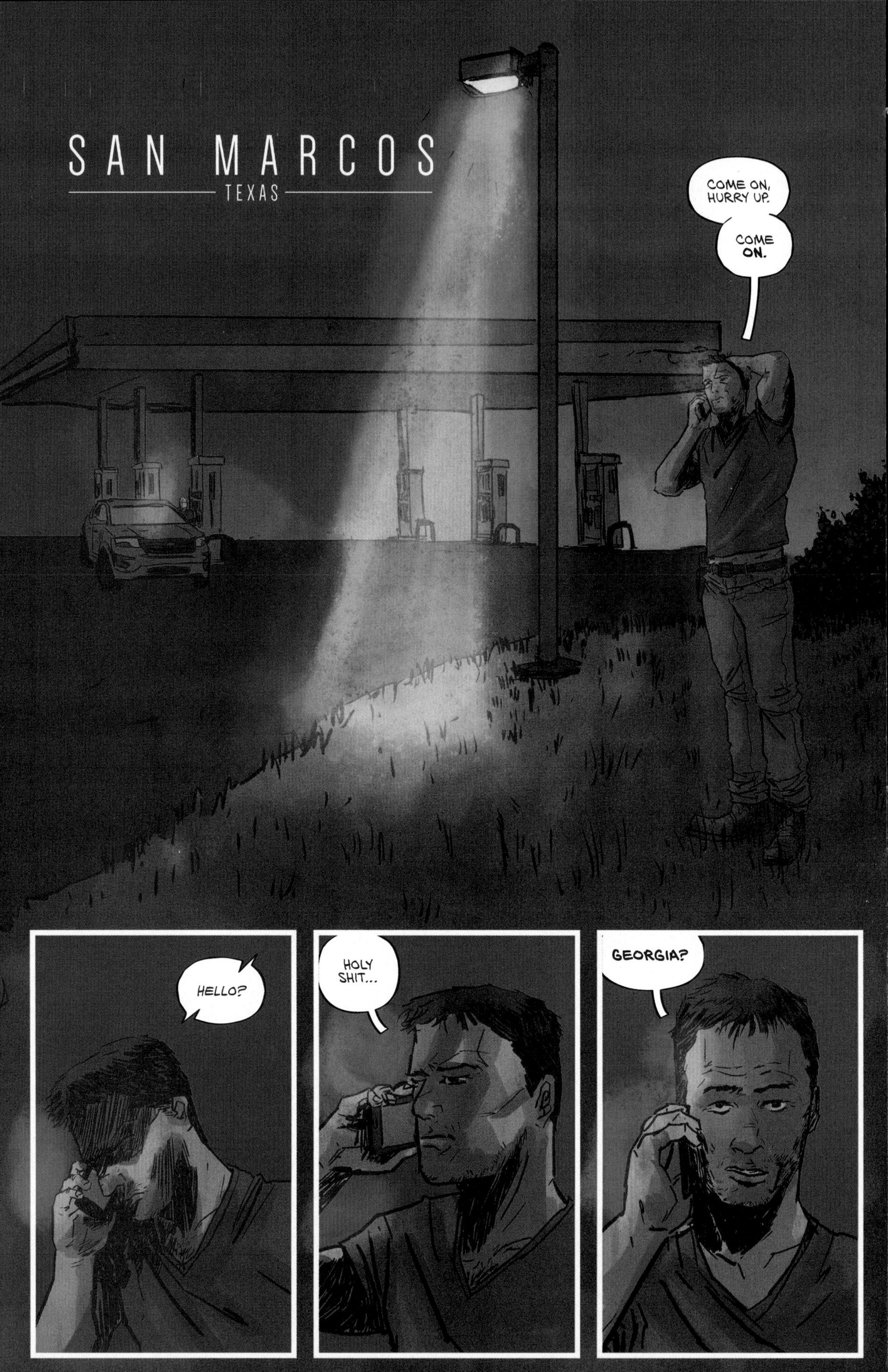
SAN MARCOS
TEXAS
COME ON, HURRY UP.
COME ON.
HELLO?
HOLY SHIT...
GEORGIA?

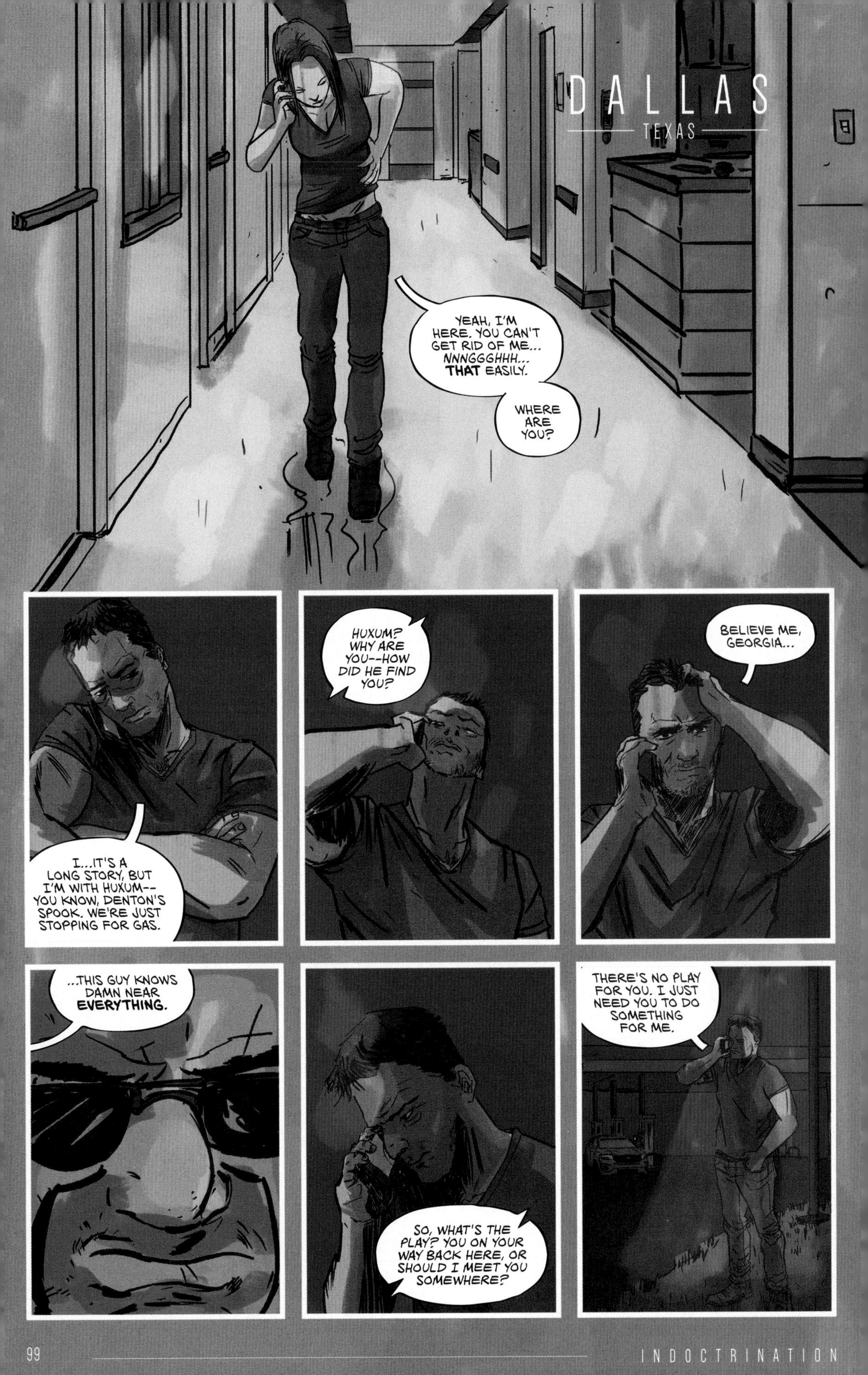
DALLAS
TEXAS
YEAH, I'M HERE. YOU CAN'T GET RID OF ME... NNNGGGHHH... THAT EASILY.
WHERE ARE YOU?
I...IT'S A LONG STORY, BUT I'M WITH HUXUM-- YOU KNOW, DENTON'S SPOOK. WE'RE JUST STOPPING FOR GAS.
HUXUM? WHY ARE YOU--HOW DID HE FIND YOU?
BELIEVE ME, GEORGIA...
...THIS GUY KNOWS DAMN NEAR EVERYTHING.
SO, WHAT'S THE PLAY? YOU ON YOUR WAY BACK HERE, OR SHOULD I MEET YOU SOMEWHERE?
THERE'S NO PLAY FOR YOU. I JUST NEED YOU TO DO SOMETHING FOR ME.

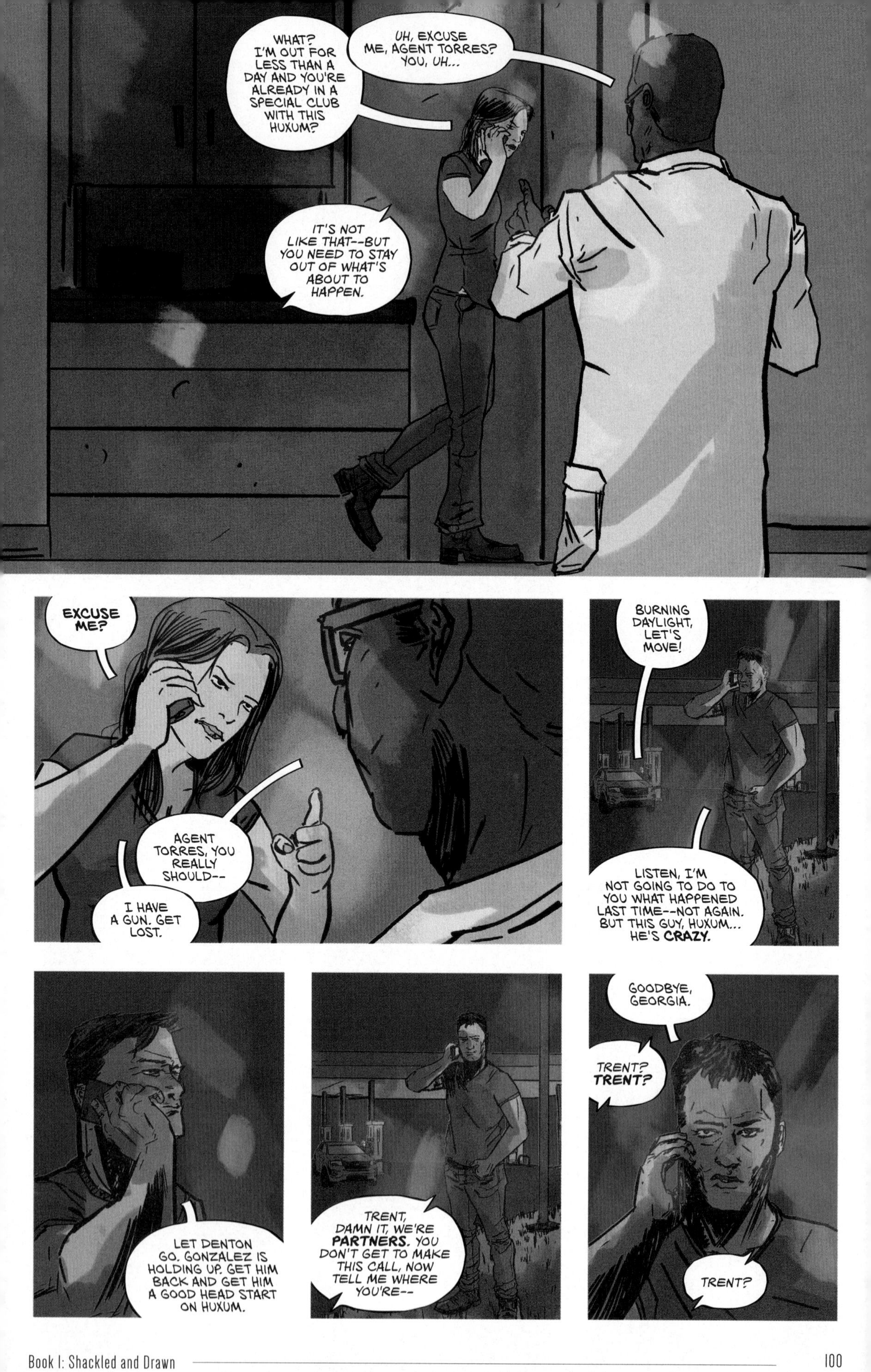
UH, EXCUSE ME, AGENT TORRES? YOU, UH...
WHAT? I'M OUT FOR LESS THAN A DAY AND YOU'RE ALREADY IN A SPECIAL CLUB WITH THIS HUXUM?
IT'S NOT LIKE THAT--BUT YOU NEED TO STAY OUT OF WHAT'S ABOUT TO HAPPEN.
EXCUSE ME?
AGENT TORRES, YOU REALLY SHOULD--
I HAVE A GUN. GET LOST.
BURNING DAYLIGHT, LET'S MOVE!
LISTEN, I'M NOT GOING TO DO TO YOU WHAT HAPPENED LAST TIME--NOT AGAIN. BUT THIS GUY, HUXUM... HE'S CRAZY.
LET DENTON GO. GONZALEZ IS HOLDING UP. GET HIM BACK AND GET HIM A GOOD HEAD START ON HUXUM.
TRENT, DAMN IT, WE'RE PARTNERS. YOU DON'T GET TO MAKE THIS CALL, NOW TELL ME WHERE YOU'RE--
GOODBYE, GEORGIA.
TRENT? TRENT?
TRENT?

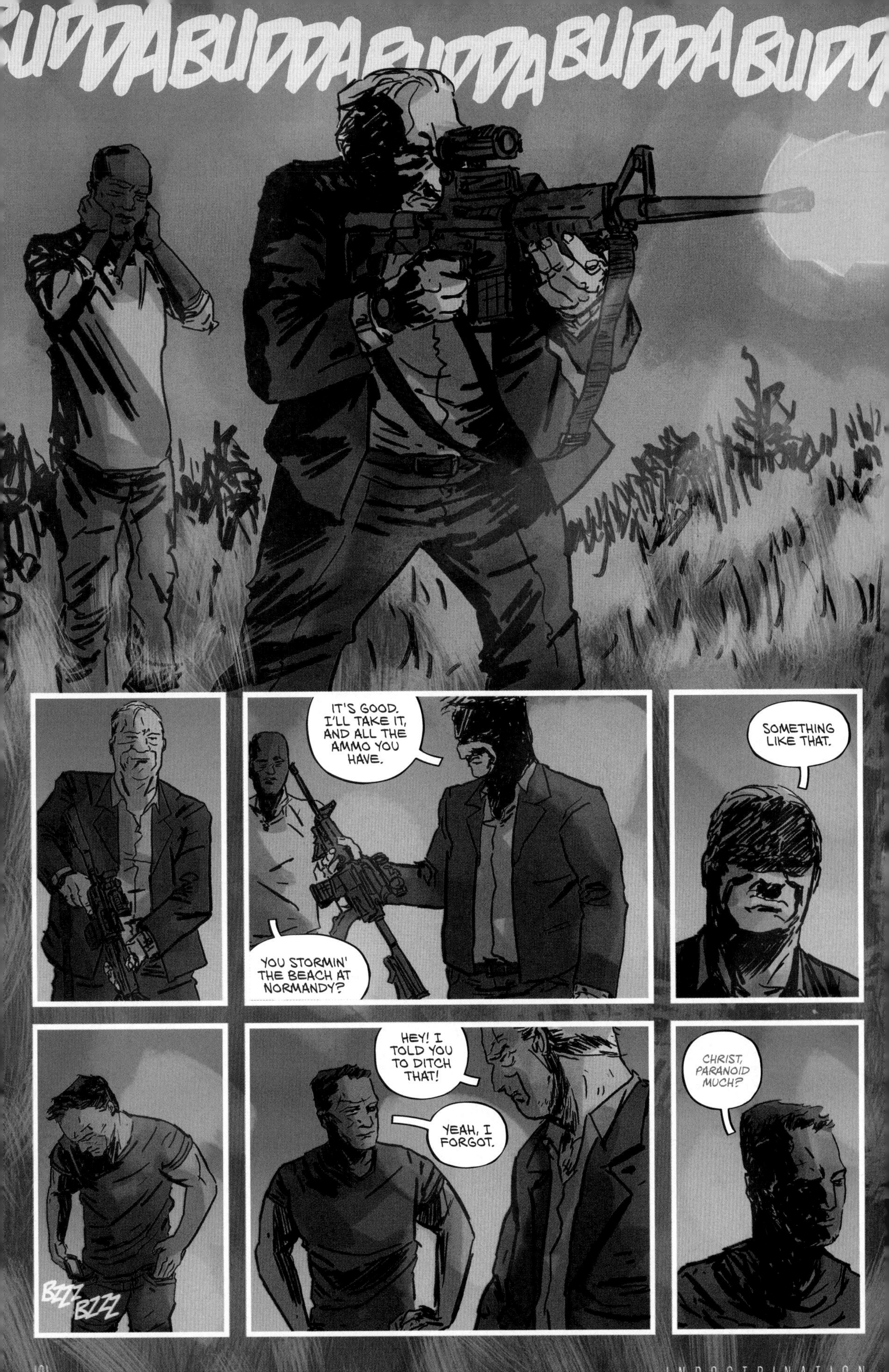
BUDDABUDDABUDDABUDDABUDD
IT'S GOOD. I'LL TAKE IT, AND ALL THE AMMO YOU HAVE.
YOU STORMIN' THE BEACH AT NORMANDY?
SOMETHING LIKE THAT.
BZZZ BZZZ
HEY! I TOLD YOU TO DITCH THAT!
YEAH, I FORGOT.
CHRIST, PARANOID MUCH?

ARE YOU KIDDING ME, GEORGIA?

Georgia:

Tell me where you're going, or I hand Wilkins over to Huxum. I'm not kidding, I'll do it.

Georgia:

Tell me where you're going, or I hand Wilkins over to Huxum. I'm not kidding, I'll do it.

YEAH, I KNOW YOU WILL.

Trent:

Alamo. Be there by sundown. Bring your battle rattle.

PHONE. NOW. I WANT TO SEE THAT MESSAGE.

THIS PHONE?

KKSSHH

THERE YOU GO.

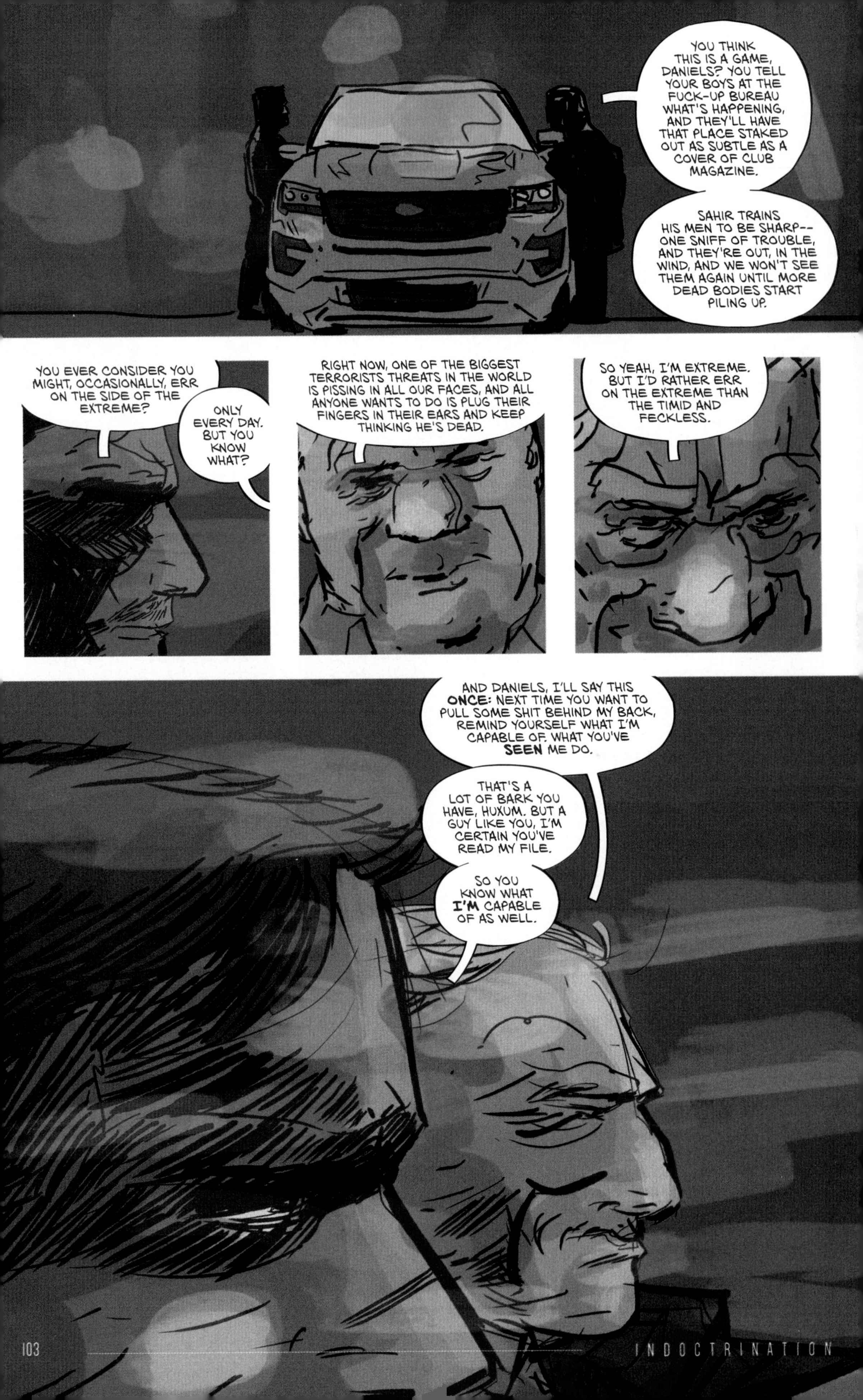
YOU THINK THIS IS A GAME, DANIELS? YOU TELL YOUR BOYS AT THE FUCK-UP BUREAU WHAT'S HAPPENING, AND THEY'LL HAVE THAT PLACE STAKED OUT AS SUBTLE AS A COVER OF CLUB MAGAZINE.
SAHIR TRAINS HIS MEN TO BE SHARP-- ONE SNIFF OF TROUBLE, AND THEY'RE OUT, IN THE WIND, AND WE WON'T SEE THEM AGAIN UNTIL MORE DEAD BODIES START PILING UP.
YOU EVER CONSIDER YOU MIGHT, OCCASIONALLY, ERR ON THE SIDE OF THE EXTREME?
ONLY EVERY DAY. BUT YOU KNOW WHAT?
RIGHT NOW, ONE OF THE BIGGEST TERRORISTS THREATS IN THE WORLD IS PISSING IN ALL OUR FACES, AND ALL ANYONE WANTS TO DO IS PLUG THEIR FINGERS IN THEIR EARS AND KEEP THINKING HE'S DEAD.
SO YEAH, I'M EXTREME. BUT I'D RATHER ERR ON THE EXTREME THAN THE TIMID AND FECKLESS.
AND DANIELS, I'LL SAY THIS **ONCE**: NEXT TIME YOU WANT TO PULL SOME SHIT BEHIND MY BACK, REMIND YOURSELF WHAT I'M CAPABLE OF. WHAT YOU'VE **SEEN** ME DO.
THAT'S A LOT OF BARK YOU HAVE, HUXUM. BUT A GUY LIKE YOU, I'M CERTAIN YOU'VE READ MY FILE.
SO YOU KNOW WHAT **I'M** CAPABLE OF AS WELL.

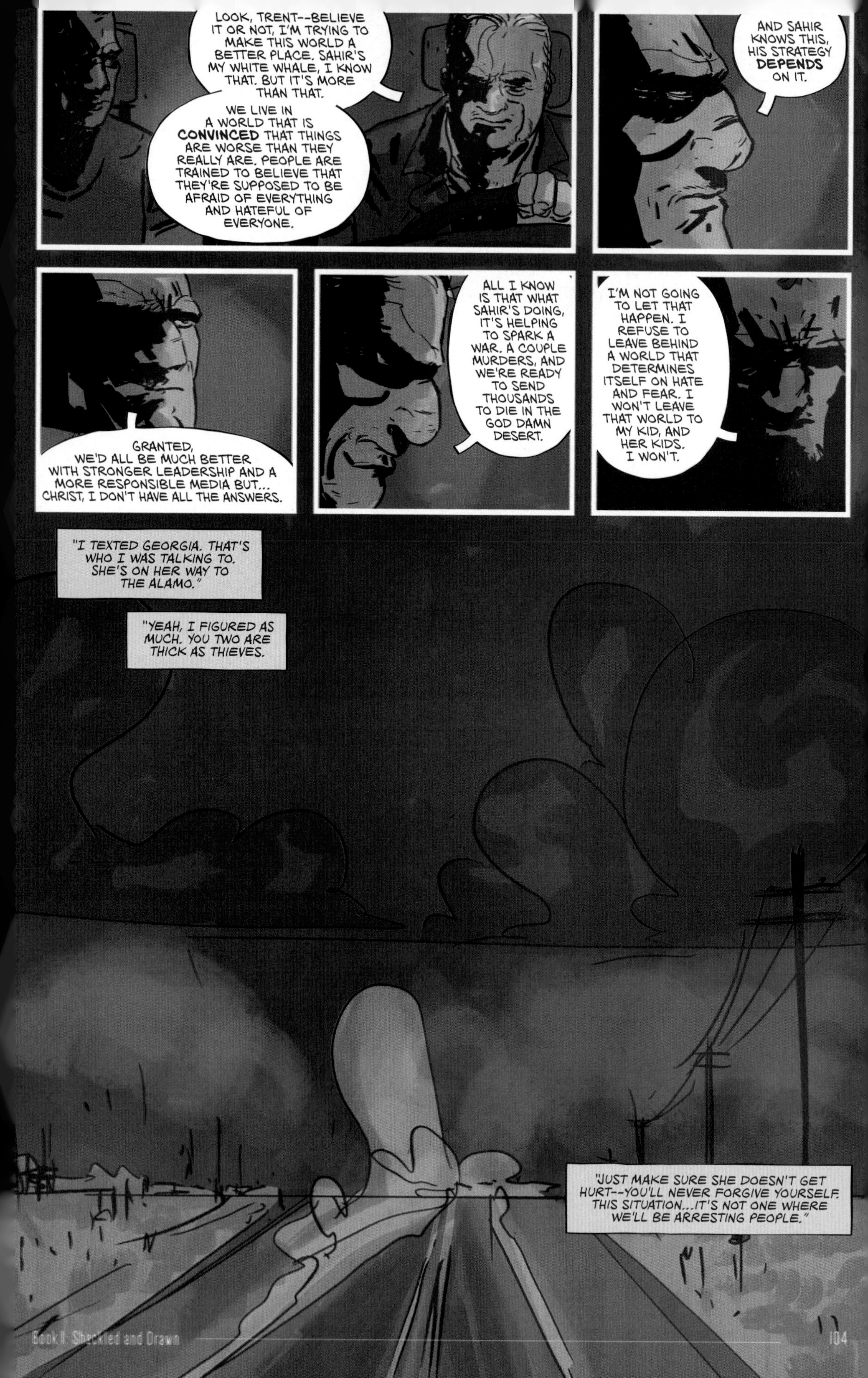

LOOK, TRENT--BELIEVE IT OR NOT, I'M TRYING TO MAKE THIS WORLD A BETTER PLACE. SAHIR'S MY WHITE WHALE, I KNOW THAT. BUT IT'S MORE THAN THAT.
WE LIVE IN A WORLD THAT IS CONVINCED THAT THINGS ARE WORSE THAN THEY REALLY ARE. PEOPLE ARE TRAINED TO BELIEVE THAT THEY'RE SUPPOSED TO BE AFRAID OF EVERYTHING AND HATEFUL OF EVERYONE.
AND SAHIR KNOWS THIS, HIS STRATEGY DEPENDS ON IT.
GRANTED, WE'D ALL BE MUCH BETTER WITH STRONGER LEADERSHIP AND A MORE RESPONSIBLE MEDIA BUT... CHRIST, I DON'T HAVE ALL THE ANSWERS.
ALL I KNOW IS THAT WHAT SAHIR'S DOING, IT'S HELPING TO SPARK A WAR. A COUPLE MURDERS, AND WE'RE READY TO SEND THOUSANDS TO DIE IN THE GOD DAMN DESERT.
I'M NOT GOING TO LET THAT HAPPEN. I REFUSE TO LEAVE BEHIND A WORLD THAT DETERMINES ITSELF ON HATE AND FEAR. I WON'T LEAVE THAT WORLD TO MY KID, AND HER KIDS. I WON'T.
"I TEXTED GEORGIA. THAT'S WHO I WAS TALKING TO. SHE'S ON HER WAY TO THE ALAMO."
"YEAH, I FIGURED AS MUCH. YOU TWO ARE THICK AS THIEVES.
"JUST MAKE SURE SHE DOESN'T GET HURT--YOU'LL NEVER FORGIVE YOURSELF. THIS SITUATION...IT'S NOT ONE WHERE WE'LL BE ARRESTING PEOPLE."

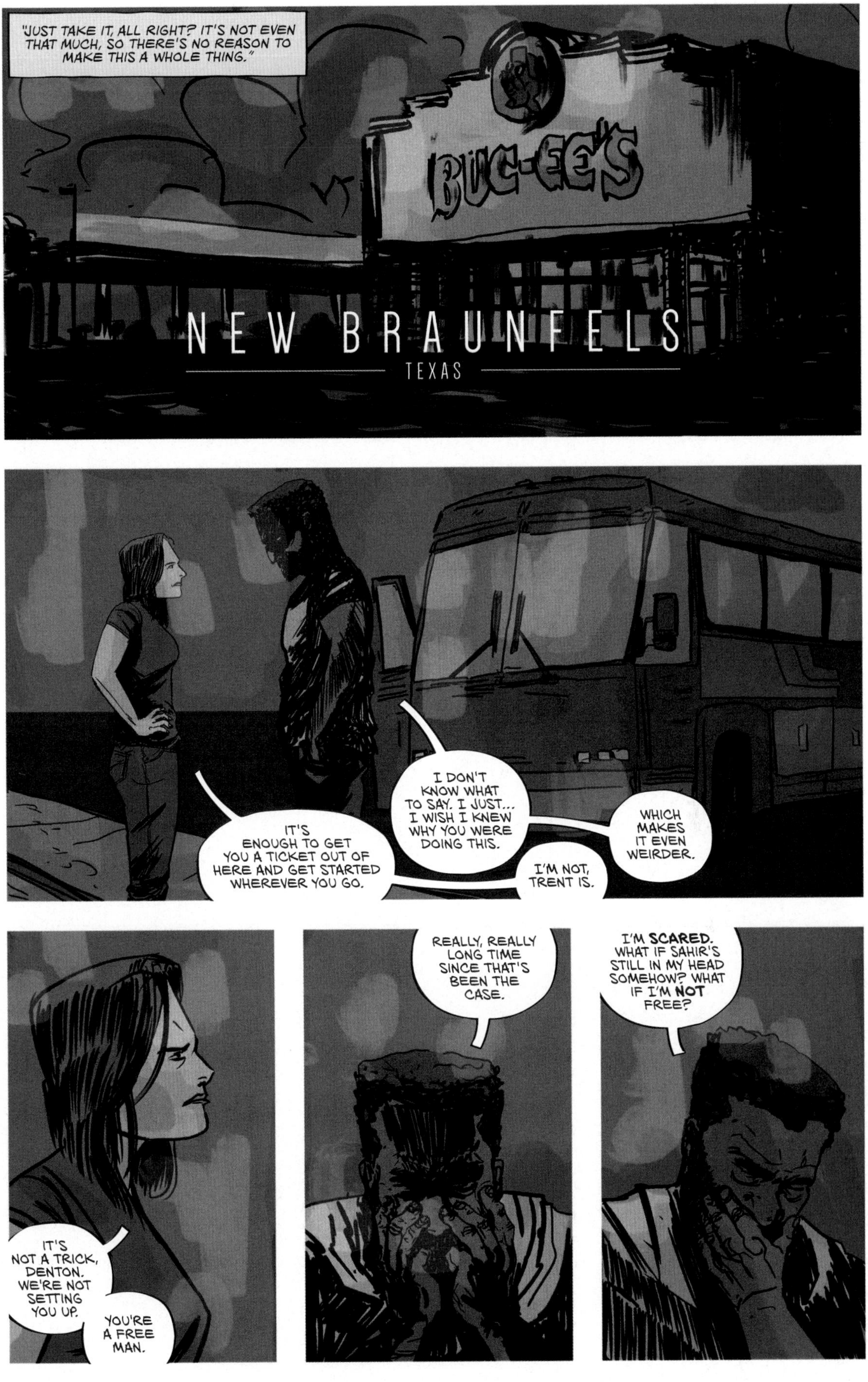
"JUST TAKE IT, ALL RIGHT? IT'S NOT EVEN THAT MUCH, SO THERE'S NO REASON TO MAKE THIS A WHOLE THING."
BUC-EE'S
NEW BRAUNFELS
TEXAS
IT'S ENOUGH TO GET YOU A TICKET OUT OF HERE AND GET STARTED WHEREVER YOU GO.
I DON'T KNOW WHAT TO SAY. I JUST... I WISH I KNEW WHY YOU WERE DOING THIS.
I'M NOT, TRENT IS.
WHICH MAKES IT EVEN WEIRDER.
IT'S NOT A TRICK, DENTON. WE'RE NOT SETTING YOU UP.
YOU'RE A FREE MAN.
REALLY, REALLY LONG TIME SINCE THAT'S BEEN THE CASE.
I'M **SCARED.** WHAT IF SAHIR'S STILL IN MY HEAD SOMEHOW? WHAT IF I'M **NOT** FREE?

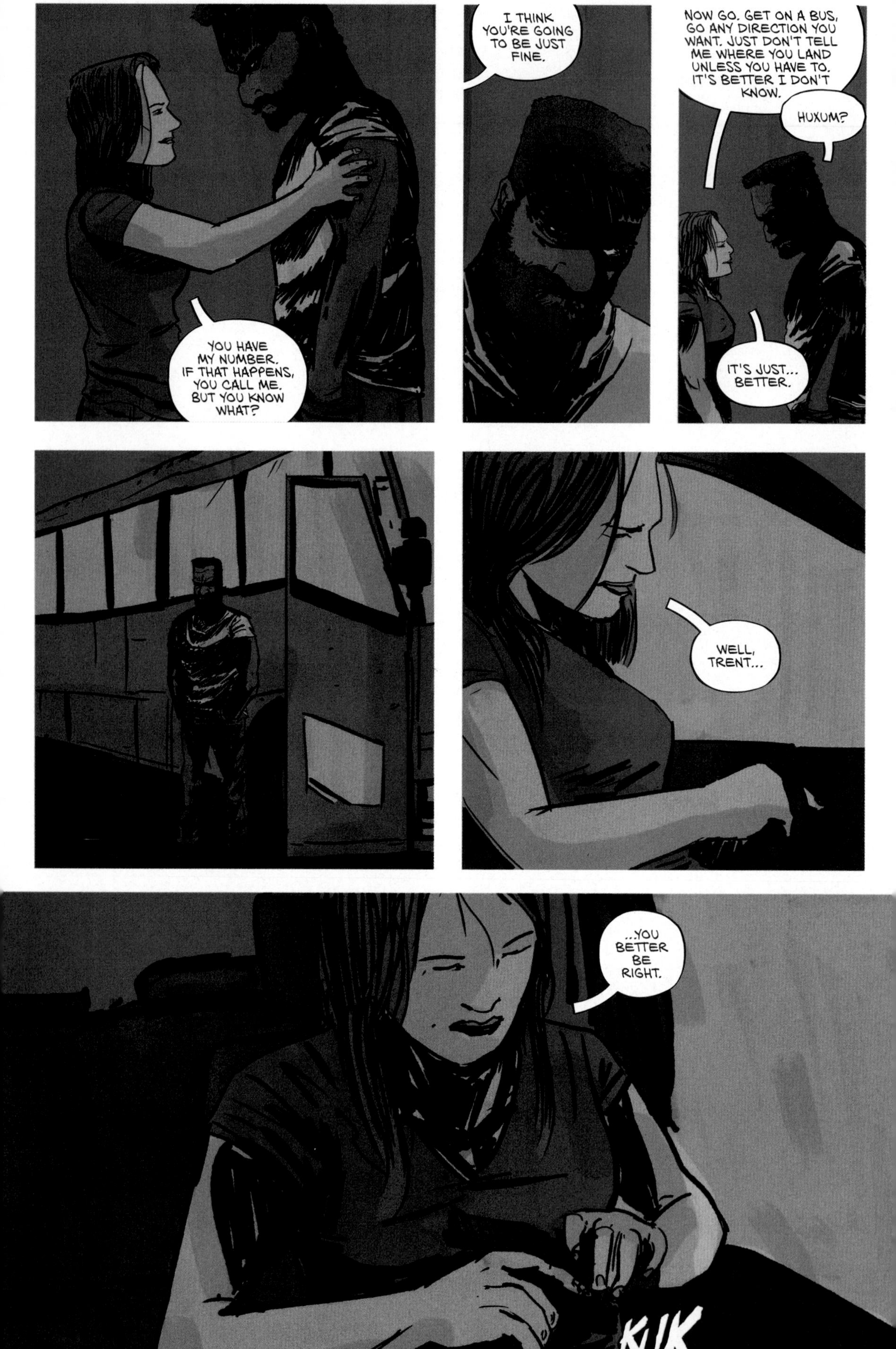
YOU HAVE MY NUMBER. IF THAT HAPPENS, YOU CALL ME. BUT YOU KNOW WHAT?
I THINK YOU'RE GOING TO BE JUST FINE.
NOW GO. GET ON A BUS, GO ANY DIRECTION YOU WANT. JUST DON'T TELL ME WHERE YOU LAND UNLESS YOU HAVE TO. IT'S BETTER I DON'T KNOW.
HUXUM?
IT'S JUST... BETTER.
WELL, TRENT...
...YOU BETTER BE RIGHT.
KLIK

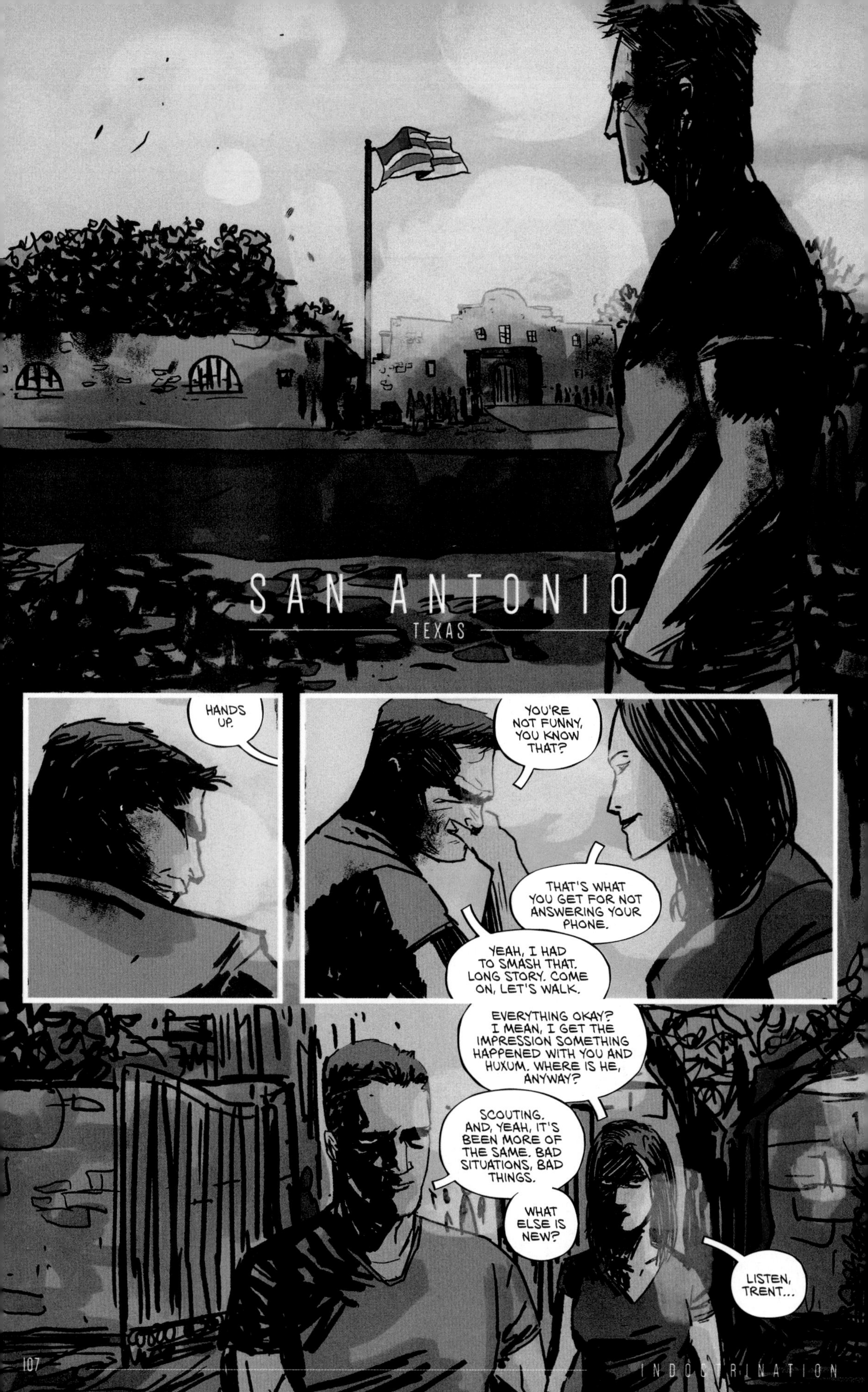
SAN ANTONIO
TEXAS
HANDS UP.
YOU'RE NOT FUNNY, YOU KNOW THAT?
THAT'S WHAT YOU GET FOR NOT ANSWERING YOUR PHONE.
YEAH, I HAD TO SMASH THAT. LONG STORY. COME ON, LET'S WALK.
EVERYTHING OKAY? I MEAN, I GET THE IMPRESSION SOMETHING HAPPENED WITH YOU AND HUXUM. WHERE IS HE, ANYWAY?
SCOUTING. AND, YEAH, IT'S BEEN MORE OF THE SAME. BAD SITUATIONS, BAD THINGS.
WHAT ELSE IS NEW?
LISTEN, TRENT...

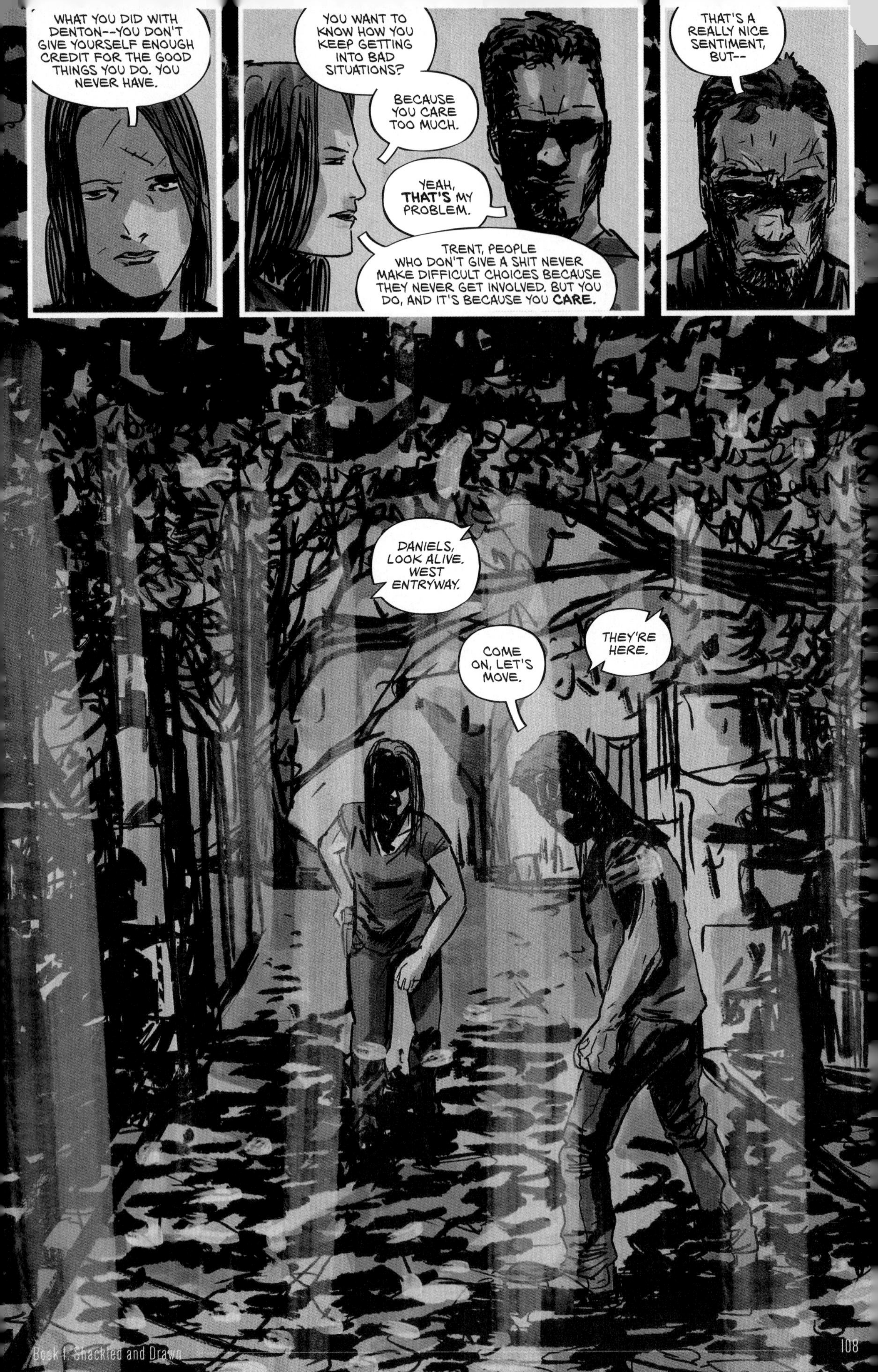
WHAT YOU DID WITH DENTON--YOU DON'T GIVE YOURSELF ENOUGH CREDIT FOR THE GOOD THINGS YOU DO. YOU NEVER HAVE.
YOU WANT TO KNOW HOW YOU KEEP GETTING INTO BAD SITUATIONS?
BECAUSE YOU CARE TOO MUCH.
YEAH, **THAT'S** MY PROBLEM.
TRENT, PEOPLE WHO DON'T GIVE A SHIT NEVER MAKE DIFFICULT CHOICES BECAUSE THEY NEVER GET INVOLVED. BUT YOU DO, AND IT'S BECAUSE YOU **CARE.**
THAT'S A REALLY NICE SENTIMENT, BUT--
DANIELS, LOOK ALIVE. WEST ENTRYWAY.
THEY'RE HERE.
COME ON, LET'S MOVE.

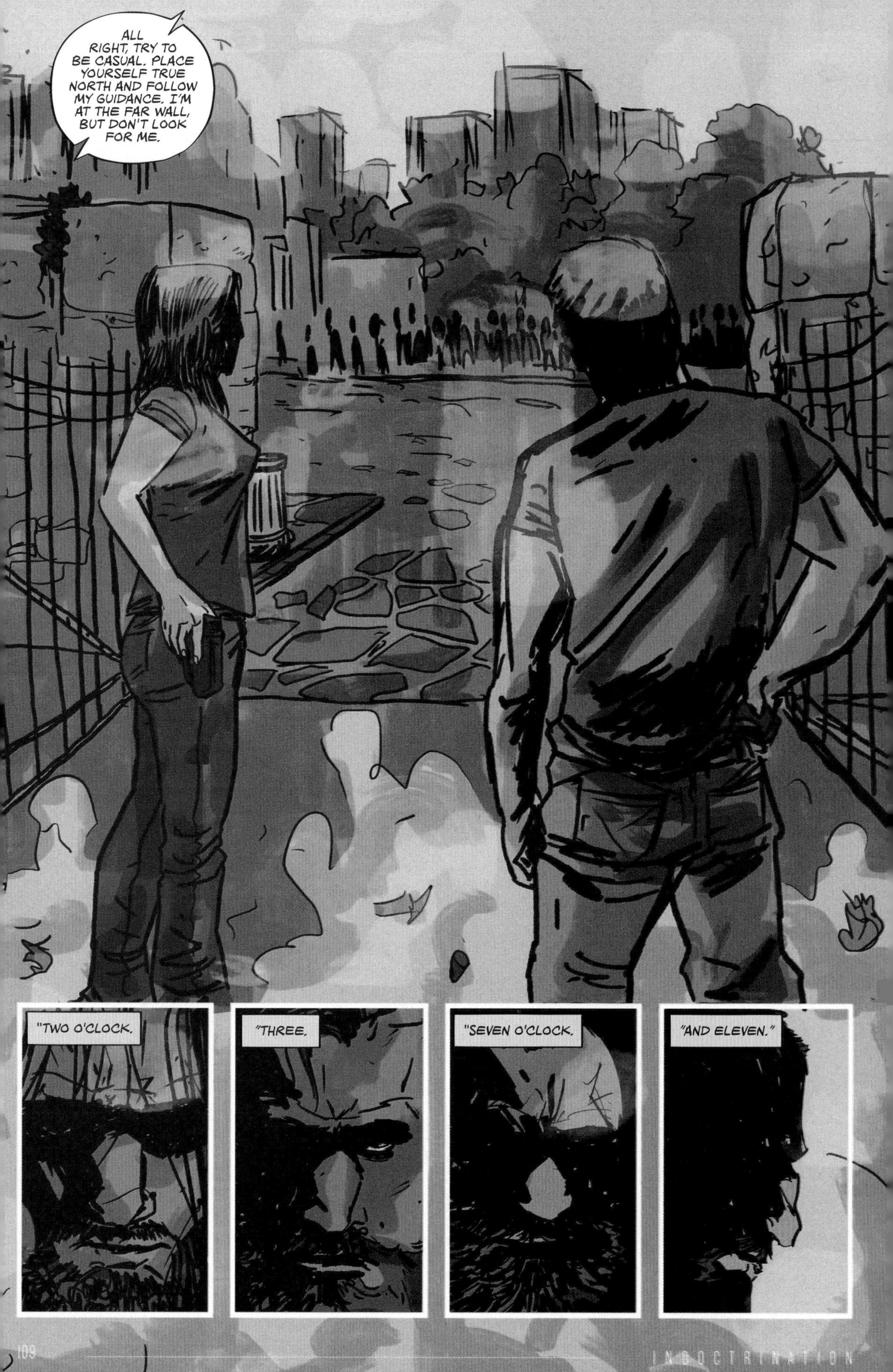
ALL RIGHT, TRY TO BE CASUAL. PLACE YOURSELF TRUE NORTH AND FOLLOW MY GUIDANCE. I'M AT THE FAR WALL, BUT DON'T LOOK FOR ME.
"TWO O'CLOCK.
"THREE.
"SEVEN O'CLOCK.
"AND ELEVEN."

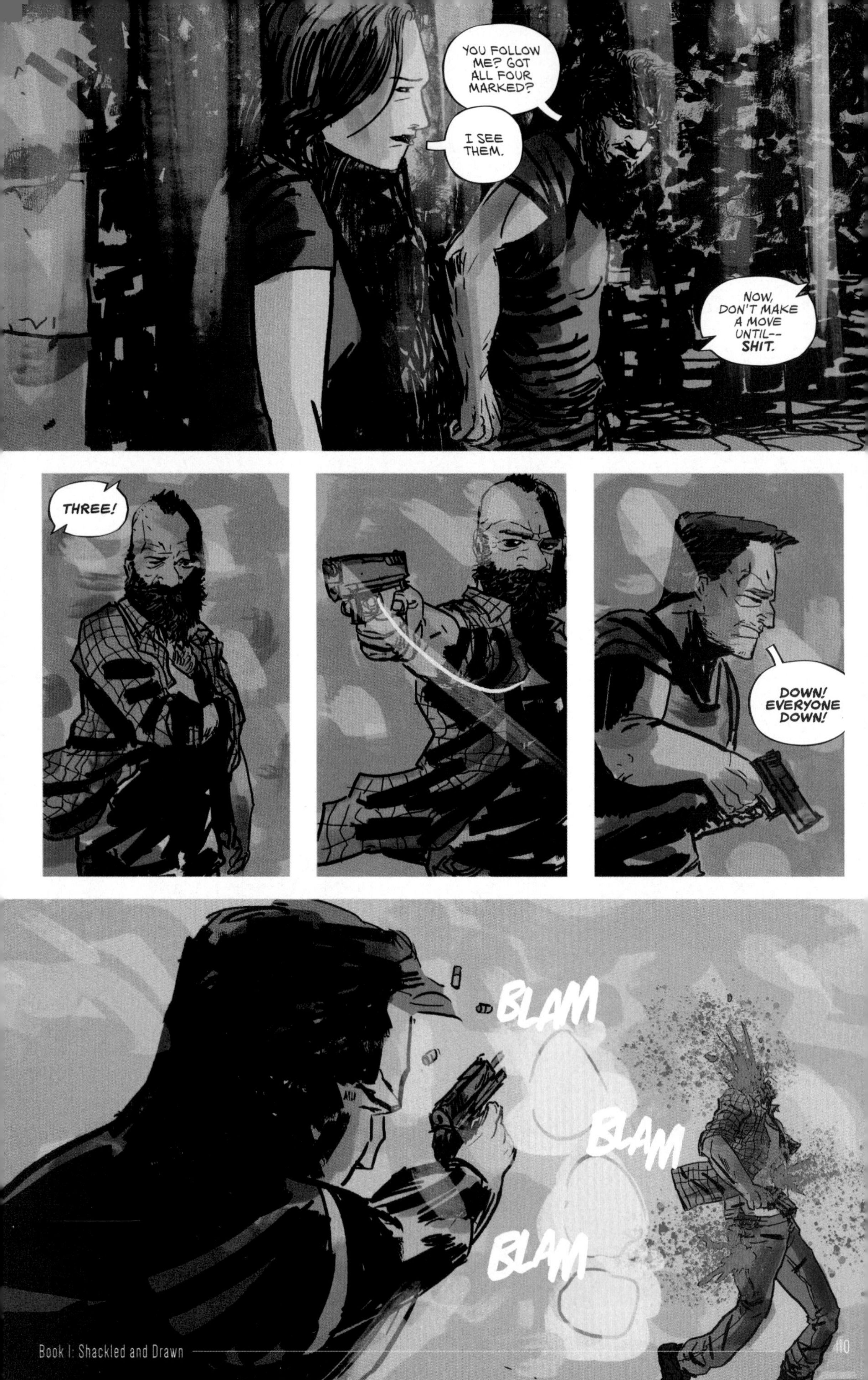

YOU FOLLOW ME? GOT ALL FOUR MARKED?
I SEE THEM.
NOW, DON'T MAKE A MOVE UNTIL-- SHIT.
THREE!
DOWN! EVERYONE DOWN!
BLAM
BLAM
BLAM

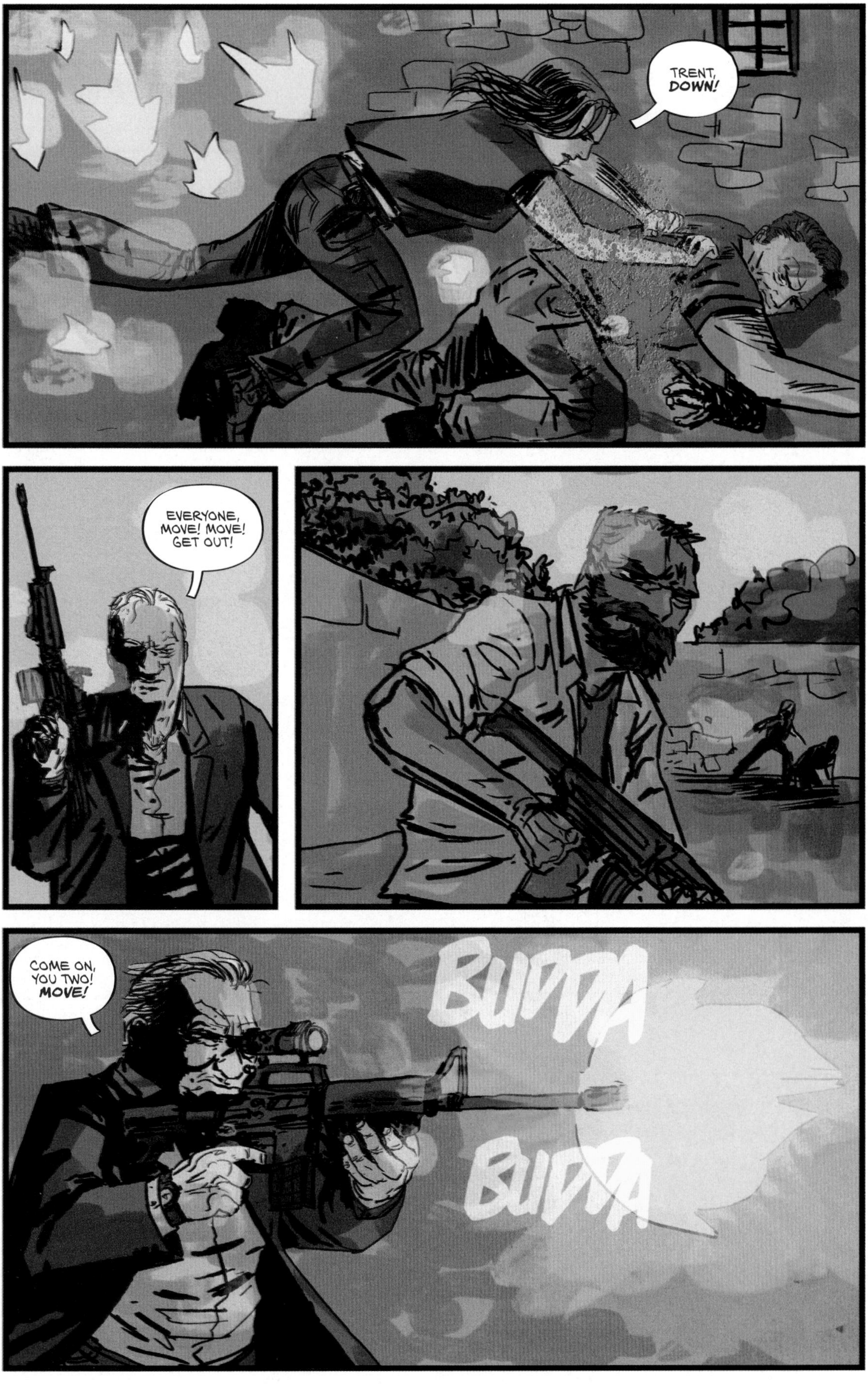
TRENT, DOWN!
EVERYONE, MOVE! MOVE! GET OUT!
COME ON, YOU TWO! MOVE!
BUDDA
BUDDA

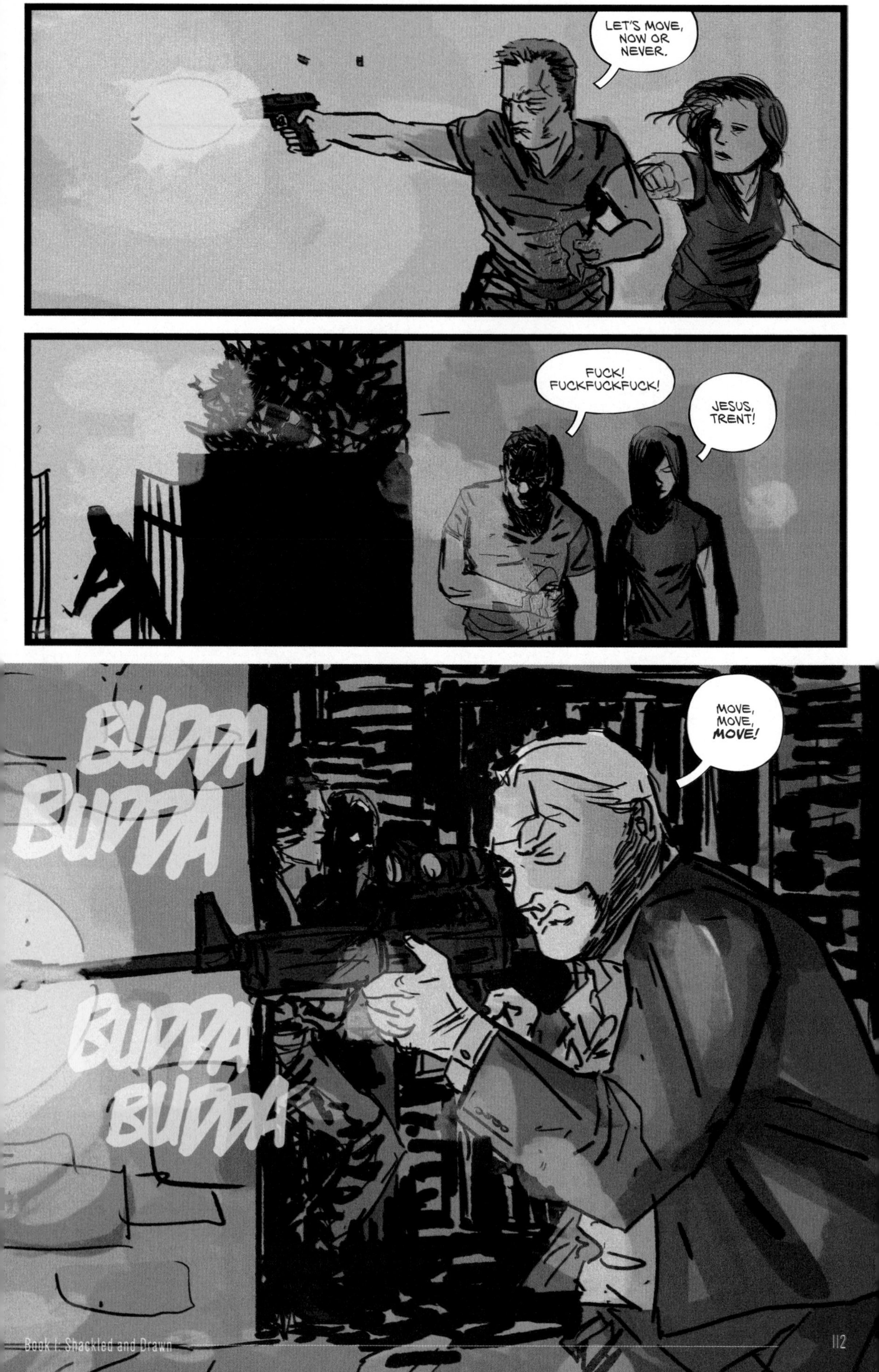
LET'S MOVE, NOW OR NEVER.
FUCK! FUCKFUCKFUCK!
JESUS, TRENT!
BUDDA BUDDA
MOVE, MOVE, MOVE!
BUDDA BUDDA

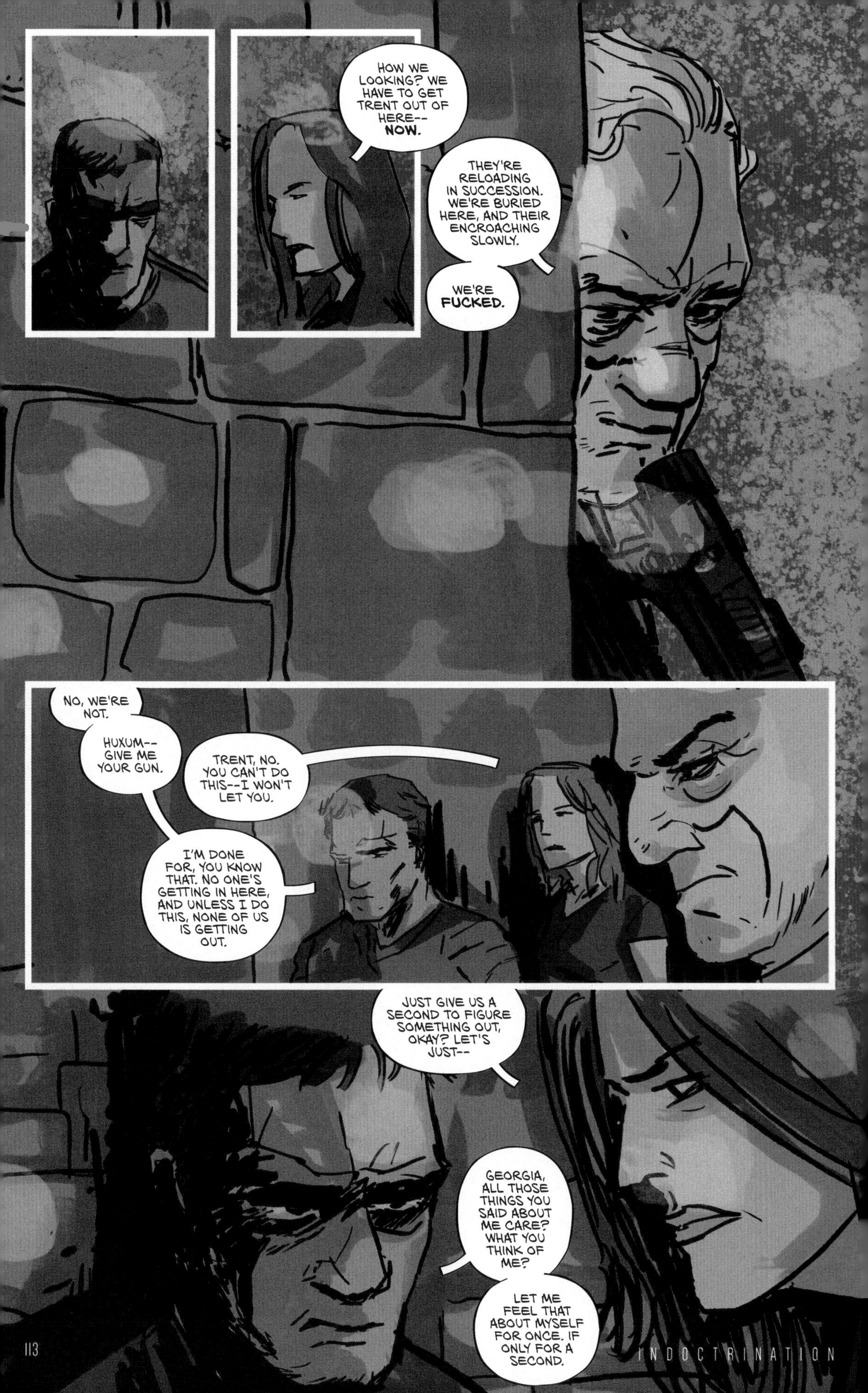
HOW WE LOOKING? WE HAVE TO GET TRENT OUT OF HERE-- **NOW.**
THEY'RE RELOADING IN SUCCESSION. WE'RE BURIED HERE, AND THEIR ENCROACHING SLOWLY.
WE'RE **FUCKED.**
NO, WE'RE NOT.
HUXUM-- GIVE ME YOUR GUN.
TRENT, NO. YOU CAN'T DO THIS--I WON'T LET YOU.
I'M DONE FOR, YOU KNOW THAT. NO ONE'S GETTING IN HERE, AND UNLESS I DO THIS, NONE OF US IS GETTING OUT.
JUST GIVE US A SECOND TO FIGURE SOMETHING OUT, OKAY? LET'S JUST--
GEORGIA, ALL THOSE THINGS YOU SAID ABOUT ME CARE? WHAT YOU THINK OF ME?
LET ME FEEL THAT ABOUT MYSELF FOR ONCE. IF ONLY FOR A SECOND.

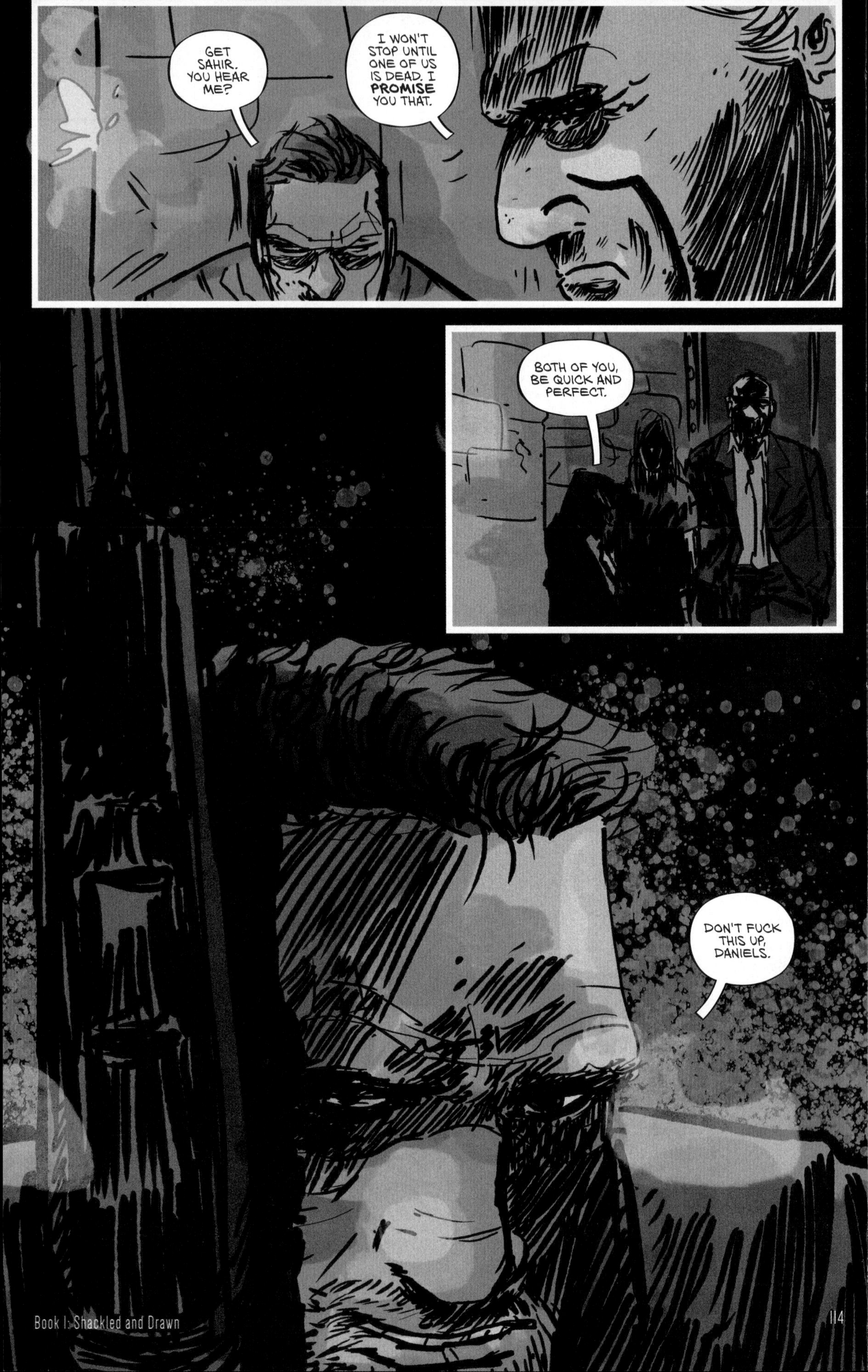
GET SAHIR. YOU HEAR ME?
I WON'T STOP UNTIL ONE OF US IS DEAD. I **PROMISE** YOU THAT.
BOTH OF YOU, BE QUICK AND PERFECT.
DON'T FUCK THIS UP, DANIELS.

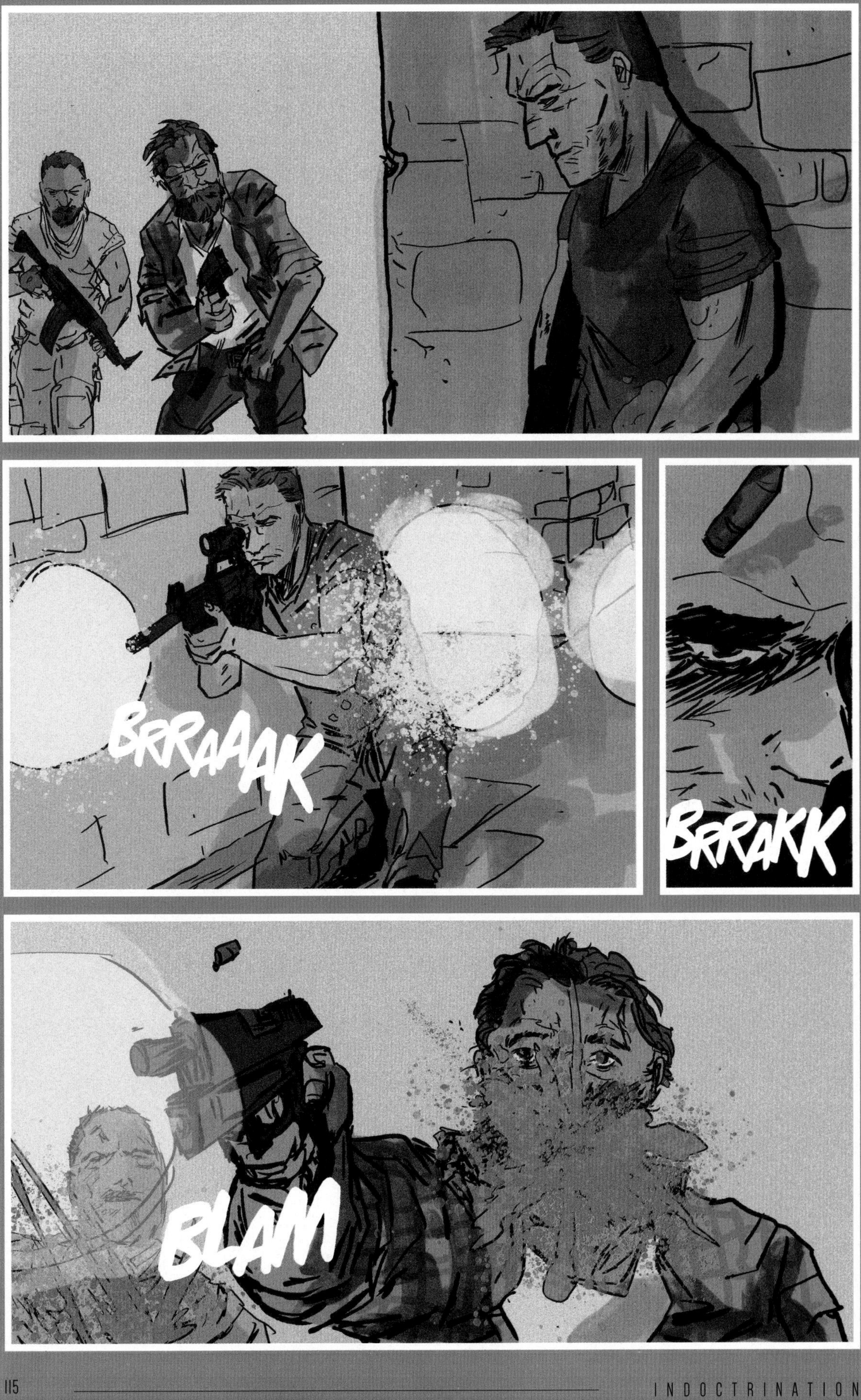
BRRAAAK
BRRAKK
BLAM

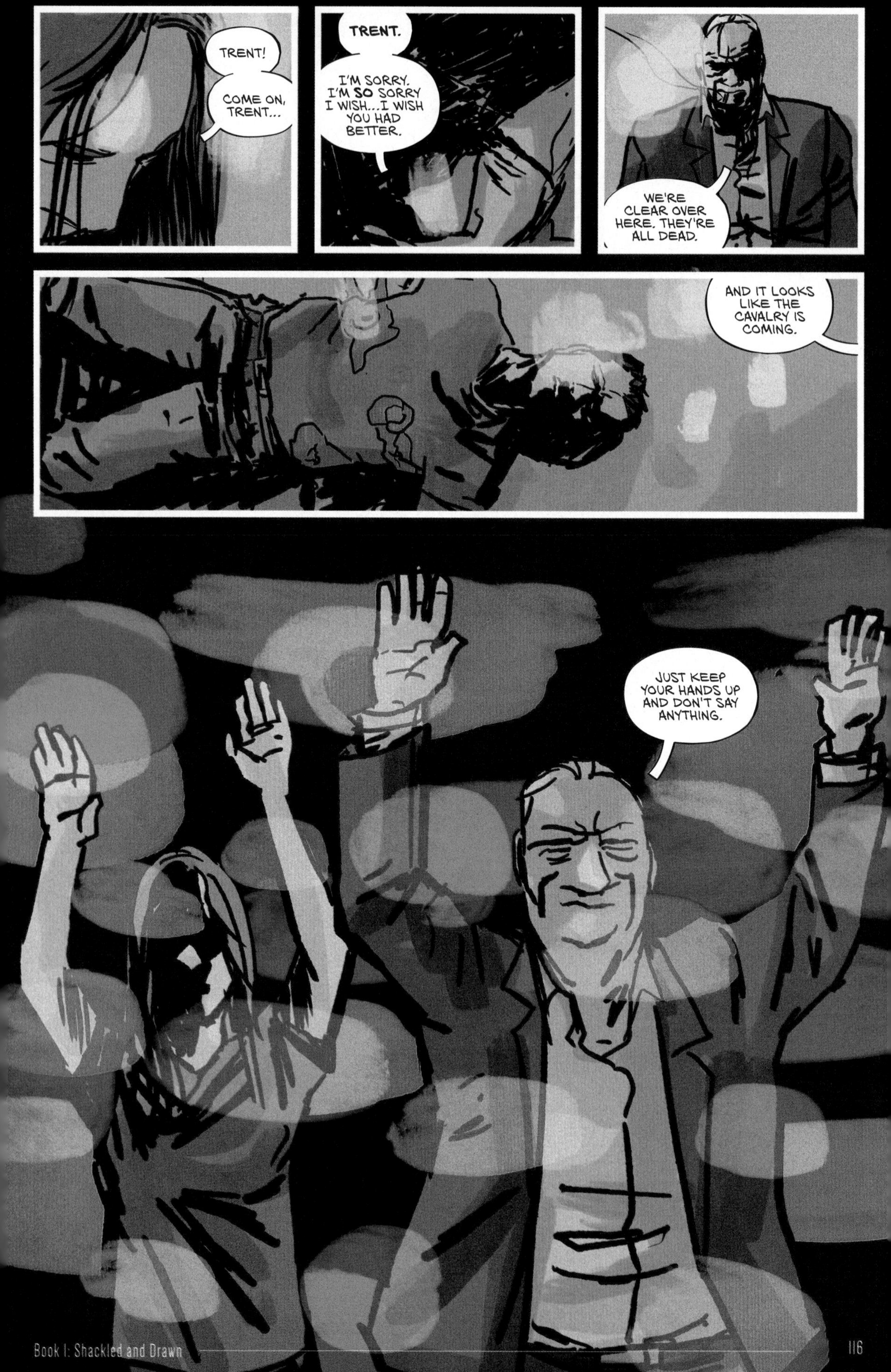
TRENT!
COME ON, TRENT...
TRENT.
I'M SORRY. I'M SO SORRY I WISH...I WISH YOU HAD BETTER.
WE'RE CLEAR OVER HERE. THEY'RE ALL DEAD.
AND IT LOOKS LIKE THE CAVALRY IS COMING.
JUST KEEP YOUR HANDS UP AND DON'T SAY ANYTHING.

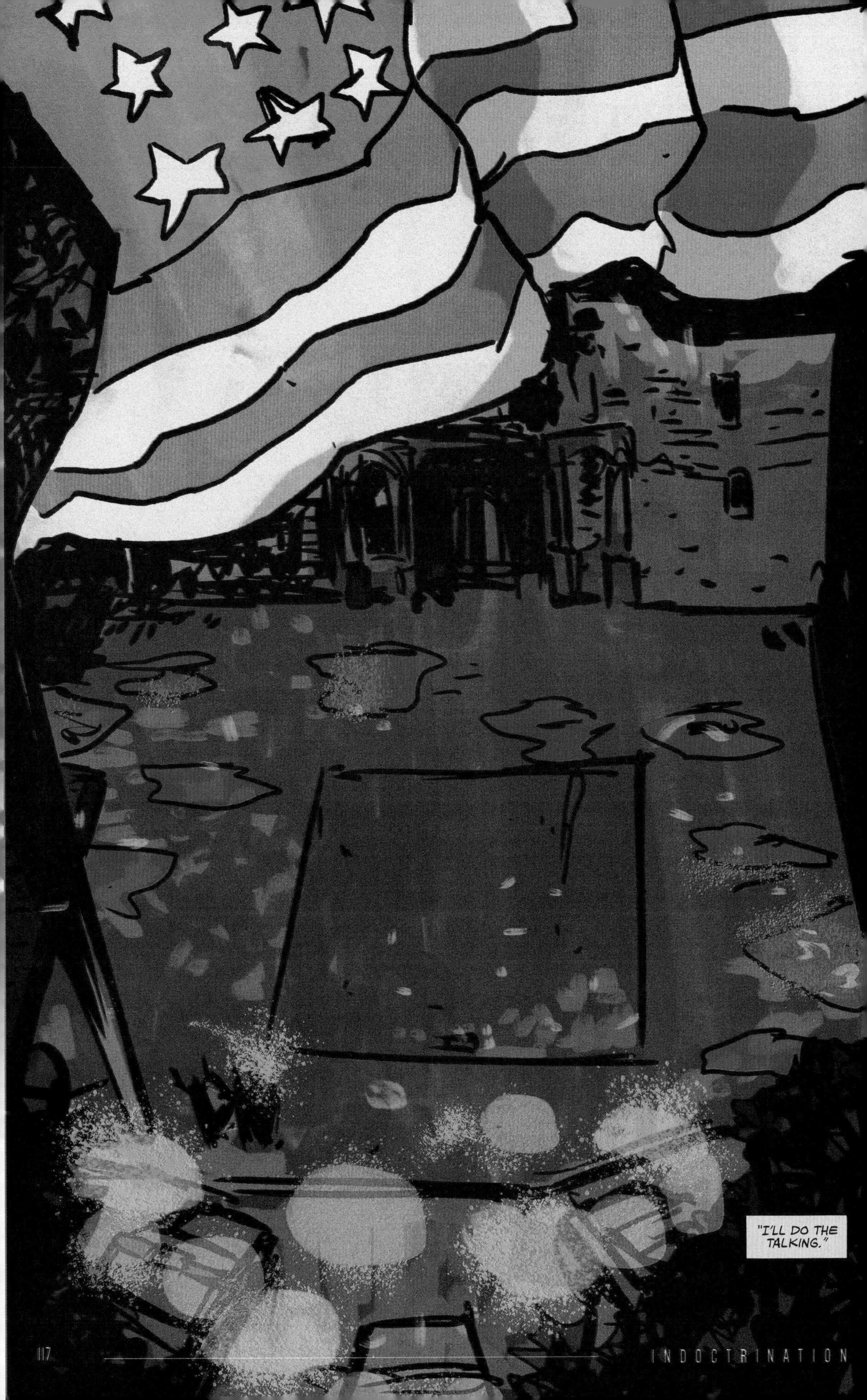
"I'LL DO THE TALKING."

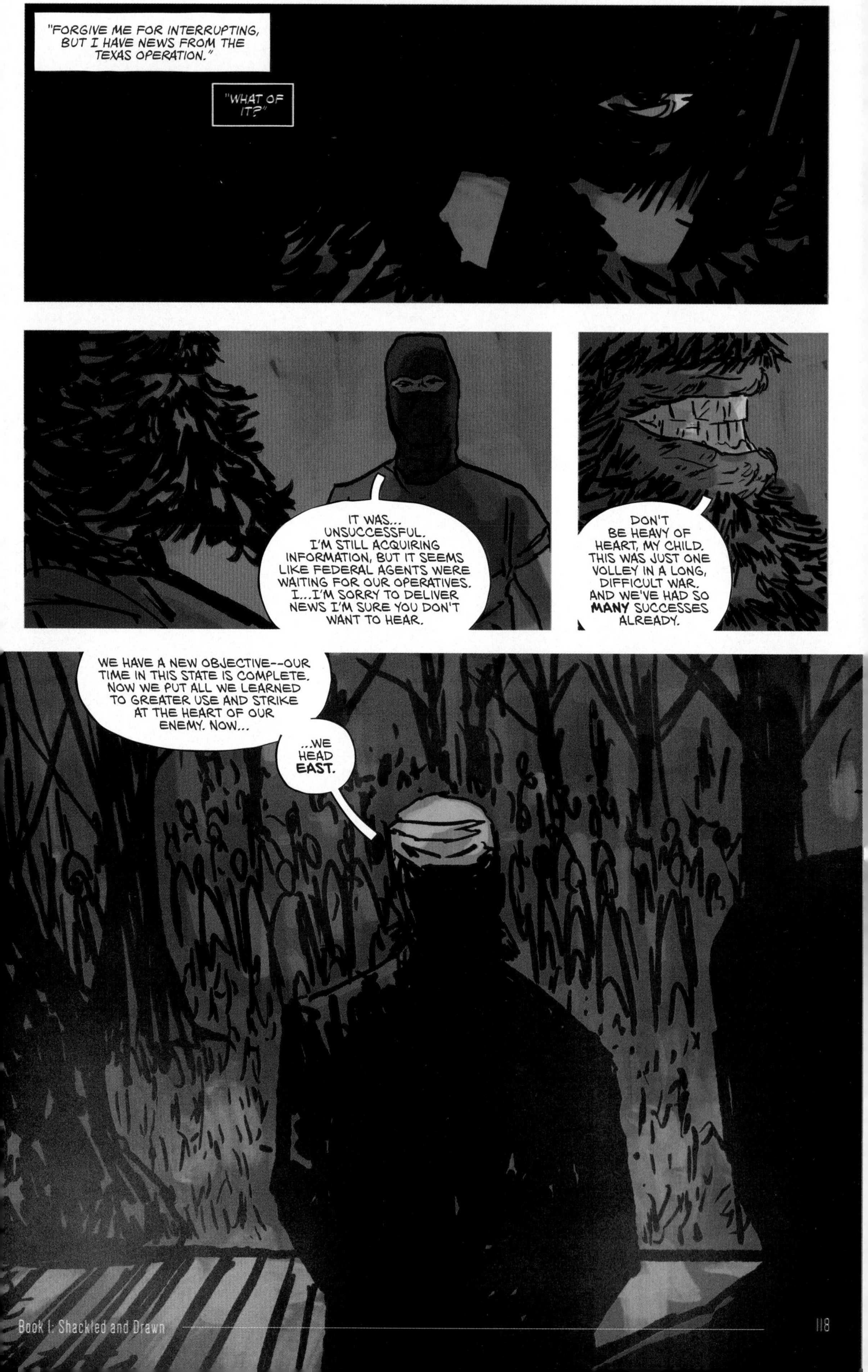
"FORGIVE ME FOR INTERRUPTING, BUT I HAVE NEWS FROM THE TEXAS OPERATION."
"WHAT OF IT?"
IT WAS... UNSUCCESSFUL. I'M STILL ACQUIRING INFORMATION, BUT IT SEEMS LIKE FEDERAL AGENTS WERE WAITING FOR OUR OPERATIVES. I...I'M SORRY TO DELIVER NEWS I'M SURE YOU DON'T WANT TO HEAR.
DON'T BE HEAVY OF HEART, MY CHILD. THIS WAS JUST ONE VOLLEY IN A LONG, DIFFICULT WAR. AND WE'VE HAD SO **MANY** SUCCESSES ALREADY.
WE HAVE A NEW OBJECTIVE--OUR TIME IN THIS STATE IS COMPLETE. NOW WE PUT ALL WE LEARNED TO GREATER USE AND STRIKE AT THE HEART OF OUR ENEMY. NOW...
...WE HEAD **EAST**.

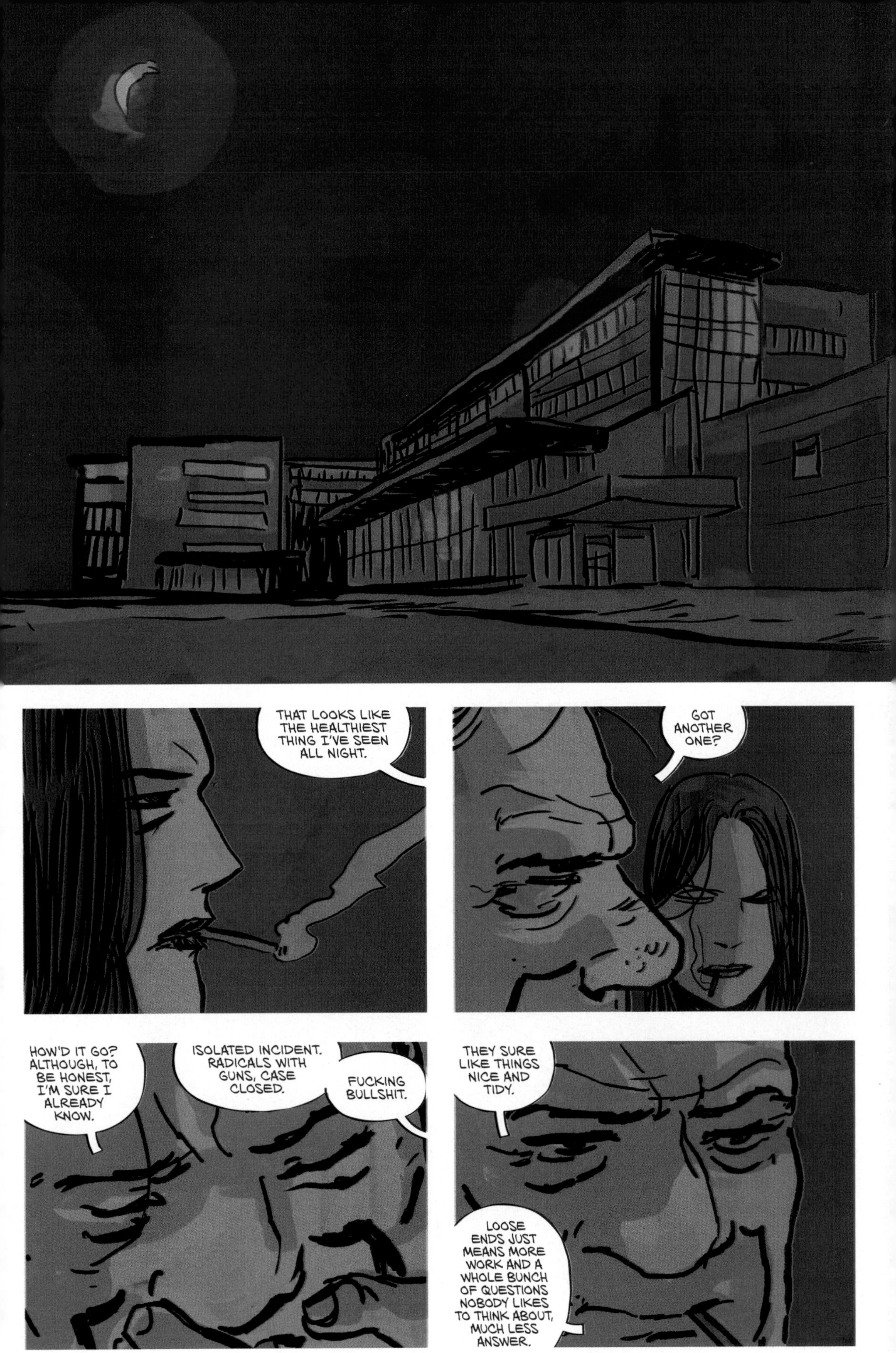
THAT LOOKS LIKE THE HEALTHIEST THING I'VE SEEN ALL NIGHT.
GOT ANOTHER ONE?
HOW'D IT GO? ALTHOUGH, TO BE HONEST, I'M SURE I ALREADY KNOW.
ISOLATED INCIDENT. RADICALS WITH GUNS, CASE CLOSED.
FUCKING BULLSHIT.
THEY SURE LIKE THINGS NICE AND TIDY.
LOOSE ENDS JUST MEANS MORE WORK AND A WHOLE BUNCH OF QUESTIONS NOBODY LIKES TO THINK ABOUT, MUCH LESS ANSWER.

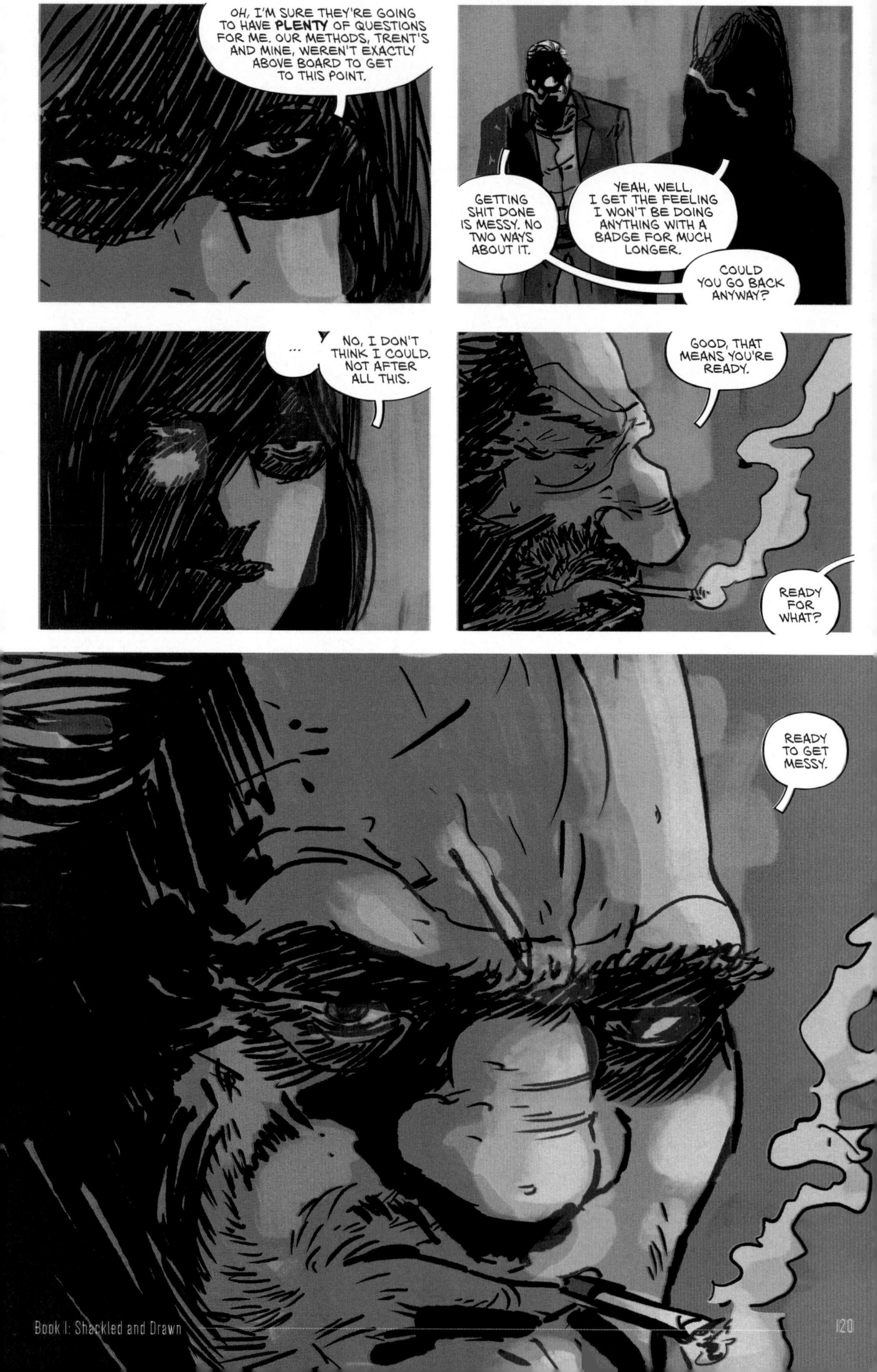
OH, I'M SURE THEY'RE GOING TO HAVE PLENTY OF QUESTIONS FOR ME. OUR METHODS, TRENT'S AND MINE, WEREN'T EXACTLY ABOVE BOARD TO GET TO THIS POINT.
GETTING SHIT DONE IS MESSY. NO TWO WAYS ABOUT IT.
YEAH, WELL, I GET THE FEELING I WON'T BE DOING ANYTHING WITH A BADGE FOR MUCH LONGER.
COULD YOU GO BACK ANYWAY?
...
NO, I DON'T THINK I COULD. NOT AFTER ALL THIS.
GOOD, THAT MEANS YOU'RE READY.
READY FOR WHAT?
READY TO GET MESSY.

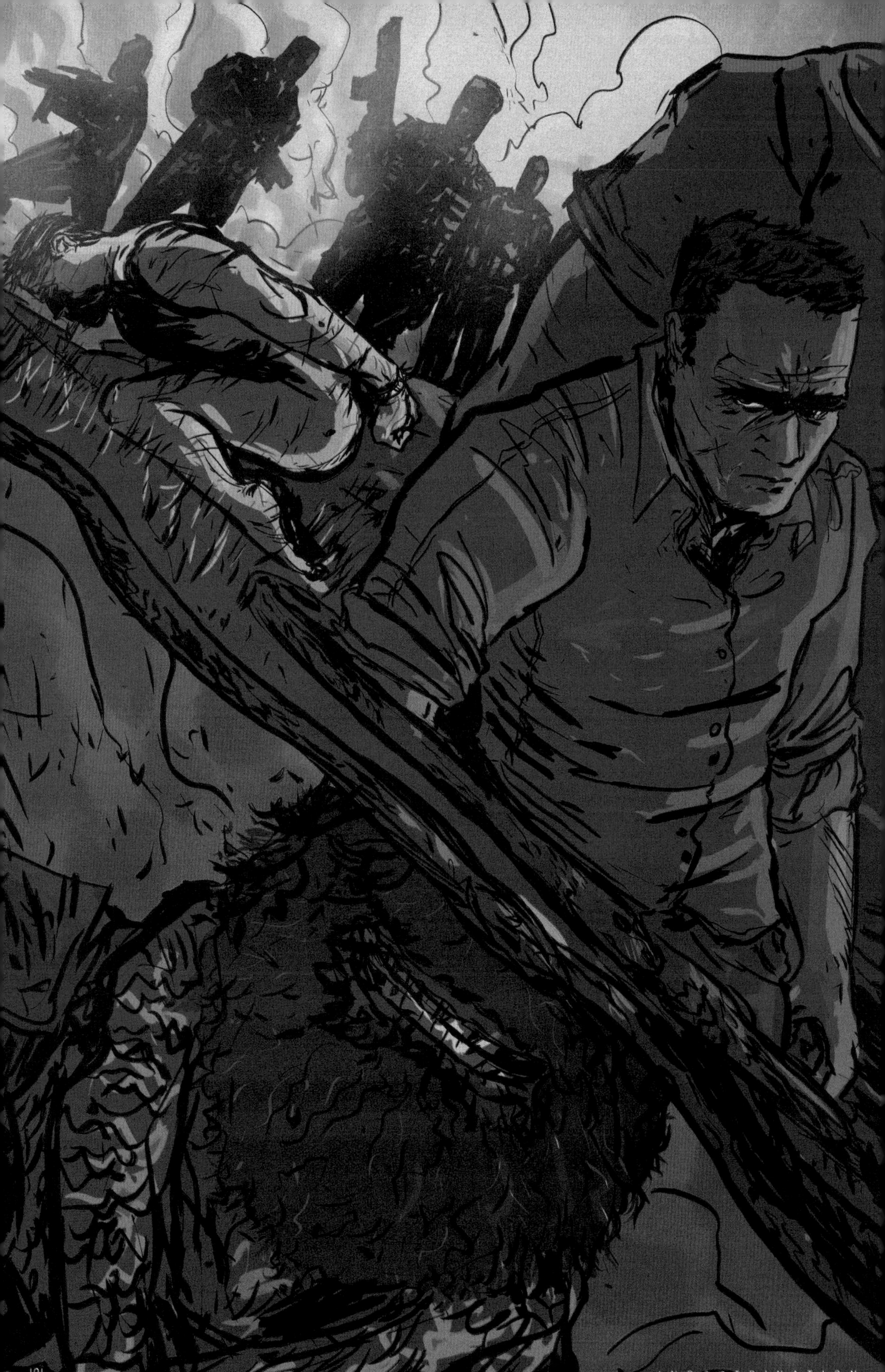

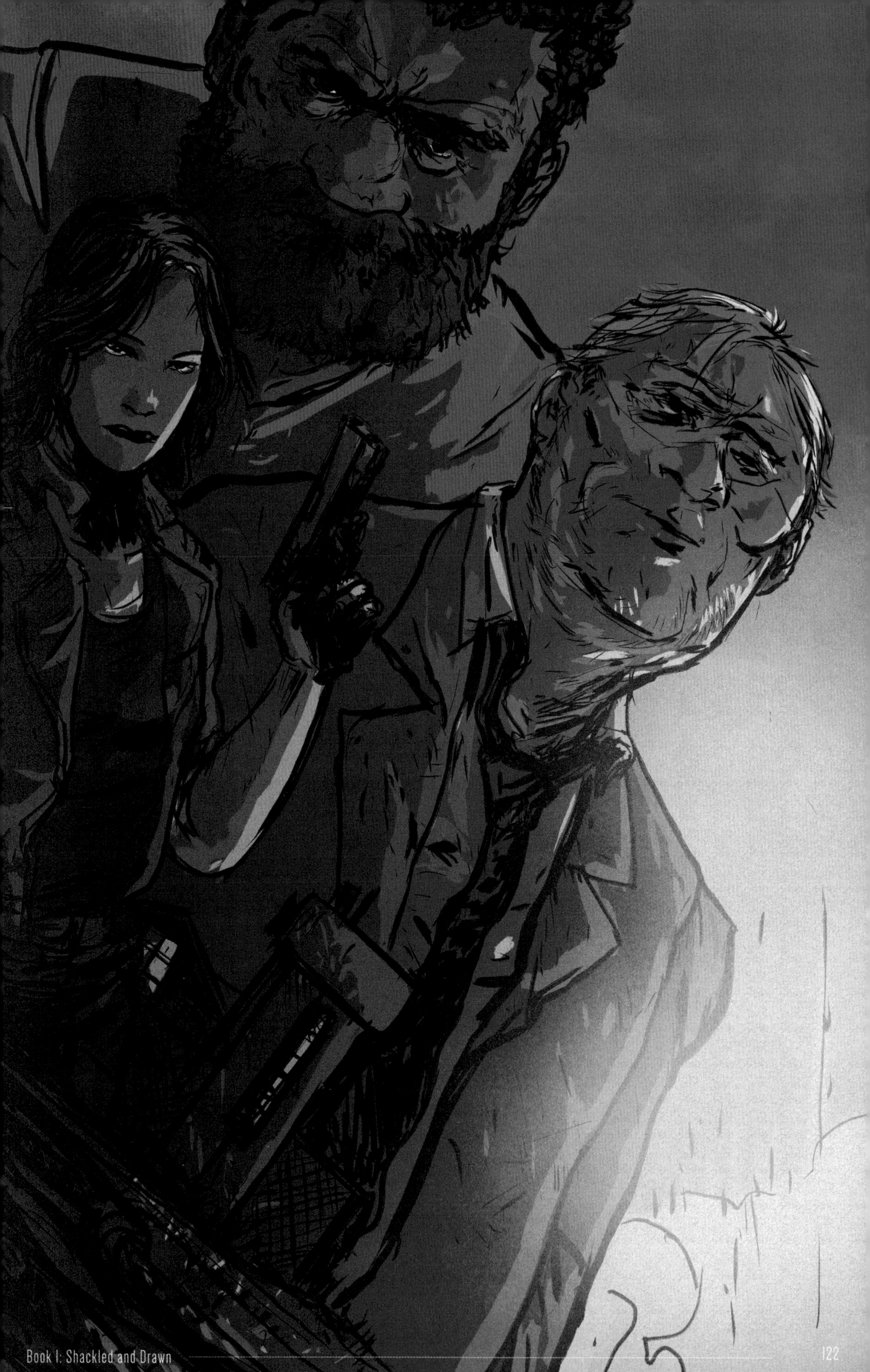

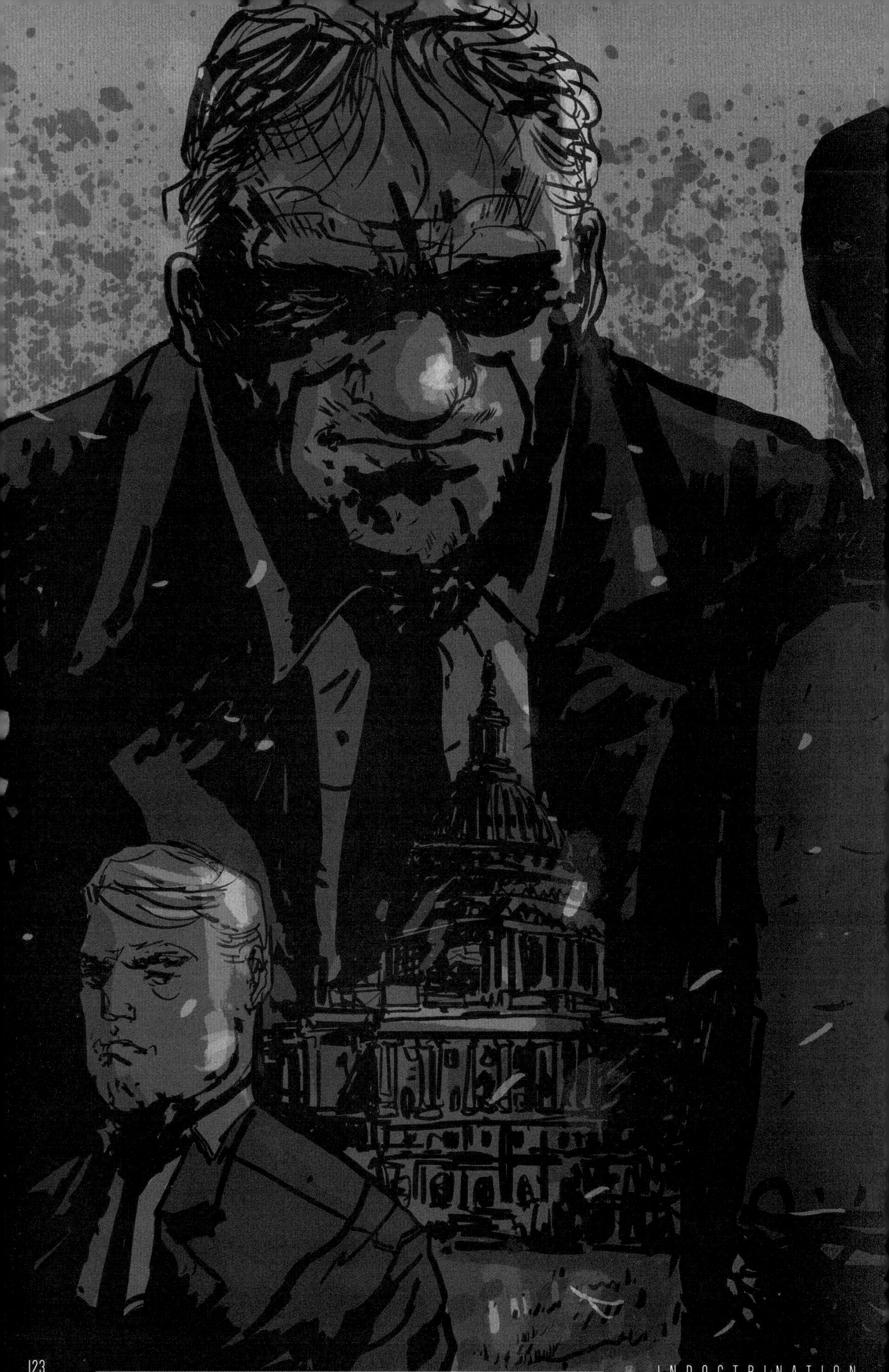

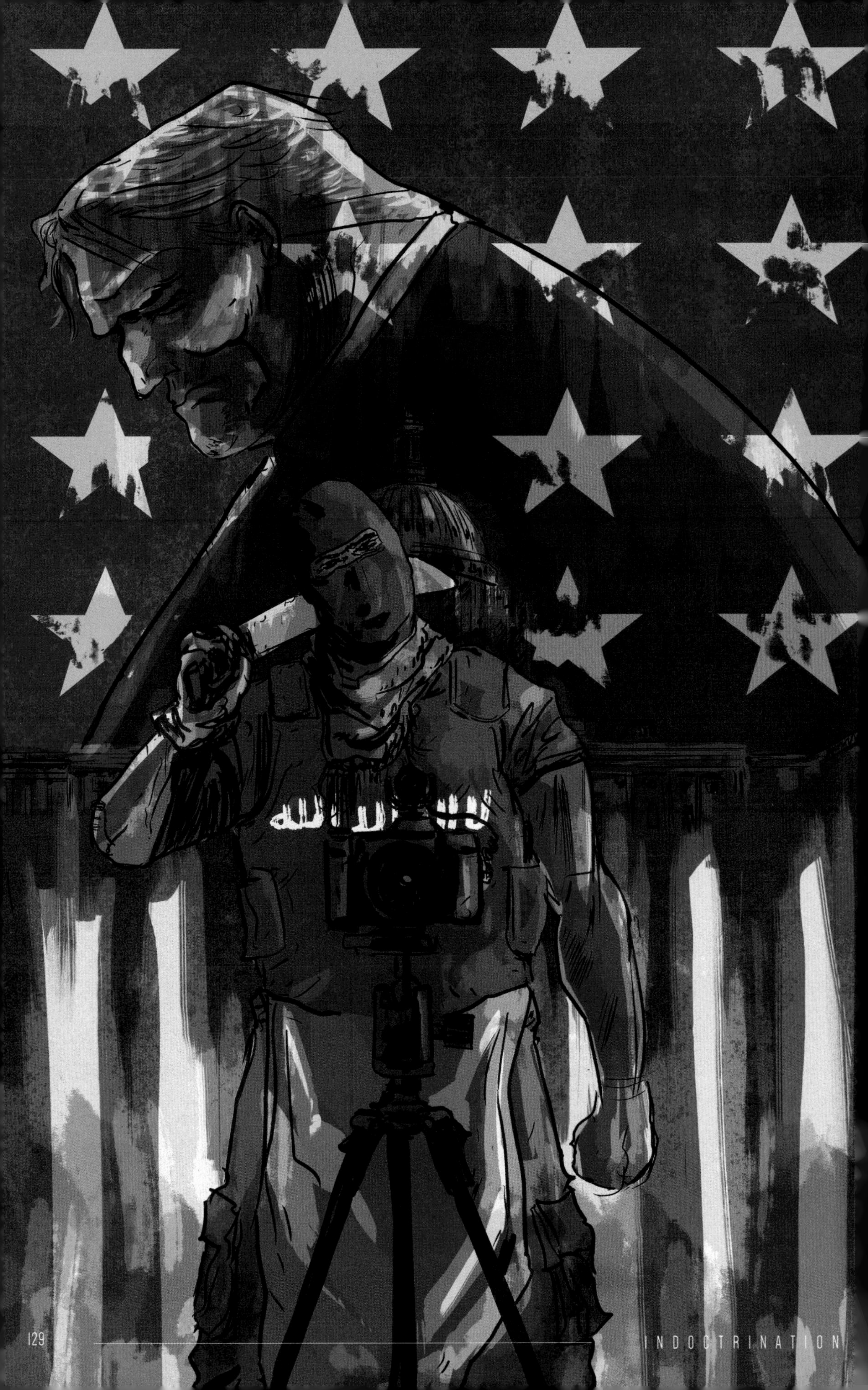

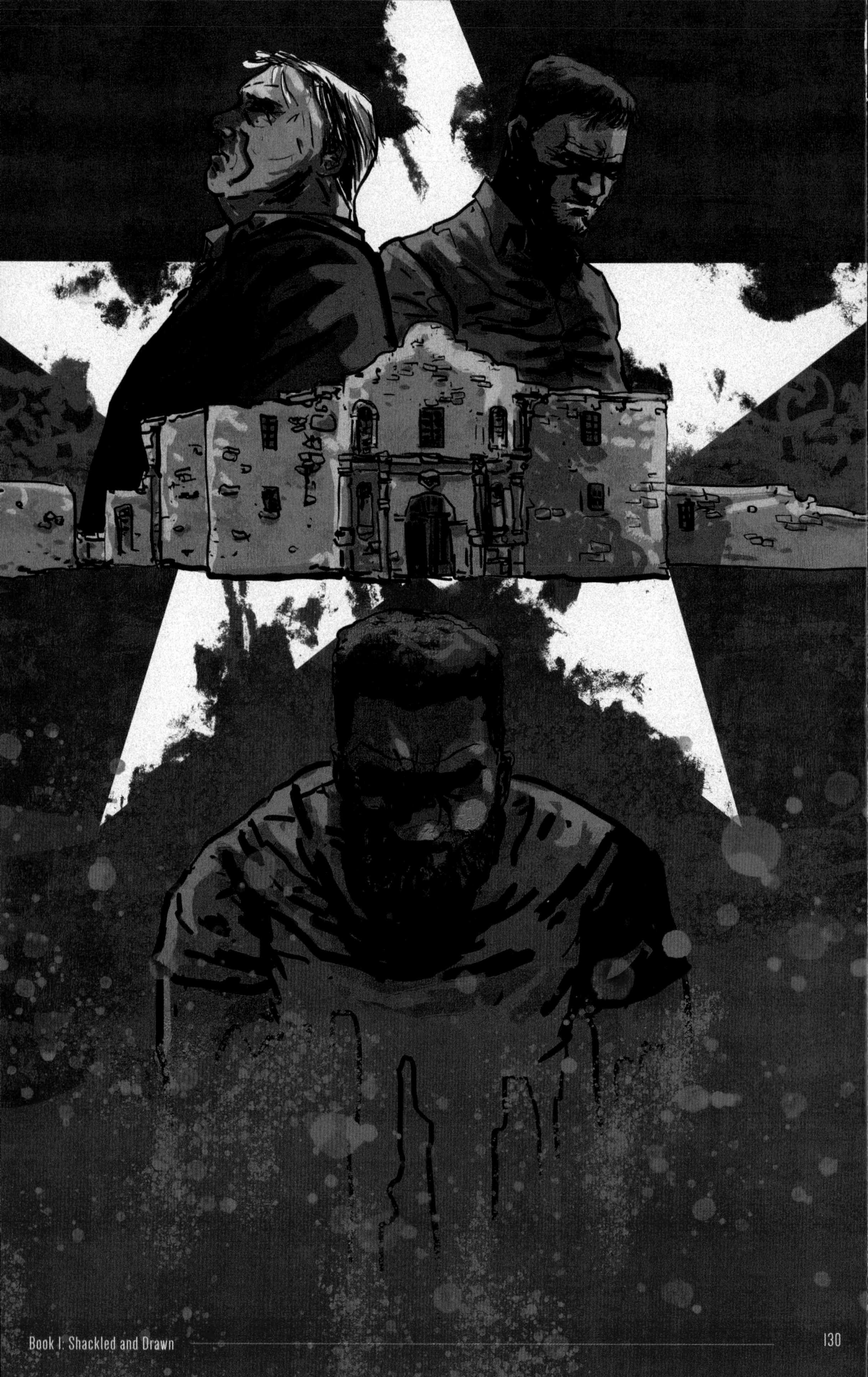

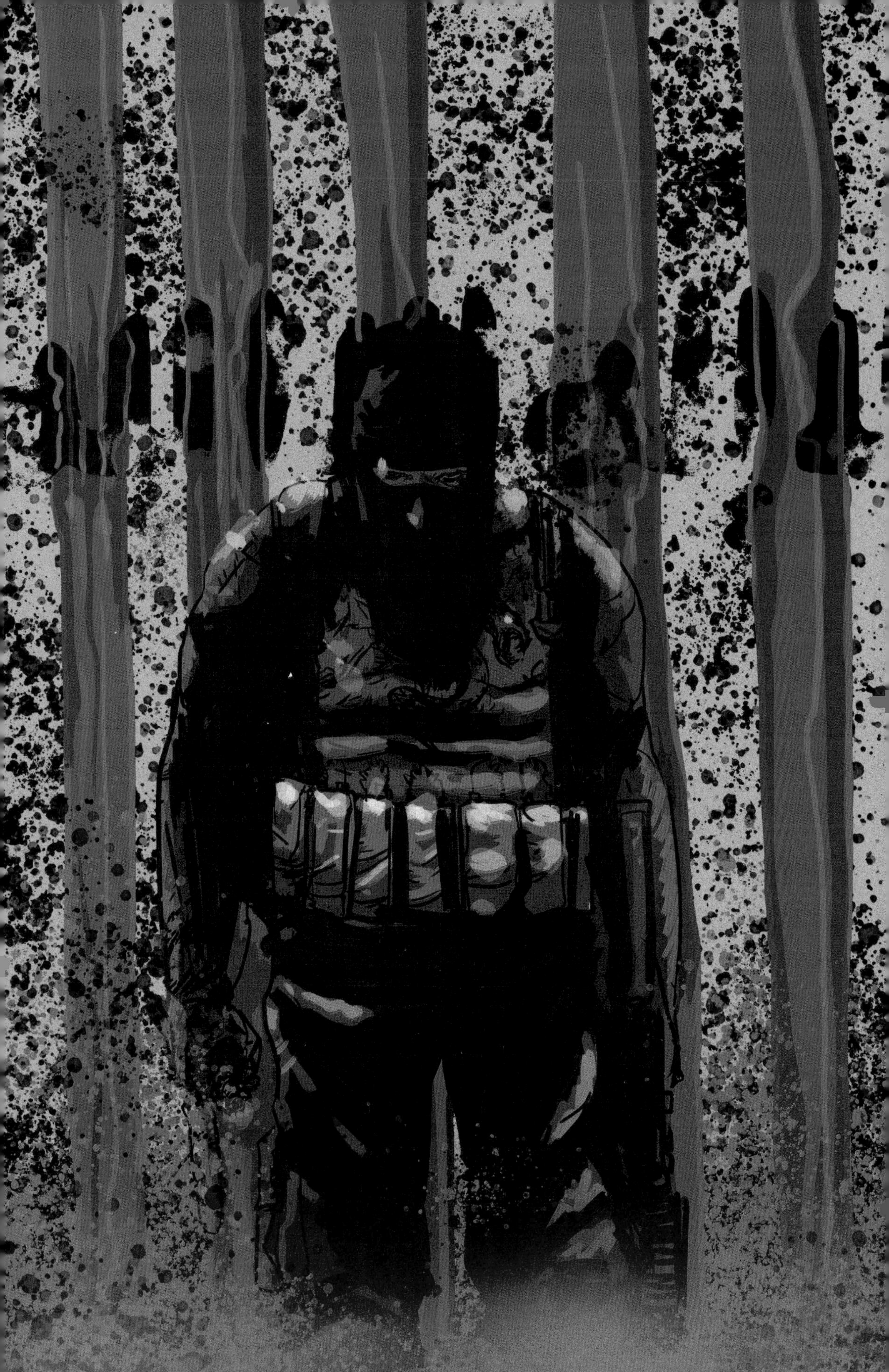

A WAR OF IDEAS

"Practical men, who believe themselves to be quite exempt from any intellectual influences, are usually the slaves of some defunct economist. Madmen in authority, who hear voices in the air, are distilling their frenzy from some academic scribbler of a few years back."

— John Maynard Keynes, 1936

"Ideology." Today, the word is a dirty one among practical thinkers, a label used to slag an argument as less than serious; dogmatic; not anchored in the facts. But what if ideas really matter? What if ideas provide the framework, good or bad, for human action?

The ideological spectrum, conventionally speaking, swings from one dangerous extreme to another. In grade school, we are taught that "right" extremism is nationalist, nativist, and often racist. Think fascism and Nazism. This is really evil, authoritarian stuff that has produced horrific outcomes in practice. The other extreme, the far "left," is populated with the failed experiments of socialism and communism. These are equally murderous ideologies responsible for the dead corpses of hundreds of millions of innocents.

History tells us, if you are listening, that when political indoctrination happens, innocents will die.

So what can we make of radical Islamic terrorism? Where does this "ism" fit in the spectrum of extremist ideas?

How do you explain a religious ideology that inspires a husband and wife in San Bernardino to abandon their newborn child for a workplace suicide mission – the premeditated murder of 14 colleagues?

How do we make sense of the cold, calculated assassinations of political satirists at Charlie Hebdo? Two brothers, Saïd and Chérif Kouachi, crashed an editorial meeting of the magazine on January 7, 2015, executing each of them, one after the next, in the head. Their supposed offense? Having drawn cartoons.

Where on the political spectrum do we drop a pin to explain the systematic execution of 89 music fans at an Eagles of Death Metal concert at the Bataclan Theater? Three Muslim men dressed in black, shouting "Allahu Akbar," sprayed the crowd with bullets. The attackers reloaded their Kalashnikov automatic rifles three or four times over twenty minutes, calmly, systemically murdering their unarmed captives.

Maybe ideas matter more that we think. Maybe, just maybe, the conventional wisdom of splitting the difference between two extremes completely misses the point. Ideas matter. Ideology matters. Bad ideas indoctrinate evil. Evil erases the value of life. Evil kills.

Good versus Evil. Right versus Left. Nazis versus Communists. Maybe a better way to make senses of ideas, good to bad, is to lump all of the murderously authoritarian "isms" on one polar end of the spectrum. Right there is any ideology that twists religion into an anti-life, by-any-means-necessary, Us-or-Them philosophy. Right there is any ostensible *higher purpose* that subjugates your life, your individual liberty – your hopes, dreams, goals, relationships, and personal eccentricities -- to someone else's political agenda.

Fuck any ideology that diminishes our sense of life – the joy of being, being different, pursuing, risking, succeeding or failing -- to some horrible, undefined master plan that reduces life to nothing more than data points, pawns that can be moved, or eliminated, like on a game board.

I know what you're thinking. I have better things to do than engage in the battle of ideas. This book forces you to consider the obvious: What if bad ideology indoctrinates your neighbors, or your colleagues, or your family?

There are good ideas and evil ideas. Right and wrong ideas. This series is all about that battle, the war of ideas. The practical among us will have to engage. Think for yourself. Fight the power. Don't be Indoctrinated.

MATT KIBBE

FREETHEPEOPLE.ORG

Matt Kibbe is a leading advocate for personal, civil and economic liberties. An economist by training, Kibbe is a public policy expert, bestselling author and political commentator. He is President and Chief Community Organizer of Free the People. He lives in Washington, DC with his unspeakably awesome wife of 30 years, Terry, and their three liberty-minded cats, Roark, Ragnar and Iko. A noted scholarly expert on The Big Lebowski, Kibbe is also an avid DeadHead, drinker of beer and whisky, and collector of obscure books on libertarian philosophy.

 @mkibbe   facebook.com/mattkibbe

INDOCTRINATION

FEAR

Fear is one of the most powerful human emotions. It can paralyze and be all-consuming. It can drive ordinary people to do extraordinary things, for better or worse. There are times, no doubt, when fear is justified and a healthy response to real danger. And there are many others when fear is deliberately manufactured — and then exploited — by those in power to further their own ends. Fear of the unknown, the unfamiliar. Those who don't share your skin color. Immigrants. Muslims. The "other." These are the targets that seem always in vogue.

The threat of terrorism, for instance, is by any sober measure minuscule. An American is far more likely to be struck by lightning than to be killed by a terrorist. However, that reality does not stop politicians and the media from hyping the threat of terrorism ad nauseam to justify endless war and spending hundreds of billions of dollars every year to "protect" us. We are warned that our enemy is hell-bent on our destruction and cannot be reasoned with. They are the embodiment of evil, as any great enemy is.

If only life were so simple, or we so innocent. You don't need to dig too deep to begin uncovering the root causes of modern terrorism. People are drawn to extremist ideologies for a wide variety of reasons and every case is unique. Nevertheless, there are common threads to many stories of radicalization that we ignore at our own peril. Those on the fringes are often moved by a volatile mix of a lack of opportunity and community, in combination with a real or perceived harm. By hypocrisy, suffering and death.

In countless cases, U.S. foreign policy is the unseen midwife to terrorism. It is "blowback," a term coined by the CIA to refer to the unintended consequences of our actions abroad — specifically those kept secret from the public. As a result, the violent reactions that our meddling provoke are perceived as coming out of nowhere. Our most reviled and feared enemies in recent decades — from Saddam Hussein and Osama bin Laden to the Islamic State — are textbook examples of blowback.

As it has since time immemorial, violence offers the allure of a quick fix, or is at least seen as a palliative. More than simply righting a specific wrong, the goal of terrorism is often apocalyptic. That does not mean bringing about the "end of the world," as it is commonly understood, but something closer to its original definition. In Greek, apocalypse literally means "unveiling," or the opening of our eyes to reality and irrevocably changing the way the world is seen.

A supposed truth that the Islamic State hopes to reveal is the intolerance of the West toward Muslims and a fundamental disregard for the value of their lives. By dropping more bombs on the Arab world and restricting Muslim refugees, we only bolster their narrative and make recruitment that much easier. Now that is a fear to be taken seriously.

ERIC STONER

WAGINGNONVIOLENCE.ORG

Eric Stoner is a founding editor of Waging Nonviolence and an adjunct professor at St. Peter's University and St. Joseph's College. He has reported from Afghanistan and his articles about militarism and the future of war have appeared in The Guardian, Mother Jones, Salon, In These Times, Sojourners, and the Pittsburgh Post-Gazette.

Waging Nonviolence is the leading source for news, analysis and original reporting about the social movements that are constantly reshaping our world. Since 2009, Waging Nonviolence has been telling in-depth, compelling stories about how ordinary people are organizing for social, economic and environmental justice and challenging authoritarian regimes, which has led to the site being blocked by the Chinese government and targeted by pro-Putin trolls.

 @wagingnv   facebook.com/wagingnonviolence

COMICS & POLITICS:
HEARING WHAT'S ON AND OFF THE PAGE

Comics can be a strange place to occupy.

While the profile of characters and stories from the medium has grown considerably over the past couple decades, it remains a very small space. Compared to other entertainment industries in America, like music, film, or even fine arts, comics bring in almost no money and have a very niche audience. Some successful people within the medium move out for better paid and recognized work elsewhere, while others never even try to enter at all. This has all made sure that comics remains small.

That size isn't an inherently good or bad thing, but it is a root cause of what I mean when I call comics a strange place. Once you make your way into comics, whether it's as a creator, a journalist, or a fan, it quickly becomes clear how interconnected everything is. The game Six Degrees of Kevin Bacon for Hollywood could be played as Three Degrees of Mike Allred in American comics.

This has the effect of making the conversations within the industry occur at a much faster rate. News and ideas spread fast and it's easy for everyone to comment. The rapidity of information sharing is balanced by a lack of central systems. There are no dedicated news sources, educational outlets, or regulatory systems in comics. It's small enough that everyone can be in the loop, but too small for traditional systems of monitoring to care.

In essence, comics has been left in its own corner and to its own devices. There are no authorities on how to discuss the subject matter, no professors to define terms and educate new entrants, and no unions to establish standards of conduct. Despite having been around for more than a century, the medium is still discovering its standards.

This is an exciting opportunity. It's a chance to help shape the basic terminology and understanding of a challenging medium without almost limitless potential. However, without those aforementioned systems in place, it's very easy for that opportunity to go awry. Advancing comics comes from advancing our understanding of comics and that starts with discourse. Discourse starts from a very basic thesis, one that applies far beyond comics:

All language is political.

Everything we say, do, create, and put out into this world holds meaning, both intentional and unintentional. From the haughtiest original graphic novel to the most derivative superhero comic, they come loaded with ideas, beliefs, and philosophy. That same sentiment applies to criticism, journalism, podcasting, and any other form of reaction. When we put something out into the world, it means something.

That meaning isn't enough by itself. Taken in a vacuum, each statement holds no value. Understanding comes from engagement. A tree falling in an empty woods makes a sound, but it doesn't make a difference. A comic may technically be speech on its own, but it doesn't have an impact until it is read. It's the acts of reading, response, and review that gives any speech meaning. This is where we discover the value of art. It's also typically where institutions like schools and critical apparatuses would help teach people how to engage. In comics we don't have those in any meaningful way, so we have to invent it for ourselves.

The danger of this is that while we all may be speaking, no one may actually be heard. Discourse requires response, and at the heart of response is change. Reading something without considering it or being open to being changed by it is not discourse, it's only consumption. If our speech and creation is to have any impact, it must not fall on deaf ears. More importantly, if we are to be impacted then we must be sure to listen.

Academic traditions encourage vigorous discourse and disagreement, creative destruction taken outside of its economic context and applied to art. Comics must create these traditions on its own. The alternative is to have a space filled with speech, but absent of discourse. It's the key to advancing the medium on all levels. Different people look for different things: artistic expansion, social justice, fairness in business. All of these topics mean different things to different people, and will continue to do so.

There's no reason why all of these things must remain stagnant though. Depending on who you speak to, you'll hear very different opinions on how far the medium has come in regards to each of these topics.

Likely the only thing you won't hear is that all of these things are the same as they were 10 or 20 or 100 years ago.

It's this continual cycle of creation and reaction and creation that is itself reaction through which any artistic medium evolves. Each thing builds on what came before, like panels in a comic book creating meaning through their connection. Whether it's an opposing response or a refinement of a movement, we are building that story together. Every panel relies on its understanding of the previous moment. If an artist ignores what is to the left, then what he creates on the right will be confusing.

The future of comics will be determined by the people in it today, and that provides a lot of power to relatively few people. They are creating and saying things of import everyday, telling stories and providing responses to them. What is uncertain is how well these things will be said and what impact they might have in the future. That is entirely reliant on the quality of communication.

Comics has the ability to create its own narrative today, to say something of value. What is being said relies on what is being heard though and that's the more significant choice.

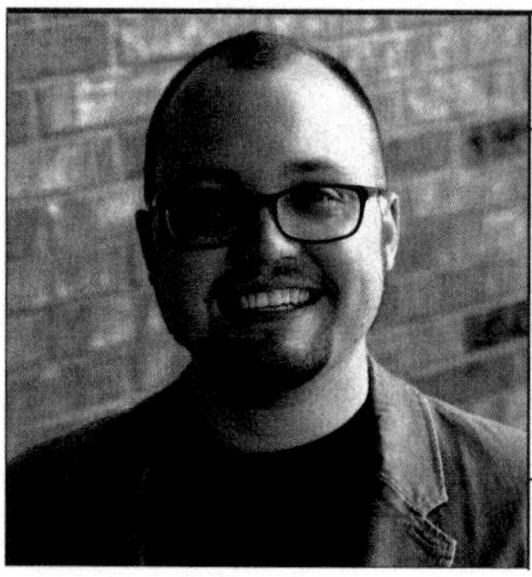

CHASE MAGNET

COMICSBULLITEN.COM

Chase Magnett is a comics critic who writes about and edits comics professionally. He emphasizes a strong analytical approach to the medium in both its form and messaging. You can find him working as the Co-Managing Editor of Comics Bulletin and a Contributor at ComicBook.Com. When his life is not being consumed by comics, he enjoys spending entire days at the movies, grilling, and googling images of pangolins.

@ReverendMagnett

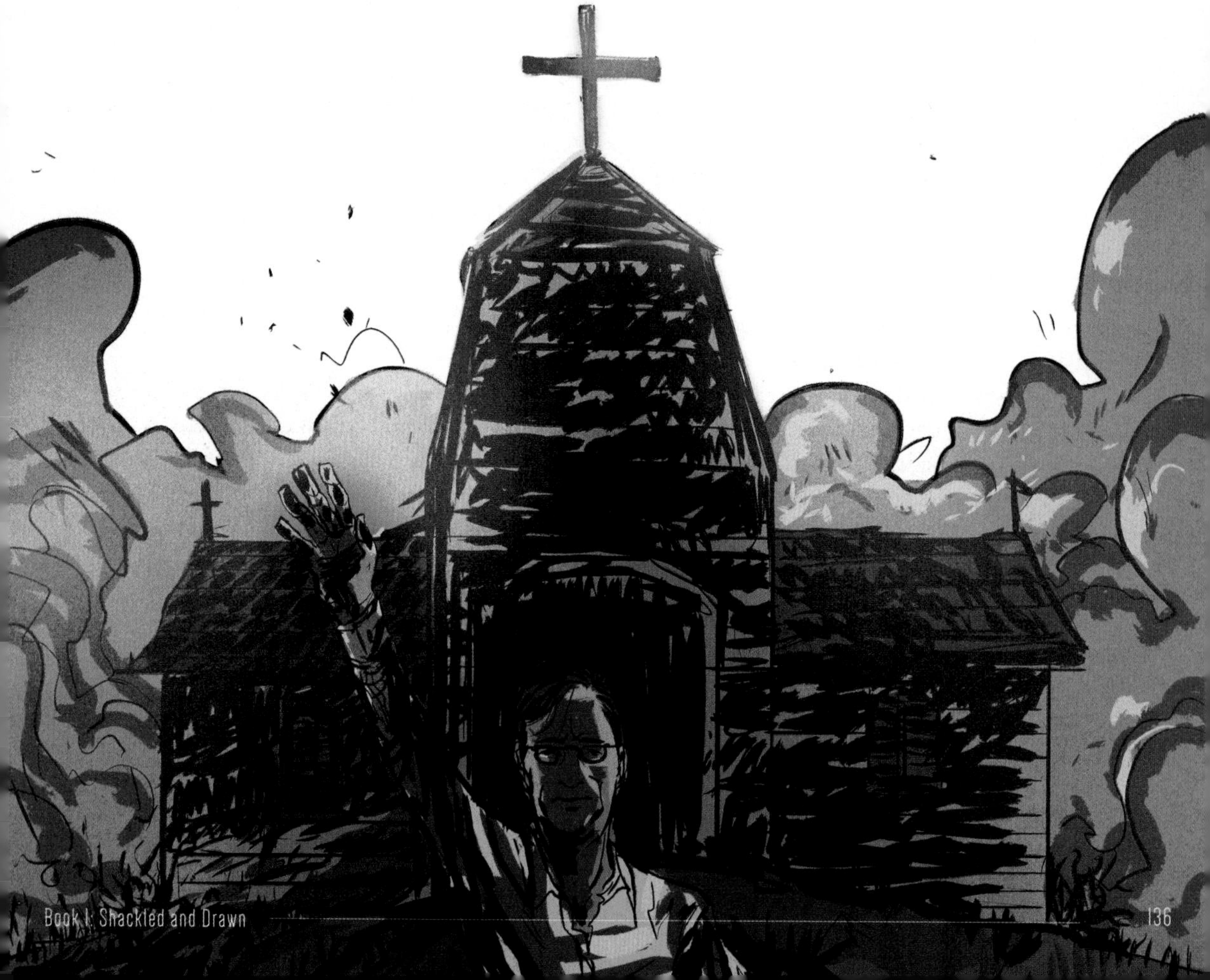

WHAT WE TALK ABOUT
WHEN WE TALK ABOUT WAR

The relationship between politics and government is an interesting one. Politics is all about taking impersonal things—plastic candidates, abstract promises, tightly scripted speeches—and making them feel personal. These people are really just like us. They're speaking from their heart. I want to have a beer with them. It's all lies of course. They're nothing like us, they're not sincere in the slightest, and they probably don't drink beer except for photo op purposes. Certainly not good beer, anyway.

Government, on the other hand, does the exact opposite. It takes things that are immensely personal—your job, your family, your health, your life—and makes them seem impersonal. Tax collectors aren't stealing your money, they're providing for the common good. We're not telling you what to eat, we just want to ensure a healthier society. We would never dream of forcibly conscripting your children into 12 years of propaganda, we just care about high quality education.

The most dishonest, as well as the most dangerous, example of this is the subject of war. There's nothing more personal than war, but you'd never know it to hear people on the news or in politics talk about it. Every day we are bombarded with euphemistic terms like making the world safe for democracy, holding people accountable, demonstrating American exceptionalism, and showing the world that actions have consequences. There's nothing particularly wrong with these terms except that they obscure the real issue, which is that human beings are being sent to kill other human beings.

When we talk about war, we don't say things like "Joe is going to kill Ahmed." We talk bigger than that. Instead, we say things like "America is at war with Afghanistan." We say these things despite the full knowledge that America can't be at war with anything, because America is an abstract concept that artlessly smashes together a set of values with certain elected officials and a specific chunk of geography. Afghanistan can't be warred upon, because you can't really win a fight against mountains and desert, even if you really wanted to try.

There are a couple of reasons why we use these metaphors. One is certainly linguistic ease, but I think the more important reason is that it masks a reality that, if we were made to confront it on a daily basis, would be too horrible to bear. It's easy to get angry and say that the US should invade the Middle East. It's a harder position to take when you think about individual Americans shooting individual Afghans, especially when many of these are likely to be innocent casualties caught in the crossfire and when you realize that our own boys have just as much chance of getting blown up as the enemy.

Politicians on both sides of the aisle don't like us to think in these terms. An enemy is always most popular and most useful when it is distant and faceless. As Hillary Clinton sabre-rattles in favor of more interventionism, more nation building, and more death in service of a bigger, bigger, ever bigger government, Donald Trump seeks to trade xenophobia and lunatic blustering for votes. Meanwhile, we are assured that killing is really about safety; war is peace; freedom is slavery.

George Orwell, who grappled extensively with the idea that the language we use shapes our thoughts and perceptions, once wrote that the language of politics "is designed to make lies sound truthful and murder respectable, and to give an appearance of solidity to pure wind." We permit government to do things to our fellow man that we would never dare do ourselves, and we largely do it because we trick ourselves into forgetting that they are men. They are the faceless, nameless enemy, best not examined too closely.

Preserving our own humanity requires acknowledging that of others. There are circumstances in which killing is defensible. There may be cases where the alternative is something even worse. But it's a cop out to pretend that war is anything other than looking down the barrel of a gun at a fellow human being and deciding to pull the trigger. Convincing ourselves otherwise is just another form of indoctrination.

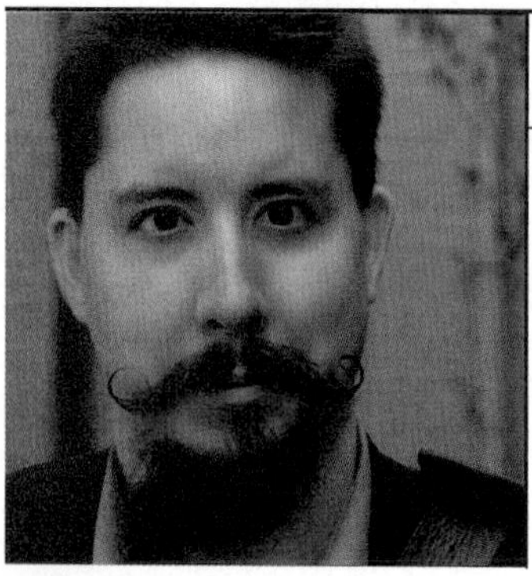

LOGAN ALBRIGHT

@loganalbright73

where his contrarian nature drove him into countless hours of heated debate at this bastion of progressive thought. Logan occasionally takes time out from his busy schedule of railing against the evils of government to play the part of musician, amateur novelist, and moustache enthusiast.

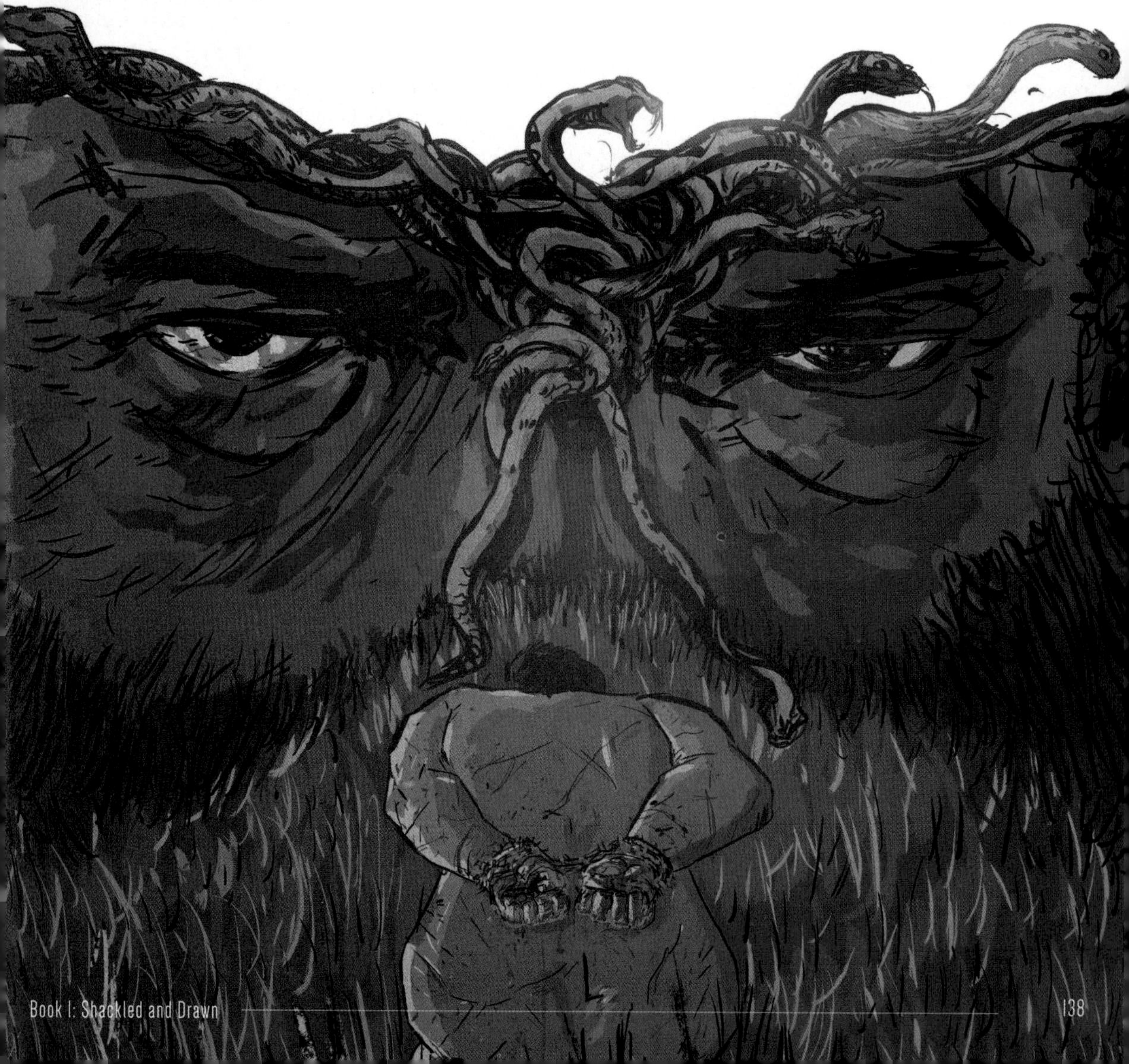

SUPPORT THE TROOPS

Here's how not to support the troops:

[Cue gratuitous "Salute the Sky!" flyover at your local NFL pregame show]

Sure, the stoke is high and you're psyched on an awesome display of air superiority. The cheers you hear are for the Red, White, and Blue! America…Fuck yeah!

This full-throated spectacle conveys legitimate and genuine admiration—but that's very different than support. And, heads up! It may do more harm than good.

Choreographed adoration of the uniformed military is dangerous to the men and women who fight for our freedoms. It produces a false aura of invincibility, dumbs down our estimation of their sacrifice, and fits out tone-deaf bros with Back To Back World War Champs tanks and tees.

After fifteen years of continuous war, nearly 7,000 American soldiers, sailors, Marines, and airmen have paid the ultimate price for their country. Tens of thousands more have been wounded. Since 2012, approximately 1,000,000 veterans have been added to the VA's compensation lists. The ongoing phenomenon of veteran suicide has claimed thousands more lives at a pace that far outstrips the national average. Some 50,000 vets sleep on the streets.

Sure, the U.S. military is the strongest fighting force in human history. No conventional force can compete. Such statements aren't up for debate. Service and sacrifice deserve our veneration. That's why public esteem for the military has been consistently high for decades. Pew's research suggests that no occupational group—not teachers, doctors, scientists, or engineers—enjoys greater regard.

But for many, this respect is superficial—as fleeting as that stadium flyby. Civilians like me echo "thank you for your service" on autopilot without any conception of what that service entails. As Matt Richtel wrote in a New York Times column titled "Please Don't Thank Me for My Service," some recent vets find "the thanks comes across as shallow, disconnected, a reflexive offering from people who, while meaning well, have no clue what soldiers did over there or what motivated them to go, and who would never have gone themselves nor sent their own sons and daughters."

This isn't to say that we shouldn't be grateful—or staggered by the planning and precision needed to maneuver four F-15s into a thunderous exclamation point on the national anthem.

But stop and think. What are we asking of these men and women? Are we taking adequate care of them when they return home? Are the civilians who put them in harm's way held accountable? How well is our military positioned to achieve victory?

This isn't an attempt to scold but to seriously question what it means to support the troops. A responsible patriot should think long and hard about the service of the men and women who would give their lives to defend our freedom. Meanwhile, the wholesale ubiquity of symbolic gestures at ball games, NASCAR races, and golf tourneys cements the status quo.

Maybe we should also ask if that's a good thing.

REID SMITH

 @reidtsmith

Reid Smith writes from Washington, D.C. where he works at the intersection of foreign policy and domestic liberty. A recovering doctoral student and think tanker, he's also a featured contributor at news outlets such as the American Conservative, the American Spectator, and Rare Politics. He tweets sparingly at @reidtsmith.

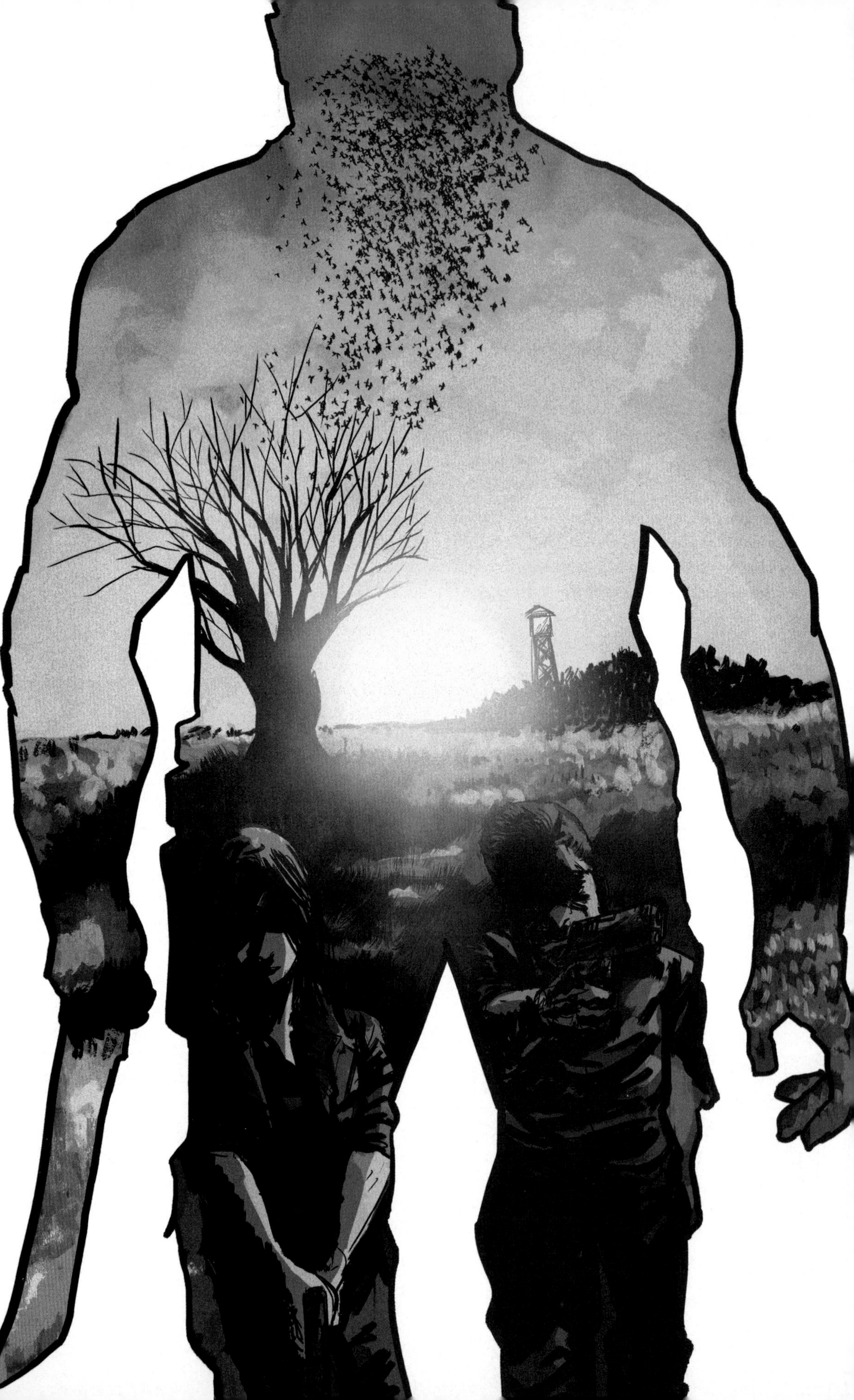